Dr Mortimer and the Barking Man Mystery

DR MORTIMER AND THE BARKING MAN MYSTERY

Gerard Williams

CARROLL & GRAF PUBLISHERS, INC.
New York

Carroll & Graf Publishers, Inc.
19 West 21st Street
New York
NY10010-6805

First published in the UK by Constable,
an imprint of Constable & Robinson Ltd, 2001

First Carroll & Graf edition 2001

Copyright © Gary Newman 2001

ISBN 0–7867–0859–X

Printed and bound in the EU

1

Of all the cases which have come my way, that of the Barking Man has been the most sensational and the widest and most tragic in its ramifications.

The discovery of the dreadfully mutilated corpse of General Pyotr Ivanovitch Ostyankin in the squalid brothel in Poland Street, Soho, in that late autumn of 1890, has of course its historical reverberations to this day, nearly half a century later, and, bearing this in mind, the reader of the year 2000 and beyond will well understand my injunction, touched upon in another account, that these records of my criminal cases be withheld from publication till not less than sixty years have elapsed.

I wish I could allude to my part in this case as the Roman poet did concerning his contribution to the Tender Art: 'I have served in the field, and not without glory.' In this instance, alas, I left the field with dubious and ambiguous honours, as the reader of these pages will learn. I hope, however, that this relation of the case will serve to cast light on one of the lesser hitherto unsolved riddles of our Imperial history, as well as to expiate some of the guilt I have felt ever since about my part in its solution.

For the first time, too, I shall be revealing the identity of the true culprit, now, as I write in this uneasy August of 1939, long since dead, and, so far as I am aware, leaving neither kith nor kin. Any scruples I may first have felt at my concealment of that person's identity were to a great extent washed away by the promptness of the police – their alacrity encouraged, I am sure, by higher powers – in closing their book on the affair. At least I knew then that no innocent person could subsequently be arrested for the murder.

I am now in my eightieth year, and it is with the prospect that I shall soon be in the presence of a Judge before Whom no secrets may be hid, and with a penitent's heart, that I lay these facts before the reader.

The main facts of the case are now history, and no more than a cursory resumption of them will surely suffice to enable the reader to follow the ensuing narrative: how the discovery of the body of the 'Butcher of Kozodieffka' in the circumstances I have mentioned above upset a veritable hornets' nest in London diplomatic circles, sparking off a paper-chase of telegraphed protests, demands and ultimatums, and how, in the manner of a sacrificial victim, the tarnished young social revolutionary and East End slum denizen Solomon Solomons was arrested and put on trial for the murder of the Russian potentate.

If ever a man was accused, tried and found guilty before his case even came to court, it was the wretched Solomons! Some wag has dubbed the press the 'Third Estate', but in no other case that I know of has the vicious licence of the penny papers had such free rein as in the Barking Man mystery. The jury were of course properly cautioned at the outset that they must discount all that they had read in the press about the case, but for them to be expected to weigh up the evidence oblivious to the then-public knowledge that Solomons was a proscribed immigrant with a long criminal record and a string of aliases in his native Ruthenia, that his mother and eleven-year-old sister had been brutally massacred in a pogrom inspired and directed by the present victim, and that he had already been implicated in an anarchist attempt on the general's life in Odessa in 1884 was to add ears to the legal ass!

Those who are familiar with my account of the Aldgate Mystery of the same year – 1890 – will know that I am the James Mortimer who left his stick behind in the rooms of Sherlock Holmes at 221B, Baker Street in the fateful year of 1889. The celebrated affair that ensued, however – the Baskerville Case – has already been more than ably chronicled by my good friend, John Watson, MD, to whom I also owe what acquaintance the reading public already has with me.

Watson's chronicles also confirm that at the time of the events I am about to relate, Holmes was engaged by the French government in matters of the highest import. I was in a position to know that Watson was equally engrossed in winding up one of the three unchronicled cases that had occupied the pair during the winter of 1890; namely, the awful affair of the Extra Cellar in Portland Place. How keenly I was to miss those trusty friends in the trying days that were to come!

With my partner in medical practice and wife of some six months, Dr Violet Branscombe, I was engaged in running the Whitechapel People's Dispensary, the little socio-medical outpost which a steady accumulation of contributory funding would later expand into the Bryant Foundation. When the events I am about to relate burst on us, we had been absent from England for some ten weeks, I having put my foot down in the November of 1890, when Violet, having assumed that summer the dual mantles of directrix of the Whitechapel Dispensary and clerk-of-works of the embryonic Bryant Foundation institute across the court from it, had very nearly driven herself into a complete breakdown. In what had amounted to a domestic *coup d'état*, I had prescribed a winter cruising on the Nile, so that when we arrived home refreshed at the end of the second week of February, '91, the chill grey streets of the East End formed a piquant contrast to our still-fresh impressions of blue skies, whispering reeds and stalking ibises.

The People's Dispensary had been Violet's conception, and among the women who brought their troubles to her there, those of the streets formed a large proportion. It was one of that category who confronted us, when, on that cold, grey Sunday morning, Violet called me in from the adjoining pharmacy to hear the woman's plea. She was a strapping blonde girl in a rather shiny pelisse a size too small for her and a hat with a crestfallen feather, but what set Iris Starr apart from all the other unfortunate women who had passed through our little outpost was the size of the debt we both owed her – Violet for her life and I consequently for most of what happiness had been allotted to me on earth.

Briefly –I do not care to recall the incident too frequently or in too much detail – Violet had, late one morning at the end of the previous September, had occasion to visit a hovel of a room in Union Street, in order to rescue a sick and ill-used child from the hands of a drunken termagant of a mother. My wife had found the woman in bed, apparently dead drunk, and, quietly disengaging the child from the folds of the filthy coverlet, had wrapped her, unresisting, in a clean blanket, before discreetly carrying the child out of the room and downstairs. Violet had hardly crossed the threshold of the street-door, however, when the mother, with a screaming swoop, had knocked off her hat

7

from behind, and seized her long hair in her fist. Meanwhile, the commotion had drawn a crowd of idlers round the door, most of whom would have been more than content to watch a good 'mill', especially one between such a tartar and a lady.

Violet stubbornly held on to the now-screaming child, while the woman tugged at her hair, pulling her head back so that her neck was fully exposed. To the horror now of the onlookers, the drunken woman with her free hand was seen to raise a flashing object above Violet's naked throat. A gasp went up from the crowd, then a woman stepped up smartly behind the maddened hag, and, seizing her bare raised arm in both her hands, leant forward and sank her teeth into the flesh. The termagant screamed, and the object she had been wielding fell to the ground. It was an open razor.

Characteristically, Violet had refused to press charges, seeking to play down the incident as a mere gesture on the desperate mother's part, but neither she nor I had any doubt as to how much we owed to Iris Starr's prompt and disinterested action. Bearing this in mind, the reader will readily understand my motivation in pursuing the case which was to unfold, in spite of the non-cooperation – nay, obstruction – of the object of my assistance, with all the strength and ingenuity at my command. Some debts can never be fully repaid.

At that Sunday meeting, Iris's broad face was smeared with a mess of tears and rouge, and she held up her clenched fists before her. I slipped across the room and leant against the windowsill.

'Iris is the sweetheart of the unfortunate Solomons, James,' my wife murmured with husky concern, as with a soothing gesture she reached out to our visitor.

We had read something of the case in a rather elderly edition of *The Times* while we had been staying in Shepheard's Hotel in Cairo over the previous Christmas, but then the immemorial enchantment of the Nile had taken us in its grip again, and we had given ourselves over to the gentler rhythms of the honeymoon we had never really had in that busy August in London. I resolved to get up the facts of the case directly.

''E never did the Soho murder, doctor!' Iris was wailing. 'As Gawd is me witness! Never! Just 'cos 'e's a foreigner, an' 'e 'angs abaht wiv the crowd in the Warsaw . . .'

The Warsaw Café in Osborn Street, Whitechapel, was the haunt where flotsam stirred by the social and political tides of Eastern Europe snagged in a sort of British eddy on its way across the Atlantic. There bearded savant rubbed shoulders with yellow-booted pimp, and over adjoining tables the blueprints for new heavens and new earths, drawn up with the help of the social templates of Marx and Bakunin, would be discussed, in competition with muttered schemes for burglaries and abductions. One got a first-rate game of chess there, too.

Violet took off her pince-nez, and, plucking out the snowy cambric handkerchief from the cuff of her mutton chop sleeve, began with her stubby, capable white fingers to clean the lenses. Her grey eyes were downcast for a while under their tow-coloured lashes, then she spoke in her warm, deep voice.

'But how came Solomons to be in Soho on the night of the murder, Iris? It is a long way from Whitechapel, after all.'

'Put up job, ma'am!' the magdalen exclaimed. 'Somebody 'ticed 'im up there, I'm sure. The busies must've known 'e'd been in that lay to do in the Rooshian general in '84, and they just set 'im up on the strength of it – for want o' somebody better. Trust 'em to pick on a foreigner!'

'But have you no more to go on than that, Iris?' my wife went on. 'If he is to be helped, there must be more than that. Without proper evidence . . .'

The reddened eyes turned as big as saucers as Iris shook her fists impatiently.

'But that's just it, ma'am!' she burst out. 'There is evidence of it: the 'ole East End knows about it, but not a word in the bloody papers – beggin' yer pardon, ma'am!'

Violet clipped on her pince-nez again, and searched the bedraggled woman's eyes.

'Please go on, my dear – the evidence . . .'

'The murder was supposed to 'appen on the Thursday midnight . . .'

'Thursday the what, Iris?' I asked from my perch at the windowsill. 'Please remember we have been away.'

'Sorry, doctor, I forgot. Thursday the 27th of last November. In all the papers. They took Monia – that's short for Solomon, ma'am – oh, my Monia!'

The absurd feather bobbed pathetically as Iris Starr covered her face with her hands and sobbed. Violet reached over the desk and patted her hand.

'Now bear up, Iris, do,' my wife urged gently. 'They took him where, and when?'

'That afternoon – the Friday, ma' am. 'E come in in the small hours. Wouldn't say where 'e'd been – not that that was anyfink fresh – an' slep' till dinnertime, then 'e went aht, an' I didn't see 'im again. They took 'im just after four ahtside the Scotch baker's in Dorset Street.'

'And what was this evidence you were going to tell us about?' Violet went on.

''E couldn't 'ave done it, ma'am – 'e just couldn't – because 'e couldn't 'ave got there in time. I was, well, walkin' down Osborn Street that Thursday night – near the Warsaw – Brummie Ida was wiv me at one time, an' she'll tell yer I was there – an' I saw Monia come aht of the Warsaw wiv a bloke called Klaff – I don't know 'is first name . . .'

'What time would this have been on the Thursday night, Iris?' I put in.

'Ooh, 'alf-eleven, maybe a bit later, and orff they both goes dahn the street to Klaff's place – just a few doors dahn from the Warsaw – but they came aht again direckly . . .'

'And was Brummie Ida with you all this time?' Violet asked.

'Yes, ma'am, an' she walked up and dahn wiv me till after midnight, then since nothin' was 'appenin' and a perishin' wind 'ad got up, she said, well, sod this for a lark – beg pardon, ma'am! – and went off.'

'Did you follow Klaff and Solomons, then?' I asked.

'Well, doctor, I was on the point of doin' it, but 'e fair goes orff the deep end if 'e gets the idea anyone's spyin' on 'im or follerin' 'im, so in the end I didn't bother.'

'Which direction did they go in?' Violet asked.

'Dahn towards the Whitechapel Road, then I lorst 'em.'

'Do you recall anyone else who might have seen Solomons coming out of Klaff's place?' Violet asked.

'No, ma'am, I've been rackin' me brain ever since, but as I said, it was fair perishin' in that wind, and the streets was deserted – anyone with any sense would've been indoors. I've asked arahnd there since, but either there wasn't nobody, or they're all keepin' shtum – you know 'ow it is rahnd 'ere.'

'But surely there must have been at least one police-patrol round there?' I said. 'Especially at that hour, when the pubs were starting to empty.'

Iris's round, bold face creased, and she gave a hoot of bitter laughter.

'No fear, doctor! On a perisher like that, they'd be 'avin' a tot of rum in some pub-guv'nor's back parlour, or like as not they'd be cuddled up in a doorway wiv one of us gels – you don't fink they let us 'ave the run o' the streets for nothin', do yer?'

Violet frowned, and stretched her clasped hands out on the desk-top.

'So you were the only one to see Solomons and Klaff come out of Klaff's lodgings, Iris?'

'I know what yer might be thinkin', ma'am, but I swear before Gawd I'm tellin' the truth. No power on earth could've got Monia from Osborn Street to Soho in the time they're sayin' 'e was there.'

'But he'd have had time,' I objected, 'especially by train, to get to Soho, if he or both of them changed direction after you'd lost sight of them. Eleven thirty or so from Whitechapel – that would leave them . . .'

'But that's just it, doctor – I saw Monia on 'is own, comin' back up Wentworth Street towards Liverpool Street station – cool as a cucumber – at 'alf-past one.'

'And nobody was with you on that occasion, either?' I asked.

'No, doctor – worse luck!'

'It all turns round what Solomons was up to between your two sightings, Iris,' Violet remarked, 'and this Klaff will have to be got into the witness box . . .'

'Doesn't look as if that 'un will run, ma'am . . .'

'Why? What do you mean?'

'Klaff's disappeared – 'ooked it, by the look of it.'

'How, Iris?' Violet demanded huskily, the lenses of her pince-nez glinting.

'Well, ma' am, as soon as I fahn aht Monia 'ad been took, I went rahnd to Leman Street – though I must say, it went against the grain – and told the coppers what I've just told you

11

– that'd 'ave been abaht seven on the Friday evenin' – an' they took me rahnd straight away to Osborn Street in a Black Maria. But when they asked Klaff's landlady where 'e was, she said that after 'e'd 'ad 'is dinner that day 'e'd up and paid 'er 'is back rent in gold – three quid it amahnted to – asked for 'is gear, which she'd been 'oldin' back against 'is rent, shoved 'is stuff in a seaman's bag, an' lit aht. Didn't tell 'er where 'e was goin' – not so much as kiss yer ar – 'and ma'am – and the coppers ain't been able ter trace 'im since – or that's their story . . .'

I exchanged glances with Violet, glances which in a trice encompassed a world of meaning. Our shared look asked the question whether we were ready, scarcely hours after our arrival back from what had been meant as a voyage of recuperation, to plunge into an affair charged with ominous implications, and this quite apart from the numerous responsibilities, left behind for weeks, of the work now to be resumed on the new socio-medical institute. Not to mention the everyday running of the People's Dispensary, our immediate responsibility that morning. However, in the face of the debt we owed poor Iris, there could be but one course of action open to us. Fortunately, it was a Sunday, so that after we had seen off the last patient after midday we should have the rest of the day to ourselves. We would have to talk. For the time being, Violet kept to the business in hand.

'When does Solomons' case come up, Iris?' she asked our visitor.

'Tomorrer, ma'am. Yer'll 'elp, then? Oh, say yer'll 'elp . . .'

'Of course, Iris,' my wife answered simply for both of us.

'Thank Gawd, ma'am! I should've known yer'd 'elp, after the way yer stood by Rosie Bartlett last year – goin' ter quod for 'er, an' all! An' you too, Dr Mortimer – yer a sport!'

Iris then said some rather extravagant things about my part in the Aldgate case the year before, which I need not go into here, but her compliments by no means relieved me of the weight of the realisation of what we might be taking on.

'Who will be representing Solomons?' Violet asked in her practical way. 'He must have legal assistance.'

'Oh, that's all taken care of ma'am – Mr Zeinvel from Crutched Friars.'

I reflected that that at least was a point in Solomons' favour, for David Zeinvel, whom I had got to know during the course of the Aldgate affair, was as clever as a box of monkeys, and in spite of his reputation among the police fraternity as a criminals' friend, I knew that he respected facts and evidence with the same scrupulousness as a dandy bestows on his clothes. I wondered, though, who would be footing Solomons' legal bill, for Zeinvel had not reached such a height in his profession as to be able to take on cases gratis. But for the moment there were more pressing matters to be considered.

'An excellent choice!' Violet echoed my thoughts. 'A most astute lawyer, and a fine man! But do you recall the name of this man Klaff's landlady, Iris? The man you say you saw Solomons with on the night of the murder?'

'Yes, ma'am – Mrs Snell – she's a real tartar! Her place is above Axelband's the piecework tailor's. You'll know it.'

Violet smiled and nodded, then got up and went round the desk to our visitor. She placed a comforting arm round Iris's shoulders, and pressed something into her hand as she led her to the door.

'Now you are not to take on so, Iris. It is all out of your hands now, and I suggest that, until you are called . . .'

'"Called", ma'am?'

'Yes, to stand witness at the trial: you have received a summons?'

'No, ma'am, Mr Zeinvel said that since the other lot ain't goin' ter call me, it'd do more 'arm than good to put me in the box. Looks as if they'd got their 'eads together. I suppose it's for the best, though.'

I had feared something of the sort, for witnesses of poor Iris's kind are generally seen by our learned friends as fit for nothing but bamboozling and bullyragging, their testimony being invariably deemed to be no better than it ought to be. On hearing this, Violet resumed her seat behind the desk, and scribbled briefly on a piece of paper, after which she got up again and rejoined Iris at the door.

'Very well, then, Iris,' she said, folding the note and pressing it in our visitor's hand. 'I suggest you go and stay at the place I've written on the note, while the trial is going on. I don't think you should be walking the streets till it's over.'

13

'Oh, no, ma'am! I can't just sit an' twiddle me thumbs while Monia's goin' through it . . .'

'From now on, Iris,' I said, 'we shall be your eyes and ears, and besides, there may well be people – powerful people – who might want to keep you quiet. I really think you should take Dr Branscombe's advice.'

The street-girl paused on the threshold, and looked intently at Violet.

'I shall be keeping you informed, Iris,' she said. 'Never fear.'

'Righto, ma'am, seein' as yer both on the case: I can see Monia's as good as aht already! I suppose this place you've written dahn's all Sir Garnett?'

'All Sir Garnett!' Violet remarked with a chuckle. 'All in order. It is a place in Hackney where girls can go who are, well, up against it. It is run by a clergyman friend of ours, but don't worry about your having to sing psalms or wash with carbolic soap, as he's a sport!'

'All right, then, ma'am – whatever you say.'

I stepped forward and slipped a couple of half-crowns into the young woman's hand.

'For the cab, Iris,' I said.

'Gawd bless yer, doctor, and you, ma'am.'

My wife smiled, then shot me a glance, and I escorted Iris Starr, still full of thanks, downstairs and out into the nearest disengaged cab, in which she would be conveyed to the Hackney women's refuge, where she would find succour under the roof of the Reverend Hilary Venables.

When I got back to the dispensary, I found that Violet had sent off the lad with the medicines, and was standing at the door in her outdoor things. She looked purposeful and determined, and I knew that, once she had assumed that expression, nothing would deter her from her object.

'They are not even going to listen to her testimony, James, but Iris shall have a voice, and we shall articulate it! I trust friend Zeinvel will be at his usual lunchtime table in Cohen's Restaurant, and I propose that we combine a little nourishment there with a confidential consultation with him.'

After we had locked up the dispensary, I escorted my wife to the restaurant in Fieldgate Street, where her surmise turned out

14

to be an accurate one, for at the usual table in the back of the room, we espied our legal friend's lacquered black head stooped over a plate of soup. As if sensing our notice, Zeinvel looked up quickly, his sharp, birdlike features framed in a sort of still alertness. Recognition quickly dawned in the dark, slightly almond-shaped eyes, and, dropping his spoon into his plate, he rose to his feet, and we strode up smiling before he could leave his seat.

'Dr Mortimer!' he exclaimed, wringing our hands in turn. 'And Dr Branscombe! I haven't seen you since the wedding – how are things with you?'

We sat down opposite Zeinvel, and, after ordering our luncheon, gave an account of ourselves. On hearing of Iris Starr's testimony, Zeinvel's face took on the impassivity of a carved mask.

'I won't disguise the fact that Solomons is up against it,' he murmured. 'There's a lot against him – or seems to be and he has powerful interests against him – very powerful interests. As to this man Klaff Iris Starr refers to – his name's Semyon Klaff, by the by – I've already spoken to the landlady, but . . .' Zeinvel gave an eloquent shrug. 'You could go and see her, I suppose,' he conceded. 'You may spot something I've missed.'

The lawyer's words acted on me like a cold douche.

'Is it so hopeless, then?' I muttered.

'Hopeless – no. I, er . . . have my contacts . . .' The aquiline face lit up with a sudden cheeky cockney grin, and my spirits rose again. 'And besides, my dear doctors, I now have you on my side!'

'What can we do?' Violet asked with husky urgency.

'Well, for one thing,' Zeinvel said, tackling a choice morsel of gefilte fish, 'one of you might be devilling for me at the Old Bailey tomorrow.'

I remembered that at that time, once a barrister had been briefed to take a case, the managing solicitor was not required to set foot in court. Violet was just about to speak when I silenced her with the sternest glare I could muster – she would *not* drive herself to a breakdown if I could help it – and leapt into the breach.

'I shall be that, er . . . devil, Zeinvel.'

15

'Capital, doctor! I was going to send along my clerk, Leonard. He's a good lad, but only a lad, after all.'

'What am I to do there, Zeinvel – what specifically . . .'

'The thing – if I may say so – you are best at, doctor – observe. I don't want a shorthand transcript of the proceedings – I can get that anyway – I want intelligent observations as to *how* those involved behave, how they react to the evidence, and so on.'

'I am your man, then, Zeinvel.'

'Excellent! Case comes up at ten thirty tomorrow in the Central Criminal Court of the Old Bailey. Be sure you get there good and early, or you'll have to stand in the corridor – it'll be one of the cases of the century! And it goes without saying that I shall always be happy to hear any new, er . . . lines you may have on the business in the meantime.'

Zeinvel suddenly laid his knife and fork methodically at either edge of the plate, and with a glance at the wall-clock, jerked to his feet, and with a quick nod and smile to each of us, shot off his parting remark as he left.

'Justice is no respecter of Sundays – I must be off. I bid you both good afternoon, and hope to hear from you, Dr Mortimer.'

Violet reached over the table and squeezed my hand.

'We must seize time by the forelock, James!'

Luncheon over, we repaired to the lodgings of Klaff the disappearing witness, but first we enquired at Axelband's, the tailoring workshop which occupied the ground floor of the building, Mrs Snell's establishment being on the top floor. I knew that such concerns as Axelband's could be kept occupied throughout the night, especially at busy periods, with piecework being delivered to pressers, and pressed garments in turn being delivered to retail tailors in time for the buttons to be sewn on for customers' orders, sometimes as far away as the West End. Could such a delivery-man have seen Solomons and Klaff on the night of the murder?

It seemed not, for Axelband, who was clearly none too pleased to be questioned yet again on the matter, insisted that he had closed his workshop, and sent home all his workers by eight thirty on the evening in question. And as for himself, he had long been in bed and asleep by the time the events we were investigating had taken place. He closed his grudging observations with the remark – not without a meaningful glance at each of us in turn – that those who had done a hard day's work slept soundly at nights.

We next tackled the rickety bare stair-treads to Mrs Snell's set of rooms up in the gods. A stout, red-faced matron in an apron, and with her grey hair in a bun on the top of her head, answered my knock, then stared at us truculently in silence. I explained our business, and she thrust her big jaw nearer mine before speaking.

'No, for the 'undredth time, I don't know where Mr Klaff is, and I don't care, neither, as long as 'e don't try to drop 'is 'ook 'ere again, which ain't likely, seein' as every flatfoot from 'ere to Timbuctoo's lookin' for 'im. Good riddance to bad rubbish, say I. Three months 'e kept 'is rent back from me, me who 'as to pay rent meself an' ain't got no other means o' support. Now if yer don't mind . . .'

'We appreciate the value of your time, Mrs Snell,' Violet said in her most diplomatic tone, at the same time slipping half a crown into the woman's hand, 'and we would not dream of trying to steal it . . .'

'Obliged, I'm sure,' the landlady said, with raised eyebrows. 'What else did yer want ter know?'

'Klaff paid off his rent arrears in gold, we understand?' I queried.

'Yerss – three sovereigns. Good 'uns, too – and the coppers took 'em away. Gave me a bleedin' receipt for 'em – what's the use o' that? I need the money now, not after the bleedin' trial – be sure I'll 'ave it back, too: I know me rights!'

'What did Klaff do for a living, Mrs Snell?' Violet asked.

'Supposed ter be a seaman, but the only ship I knew 'im ter serve on was the SS Ear'ole! 'Ung round the Warsaw for much o' the time. Didn't keep reg'lar hours – in and out all times o' the day or night. No use askin' 'im questions, neither – 'e'd just jabber back at yer in 'is own lingo – "me no savvy" style.'

'Did he have many visitors?' Violet asked.

''Ere? No, never. None that I noticed, any road.'

'And you've no notion how he came by his sovereigns?' I asked.

'I've no idea: all I care abaht is that 'e owed three of 'em ter me, an' I'm 'avin' 'em back!'

'What was Klaff like, Mrs Snell?' Violet asked.

17

The landlady sniffed, and turned down her mouth like a drawn bow.

'Funny little feller – dirty sort o' cove – full o' foreign ways. I've seen the coatmakers' nippers in Spitalfields foller 'im in the street, 'ollerin' "Our better friend! Our better friend!" in their funny English, though it's a wonder they know any English at all, cooped up nearly all day in them sweatin'-shops, an' all . . .'

We left Mrs Snell to her grievances, and made our way down into the street again, where I turned to Violet.

'What an odd thing for children to shout after a man,' I remarked. '"Our better friend . . ."'

2

While the light lasted, we decided to visit the scene of the crime: the notorious house in Poland Street where the storm petrel of the Russian war party had met his dreadful end the previous November. As the cab bore us through the still, cold afternoon up Charing Cross Road towards Manette Street, we discussed our findings so far. I began the summing-up.

'Two men – one of them with a known interest in the victim – are seen together one night in November last an hour on either side of a gruesome murder. The next afternoon, one of the pair is flush with gold, pays his back-rent, and disappears, the other sleeps through the morning and early afternoon, and, seemingly unsuspecting, is arrested and charged with the murder. How does it seem to you?'

'Thirty pieces of silver . . .'

'Mmm . . . betrayal. Yes, possibly: it certainly doesn't look like coincidence.'

'Our abscondee also happens to be a key witness,' Violet mused aloud.

'Yes, nobbling is another possibility.'

Violet smiled fondly.

'A penny for them, my dear . . .' I said with a chuckle, giving her hand a squeeze.

'Papa used to say' (I might add that Violet's late father had been none other than Colonel Hereward Branscombe of the Chitral Scouts, the Hero of Maiwand) 'that once the Russian Bear broke loose into the Dardanelles, he would only have to slap his paw down over the Suez Canal, and the British lines of communication with India would be throttled.'

'Yes,' I agreed, 'there is the political aspect to be considered, too. Ostyankin's deliberate provocations on behalf of the Russian war party against Turkey's Balkan possessions were designed towards that very end. There are no doubt many in the chancelleries of Europe – not excluding those of Great Britain – who rejoiced to hear of his demise. A political assassination is not to be ruled out. Deep waters, and there's another thing: the sovereigns . . .'

'What sovereigns?' Violet asked.

'Klaff's apparent windfall. Why did the police take away the sovereigns which he used to pay off his rent arrears? The coins must have some relevance to the case. Still, it is early days yet, and – ah! Manette Street . . .'

Soon the hansom was skirting Soho Square, then negotiated the teeming alleys to cut across Wardour and Berwick Streets. We turned right up D'Arblay Street and emerged at last into Poland Street. I tapped the canopy above me with my stick, and instructed the cabbie to wait on the street corner, and we alighted, to continue on foot to the junction with Noel Street. It was quiet enough on this dull, cold Sunday afternoon, but what company was abroad was not, in the words of the Waxworks Lady in *The Old Curiosity Shop*, 'partick'ler select'. Characters one might have run up against in the backstreets of Marseilles or Naples eyed us insolently from the doorways of French or Italian eating places, and the odours of black tobacco and coffee mingled with those from gutter and alleyway. One outrageously dressed beanpole of a woman in an unlikely hat which was topped with an ostrich feather about a yard long stepped out in front of us, and, seeming to dismiss Violet with a contemptuous waggle of thumb and wrist, asked me in raucous French if I would like a change. To her evident dismay, my wife retorted in gutter French that if she didn't clear off, she'd smash her face in!

'Sometimes it is the only way,' Violet murmured, as she tugged me away from the scene, the woman remarking behind us that you couldn't try to get an honest living round here without being threatened with violence, to the accompaniment of derisive laughter from the open door of a café. I should explain that my wife had been forced by the virulence of male prejudice in England against women doctors to take her medical degree at the Sorbonne, and her French vocabulary was extensive.

I tightened Violet's linked elbow in mine, and we quickened our pace. At last we reached the crossing with Noel Street, and, brushing past a yawning woman in a muddy-hemmed cast-off serge costume and feather boa who was positioned under the corner lamp-post there, we crossed the street and walked up to the area of the fatal house, which was marked by a policeman on guard. We discreetly re-crossed the street in order to have a wider view of the building. Poland Street had seen better days, its façade having lost its integrity through the insertion of shop windows in some of the ground-floor premises, and it was clear that many residential buildings there had been divided into dingy human rookeries, no doubt to provide refuges for the sort of fly-by-nights we had just brushed with. Dirt and poverty were the prevailing impressions, but there seemed to be something of the original residential sedateness of the street about No. 11, the murder house. In spite of grime and dilapidation, the front of the building kept its chaste eighteenth-century design, complete with wrought-iron railings and fine door-case. Half-a-dozen railed steps led up over the area-well to the front door. There were two further floors beside the ground floor, together with an attic-storey. A zone of solitude extended for a radius of about twenty yards round the policeman.

We swept our gaze up and down the street, noting here and there isolated buildings which seemed also to have retained their original function as private dwellings.

'Perfectly situated for *maisons de tolérance*,' Violet remarked. 'Discreetly and shabbily comfortable inside, no doubt, and convenient for the so-called respectable who would indulge their vices in the appropriate quarter of the town. The fleshly paradise for the sexual hypocrites of the capital!'

We crossed again, and went round the back of Poland Street, which presented a vista of mews and outhouses, few of which seemed to have retained their original purpose of stabling coach-horses for the solid folk who must once have inhabited the quarter. The majority had no doubt been converted to work-shops given over to various sweated trades. Again, filth and dilapidation had smeared the place with their greasy fingers. We noticed how little depth No. 11 seemed to have in comparison with the surrounding houses.

'It seems to be only one room deep,' Violet remarked. 'Let us go round to the front again.'

'Yes,' I said as I complied, 'though perhaps that is because more buildings have been added on to the backs of the neighbouring houses.'

We braved the hawk eyes of the constable at the foot of the

steps up to the front door of No. 11 and examined the house close-up.

'Ah!' Violet exclaimed lightly. 'I thought so. Look at the door- and window-cases, James, and compare them with those of the surrounding houses.'

I am no architectural historian beyond the extent of knowing Georgian from Jacobean, but it was clear to me that the features my companion had pointed out, though generally eighteenth-century, were quite different from those of the surrounding houses. This shallowness of structure would later have an important bearing on the case on which we were now launched.

'I suspect that No. 11 was an earlier house,' Violet went on, 'originally standing on its own, and the rest of the street was built round it. One comes across this in streets built or extended in the late eighteenth or early part of this century, when there was a positive frenzy of building in London. The wasteful modern habit of knocking houses down to accommodate new streets does not seem to have caught on among that generation of speculators.'

'No, their motto seems to have been one of the most rents for the least expense.'

We decided that that would suffice for a preliminary reconnaissance, and, rejoining our cab, we instructed the cabbie to drive us to the Junior Minerva Club in Coptic Street, a forum for young women of the most advanced ideas, and where Violet had been a resident member before our marriage. We took tea there, then retired to the club library, where we spent the rest of the late afternoon and early evening among the back numbers of the more respectable newspapers, getting up the background to the events in Poland Street. When we finally returned to our rooms in Henrietta Street, we had much to discuss.

Our new concern emphasised the need for a new division of labour between us, and that evening the issue was finally hammered out. From now on, I should assume the role of clerk-of-works of the new Whitechapel clinic-under-construction that was taking shape before our eyes in the burnt-out shell of the former People's Dispensary, across the little court in which we held our present clinic. In fact, Jim Postgate, the foreman appointed by Dobson and Harkrider, the builders whom we had contracted, was perfectly capable of running the show under his own steam, testimony to which was the fact that the works were running slightly ahead of time. I did not stress this fact to my wife, who would naturally have ascribed this state of affairs to her own hectic interventions before I had put my foot down the previous autumn. All, then, was proceeding on course, and when first thing on Monday morning I briefed Postgate on the Whitechapel site, he greeted the news that my 'missus' would no longer be directing operations with an undisguised sigh of relief. I saw to it that all was in order – no new materials to be ordered or bills met on the spot, and no fractious suppliers or sub-contractors to be 'geed-up' – and left him to it with the injunction that on no account was he to let things slacken, for 'she' would be sure to be watching from the dispensary across the court. From the expression on his face, I could see that my warning was scarcely necessary!

While I was thus left free on the new dispensary side to act as observer in the court case that was about to unfold, we had asked Jane Bonsor, who had given us yeoman service in the past, to take over my normal duties in the dispensary *pro tem*. Jane had been the baby of the little band of young women among whom Violet had pursued her medical studies in Paris, and as our medical endeavours in Whitechapel developed, she would come to play an increasingly important role. For the moment, however, my business was in the Central Criminal Court of the Old Bailey, and I made haste for the Strand.

I arrived just after nine thirty, and I was glad that I had come an hour in advance of the opening of Solomons' trial, for the crowd of would-be spectators packing the corridors was so great that I heard it said that it almost rivalled that which had assembled to watch the trial of Adelaide Bartlett in '86, when the numbers of latecomers had to be restricted to those who held tickets previously issued by the sheriffs. I did however manage to fight my way to a place on a bench just four rows back from the lawyers' table which fronted the jurors' box. By turning my head slightly to the right, I had a first-rate view of the witness box, which stood between the jury box and the judge's bench farther down on the right, which in its turn faced across the great, high-ceilinged chamber to the dock against the left-hand wall.

I sought to divert myself amid the pre-opening hubbub by

surveying my neighbours on the spectators' benches. An almost solid array of suet-pudding-fed middle-class English faces, the men in dingy serge and the women in out-of-doors bombazine, with here and there a pillbox-hatted Tommy Atkins on leave. There was an odour of damp clothes and stale tobacco, with an occasional contribution of patchouli and mothballs from the ladies. I began to make out phrases and sentences amid the general murmur.

'I mean, he tried to do him in in Russia: it was in the paper . . .'

'Open-and-shut case, if you ask me . . .'

'Nothing but a pack of bloody foreign anarchists and red socialists – I'd send all the buggers back, if I had me way . . .'

'Let's have fair play and all that, but what I say is, if this sort of thing's allowed to run rampant, we'll none of us be safe at nights . . .'

'Yerss, give 'em an inch and they'll take an ell . . .'

The correspondence of class, appearance and demeanour between those who fill the public benches at an English trial and those who go to make up the average jury is remarkable, and I felt that if the sentiments of the 'twelve good men and true' who, primed by three months of newspaper-inflamed prejudice, were soon to sit in judgment on Solomon Solomons were anything like those of my fellow spectators, the outlook must be dim indeed for the accused.

A figure stood out from the row in front of me, just three observers down on my right. A compact, smartly dressed female form, with her blonde hair drawn up under a neat little black hat, from which a veil descended to cover her face. She was gazing straight ahead of her, and seemed to disdain the comments of the uncouth tradespeople who surrounded her. What, I wondered, would a lady be doing in this *galère*?

My musings were interrupted by a stir in the chamber: the judge and his retinue were coming in. An official called out the prescribed Norman French rigmarole, and the court rose. Drama was in the air as the jury were sworn in, one by one, then the charge was read out. All eyes were now on the slight, lightly bearded figure with the sharp, high features of some Assyrian high priest who now stood in the dock across on the left-hand wall. Solomon Solomons stared straight across at the judge's bench, his slim left hand dangling nonchalantly over the edge of the dock.

The accused was challenged, and his quiet voice fell calmly into the hushed chamber: 'Not guilty,' and, surprising as it may seem to the modern reader, that was all that the court was to hear from him, for until the Criminal Evidence Act came into force in 1898, defendants were not allowed to speak in their own defence. Nor for the reasons I have already indicated did I have the reassurance of seeing my old friend David Zeinvel at the lawyers' table.

Solomons having pleaded not guilty, the counsel for the prosecution was called upon to outline the case and introduce the evidence-in-chief, and here a stir ran through the court, for appearing for the prosecution was none other than Sir Edward Clarke, the Solicitor General. There could have been no clearer indication of the interest the government had in the case than that Sir Edward should appear for the Crown, for apart from the weight and prestige attached to him on account of his distinguished career at the bar and in politics, as well as for his skills as a jury orator – he would be chosen by his party to reply to Gladstone's historic Home Rule Bill two years later – he would enjoy because of his office a crucial procedural advantage which will emerge in the course of my narrative.

'At half-past seven in the morning of Friday the 28th of November last,' Sir Edward began in his dry, clear voice, 'Police Constable Edwin Luckham, while patrolling his beat along Great Marlborough Street, Soho, was approached by Mrs Eliza Donkin, who asked him to come with her to No. 11, Poland Street, where she had just minutes before arrived for her work as cleaner, saying that she had found the dead body of a man in one of the bedrooms. Constable Luckham then asked her if she had sent for a doctor, and she replied that the man was beyond all that, and that, in her own words, he had been "done in worse than Jack the Ripper".'

Sir Edward paused for a moment, and a light murmur rustled through the court.

'Constable Luckham then accompanied Mrs Donkin to No. 11, Poland Street, where he was led into a bedroom, where he found the dead body of a naked man of late middle-age, dreadfully mutilated and tied spreadeagle-fashion by the wrists and ankles to the posts of a brass bedstead. Constable Luckham then summoned assistance by blowing his whistle out of the window of the room, which gave out on to the street, a colleague of his arriving within three minutes. This colleague, Constable Matthew Divitt, went immediately in search of medical assistance, then to inform his superiors. Constable Luckham examined the body on the bed without attempting to move it, satisfied himself that life was extinct, and asked Mrs Donkin who the man was. She replied that she did not know, and that she had only ever cleaned the place when it had been empty. On being asked who the regular tenant of the house was she again disclaimed knowledge, saying that she had got the job from the house-agents, who also paid her wages, and that she did similar work for them in other houses in the district. It has since been ascertained that the tenant on the agents' books is a Mr De Kok, who has yet to be traced.

'Detective Sergeant Houlsby then arrived from Great Marlborough Street police station, the time being ten to eight. He was accompanied by a local physician, Dr Reginald Pinnock, who satisfied himself after a cursory examination that the man on the bed was dead, whereupon Sergeant Houlsby instructed Constable Divitt, who had arrived with the doctor, to go back to the police station to fetch expert medical assistance, and ordered Constable Luckham to position himself at the front door and to make sure that no one entered or left the building unsupervised. Sergeant Houlsby then dismissed Dr Pinnock, and made a thorough examination of the room. He found no evidence of a struggle, and that there was a shapeless mass of burnt cloth in the grate of the fireplace, with indications that the fire had been doused at some time. Sergeant Houlsby detected a smell of chloroform on the pillow of the bed, but found no mud, moisture or any suspicious-seeming discoloration on the carpet, which was deeply piled and laid from wall to wall. All four windows of the room – two on the street side, two looking out on the mews at the back – were shut, but none of the catches had been secured. Detective Sergeant Houlsby then went through the contents of a full set of male clothing which were draped over an upright chair at the side of the bed, and from an examination of papers found in the pockets was able to ascertain that the owner of the clothes was General Pyotr Ivanovitch Ostyankin, who, it

26

turned out on subsequent investigation, had been staying at the Cadogan Hotel under the name of Monsieur Lefranc, and had left there at nine thirty on the previous evening in company with another gentleman, a Mr Alexander Miller.

'At about half-past eight the police surgeon, Mr Calton-Freke, arrived at No. 11, Poland Street, and made a thorough examination of the body, discovering that, apart from the extensive mutilations he had suffered, the dead man had received a fatal stab-wound through the heart. The dead man was later identified as General Ostyankin.

'Now at about ten past four on that Friday afternoon a man was arrested for acting suspiciously in Dorset Street, Whitechapel, and was detained for further questioning at Leman Street police station. He was in possession of eighteen pounds in gold sovereigns, and was unable to give a satisfactory account of how he had come by that sum of money. Evidence however came to light later on in the day that established the strong likelihood that the sovereigns had been drawn by the deceased General Ostyankin from Coutts Bank in the Strand on the previous morning, Thursday the 27th November.

'The man arrested in Dorset Street on the Friday afternoon was the accused, Solomon Solomons, and the Crown will set out to prove that the said sovereigns in his possession were the identical coins drawn by General Ostyankin on the previous day, and that Solomons did at some time between the hours of midnight on Thursday the 27th of November last and two in the morning on Friday the 28th wilfully murder him.'

The judge, Lord Justice Calthrop, slowly made a note, then, peering over the cut-off lenses of a pair of antique reading-glasses, indicated that Sir Edward might call his first witness, who was PC Luckham. The constable merely confirmed what counsel for the Crown had said in his opening speech, except for the further detail, under cross-questioning from the defence counsel, the then-unknown junior barrister Francis Carmody, that the back door of No. 11, Poland Street had been locked when he had searched the house on his arrival, and that there had been no signs of forcible entry at back or front.

The next witness, Mrs Eliza Donkin the cleaner, corroborated Sir Edward's statement, but added, under Carmody's cross-questioning, that the front door of the house in Soho had been locked when she had arrived for work, as had been the back door, when later she had checked it with PC Luckham.

Detective Sergeant Houlsby was then taken through his testimony by Sir Edward, after which the defence counsel asked him if there had been much blood in the vicinity of the bed. A great deal, the sergeant had replied, including marks up to a yard up the wall behind the bed-head. On further cross-examination by Carmody, the CID man confirmed that there had been no sign of a struggle in the room.

Calton-Freke, the police surgeon, gave an amplification of what Sir Edward had said in relation to his initial inspection of the body of the victim, but the next witness, Sir James Ettrick, the distinguished pathologist, was the big gun among those who had testified up to that moment.

After establishing the surgeon's credentials – no brief process – Sir Edward launched into his examination of the cause and means of death.

'In your opinion, Sir James, at what time did the deceased meet his death?'

'Judging by the state of rigor and the degree of lividity of the body at the temperature of the room recorded by my colleague Mr Calton-Freke, I should say between midnight and two in the morning.'

'No later than that?'

The bearlike man's small dark eyes almost disappeared under the bushy grey eyebrows as he pondered the question for a moment.

'Certainly not later than that,' was his reply. 'In fact, I should be inclined to put it nearer midnight than 2 a.m.'

'Could you describe the deceased's injuries, Sir James?'

'In terms a layman might understand,' added the judge with a weary sigh. 'If you please . . .'

'Deceased,' Sir James began, 'had had his left ear partially torn off and had been cut and stabbed repeatedly about the face in a series of about thirty superficial, random blows, the soft tissue of the nose having been cut away entirely. Deceased's genital organs had been cut off and from the state of the inside of the mouth, I infer that there had been an attempt to force them into the mouth, probably after death. The most serious single injury, however, was a deep, straight stab-wound through the heart.'

'And that,' the prosecution counsel remarked, 'was presumably the cause of death?'

'Lacking exact knowledge of the sequence of the blows, I'm inclined to say, yes, that would have been the most likely immediate cause of death, though the shock and loss of blood occasioned by the other injuries, and particularly the genital wounds, could easily have proved fatal in themselves.'

'And what in your opinion might the murder weapon have been?'

'A sharp, two-edged, straight blade about eight inches long and an inch wide.'

'Such as might be the blade of, say, a stiletto?'

Sir Edward seemed to give an extra sibilance to the initial consonant of the last word, and there was a sort of answering murmur from the body of the court. A stiletto – the sort of knife a foreigner might use . . .

'Yes,' Sir James grunted. 'Something of the sort.'

'And would you say the wounds had been caused by a single hand?'

'Mmm . . . difficult to say, but from experience, I should say yes.'

'Apart from the odour in the room and the traces on the pillowcase, were there medical indications that chloroform had been used on the deceased?'

'Yes, the autopsy indicated it had been inhaled as vapour, rather than ingested as a liquid.'

'Had it been expertly administered, would you have said?'

'Insofar as the patient didn't die of it . . .' was Sir James's wry retort, to answering laughter from the court.

'And what would have been General Ostyankin's general state of health, before he came by these terrible injuries?'

'A1 – a most robust subject for his age and weight.'

'What was your general impression of the general's wounds, Sir James?'

The big grey man's voice came over low and sombre. 'I have been a member of the medical profession for over half a century, but I think they were the worst injuries I have ever known one human being to inflict on another.'

'Thank you, Sir James. I have no further questions, my Lord.'

Francis Carmody was on his feet before the judge had finished his nod.

'What was deceased's height and weight, Sir James?'

'Five feet eleven, and sixteen and a half stone.'

The defence counsel swung his gaze over to his client in the dock and smiled at the slightly built figure who stood there with such a languid air, and, once the heads of spectators and jurors had ranged in that direction for a moment, Carmody returned his attention to the pathologist.

'If you'll allow me a personal remark, Sir James, you yourself look a pretty powerful man – no stranger to the rugger-pitch in your time, I'll warrant.'

'I've propped up a few forward lines, yes, and I daresay I carry as much beef as the next man.'

'Even in your salad days, Sir James – again please forgive the observation – would you have cared to tackle a sixteen-and-a-half-stone man – however well-chloroformed – and, unaided, haul him on to a bed two foot six off the ground?'

'No, sir, I would not, and in any case, that's what hospital porters are for!'

More tittering in court.

'Thank you, Sir James,' Carmody said with an unabashed smile. 'No more questions, my lord.'

'You may step down, Sir James,' the judge said in his dry, rustling voice. 'It being a quarter to one, I think we might retire for luncheon. The court will meet again at two o'clock.'

3

I joined the general scurry towards the exit, though – Lord knows how! – a racing pack of pressmen was already well ahead of the vanguard in the corridor. Once outside, I walked briskly down the Strand to where it joins Fleet Street, then made for Wine Office Court and the Cheshire Cheese, where I laid claim to a pew and ordered beefsteak pudding and a pot of ale. I sorted out my impressions while I waited for my meal.

The defence counsel, Carmody's, strategy – a clear case of his having to make forensic bricks without the vital straw of corroborative witnesses – was becoming clear. A lone man – there had been nothing in the indictment about accomplices – slightly built and with the look of a scholar or seminarist rather than a bravo or bully, was supposed to have overpowered and chloroformed a hulking man nearly six feet tall, stripped him, and, unaided, hauled him on to a bed and tied him to the posts by his wrists and ankles. I saw too the drift of Carmody's questions as to whether the doors of No. 11, Poland Street had been locked on the arrival of the cleaner, and, after her, Constable Luckham, and whether there had been any signs of forcible entry: the murderer had either been admitted or had been in previous possession of a key. Francis Carmody had evidently decided to let the facts act as the principal witnesses for the defence. The case had gripped me, and I positively bolted my beefsteak pudding and swilled down my ale before dashing back into the roar of Fleet Street, such was my eagerness to regain my seat on the public benches in the Central Criminal Court.

Back in the Old Bailey, the next witness to be called was Emilio Quandt, the clerk who had booked General Ostyankin into the Cadogan Hotel under the name of 'Monsieur Lefranc' on Monday the 10th of November and had later taken the general's key when he had gone out, never to return, at half-past nine on the fatal evening of the 27th, accompanied by a gentleman who would appear presently to give his testimony.

To return to Quandt the hotel clerk, he gave his impression

under Carmody's cross-questioning that the Russian militarist had been in high good humour when he had left the hotel that evening, even quipping in response to the clerk's solicitous warning about the rising wind that, whatever the weather, 'the night had been made for love!' Sir Edward coughed loudly at that point, as if to break the expectant silence with which the court had received this last remark. Mr Carmody had no more questions to put to the witness.

Next to testify was James Withers, the cabbie who had conveyed the deceased and his gentleman companion from the Cadogan Hotel directly to Kettners restaurant in Romilly Street, where they had been put down just before ten o'clock. Withers had been unable to gauge anything as to the mood or demeanour of his two fares, nor had he caught the drift of anything they had said.

Fritz Moritz, head waiter at Kettners, next stepped into the witness box. He had been busy as usual that Thursday evening, but in the intervals when he had noticed Ostyankin, who had patronised the restaurant quite frequently over the years, the Russian had seemed to be in serious conversation with his companion. On being challenged by the defence counsel as to the 'seriousness' of that conversation – had the two men seemed to be arguing or quarrelling? – Moritz replied no, merely 'seriously talking, as one might about business,' and that Ostyankin had paid the reckoning with a sovereign and tipped him the change, before leaving quietly at about eleven thirty with his companion, to be driven by the next witness, cabman Edwin Mordew, directly to the opening to back Poland Street, near the intersection with Noel Street. Carmody asked whether the cabbie was sure it had been the back street Ostyankin had entered by, and he replied that, yes, he had distinctly seen the tall, stout gentleman disappear up it into the darkness. He had then driven the other gentleman to Farm Street, where they arrived at about a quarter to midnight, and the latter had descended and paid the fare.

The defence counsel having no further questions, and the cabman having been stood down, the judge engaged in some no-doubt technical interchange with the Solicitor General, and my attention wandered to the front row again. The smartly dressed, veiled lady was still there, and I now noticed her small, perfectly moulded torso. I mused idly that, if the face under the veil matched her figure, we must have a Pocket Venus in our midst.

'Your name is Alexander Miller?'

Sir Edward Clarke's voice broke in on my reverie, and I glanced up at the new occupant of the witness box. He was a smallish, plump man in the late forties, with thinning ginger hair and a not-very-successful beard. He had what I have heard termed an 'honest Scotch face', but the accent in which he gave his answer to the prosecution counsel did not confirm this impression, as the high, almost feminine voice belied the plain, blunt features and stubby root of the body.

'That is my name, sir,' came the flutily cultured tones, in which there yet lurked the hint of foreign fields.

'You are a Russian subject, and reside at 8, Farm Street?'

'Both correct, sir.'

'What is your occupation?'

'I am an import agent in the timber trade, and I act as *homme d'affaires* to several gentlemen with interests in that line.'

'Is that the relation in which you stood to the late General Ostyankin?'

'Yes, sir, our relations were on a business footing.'

'Had you known the general long?'

'I first met him at a social gathering in St Petersburg about twenty years ago, and he asked me to look after his business interests here in England. The general was of a powerful land-owning family, and owned extensive forests in Finland.'

'Did you know the purpose of his last visit here last November, apart from a wish to keep an eye on his business interests?'

'No, sir, I did not enquire about the general's other interests: an *homme d'affaires* must above all be discreet, or he would soon cease to be one.'

'Quite, Mr Miller. And during your last conversation with him in Kettners restaurant on the evening of the 27th of November last year, what did you talk about?'

'We talked of a forthcoming visit he wished me to make to the North of England, in connection with a cargo of timber that was to be landed from Mariehamn.'

'Did the general seem at all apprehensive or worried on that evening?'

'On the contrary, he was in good spirits – at his ease.'

'And as far as you could see, did these good spirits accompany him to Poland Street, where he left you that night?'

'Definitely, sir. We had arranged to meet the following Monday to discuss the final details of my trip north, and that was our main topic of conversation in the cab to Poland Street.'

'Did you go straight home on getting out of the cab in Farm Street?'

'No, sir, I went down to the house of a Russian friend of mine – also on Farm Street – where we used to get together with others for cards and Russian talk.'

'Unannounced,' the judge broke in drily, 'and at nearly midnight?'

The stubby ginger man giggled and spread out his hands.

'We Russians are *sans façons*, my lord – how do you put it? – we do not stand on ceremony, and, as for midnight, why for us the evening is just beginning then.'

'I see,' Lord Justice Calthrop said uncomprehendingly. 'Please carry on, Sir Edward . . .'

'How long did you stay at this, er . . . informal gathering, Mr Miller?'

'From just before midnight till about half-past two in the morning, then I went straight home to bed.'

The Solicitor General nodded and changed tack.

'And can you suggest any reason why, judging by the general's conversation and demeanour in your presence that evening, he might have faced the dreadful end that awaited him in the house in Poland Street?'

'None, sir, as God is my witness. If there was a carefree man in London that night, it was General Ostyankin.'

'Thank you, Mr Miller. No further questions, my lord.'

A glance from the judge, and Francis Carmody was up on his feet.

'You will be aware that General Ostyankin is one of the most talked-about figures in Europe, Mr Miller?'

A shrug from the timber-agent.

'Politics – I know nothing of that, sir. I am a businessman.'

'You are a member of a distinguished St Petersburg service family, are you not, Mr Miller?'

Another shrug.

'Your most illustrious ancestor was a Scottish master shipwright, Hugh Miller, who was invited to Russia nearly two centuries ago by Tsar Peter the Great to help rebuild the Russian Navy?'

'That is so, yes, and we have done our best for Russia since then.'

'Too modest, Mr Miller! You number among your ancestors two field-marshals and an Imperial privy counsellor, do you not? And I believe your elder brother is today a senior member of the Russian diplomatic corps?'

Miller slashed his hand dismissively in the air.

'Yes, yes, that is so.'

The counsel for the defence turned to face the jury, and smiled scornfully.

'I see, Mr Miller, and you say you know nothing of the late General Ostyankin's politics?'

Yet another shrug.

'That is not an answer!' the judge snapped.

'I am sorry, my lord – no, I did not know anything about the general's politics.'

Carmody returned to the attack.

'Can you shed any light on the late general's comment as you both left the Cadogan Hotel on the night of the 27th of November, as related to us by the booking-clerk there, that "the night was made for love"?'

A rather unconvincing smile creased the Russian's homely features.

'Oh, the general was a very jovial man, sir, always joking!'

Mr Carmody did not smile.

'How long have you lived in London, Mr Miller?'

'I have my office here – in Leadenhall Street – but I also have an office in Petersburg, and . . .'

'*Lived* here, Mr Miller – on and off. How long?'

'Twenty-two years.'

'Then you will be familiar with Soho?'

'Mmm . . . not so familiar, sir. My business does not take me there.'

'And does your pleasure ever take you there?'

Sir Edward was on his feet in an instant.

'My lord, that is an entirely impertinent question!'

Lord Justice Calthrop peered censoriously at the young defence counsel over his half-track spectacles.

'I am inclined to agree with you there, Sir Edward. Mr Carmody, what is the point of your question?'

'My lord,' the young barrister replied, 'I seek to find out from the witness whether, after more than twenty years' residence in London, he is at least aware of the reputation of Soho as a quarter of vice and prostitution notorious throughout Europe.'

'I see, then pray do so, without prevarication or insinuation.'

Francis Carmody did so, but Miller's floury dumpling face betrayed no emotion as he made his reply.

'I stand by what I have said, sir. I do not know Soho, and I do not go there for business or for pleasure, nor do I know or care why General Ostyankin went there.'

With a little shake of the head and an incredulous smile for the benefit of the jury, Carmody looked down and shuffled his papers on the table.

'No more questions, my lord.'

Francis Carmody was making his mark, and all eyes were on him as he flopped back down into his seat. It seemed as if he had caught the eye of the intriguing veiled lady in the row in front of me in particular, for as soon as Miller had left the witness box and disappeared through the door behind, she raised her veil and looked towards the lawyers' table. A very fair, kittenish face, its striking prettiness marred only by a thin, set-lipped mouth, whose hardness no salve would ever conceal.

A Dr Fedoroff then entered the witness box, to testify that Miller had called at his house – 19, Farm Street – just before midnight on the night of the 27th of November, at the very moment when he was on his way out to deal with an emergency call in distant Highgate. Providentially, Miller had been able to take the doctor's place at the card table with three other Russian guests in time to prevent the breaking-up of a convivial game of whist. Miller had remained at the table till half-past two on the Friday morning, when Dr Fedoroff had returned from his call, and the party had finally broken up.

Jules Cazes, Dr Fedoroff's French manservant, then stepped

into the witness box to testify that he had let only one gentleman out from the card party that night – a Major Tvardoffsky, who had left in a rather downcast state, judging by his looks, and with the words: 'I've won enough hearts for one night, I think,' Mr Miller, who was known to the servant, had left with the other two gentlemen after the doctor had returned at half-past two.

Lord Justice Calthrop then intervened gravely, addressing the jury.

'I should point out here that, as far as the enquiries of the police have been able to ascertain, the other three participants of this card party – apart from the witness Alexander Miller – left the country immediately after the death of General Ostyankin had become public knowledge, and that subsequently this court has been unable to bring them here to testify. As it is nearly five o'clock, I shall now dismiss the court until half-past ten tomorrow morning.'

We all rose as the judge retired amid a string of bawled-out medieval jargon. I was astonished at how quickly the time had flown, and what a strain it had been to concentrate on all the testimony heard. My head was abuzz with speculation as I drifted on the tide of humanity into a darkling Fleet Street, where a damp, pearly fog was beginning to descend. No cab could be obtained for love or money, so I made my way briskly to the Temple station, where I presently boarded the 5.04 District train for Whitechapel.

I had much food for thought as I sat in the crowded, dimly lit smoking carriage, and meditatively rolled a cigarette. It was clear first and foremost that politics had loomed very large in the Poland Street case, quite apart from the late victim's prominence in that field. The witness Miller's diplomatic economy with words, his evidently high connections in Russian politics, the three mysteriously missing witnesses to his presence at the card game in Farm Street – all of them army officers – all of this pointed to affairs of state. Anyone opening a morning paper in those days could hardly avoid being aware that Russia was divided between Orthodox and Westernising parties, and that large sections of the armed forces were affected to the former traditionalist, expansionist faction, of which General Ostyankin had been one of the leading lights. There would no doubt have been many, too, on the opposite side who must have welcomed the news of his elimination with joy. To which faction – if any – did Alexander Miller and his gambling cronies belong?

And where would the British government stand? At all costs the revelation of a possible British official involvement, or that of one of our Balkan allies – Turkey in particular – in the crime must be avoided. The alternative did not bear thinking about. No, official Britain's ideal culprit would be a Russian, and one with revolutionary or criminal antecedents. Solomon Solomons filled the bill to a 't', and I could not doubt that the British authorities would do all in their power – short of directly thwarting the legal process – to hasten his conviction.

I blew a smoke-ring into the overbreathed air of the carriage, and recalled Klaff, that other potential witness who had also disappeared immediately after news of the general's death had come out. Like migrating swallows . . . And where did I stand in all this? Certainly I held no brief for the politics of the bomb and the knife, however grievous the wrongs that might have incited them. Fair play and charity were my chosen weapons against society's ills, with strong, just laws as a shield. And apart from the great debt Violet and I owed to Solomons' distracted sweetheart, the thought that three great empires might be in league under the prosaic London skies to destroy an innocent stranger could not but awaken in me the fighting spirit of a free man. I got up and crushed my cigarette firmly under my boot as the train screeched into Whitechapel station. We should see.

4

After evening surgery I related the events of the trial to Violet over supper in our rooms in Henrietta Street, and she immediately agreed with my initial diagnosis that, as with the proverbial iceberg, nine-tenths of the case was submerged from the public view.

'There can be no doubt that politics plays a major part in this affair, James, and, as you point out, the choice of the Solicitor General to lead for the prosecution confirms this. How they must be longing to get the whole business over and done with!'

Something occurred to me, and I laid down my knife and fork on my plate.

'It is curious, Violet,' I remarked.

'What is, my dear?'

'The testimony of the French servant of the Russian doctor in Farm Street, where the card-game involving Miller and the three others was supposed to have taken place on the night of the murder.'

'Whist – at Dr Fedoroff's house. Yes?'

'About what the Russian officer who left the card-game at half-past midnight was supposed to have said to the servant.'

'Mmm . . . that he'd won enough hearts for that night, or something of the sort – odd remark to have made – but I suppose that, the company being Russians, a certain amount of drink had been taken on board by then, and who knows what nonsense a man may talk when he's a bit squiffy!'

'It's not the quality of the remark I mean,' I elaborated, 'but, well – hearts. I believe your late father was rather fond of cards, Violet?'

'Yes, a man's not much use in an Indian mess in peacetime if he can't join in card-games. What of it?'

'From what he may have told you, can you think of a game where *winning* hearts might make one gloomy, as the departing Russian guest seemed, according to the French servant?'

'Ah, I see what you mean. Well, the actual game of Hearts

comes to mind: in Hearts you lose a point for every heart you take.'

'That will have been it, then. And how many players are needed to make a game?'

'Oh, three to six or more: there are a number of variations of the game.'

'But starting with three?'

'Mmm . . . generally, yes, especially in a small gathering. You think the arithmetic may be significant, then?'

'May be something in it: if only they could bag those absconding witnesses . . .'

We left the table to the maid-of-all-work to clear away the supper things, and retired to the front parlour, where, changing the subject to the building-works – ah, those works! – Violet discussed ways and means until, at no late hour, we turned in for the night.

The second day of the trial found me in the same place on the public benches, and I noticed that the Pocket Venus was also in her place of yesterday in the row in front. This time she had discarded her veil, and presented her fair, cold face candidly to the proceedings. Again, what thin, set lips! For the rest, the gently growling, no-nonsense London burghers in their broadcloth and bombazine, and that indefinable tension and excitement inseparable from murder trials, then the subdued rustle and roar as the court rose for the judge and his retinue, and the drama recommenced.

'You are Police Constable Ernest Seddon, and you are attached to "H" Division of the Metropolitan Police?' Sir Edward Clarke's voice rang out.

'Yes, sir.'

'Please tell the court what occurred while you were on your beat in Whitechapel at about ten past four in the afternoon of the 28th of November last.'

The constable took out his notebook, opened it, and began a stilted recitation.

'I was checking the lock of an empty shop at the corner of Chicksand and Spelman Streets at approximately 4.10 p.m., when I noticed a lone man on the opposite side of Chicksand Street behaving suspiciously.'

'How, suspiciously?'

'Well, sir, he was tugging and rattling at the door of a house there, then stepping back into the road and looking up at the windows, which were unlit, though at that time of the year it was already getting dark. What's more, I'd seen a man of a similar build to him doing exactly the same thing earlier on in my shift, at about twenty past one that afternoon. I waited till he'd given over rattling and was moving off, then I stepped out of the shadow of the shop doorway I'd been in and followed him carefully up around Fashion Street and up into Dorset Street, where he stood hesitating-like outside a common passage there.'

'That turned out to be in fact where the man lived, was it not?'

'That's right, sir. Well, I walked up to him and asked why he had been trying the door of the house in Chicksand Street. He said someone had told him there might be the chance of a job there, but that it had turned out to be a frost, and he was angry about it. I then said he'd been there before this afternoon, hadn't he? He said he had, but he'd decided to give it another go. I then asked him his name and where he lived, and he said Joseph Morris, and that he lived in a seamen's lodging house on Ratcliff Highway. I then said, well, what are you doing hanging round here? He said he'd been looking for a pal who had a room off the passage, and I said I'd been watching him, and he'd not been in the passage. I then asked him to turn out his pockets on to a nearby window-ledge, and he asked why, he hadn't done anything wrong, and I said it was all one to me whether he did it there in the street or down at the station. He said all right, then, and I raised my lamp while he emptied his pockets on to the ledge. There was only an old handkerchief, a couple of broken cheroots, a vesta box, a sixpence and four pennies. I noticed then that after he'd seemingly finished he'd kept his left fist clenched, and I asked him to open his palm, but instead he darted three or four steps back and pulled out a revolver from somewhere. I threw the lamp in his face, and he let slip whatever he had in his left hand, and I heard a tinkling sound on the ground as I dashed forward and grappled the gun out of his hand and wrenched his arm up behind his back, while I drew my whistle with my free hand and whistled for assistance. He then hacked my shin with his heel, and the pain made me let slip my grasp,

41

so that he was able to dash off down the street. I was joined in a few minutes by a colleague, with the suspect handcuffed and in charge. My colleague, PC Yeatman, said he'd spotted the man shinning over a backyard wall behind Dorset Street, having evidently dashed through another common passage in order to give me the slip by cutting through the buildings and coming out in another street. We later questioned the inhabitants of the street, and it turned out that he'd in fact made his dash through the passage of No. 44, through the rooms of Mr Isaac Flitterman. But before that Constable Yeatman and I picked up the things the suspect had dropped. They were eighteen sovereigns. Together we took the suspect with us to Leman Street police station, arriving there at approximately ten to five. There he was charged with loitering with intent to commit a felony, threatening behaviour, and obstructing a police officer in the execution of his duty. He was then detained, and I resumed my patrol.'

'And do you see this suspect in court today?' the Solicitor General asked.

'Yes, sir, he is the accused in the dock.'

'No more questions, my lord.'

A glance from Lord Justice Calthrop, and Francis Carmody was on his feet.

'Constable Seddon, you had ample opportunity to take a good look at the suspect in the light of your lamp when first you stopped him and questioned him?'

'Yes, sir.'

'Did you see any blood on his person or clothing, or any signs – cuts, scratches, swellings, bruising, black eyes – indicating that he may have been involved in any recent violence?'

'No, sir, none.'

Carmody picked up a labelled object from the table in front of him and brandished it languidly in the faces of the jury.

'And when he drew this revolver in the threatening fashion you describe, did you notice by which end of the revolver he held it – like this?'

With those words the counsel for the defence grasped the revolver by the butt, and, with considerable violence of gesture, and with finger on the trigger, he thrust it up towards the constable's face.

'Why no, sir, not like that.'

42

Carmody took a step backward and flipped the revolver round in his hand, so that he was grasping it by the barrel, then advanced a step towards the witness box with the revolver poised like a club in his upraised hand.

'Like this, then?'

'Yes, sir, that's more the style.'

I could see by their expressions that the weight of this clarification had not been lost on the jurymen: a man who has just killed would surely use a revolver for its designed purpose, and not as a defensive club, if on the brink of capture.

'And when you grappled with the suspect,' Carmody went on, 'did you smell any strong chemical smell on him?'

'Can't say I did, sir: I had other things on me mind besides what he smelt like!'

The jurymen's faces relaxed, and some chuckled – a point down for the defence.

'No further questions, my lord.'

I sat back in expectation as the next witness came into the box.

'You are Detective Sergeant Frederick Wensley,' Sir Edward said, 'also of "H" Division of the Metropolitan Police, stationed at Leman Street?'

'I am, sir,' the thickset young man with the hard face and walrus moustache rapped from the box. I knew Frederick or 'Weasel' Wensley, as he was known to the East End underworld, from my involvement in the Aldgate affair in the previous year. Detective Sergeant Wensley's character could be summed up in three words: ability, pugnacity and tenacity. Let the Weasel get his forensic teeth into you, and God help you!

'Please tell the court what took place when you entered Leman Street police station in the late afternoon of the 28th of November last.'

'Well, sir, I had a few words with the desk sergeant, as I always do when I come in from outside duty, on what had come up while I'd been out, and he told me about Constable Seddon's tussle with the accused. The desk sergeant showed me the sovereigns that had been found on the suspect, and I noticed that one of them bore the date 1881. Now the Royal Mint happens to be situated in "H" Division, and I knew that it was closed for renovation from '81 to '83, and that no sovereigns had been minted over that period. I remarked on this to the sergeant, and he replied that the coin seemed genuine enough as to weight and so on, but I decided to follow the matter up when I could find time from the cases I had on hand. Well, on the Saturday morning – the 29th – we received notification from Scotland Yard that we were to keep on the lookout for colonial sovereigns, in connection with the Poland Street murder case. I naturally remembered the sovereign the desk sergeant had shown me on the previous morning, and went to work on the suspect . . .'

I thought I could imagine what lay behind those words: 'went to work on'!

'Well,' Wensley went on, 'as my interrogation proceeded, it soon came out that the man's name wasn't Joseph Morris at all, and we found out that he had no connection with any seamen's lodging house in Ratcliff Highway. He finally admitted that his name was Solomon Solomons – the accused – and that he had been in the vicinity of Poland Street in the early hours of the Friday morning. He insisted, however, that he only arrived there at about a quarter past two and that he had spent the time up till then in various public houses in the East End before setting off on foot for Soho. I should say that, in connection with this, and acting on information received, we checked at the lodgings of a man called Klaff in Osborn Street, this Klaff having been alleged to have been with Solomons from eleven thirty till one thirty, but we found that he had packed his things and left on the same Friday afternoon, and we've been unable to trace him since then.'

'Did you ask the accused if he'd been to the house in Poland Street before?'

'Yes, sir, and he said he hadn't, but that he'd heard that General Ostyankin used to frequent the house at No. 11, and that he was a very bad man and needed watching. He said he went there in the hope of getting evidence against him in some act of wrongdoing, with a view to reporting him to the police.'

'And how did he explain his possession of the eighteen sovereigns?'

'He said he just found them scattered round the back entrance to No. 11.'

'I see,' the Solicitor General remarked drily, 'fairy gold . . .'

There was scattered low laughter throughout the court.

44

'What did you say to that, Sergeant?' Sir Edward continued.

'I asked the accused what he was doing at the back entrance of No. 11 if he'd never been there before. How did he know he had to watch there for the general instead of at the front door?'

'And how did he explain it?'

'He said it was common sense that someone up to no good would go in by the back entrance. I then confronted him with the fact that two of the sovereigns he claimed he'd found were marked colonial coins issued to the general at his bank that very morning, and, in view of this, would he like to change his story? He stuck to his account of his having found them as he'd described, and I then, after consultation with my superiors, cautioned him and formally charged him with the murder of General Ostyankin.'

Francis Carmody had no questions, and a sharply-dressed young spark of the city clerk type was next sworn in.

'You are James Tolley,' Sir Edward's dry voice rang out, 'and you are at present employed as a clerk with Coutts Bank in the Strand?'

'That is correct, sir.'

'Please tell the court of the circumstances surrounding the visit of the late General Ostyankin to the bank on the morning of the 27th of November last.'

'Well, sir,' the young man began to explain in an eager manner, 'just before the general came in at about eleven o'clock – I knew him by sight, and had served him on more than one occasion in the past – I'd referred a sovereign back to the chief cashier because of the date on the reverse. The date on the coin was 1881, and I knew the Mint had been closed during that year. Well, sir, the chief called me in and shoved a magnifying glass in my hand, then handed me the coin I'd sent back – it was the old type of shield sovereign – and said: "Now then, young feller, just take a dekko at the reverse of this coin, and tell me if you see anything out of the ordinary." I took a look through the glass at the reverse, and saw a little capital "S" stamped just above the rose at the bottom of the coin. I told the chief what I'd seen, and he said: "That's 'S' for Sydney: it's an Australian minting. Perfectly in order." Well, sir, I took the coin back, and examined a few others at my desk, finding another marked with an "S" and

45

dated 1880, and counted them straight into the twenty drawn by my next client.'

'Who was General Ostyankin.'

'That's right, sir.'

The Solicitor General paused till there was dead silence in the court, then fixed his rather sombre eyes on the members of the jury. He then swung his attention back to the beaky-nosed young man with the plastered-down hair in the witness box.

'Mr Tolley,' Sir Edward said slowly, deliberately and distinctly, 'is there the slightest shred of doubt in your mind that you gave those two sovereigns – one dated 1880, the other 1881, both with the tiny capital letter "S" just above the rose at the bottom of each reverse – to General Ostyankin on that fateful Thursday?'

His pomaded head at a cocky angle, the young clerk answered promptly and cheerfully: 'Not the slightest doubt, sir.'

Sir Edward gave the jury another telling look, then addressed the judge.

'No more questions, my lord.'

Counsel for the defence did have a question, though, a seemingly simple and rather weak one, one would have thought, but whose effect would tell when he cross-questioned the next prosecution witness.

'Mr Tolley, how many sovereigns in all would you say you handed over on the morning in question to your various clients? Very roughly . . .'

The young spark chuckled.

'Well, sir,' he said in a worldly, distinctly pitying tone, 'we are talking of Coutts, you know . . .'

'Dozens? Scores? Hundreds?'

'Certainly hundreds, sir.'

'And without the cashier's magnifying glass' – there was a titter from the body of the court – 'how many dating from either side of the period 1881 to 1883 would you have spotted as colonial coins?'

The stripling's self-confidence seemed to totter momentarily.

'I'm, er . . . sure I don't know, sir.'

'No more questions, my lord.'

The next witness to be called was a bespectacled savant from the Colonial Office, a big swell in the field of Imperial economics. Sir Edward got him, at some length, to dot the 'i's' and cross the 't's' of the young bank-clerk's testimony. As he finished his dry monologue, I felt as if I could have faced a stiff examination question on Australian monetary policy. Carmody was straight on his feet, a couple of sheets of notepaper in his hand.

'Mr Woodnutt, can you tell the court how many sovereigns emerged from the Sydney mint in the years 1880 and 1881?'

The spare man in the spectacles coughed and spoke faintly.

'Not being in possession of exact figures at the moment, I should hesitate to hazard a guess, then there is the point to be considered that no separate figures exist for shield- and Pistrucci sovereigns . . .'

Carmody consulted his sheets of paper.

'Very well, then, Mr Woodnutt, allow me to help you with a round figure, which I have compiled from the abstracts of the Sydney mint. I take it you accept that authority?'

'Certainly.'

'Good. Very well, then, for 1880 the figure is one million four hundred and fifty-nine thousand, and for 1881 one million three hundred and sixty thousand. Now I concede that it would be impossible to ascertain just how many of those coins fetched up on these shores . . .'

'Quite impossible!' the statistician snapped.

Carmody swept the jury benches with his impudent grin.

'But I think it within the bounds of reasonable conjecture that on the night of the murder there were more than two of them in circulation in this great city!'

Open laughter broke out in more than one place in the crowded chamber, but Lord Justice Calthrop's Medusa stare soon restored silence.

'No more questions, my lord,' Carmody said brightly.

Lord Justice Calthrop then asked if any more expert witnesses were to be called for the Crown, and, Sir Edward answering no, the judge dismissed the court for luncheon, which I again took in the Cheshire Cheese. After the court had reassembled, I noted that the fair spectator in the row in front of me had not returned, and indeed, she missed little in failing to do so, for the rest of the day was taken up by a positive file of witnesses, many of them common types to all who have had to do with lunatic asylums, who had seen a strange, foreign-looking man in the vicinity of Poland Street at the time of the murder. Naturally, they all

47

positively identified Solomons as that man, and, equally natu-rally, the defence counsel was able promptly to set at naught their rambling, self-contradictory statements. I wondered if the jury had drawn the obvious conclusion from this evidently desperate attempt by the prosecution to supply a want of serious witnesses to the accused's true activities in Poland Street at the fatal hour. It was with no small relief that I found my way back into the Strand after the conclusion of the day's proceedings, and set my course for Whitechapel and evening surgery. I tried to put myself in the place of an average member of the jury: those eighteen sovereigns would take a precious deal of explaining away.

5

I fear that all of the next day – Wednesday – was taken up in the Old Bailey by the Casey's Court of assorted, so-called sight-witnesses that had bedevilled the previous afternoon, and with the same result as the pale sunlight faded from the used-up air of the Central Criminal Court – stalemate. Mercifully, though, just before four that afternoon, the Solicitor General announced that the evidence for the prosecution was concluded, and, on the judge's asking Francis Carmody if he wished to proceed straight away with the presentation of the defence evidence, the latter demurred, and we were again freed like end-of-term schoolboys.

Again, everything brought against Solomons so far had been circumstantial; all, that is, save the sovereigns. In my heart of hearts I could not suppress the suspicion that, as the prosecution would have it, Solomons' possession of those coins could scarcely have been accidental. And then there had been the paucity of any material bearing on the accused's activities anterior to the death of the Russian militarist: what had Solomons been doing on the rest of that Thursday, the 27th of November? Who had been his companions beside the elusive Klaff? Iris Starr had told us of her sweetheart's secretive life and nature, and we knew from the lamentable press exposure of his former political activities that a professional revolutionary's life could scarcely be a public one, but it really began to look as if the authorities' attitude was one of Here is the culprit, he murdered Ostyankin, it remains only to hang him. I now found myself to be positively riveted by the affair, and I blush now at the recollection of what, in the light of my growing obsession, the quality of my services at the dispensary must have been! That evening I could talk of nothing but the case, which, I consoled myself somewhat in the humbugging vein, would at least have the salutary effect on Violet of diverting her from her eternal preoccupation with the construction of the new dispensary. On the following morning, then, I reclaimed my place on the public bench in the Central Criminal Court with renewed eagerness as Francis Carmody, brisk and confident as ever, opened the evidence for the defence. A name was called, and a raw-faced giant in a reefer jacket, gripping a nautical cap in his huge red paw, awkwardly addressed the Bible presented to him in the witness box, and was sworn in.

'Your name is John Burton Gaselee, and you are second engineer on the *Tacoma Breeze*, at present berthed in Victoria Dock?'

'That is correct, sir,' the man replied in unmistakably Yankee tones.

'I believe you spent several days in London last November, while your ship was unloading cargo?'

'Yes, sir, that was at the East India Dock – Chinese ginger, tung oil and so on. Docked on, let me see . . . Yessir, that'd be the Monday – I guess it'd have been the start of the last week in November.'

'Monday the 24th of November, according to *Lloyd's List*, sailing again on the afternoon of Friday the 28th.'

'Yes, sir, we had to pick up a cargo at Rotterdam on the Saturday morning, then outward bound for Surinam, then we were jinking up and down the Mosquito Coast till we loaded up with bananas at Kingston and made for London at the end of January. We just hit town yesterday morning, in fact.'

'Please tell the court what brought you here so promptly, Mr Gaselee?'

'Name I read in one of your papers, in connection with this Russian general case: there's hardly anything else in the news beside that these days.'

'And what name was that?'

'Klaff.'

There was a leaning-forward, a slipping-back of hats and a gripping of form-backs on the public benches. Carmody paused a little for effect.

'What about this Klaff, Mr Gaselee?'

'Why, I was in a saloon in Limehouse – the Lord Raglan – during my trip here last November, and who d'ye think I saw there with another guy but my old shipmate, Semyon Klaff! I'd gone a few trips with him on a sealer in the Aleutians way back in the early eighties. He was a seacook, a Russian like most of the crew, and I picked up a bit of the lingo from them. He became quite a mate of mine.'

'When did this, er, reunion in the public house in Limehouse take place, Mr Gaselee? Can you remember the exact date and time?'

'Yessir, because we sailed the next afternoon, which was Friday the 28th of November, as you've just said, sir. It was the Thursday night.'

'Please tell the court more about the meeting in the public house, Mr Gaselee.'

'Well I was already a bit, well, merry, by the time these two fellers came in around midnight . . .'

'Why midnight, Mr Gaselee? How can you be so precise?'

'Bartender there calls time at midnight, sir – locks the front door behind the last arrivals, and they were the last arrivals. I recall there was a bit of a ruckus when they came in, folks cheering, and so on: just in the nick of time sort of style. They didn't look any too pleased, just grabbed a couple of beers at the bar and sneaked over to a little table in the corner of the house, but I couldn't help looking their way from time to time, the guy with the moustache looked kind of familiar, then the penny dropped – Klaff! I sort of yelled out the name and went over to their corner. I tried out my little store of Russian, but Klaff didn't seem to know me, or want to know me, and the other little guy just fixed a look on me like a rattlesnake whose tail you're standing on! I remember that look. Well, sir, as I've said, I was fairly well-oiled by then, and you know what they say: sailors don't care! I wasn't offended, so I just went over to the bar and sweethearted the barmaid into giving me three very last beers and went back and kept on until Klaff gave me a kind of soapy smile and we started talking about old times.'

'And did Klaff or his companion give any indication of what business they may have been about that night?'

'Business? No, sir – not that the other guy said much, and nothing directly to me – just sort of chit-chat between old shipmates.'

'And this went on till when?'

'Well, the bartender finally started shooing everybody out around one, and Klaff and the little guy were among the first to leave.'

'Did you follow your old shipmate and his companion out?'

'Me? No, sir: I'm damned if I didn't try for another beer, but there was nothing doing, and I guess I was the last man out.'

'Do you see Semyon Klaff's companion in the court today?'

'Sure do, sir – that's him over there.'

Gaselee pointed straight at Solomon Solomons, who still regarded the spectacle in the court as if he were a disengaged theatre-goer.

The defence counsel smiled and thanked the lofty seafarer, then Sir Edward got up again and spoke.

'Mr Gaselee, you have stated that you were "well-oiled" and "merry" on the occasion when you say you ran into the man Klaff in the public house in Limehouse; also that you have no really clear recollection of what you talked to him about, or indeed that there was any sign on his part of his having recognised you. Am I being fair in saying that?'

'No, sir, we definitely knew each other after the first few words, and I distinctly recall having talked about our time on the sealer, though the details escape me.'

'I see, but has it not occurred to you that your words – uttered in a foreign language of which you have no more than – how did you put it? "a little store" – were completely misconstrued by your interlocutor, who may not have been Klaff at all, but who may simply have given you his "soapy" smile in order to humour a clearly very powerful man well gone in drink?'

'No, sir, it wasn't like that at all. Besides, I can hold my liquor with the best of 'em, and as for English beer – well, sir, I hope you'll pardon me, but d'ye know what we say about English beer Stateside? Best left inside the horse!'

There was open laughter at this point, both from the spectators' benches and the jury box, and the Solicitor General shook his head at the judge with a scowl and flopped back angrily into his seat as the seaman was dismissed from the box, and Francis Carmody recalled Sergeant Wensley to testify.

'Sergeant Wensley, I believe you conducted an identity parade yesterday afternoon, in which my client took part, and in which the last witness, Engineer Gaselee, was asked to pick out the man he said he'd seen in the public house in Limehouse with Semyon Klaff?'

'Yes, sir, that is the case.'

'With what result, Sergeant?'

'Mr Gaselee picked out the accused, Solomons, sir.'

'Did Mr Gaselee hesitate or go back on his decision at any time during the proceedings? Please tell the court exactly how he went on.'

'He didn't hesitate at all, sir, just walked straight down the line till he came to the accused, then pointed at him. He didn't go back on that.'

Sir Edward did not seek to challenge the sergeant, and the next witness was called, one Sidney Arthur Wellcome, a long, thin, shabbily dressed man with the livid complexion of a consumptive. It appeared that Wellcome, a private schoolmaster out-of-a-place, had the previous autumn taken to sleeping on the roof of a bakery outhouse in back Poland Street in order to catch the warmth of the flue-base, and recalled that at precisely 2 a.m. on the night of the murder, kept from sleep by the driving wind, he had spotted from his vantage-point a small, slightly built man hesitate under a street lamp in Noel Street, then look round him before ducking into back Poland Street. That man, Wellcome asseverated, was Solomon Solomons.

'You are very precise about the time, Mr Wellcome,' the Solicitor General said, opening his cross-examination. '*Exactly* 2 a.m? I assume from the, er, informality of your lodging that night that your watch must have been lying in some pawnbroker's . . .'

'Irretrievably, sir,' the wretch with the leaden skin sighed in cultivated tones, 'but the church bells of St Thomas' in Kingly Street are the infallible companions of my night watches. They are all too accurate in marking the passing hours.'

'I see. I believe that you were dismissed from your last teaching post on account of over-indulgence in drink: is that the case?'

The defence counsel sprang to his feet.

'My lord, I must protest!'

Lord Justice Calthrop looked severely upon his august colleague.

'I am bound to say, Sir Edward, that unless you can immediately explain the relevance of that question to this case, I shall not be able to allow it.'

'My lord, I merely wish to explore the value of the witness's testimony in relationship to the sad fact of his weakness.'

'Have you then reason to believe that he was inebriated at the moment when he says that he saw a man enter back Poland Street at the time in question?'

'Not specifically, my lord.'

'Then you may not pursue that line of questioning with him.'

'As your lordship pleases: I have no further questions to put to this witness.'

The Solicitor General resumed his seat with his forensic feathers thoroughly ruffled, and Francis Carmody recalled Sergeant Wensley to the witness box.

'Sergeant Wensley, I believe that you called the last witness, Mr Wellcome, to identify the man he said he had seen from the bakery rooftop on the night of the murder in an identity parade undertaken on the 4th of December last?'

'That is so, sir.'

'With what result?'

'He indicated the accused, Solomons.'

'First time?'

'Straight off, sir.'

'Thank you, Sergeant Wensley: no more questions, my lord.'

The Solicitor General having none, either, what was to be the last defence witness was called and sworn in. He was a short, bullet-headed man with ill-shaven, powerful jaws.

'Your name is Emmanuel Shalit,' Carmody began, 'and you are a tailor's improver and messenger of 118, Wardour Street?'

'That's right.'

'I understand that your job as a messenger involves your wheeling a handcart round the Soho and Regent Street areas at all hours of the night?'

'That's right, I have to collect piecework from pressers all over Soho, then take the work to my place till it's time to take it in the early morning to the bespoke tailors in the West End – Conduit Street, Savile Row and so on.'

'Can you describe your route into the early morning hours of Friday the 28th of November last?'

'Yes, all that time was very busy – it always is as you get near Christmas – and I was collecting and going back and forwards along Berwick and Noel Street from about nine on the Thursday

54

evening till nearly two in the morning. I went and told the police as soon as the case came into the papers the next day.'

'Most commendable. You would be continually passing and repassing the opening to back Poland Street all that time.'

'Yes.'

'And in all that time till you finally returned to your workshop in Wardour Street with the piecework around two in the morning, did you see anyone lurking in the vicinity of back Poland Street? Anyone skulking or watching? Anyone at all out of the ordinary?'

'No, I can't say I did.'

'Trust one sheeny to stick up for another!' I heard someone mutter on the public bench behind me, to an answering snigger from his interlocutor.

'And would you tell the court why during this busy period you should find leisure to look into alleyways and passages as you went along?'

'Some years ago I was set on and beaten senseless by three men who came at me from a passageway off Berwick Market: they took all I had. Now I'm always careful: instinct.'

'Thank you, Mr Shalit,' the defence counsel concluded. 'No further questions my lord.'

'Have you any questions, Sir Edward?' the judge asked the Solicitor General, who got up in a weary sort of fashion.

'No, my lord, I have nothing to say except to remark how highly peculiar it would be for a man who decides to keep secret watch in a dark alley *not* to take measures to ensure that he is not observed from the main street!'

Sir Edward sat down, and the defence counsel rose.

'My lord,' Carmody said in an equal tone, 'I have no more questions to put to the witness, and I do not propose to call any more witnesses or present any more evidence.'

'Very well,' said Lord Justice Calthrop. 'I think then that it would be clearly undesirable that counsels' closing speeches should be interrupted by the weekend, therefore I propose that the court adjourn till half-past ten on Monday morning.'

The court then rose, and I joined in the rush for the exits, until the general scrimmage catapulted me into the Strand, and my eye was caught by something familiar in a pretty female face, whose owner was leaning out of the window of a cab. In it

I recognised the Pocket Venus, my fellow watcher on the public benches of the court, whose evident interest in the proceedings – along with her veil – seemed to have been discarded after Alexander Miller had stepped down from the witness box. I craned my neck over the heads of the crowd and saw a solid, respectably dressed female step into the hansom, whereupon my Venus addressed a clear cry to the cabbie: 'No. 4, Montelimar Close, Hampstead!' It was a hard, precise voice. The door of the cab snapped shut, and the vehicle was quickly lost to view.

6

It was but a quarter to two, and I found myself somewhat at a loss as to what to do next, but it occurred to me later while I tackled a cut off the joint at Simpsons, that, the potential Russian witnesses – not to mention the seafaring Mr Klaff – having most likely vanished abroad, I might profitably use the time till evening surgery in following up the enigma of Mr – or might it be Mynheer? – De Kok, erstwhile lessee of No. 11, Poland Street, and, for all the progress the authorities seemed to have made in locating him since Ostyankin's murder, the Invisible Man.

Having secured a table at the venerable Fleet Street eating-place, I took a draught of Dublin porter while I awaited the arrival of the trolley with the joint, and considered De Kok. A Dutch or Flemish name, then, one of convenience or that of a remote agent. If the latter, then he could surely be no man of standing in business, if the Poland Street premises were put to the use now generally accepted. I should choose, then, for my working hypothesis, a small commission-agent, of whom the human rookeries of the city accommodated, in convenience-addresses and desk-corners, virtually as many as their eaves sheltered starlings.

The trolley arrived, and I was cut a succulent slice of beef and dealt out a couple of fine floury potatoes. Having dismissed the waiter, I dressed my beef with mustard and set to. Now it will no doubt already have occurred to the reader that the police must themselves have come to exactly the same conclusion as myself regarding the possible identity and whereabouts of the bearer of the name on the lease of 11, Poland Street, but there I would make a condition. The police authorities have their official routines, tried and tested it may be, but they are routines nonetheless, and many illuminating trifles may slip through a net of uniform weave, be its meshes never so closely set. The gleaner's eye may spot what the reaper's may have missed in his wider swath.

Replete, I stepped out into the jangling Strand, and set off in the direction of Charing Cross and its bookshops, where I laid out a few shillings in trade directories, and walked down again to a bench in the Temple gardens to study them. Among the businesses and agencies, there was a sprinkling of Decaps, a relative plethora of De Jongs and a scattering of De Witts, but only two De Koks, which fact, though it narrowed my field severely, had the advantage of allowing me to complete that side of my enquiries in what remained of the afternoon – or so I thought. My first port of call, which was but a few hundred yards away in Bouverie Street, was an agency which specialised in the import of inks, but the name turned out to be of no more than academic interest, for, it seemed, that particular De Kok had been the founder of the firm, who had passed away in 1796, his name dying with him.

The second De Kok was not to be reached quite so easily, being an assembler and repairer of fairground steam organs, whose premises were sandwiched between a battery of pianoforte workshops and showrooms in the Clerkenwell Road, to which I repaired by cab. Having arrived at the works, I stepped inside a sort of glass booth, and addressed a clerk of harassed and lugubrious expression, who asked me to wait while he summoned up the boss, who turned out to be a large, walrus-moustached man in oil-smeared mechanic's dungarees. He was sweating, and had clearly been interrupted in some operation of the steam organ-maker's mystery.

'Yes, please?' the rather lubberly-looking man snapped at me, the slightly plosive 'p' betraying the Fleming or Hollander. 'You have business with me?'

'Well, sir, I was hoping you might be able to help me in some enquiries I am making. First, I understand your name is De Kok . . .'

The man fairly blew up.

'For de thousand time,' he roared, his accent thickening as he warmed to his task, 'as I have told de police, and as I am telling you, I am nod De Kok, nor am I de bloddy hen! I am De Ko – Willem De Ko!'

'I beg your pardon, sir,' I stammered, 'but I understood that your name is spelt . . .'

'Yes,' the organmonger sighed in mock-patience, as he stooped and brought his angry red face level with mine, 'I know quide well how to spell my name, but de last "k" is silent – do you understand det?'

'I'd no idea, sir, believe me . . .'

'And believe dis – you don't come in here without warrant – nod a step more! What wit de police trying to say I am some kind of whoormaster in Soho – mixed op in murders and I don't know what all – I who have lived and worked in England since thirty years and more, paying my taxes and obeying de law . . .'

It was thus under heavy fire that I retreated from the premises and took to my heels, but what I had just learned had set off a train of thought in my mind, one that would eventually bear fruit of a most unexpected kind. So De Kok was in fact pronounced as De Coe. What, then, if both my original surmises as to the name – i.e. that it was an assumed one, and that the bearer of it was a mere agent or catspaw – were true? I stopped in the deep doorway of a bicycle-shop, and pored in my directories again. I found the page, and, using my index-finger as pointer, worked down the list. Codner, Cody Leonard, Cody William . . . Ah! This was more like it! Coe Albert, Coe Bertram, Coe Desmond. I paused. Desmond Coe, Commission Agent. D. Coe – De Ko(k) . . . What if . . . The name had an added advantage for undercover purposes, for the bearer would be automatically alerted against all enquirers ignorant of its true pronunciation: 'You may not remember me, Mr De Kok . . .' I read on, and the entry gave his specialisation as the horsemeat and leather trade, with an address in Cornhill, which was my next stop. Dundee Buildings, however, had not known Desmond Coe since last winter, the caretaker giving me the address of the agent's last private address, for which I immediately made tracks.

This was a tall private house on Warwick Square, in the unexceptionable purlieus of Pimlico, where, after I had introduced myself and given a sound business reason for being interested in the whereabouts of the elusive knackers' agent, I was shown Coe's room by Mrs Gedge, his erstwhile landlady.

'Just took himself off,' the long, thin woman with the black hen's eyes explained to me, 'without a by-your-leave. Just him and his little Gladstone bag. Left nothing behind – except an almighty stink in my kitchen, that is . . .'

'A stink, Mrs Gedge?'

'Burning varnish. I'd just come back from my sister's after having had tea there, and I smelt it as soon as I came up to the area. I went straight down the area steps to see what was going on, but the maid was nowhere to be seen: when the cat's away . . .'

I could scarcely help smiling at the landlady's so-accurate self-description.

'. . . then I opened the window, and raked the stove out. It was all charred wood and an iron thimble-thing – there was another lump of iron, too.'

It sounded to me like the remnants of a walking-stick, with the 'iron thimble thing' describing the ferrule.

'Have you still got the, er . . . thimble-thing, Mrs Gedge?'

'What? Of course not! Raked it all into the cinder bucket and put it out for the scavengers. I had something to say to the maid when she deigned to turn up again, I can tell you!'

Why should Coe want to burn a walking-stick, I thought?

'When exactly did Coe, er . . . take himself off, Mrs Gedge?'

'Last Friday in November, leaving no forwarding address.'

'You seem very sure of the date, Mrs Gedge,' I remarked. 'It has been ten weeks, after all . . .'

The beady eyes looked me up and down with some disdain.

'You'd remember, too, if you lived on your rents!'

'Ah, I see: the last Friday of the month would have been his rent-day.'

'I'd his month-in-advance, of course, and this stuff . . .'

The landlady nodded down at a large, battered suitcase, which stood beside a most businesslike American rolltop desk.

'May I?' I ventured.

'Help yourself, I'm sure: neither's locked, and you won't find anything worth a farthing in either. The desk's his, too, and my present lodger here's none too keen on it: Lord knows what I'm to do with the thing. What if Mr Coe were to turn up and claim it?'

The woeful lady left me for more important things, and I pounced immediately on the suitcase, a stout cowhide receptacle of the old school bearing under the handle a cheap tin label of the sort one might punch out for oneself in any big railway station. The label read: 'D. Coe.' Inside the case were a looped bundle of worn leather bootlaces, a pair of small brown boots with cracked soles and heels worn at the outer edges, and a few clean but frayed shirt-collars. Certainly, what I had seen so far did not betoken affluence, and the remaining objects in the case – half a dozen bookmakers' receipts – Newmarket, Brighton and Sandwich – suggested a possible reason for this. One or two of the receipts were for five, and one for as much as ten pounds, and I clucked my tongue against my upper teeth as I reflected that no working- or professional man could go it at that rate and keep up a decent standard of life.

I replaced the objects in the case and awaited the return of the landlady some five minutes later.

'You said that Coe left with only a little Gladstone bag, ma'am: surely then he must have left more clothes than this behind?'

Mrs Gedge bridled, and her pinched features took on an even more sniffy expression.

'I'm within my rights!' she snapped. 'In lieu of rent!'

'Indeed, ma'am,' I hastened to agree. 'Fair exchange is no robbery, and your rent was due . . .'

'I should think so, too!'

'But couldn't you – in confidence, mind – recall what articles of Coe's you, er . . . realised?'

'Hmph, let me see: three suits, two pairs of boots and a pair of low summer shoes, along with a dozen shirts and various other bits of haberdashery. There might have been one or two other things, but I've forgotten what they were.'

'It was approaching winter when he left here, Mrs Gedge, and you don't mention overcoats, so I suppose he'd have been wearing his only overcoat?'

The landlady looked thoughtful.

'Now you mention it, as a matter of fact, he had two of them: the Inverness caped one, and the baggy black one that didn't really fit him – must've bought it off a barrow . . . He must have taken one of them with him.'

Curious, I thought, when one is leaving somewhere in a hurry with only a Gladstone bag, to choose to stuff a heavy overcoat in it. It must have taken up nearly all the space in the bag. And why burn one's walking-stick before setting out on a journey?

I replaced the objects and closed the case before examining the desk. I daresay one of the omniscient human sleuth-hounds of fiction might have solved the case straight off on the strength of what I had just seen, but all my modest talents could lead me to deduce from Coe's things were the facts that he was a man with small feet and a tendency to bow-leggedness who appeared to have laid out most of what he earned from the trade in dead horseflesh on futile attempts to get rich from the sporting activities which employed the living variety.

I straightened up and rolled up the wooden top of the desk, to reveal a sheaf of invoices headed mainly in French, their addresses consonant with Coe's interest in the horsemeat and leather trade, then as now concentrated in France and Belgium. For the rest, a few dusty, dog-eared blank envelopes, and the last few sheets, held together by gum at one edge, of a scribbling-pad. I examined the drawers and carefully tested and tapped the panelling of the desk for concealed compartments, but found nothing more. I returned to the open top, and something occurred to me. I took out the remains of the scribbling-pad and carefully tore off the top sheet, which I slipped, uncreased, into my notecase, after which I rolled down the desk-lid again, stood upright, and took a good look round the room. Nothing in the dimensions, fittings or furnishings suggested anything to me, so, after I had slipped my hand down the back of the cane armchair and peered behind the bed-head, I picked up my hat, gloves and cane from the occasional table where I had laid them, made my way downstairs again to Mrs Gedge's parlour, and rejoined that lady, who asked me if I had quite finished.

'I must admit, Mrs Gedge,' I prevaricated, 'that my dealings with Mr Coe were carried out exclusively in writing, so that I have never actually laid eyes on him. I hope I do not trespass too much on your time and good nature if I request a short description of the gentleman?'

'Description? Nothing to crack on, really. Shortish: about five foot four or five, I suppose, a bit bandy-legged like so many little men, neither fat nor thin, rather heavy features with a thick moustache. About forty, I should say. Close – you hardly heard him squeak – and no visitors. Not one in all the four years he's been here . . . Hardly ever saw him in his room after he'd had his breakfast, either.'

'References?' I ventured.

'No – cash down!' the woman snapped. 'References are as references do has been my experience!'

'And how did he dress?' I went on.

'Neat and quiet – like yourself – oh! – except on quarter-days . . .'

'Quarter-days?'

'Yes, always stepped out in full fig on quarter-days: regular swell, with his morning-coat, spats and topper.'

I reflected that the higher class of rents and leases were paid on quarter-days: rents on substantial properties; in Poland Street, for example . . .

'And did Mr Coe have any scars or distinguishing marks on him, Mrs Gedge?'

'No – but wait a minute. I brought up a telegram to his room one morning before breakfast – the boy wanted an answer to it – and I saw him at his washstand with his sleeves rolled up. He had a tattoo on his left arm: the Three Legs of Man.'

I thanked the landlady and stepped back out into the square. I could hear Big Ben striking five, and I made haste for nearby Victoria Station.

I just had time in the pharmacy that evening before my duties began in earnest to spread out the blank sheet of paper I had removed from the pad I had found in Desmond Coe's desk in Pimlico, and, having weighted two ends with brass scale-weights, I carefully shaded the entire surface of the sheet with a soft blacklead pencil. My fingers trembled with excitement as the following words, in cursive script, stood out from under the grey surface: 'Warwick Wednesday seven fresh parcel.' It was Lombard Street to a china orange that this was 'Mr De Kok's' handwriting, and my head was abuzz with the implications of this as I struggled to concentrate on my pharmaceutical duties. I could hardly wait for the steps of the last evening patient to die away down the stairs before I burst into the adjoining consulting-room and blurted out my news to Violet.

'Why,' she exclaimed, 'if this is the so-called De Kok's handwriting, the police will be able to compare it with the specimen signature at the estate agent's of whoever engaged the rooms in Poland Street. It could materially change the course of the trial.'

63

'Violet,' I said, 'I think it is time I made my first report to Mr Zeinvel.'

'Yes,' my wife agreed enthusiastically, 'we must step round to Crutched Friars immediately and lay the facts before him. What a godsend it is he is directing Solomons' defence!'

Despite the lateness of the hour, we found David Zeinvel still bent over his desk-lamp in his Dickensian eyrie in the lawyers' warren. The lamplight shone brilliantly on his lacquered hair, and the crazy shadow his profile cast on the blotting paper before him created the illusion that some beaky bird of prey had perched between lamp and desk. As soon as we were ushered in, he sprang to his feet and wrung my hand.

'Welcome, welcome, Dr Mortimer! And you, ma'am!'

Violet smiled and nodded back.

'Please accept our apologies for calling on you at this hour, Mr Zeinvel, but we have something to tell you which I am sure will interest you.'

'First report, hey, doctor? Something caught your attention at the Old Bailey? Then you're doubly welcome. I believe we have some decent sherry somewhere . . .'

'No, thank you, Zeinvel!' I refused for both of us. 'It is to do with Solomons.'

My legal friend sat down, and, cupping his chin in his hands on the desk-top, he looked at me with a new calculation and caution as I provided him with the details of what I had discovered during my afternoon wanderings.

'This may be crucial indeed,' the solicitor said in a calm voice. 'I'm glad too that you have come straight to me about it: I shall lay this matter before the police first thing tomorrow morning. Would you let me have the paper?'

I handed over a manila envelope, and Zeinvel carefully slipped out its enclosure and studied it under the lamp.

'Won't I be needed to swear to my having found it?' I asked, but Zeinvel dealt with this as he always did with potentially compromising queries: by changing the subject.

'This is the most delicate case I have ever handled, doctor,' he remarked simply as he slipped the piece of paper back in the envelope and locked it in the top drawer of his desk. 'You will appreciate that I cannot discuss the details of the case with you while it is still *sub judice*, and in that respect, I most earnestly advise you to keep this to yourselves.'

There was a solemn shared moment of silence, then the conversation became general, culminating in an invitation from Zeinvel to lunch with him again the next day at Cohen's Restaurant in Fieldgate Street. At last we rose, and the dapper figure got up from his desk and showed us to the landing. In spite of his earlier legal admonition, I could not resist a parting shot.

'Man to man, Zeinvel,' I said as we stood on the stair. 'Is Solomons innocent?'

'Oh, yes, doctor,' Zeinvel said in a matter-of-fact voice, and bowed us out.

7

Violet and I held a council-of-war that evening after supper, and I mentioned my striking fellow spectator in the Old Bailey that day, whom I had dubbed the Pocket Venus.

'Interesting that she kept her veil down throughout the time Miller was giving his testimony,' Violet commented, 'then raised it as soon as he had left.'

'Yes,' I replied, 'as if she didn't wish him to recognise her.'

'It may have been coincidence of course, and though I'm not sure I entirely approve of your somewhat eager interest in this so-called Venus, it might be worth considering. We must bear that address she gave the cabbie in mind: what was it again?'

'4, Montelimar Close, Hampstead.'

'By the by, James,' Violet remarked, changing the subject, as we faced each other across the cleared table, coffee-cups at our elbows, 'Hilary Venables at the Hackney women's refuge sent me word today that he accompanied Iris to visit Solomons in Wormwood Scrubs, and that she has told him of our offer to help.'

'In that case, I think it might be interesting if I went up there myself tomorrow morning and made his acquaintance.'

'A capital idea, but do not forget our luncheon appointment with Mr Zeinvel at twelve thirty.'

'No fear of that – I can hardly wait for his comments after he's been to see the police about De Kok; or should we say Desmond Coe.'

On that note, we retired for the night, and at eleven the next morning it was with some awkwardness, that, in the bare brick visitors' room in Wormwood Scrubs prison, I sat face-to-face across a wire screen with the finely-modelled features – their priestly cast emphasised by the black goatee beard – of the accused in the Ostyankin case. There was a short silence, during which I suppose I must have cast a fugitive glance round the chamber, only to meet what I took to be cold suspicion in the eyes of the guard who sat regarding us from a kitchen-style chair next to the louvred iron door. At last Solomons relieved me from my embarrassment.

'Iris has told me about you,' he said in a sharp, high voice, with only the faintest of foreign accents. 'Your wife cares about women – and you: What do you care about?'

'I care about justice.'

The bearded young man gave a snort.

'Justice – in this society!' he remarked with a bitter laugh, waving his arms round the room. 'Where the big thieves lock up the little thieves!'

'We must all do what we can, Mr Solomons. We must work and hope, so that some day . . .'

'Jam tomorrow, hey, doctor? That's what you English say, isn't it? Well, I want my jam now. My full share. I am not content to wait till the middle classes wake up and remember to pass me the empty jam-tin to scrape.'

'Perhaps you'd prefer to wake them up with a bomb?' I countered, and the dark, hooded eyes of my interlocutor narrowed. He made no reply, and I realised that I had started off on the wrong foot.

'There is no time to lose,' I went on, 'least of all on political bickering. Shall we agree once and for all to disagree on that point?'

Solomons smiled lazily, shrugged and nodded. 'Go on, doctor. I see you are not ready yet.'

'I do not know whether you are guilty or not guilty of the murder of Ostyankin . . .'

'Sadly – to my everlasting regret – I am not, but, still, go on.'

'Well, be that as it may, what I am convinced of now is that the scales of justice are being weighted against you, probably by very powerful interests, and for your sake and Miss Starr's . . .'

'She is a good comrade, my Iris,' the prisoner said, with his dreamy nonchalance. 'We share everything. Everything. I suppose you think I live on her, that I am a fancy man, a pimp, as they say in the filthy newspapers, but what can you know? You who earn four, five hundred pounds a year, whose feet are always dry when it rains, and who believe that one day perhaps there will be justice . . .'

I looked anxiously at the clock above the iron door: I had not much time left.

'I have pledged Miss Starr that I will do what I can to help,' I said, an urgent tone creeping into my voice. 'Please tell me all you know about the case.'

Solomons showed the same languid air of unconcern as he wasted another ten seconds studying me.

'About Ostyankin, I will tell you nothing, Dr Mortimer. About myself or my affairs – again I will tell you nothing. I am a free man, and I accept the consequences of my actions.'

'Really, Mr Solomons, it occurs to me that you are not fully aware of the seriousness of your situation.'

Another intolerable, yawning pause, and I fidgeted in my hard-backed chair as I again glanced at the clock in front of me. Five minutes left of my allotted visiting-time.

'But because you have been kind to Iris, doctor, I think I will tell you something.'

I leant forward eagerly.

'About Poland Street . . .' came the lazy drawling voice.

'Yes, yes, go on – about Poland Street?'

'I have watched Poland Street,' Solomons said in a whisper so faint the guard sat up and began to take extra notice. 'Yes, how I have watched it! I will tell you who goes there to visit No. 11.'

Even today I hesitate to reveal some of the names the young revolutionary recited in his dry, faraway whisper. Suffice it to say, they included those of some of the proconsuls of the British Empire, and I was aghast at the implications of this, should this mad-sounding recitation prove true.

'But you should have said so already to the police!' I stammered. 'Perhaps one of them at least could, under immunity, have been persuaded to . . .'

A peal of high, cracked laughter interrupted me.

'And do you think I have not told them, doctor? Do you think also that they would take action against such highly placed people? Even to knock at their doors? If so, you are a child – a child! Your rulers are beasts of prey, doctor, with the appetites of beasts. Just as farmers farm cattle, they farm the people! Only to eat them up eventually! Do not dream of talking to them about justice!'

I sat and goggled, then the guard at last rose and signalled me to leave, but before he reached us Solomons had time to finish his revelation.

'And before each beast enters No. 11, there goes in a woman with his little prey – blindfolded! Good luck, doctor! May you find justice.'

I left the awful place with Solomons' mocking laughter ringing in my ears, and, having passed gratefully through the wicket gate of the prison, made reflectively along Du Cane Road for East Acton station. Once in the train, and having changed on to the Circle Line at Notting Hill Gate, I pondered on my meeting with Solomons. I came to the conclusion that pride – the pride of the devil – was the main trait of Solomons' personality. He had certainly shown not a trace of gratitude for the pains I was taking on his behalf, an attitude all the more irritating in view of his point blank refusal to tell me anything about his activities on the day of Ostyankin's murder, or indeed anything about himself at all. And yet what integrity! What was that he had said about being a free man? To weigh up a whole society in the light of one's own bitter experience, to find it wanting, then to act on one's diagnosis even if it led to the gallows. Yes, there was something in that. And then, what should I have been – I with my comfortable, assured place in the scheme of things – had I suffered what Solomon Solomons had suffered? To come home, a mere boy, and find one's mother and sister murdered, one's whole world swept away, and all because one worshipped a different God from that of the established, Orthodox order. As this case unfolded, I was to find my cosy assumptions as to the nature of society challenged as never before.

I arrived at the Whitechapel Dispensary just as Violet was getting ready to go out to our luncheon appointment, and as we walked the short distance to Fieldgate Street, I told her of my meeting with Solomons. When I related his parting remark to me, about little girls allegedly being led blindfolded into the house in Poland Street for the use of highly placed lechers, she stopped against the stream of the raw commerce of dinnertime Whitechapel Road and faced me, her eyes narrowed, and her lips set in a hard, pale line.

'If, as Solomons suggests, James, the, er . . . trade in Poland Street is so specialised, it is even more likely that its patrons will be prepared to take strong measures to protect it – and themselves. We are reminded yet again that we risk treading on very powerful toes.'

My wife looked thoughtful for a moment or two, then, locking her elbow again firmly in mine, strode on with me in grim silence towards our destination.

Over luncheon in Cohen's, Zeinvel, as dapper and unruffled as ever, lightly dismissed my account of Solomons' – to me – new allegations.

'Hearsay,' he said, as he relished the borscht soup, 'and in any case, the police would scarcely wish to trespass into that social and political minefield. Their pensions – and perhaps even more – might well be at stake. No, they have their case cut and dried, doctor, and we will have to produce something more than general accusations of vicious goings-on to shake their confidence in it.'

I bridled somewhat at what seemed an omission in Zeinvel's statement.

'But the information I gave you yesterday evening about the agent De Kok, and his possible part in . . .'

Zeinvel replaced his spoon in the hollow of his empty plate, and looked at me.

'Ah, yes, doctor. De Kok. It looks as if you won't be called to give evidence – or even be questioned – about your findings in Pimlico after all: in fact, the police were not particularly keen to know how I had come by the information.'

'You mean they have simply ignored it?' Violet put in, her voice husky with suspense.

'No, no,' Zeinvel said, as the waiter arrived with our fish. 'Let me explain. I presented the information to them just as you had recounted it to me . . .'

'Who was the officer in charge?' I asked.

'Sergeant Wensley.'

'But surely he doesn't carry enough seniority to handle something like this, in spite of his ability,' I objected.

'I suspect he is acting as a sort of gamekeeper's retriever, but who exactly the head gamekeeper is in this, I'm not sure: it's a murky case. At any rate, I presented the information and the slip of paper with the message. The police were interested, but as soon as they'd compared the writing on the paper with the house-agent's specimen signature in their possession – and found that the two matched – all the wind seemed to go out of their sails. Wensley explained to me that they'd received a report from Belgium on Monday that the body of a man – an Englishman, judging by his clothes – had been fished out of the Bonaparte Dock in Antwerp. He was a man of about forty, five feet four inches tall, wearing a heavy moustache and with a tendency to bow-leggedness, and bearing on his left forearm a tattoo of the Three Legs of Man.'

8

It was with a growing sense of foreboding that I emerged into the Vale of Health on the heights of Hampstead an hour after our luncheon with Zeinvel. Our lawyer friend had compared the relationship of Sergeant Wensley and his putative hidden masters to that of a retriever and a gamekeeper. It seemed to me, then, that this recovery of the body of what we could only conclude was Desmond Coe, alias De Kok, might well be the hidden gamekeeper's first warning display of trapped vermin. It was increasingly being borne in on us that we were punching above our weight.

I set my jaw anew, and enquired of an early muffin-man where Montelimar Close might be, to be directed to a discreet loop of villas, with entry and exit on to North End Way. Each villa was surrounded by its picket of laurel or holly, and the massed evergreen foliage, greasy with winter moisture, emitted that curious atmosphere of oppression that always seems to go hand-in-hand with that type of vegetation. A fog, rising from the city below, did nothing to alleviate this mournful aspect. I shivered slightly in my ulster as I paused before the polished brass plate on the stout stone gate-post of No. 4. I read: 'The Magnolias Nursing Home', then peered through the iron-grilled gate at the low-lying, though substantial two-storey building at the bottom of a longish drive, which was crowded in on both sides by dense, dripping shrubbery. I pulled up my coat-collar round my face, lifted the heavy iron latch of the gate, and stepped down the gravel to the front door, to one side of which was an extensive conservatory, sporting iron pinnacles and curlicues at every peak. There were figures in invalid-chairs behind the glass walls, and I made a path with my stick through the undergrowth till my face was right up against a pane. I could now study the inmates in some detail, and it was with an involuntary shudder that I recognised the conditions I had observed in the patients on my first visit, as a medical student, to a ward in the Charing Cross Hospital devoted to sufferers in the final stages of syphilis.

But what had a Pocket Venus and a staid matron to do in this place? Were they staff? Visitors? Volunteers?

'Can I help you, sir?' came a quiet voice behind me, and I swung round, startled, to find myself face-to-face with a sturdily built man in hospital whites.

'Ah!' I exclaimed. 'I fear I have come to the wrong house.'

'I see, sir. I'll just show you to the gate, then.'

'No need, I can find my way out,' I stammered, beating a retreat back through the bushes and down the gravel drive to the street. I must not show my hand yet. I hurried along the close in the opposite direction to the one from which I had entered it. The next villa in the row, No. 5, was empty, with a 'For Sale' sign protruding above the canopy of laurels that encroached on the tall, spiked front gate. I had an idea, but that would wait till its due time. In the meantime, I made for the East End, and evening surgery.

That night, at supper, I told Violet of my findings in Hampstead.

'It seems ominous, James, but it may have nothing to do with the case.'

'Odd, though, that they should go straight from the court to the clinic.'

'If the respectably dressed lady you describe – the one who joined, er . . . Venus in the hansom – had been in the court, whose testimony would she have heard? I've forgotten some of the details.'

'Gaselee the American sea-going engineer, the poor drunken schoolmaster, Wellcome, and Shalit, the tailor's delivery man – alibis for Solomons.'

'I see – suggesting that her particular interest was in Solomons and his plight. So we have Venus watching Miller, and Matron watching Solomons. An intriguing conjecture, perhaps worth future examination if either of the ladies comes into our ken again, James, but you may be interested to learn that I have been engaged in my own investigations this afternoon!'

'Ah! Do go on.'

'Yes, à propos the allegation of Solomons that under-aged girls were being used by society lechers in Poland Street. If that had been the purpose of Ostyankin's visit there on the night he was murdered, what became of the little offering?'

'Perhaps she was used somehow in the murder plot? She would have been spirited away, no doubt, failing something worse . . .'

My wife's back stiffened in her chair, and a dark expression came over her face.

'Yes, James, something worse. We are looking into the pit . . . But there may be a happier – if I can use such a word in this connection – outcome. Perhaps the general met his end before his, er . . . titbit could be offered him.'

'Yes, I see, the procurer or procuress turn up with their blind-folded charge, only to find – what?'

'If it is Ostyankin's corpse, and they have no part in that particular plot, they will have made themselves scarce pretty quickly.'

'But then they would presumably have kept the little victim for another occasion, another client.'

'Perhaps, James, but they would have seen that this time they had landed in a hanging matter. Their instinct would have been to bolt, to get away as quickly and as far away as possible.'

'The little girl would have been dumped somewhere? But where?'

'That is what has engaged me this afternoon, James. I have been visiting some likely refuges and places of rescue where such an abandoned child may have fetched up. My sources are extensive, and, as you know, many people will speak to me who will not speak to the police.'

'Have you learnt anything, then?'

'Not yet, but it is early days. I have merely touched the surface of all the possibilities, and I intend to press on with my enquiries. One thing seems certain, though: the police will scarcely wish to tread along that path, if what Solomons has said about the status of some of the visitors to Poland Street is true. I think I can guess, too, what the "fresh parcel" in Coe's cryptic message refers to: what was it exactly again?'

'"Warwick Wednesday seven fresh parcel,"' I replied.

'Warwick presumably refers to Coe's lodgings in Warwick Square, but I can scarcely imagine him soliciting the delivery of "fresh parcels" there, under the jaundiced eye of Mrs Gedge!'

'No, indeed, and which Wednesday? It may of course have been all perfectly above board, and the parcel may have been no more than that, in connection with Coe's legitimate business activities: samples, or something of the kind.'

'It occurs to me, James, that the economical nature of the wording – the sort of way one would arrange a telegraph-message – also indicates a possible newspaper advertisement. Perhaps it might be worthwhile if you called round the newspaper offices in the morning?'

'A good idea, and after morning surgery and luncheon, we might both redouble our enquiries among the foundling refuges.'

Having drawn up our next day's plan of campaign, we turned in for the night, and, next morning, directly after breakfast, I repaired to Fleet Street, where, at the offices of the *Daily Telegraph*, Violet's theory bore fruit. Not only had Coe's message appeared in the issue for Monday, the 24th of November last, but in identical form – except for the days stipulated – at intervals of two to three weeks as far back as the beginning of the previous year and beyond. I noted these dates down, and, in a change of plan, set off for Wormwood Scrubs prison, where I was again able to secure an interview with Solomon Solomons, who greeted me with the same unconcern as on my first visit on the previous day.

'Well, doctor,' he said with a slow, lazy smile, 'have you found justice yet?'

'No, not yet, but I have been watching you . . .'

'Oh, is it so, then? You have been perhaps scraping a hole in the wall of the cell next to mine, like the Count of Monte Cristo?'

'Let us say I have a crystal ball, in which I can descry not only the future, but the past. I look into the ball, and the mists clear: it is night, and the place is the alley behind Poland Street. You are there, and it is as if I am looking through your eyes. But wait, the mists are descending again, the night passes – again and again – and I am seeing the same scene repeated. I see a woman, and she is leading along a blindfolded little girl . . .'

Solomons snorted contemptuously.

'How amusing, doctor, but I remember telling you that yesterday morning.'

'But that isn't all, Mr Solomons,' I continued. 'My powers extend beyond the boundaries of time, as well as space – the sightings occurred on Monday, the 24th of November, Wednes-

75

day the 19th, and Wednesday the 12th – two days after General Ostyankin arrived in England. Do you find that interesting?'

The prisoner was now sitting bolt upright in his chair across the chickenwire grille, and the lazy smile was quite wiped from his face, which was a shade whiter even under the prison pallor. He glared at me for a few moments before speaking, and I knew that I had hit the mark.

'I know many who would kill for that crystal ball of yours, Dr Mortimer, including your authorities. If I were you, I should not let them know you have it.'

'Thank you for that confirmation,' I said, rising and nodding towards the turnkey. 'I trust we shall have you out of here soon, in spite of your best efforts to the contrary!'

I discussed my latest findings with Violet, in a spare moment at the dispensary.

'That bears out our suspicions about the message on Coe's notepad,' I said. 'Advertisements were placed in the *Daily Telegraph* a day or two in advance of Ostyankin's visits to Poland Street, so that suitable, er . . .'

'Prey?' Violet put in. 'A honeypot to tempt the bear . . .'

'Exactly. So that suitable prey could be procured for him, and we can safely conclude that the similar advertisements placed before his last visit to England were inserted in the paper with a view to catering for other distinguished *habitués* of the house in Poland Street.'

'But where does Warwick come in?' my wife objected. 'It is preposterous to suggest that the so-called parcels were brought to Pimlico to be looked over!'

'Mmm . . . yes, that is still to be determined, but I think we are on the right track.'

Violet looked thoughtful for a moment.

'Solomons' surprise when you revealed the dates of his vigils in Soho on the nights when little girls were procured suggests that the police have not been able to get the exact dates out of him.'

'That issue was skated over at the trial: so much seems hidden in this case. Still, I think we can claim to have made some progress. I even think we have deserved a little treat . . .'

My wife's grey eyes widened behind her pince-nez.

'A treat, James?'

'Yes, I was thinking of a little excursion to the salubrious heights of Hampstead after luncheon tomorrow, on – how does the song go? – a bicycle made for two . . .'

9

Conforming our timing to that of the sick-visiting habits of respectable folk of a Sunday – after a late luncheon – we arrived on our hired tandem in the vicinity of the Vale of Health at half-past two, and in that winter season the sun was already westering in dull gold. Violet was as charming as ever in her bicycling *tenue* of Jaeger tweed Norfolk jacket and bloomers tucked into the stout woollen stockings that emerged from her neat brown boots. A jaunty little tweed trilby set at a rakish angle on her gathered-up hair and a pair of tinted goggles completed the ensemble. I had merely donned country togs and a reversed cricket cap, which, with the addition of goggles, I hoped would enable me to pass as a fresh air fiend. We had hoped that any folk who might then be out taking an afternoon stroll would not be surprised by anything that a couple of bicycling faddists might get up to, and, apart from the occasional shaken bonnet or clucked palate, we were proved right in this. Indeed, a feature we had not bargained for was the fact that we were not the only ones thus occupied, and, more than once, I was obliged to acknowledge the salutes of fellow Jehus coming in the opposite direction by raising my disengaged forefinger to the rim of my goggles.

We must have swung round Montelimar Close and round again half a dozen times – keeping weather eyes open for our hoped-for visitors at No. 4 – until, hopefully having established our credentials with any curtain-peepers in the vicinity, we stopped and dismounted. We then propped our machine against the gate of the empty villa next to No. 4 in order to effect some diplomatic repairs to our back tyre.

'They are either not coming,' I muttered uneasily, as I glanced up and down the road, which was deserted, 'or they are already inside. I'm going to slip into the garden here, and take a look through the fence.'

Violet looked round her quickly.

'Up you go, then, James – the coast is clear.'

Violet steadied the bicycle as I hopped up, and, resting my foot on the front seat, carefully negotiated the spikes of the high gate and flopped down onto the drive on the other side, while my co-pedallist went on with her Barmecide tinkering. I slipped into the rank shrubbery, getting a soaking for my pains, then, reaching the spiked railings with No. 4, I sought a gap in the neighbouring hedge that would allow me a clear view into the conservatory which covered most of the wall of the nursing home. This done, I whipped out the small, brassbound field-glasses that had rendered me such sterling service in my hours of leisure from my general practice days in Dartmoor, and settled down to my observations.

There were half a dozen of what looked like visitors, some seated, others standing with their backs to me. I focused and refocused my glasses, taking all the advantage I could of the waning light of the February afternoon, and cursing the capricious glinting of the sun on the conservatory-panes until, yes – that looked like them. The elder lady was standing facing the window, with an arm round the shoulders of a figure who, with a jerky, stilted gait, was trying to move across the room, while a neat female form had a restraining hand clutched around his elbow. I screwed the glasses into even finer focus, and was able to recognise the pretty fair face of the Pocket Venus of the Old Bailey.

I studied the poor husk the women were tending, fixing his image in my memory. Here was stark tragedy. I continued my surveillance amid the mournful reek of old soot and dank greenery for some ten minutes more, the soughing of the breeze in the leaves being punctuated by the increasingly frantic squeaking of Violet's inflator, then it became clear that the young man's visitors were preparing to leave. I scuttled back down behind the hedge, and, holding my breath, levelled the field-glasses on the front door.

Two other couples preceded them, then my birds appeared, not ten yards away. They were almost abreast of me, when the Pocket Venus drew a handkerchief from her sleeve and dabbed at her eyes. Thanks to the power of the glasses, I was able to notice that the otherwise spotless handkerchief was stained at one edge with an unmistakable shade of purple. I smiled and tucked away the glasses, for by then the women were lost to view.

I started to make my way back to Violet and the tandem, but I was stopped in my tracks by a loud and hearty man's voice from the vicinity of the gate of No. 5. I crouched down and remained silent.

'My dear young lady!' the voice was booming. 'It is a clear case of a torn inner tube, and all the pumping in the world will not put it right . . .'

'I assure you, sir,' came Violet's low, husky voice, 'it is merely low air-pressure. There! It is firmer already.'

'It will be no trouble at all, ma'am: I can have that tyre off in a twinkling . . .'

And so the badinage continued for what seemed like an age, as I squatted impatiently in the leaf-litter. At last the hateful, officious voice ceased its booming, and I crept tentatively forward, until I saw that Violet was alone again. She looked up and nodded.

'The road is clear again, James – can you see them?'

I gazed down the street.

'Yes! They are getting into a cab – it's going off in the direction of North End Way. Quickly!'

We leapt into our seats and pedalled hell-for-leather, until we could see the cab plainly before us. Soon we had left North End Way behind us, and were bowling down after the cab into the fog and smoke of central London. I put out my right arm as we swung into the Finchley Road, with the cab just in front of us. We were gaining on it, and both of us instinctively slowed our pedalling, when a done-in-looking horse pulling an overloaded cart emerged suddenly in front of us from Circus Road and blocked our way. We were forced to brake with such violence that our machine reared like a bronco, then slithered with screeching tyres into the kerb, where we toppled over in a heap.

'Bleedin' scorchers!' the carter yelled back at us, as I helped Violet to her feet at the kerbside. 'Bloody cycles oughtn't ter be allowed on the roads!'

'Give a thought for that poor horse, you brute!' Violet cried after him, as, after giving our machine a quick look-over, we remounted and proceeded at speed down the road, but there was no sign of the hansom.

In no time at all we were at the intersection where the Finchley Road begins to skirt Regent's Park, with Prince Albert Road branching off to the left, and St John's Wood to the right. I put out my hand, and we pulled up at the kerb, where, dismounting, we propped up the tandem. We looked carefully in all directions, but could see neither hide nor hair of our cab.

'Straight down Park Road!' Violet urged. 'We can't go in all directions at once, so we may as well head down into town. That'll be their most likely route, by the law of averages . . .'

We rode at the fastest pace we could without resorting to downright scorching, and my pulses quickened as, just as we were coming to the Regent's Park roundabout, I spotted a solitary hansom, going along at a sedate pace amid the sparse Sunday traffic.

'It could be them!' I shouted back at Violet.

'Yes, I can't see any other cabs!'

We slowed down again, and dogged the cab as it turned down Cleveland Street, and, as the traffic, like the thoroughfares, became progressively denser, I had to keep my eyes peeled as other hansoms started to jink into view on all sides. Fitzroy, Charlotte and Rathbone Streets went by until the cab finally came to a halt at a building on Soho Square. I signalled, and turned towards the opposite side of the square, where we stopped and pretended to inflate a tyre, while, to our satisfaction, we espied the elder lady of our pair get out of the cab and enter a building.

'It's the Working Girls' Club!' Violet exclaimed huskily.

I had heard of this admirable institution, where a single girl in London might find homely accommodation at moderate rates.

'The lady cannot possibly be an inmate,' I remarked. 'She may well work, but "girl" . . .'

I stowed away the inflator, and we gave chase, but lost the hansom amid a hugger-mugger of traffic somewhere in that densely packed triangle whose sides are formed by St Giles, Charing Cross Road and Shaftesbury Avenue. We soon gave up the hunt as hopeless and pulled for home, where, after we had bestowed our tandem in the area, we went indoors for a change of clothing and a rest, then took a leisurely tea, in the course of which we discussed the events of the afternoon.

'Can it be coincidence that the Working Girls' Club is a mere stone's throw away from the house in Poland Street where the Russian general was murdered?' Violet remarked at one point.

'The older I get, my dear, the less I believe in coincidence. Effects have causes. I feel it in my bones that we are on to something!'

'Mmm . . .' Violet murmured. 'Venus keeps her veil lowered while witness Miller is present in court, then lifts it the moment he leaves. She later picks up a stately lady from the same court hearing on a later day, and they drive off together to Hampstead. Today they drive back together from the same place in Hampstead to Soho Square, which is in the same quarter as Poland Street, ergo Venus and the Matron are connected with the case. A pretty speculation, James, and an enjoyable Sunday ride, but we've nothing else to go on.'

I relished a particularly luscious morsel of Dundee cake, and smiled lazily.

'On the contrary, my dear, we have that distinctly promising purple stain on Venus's handkerchief . . .'

10

On the next morning, Monday the 23rd of February, I sat again among the spectators in the Central Court of the Old Bailey and listened to Mr Francis Carmody's closing speech for the defence. Lest at this turn the reader should think my memory at fault in thus describing the order of speaking of the respective counsel at an English trial, I should explain the advantage – which I have touched upon earlier on – enjoyed by a senior law officer like the counsel for the Crown, Sir Edward Clarke. It is simply that as Solicitor General, Sir Edward enjoyed the exceptional prerogative of speaking after the defence counsel. In such cases, the prosecution has, literally, the last word. Carmody would, then, have to stretch his abilities to the very limit to see that his arguments were not effaced in the minds of the jury by the legal heavyweight who was to follow him. The tension in the chamber was almost tangible as he proceeded methodically to a verbal recall of all the testimony, for and against his client, which has already been described in this account. It was not, then, until past two that afternoon that he came to his final peroration, the strained concentration on the faces of the jurymen being plain to see.

'One thing,' the young barrister began, 'is beyond dispute: General Ostyankin met his death by bloody murder in the bedroom in No. 11, Poland Street. The murderer – I use the singular advisedly, for it is a remarkable feature in this case that there has been no suggestion or indication of an accomplice – must of necessity have been present in that room of blood, full as it was with the stench and stain of chloroform.'

Carmody paused and raked the jury benches with his glance.

'Gentlemen of the jury, the murderer must have been there.'

Another pause, then the slightly built form swung round and glanced for a moment at the battery of his legal opponents on the lawyers' table.

'Yet, astonishing as it must seem to you all, gentlemen of the jury, the Crown has offered not a single shred – not a jot or tittle – of evidence that the accused was ever in that room. My learned friend's silence on the matter when he comes to exercise his august prerogative to speak after me will be eloquent enough testimony to this. Not a scrap of evidence, then, that Solomons was in the fatal room, and it is evidence, and evidence alone, that you are concerned with here. What, then, is the case against the accused? It is composed of two strands. First, his admitted presence in the back alley of Poland Street, opposite the back door of No. 11, two hours and more, according to the testimony of excellent witnesses, *after* the latest time General Ostyankin could have met his death. At least two full hours *too late* to have had any hand in the deed itself. I hasten to add, gentlemen, that you are not concerned today with the exact reason why Solomons was there at all, but with weighing the evidence as it bears upon the circumstances of General Ostyankin's death. The second strand of – I will not dignify it with the name of evidence – shall we say, rather, contrivance? – appears to be founded on the zany supposition that, of all the millions of colonial sovereigns then as now in circulation throughout the Empire, there were somehow no more than two in circulation in this great city on the night of the murder, and that those momentous two linked victim and accused.'

Carmody scanned the faces of the jurymen for a moment, then, flapping his arms out penguin-like from his sides and bringing them back smartly, his eyebrows shot up in a helpless expression, and he finished with a sort of exasperated sigh.

'And that, gentlemen, for what the case for the Crown is worth is *it*. To put it bluntly, the Crown has given you no real evidence to go on, therefore the task before you is an easy and happy one: merely to give utterance to the fact that is staring you all in the face; that Solomon Solomons is not guilty.'

Francis Carmody turned and bowed stiffly towards the judge, then resumed his place on the lawyers' table, whereupon Lord Justice Calthrop adjourned the court till the following morning. I rose and began to leave, this time seeing no one I could recognise among the departing throng. Carmody, then, I thought, had made the most of the hand he had been dealt in emphasising the merely circumstantial nature of the Crown's case, though they were formidable enough circumstances. What *was* Solomons doing in the back alley of Poland Street, however long after the murder had taken place he had arrived there? And the sovereigns – the colonial gold – how did they come to be in his possession? I was assailed by a black doubt: what if after all Solomons *had* killed Ostyankin in the bedroom in Poland Street, then simply robbed him of his money? The commonsense conclusion . . . No, if Solomons was to be got off, it would be essential to prove how, without entering the fatal room, he had come into possession of those sovereigns. And what was the plain, bluff juror to make of Solomons' presence in the alley in the light of what he had for weeks on end been reading in the daily paper? Ostyankin had done in Solomons' mother and young sister in Russia. Solomons had already had a crack at the general there, and now he had had a go at him in Soho the previous November, as any man as is a man would have done. Pulled it off this time, no doubt. In his place I might have had a crack at that Rooshian meself: nasty piece of work – better dead, in fact. Good riddance to bad rubbish. Bad luck Solomons had been caught, though – clever wheeze of that copper's with the Australian sovereigns. Still, you couldn't just do a bloke in on a grudge: law would have to take its course now. Or something like that.

I set off down the Strand for the warmth and beefy savours of Simpsons. With some food inside me, I felt more equal to my next task, which had been suggested to me by a perusal of the invaluable Ward's directory after breakfast that morning. Scanning the directory, I had found the timber agency of Alexander Miller, the 'off and on' denizen of London and quondam *homme d'affaires* of the murdered Russian general. His interest in the timber trade, then, must be a very real one: certainly there would have been nothing illusory about the rent of an office in Leadenhall Street, and even less so one in the newish redbrick palace of commerce I found myself surveying after a fifteen-minute cab-drive.

Miller sported his brass plate on a frosted glass-topped door off a corridor on the third floor, which was flanked on either side by those of the suites of shipping companies holding household names. I had entered the corridor with no thought of bearding Miller in his lair, so to speak, it having long become clear that discretion must be of the essence in the investigation of this case.

It was rather with the intention of getting the lie of the land, for it has been my experience that a glance at the everyday surroundings of a subject – where he works and lives and has his being – may reveal aspects of him that a thousand words of description or reminiscence from the lips of third parties may leave untouched. So it was in this case, for on the wall just off the glass-topped door was a glass display-case, inside of which was a typewritten sheet, down the side of which were affixed little cigarette-card sized samples of what looked like paint-colours – so many studies in brown. Casting my eyes up and down the empty corridor, I drew a magnifying glass, newly purchased that morning from Messrs Negretti and Zambra in Holborn Circus, and, bowing over the display-case, I brought the weighty lens up against my spectacles, and studied the typewritten sheet and its fixtures. Veneers, Baltic and Mediterranean, with descriptions and prices, along with an invitation to consult the complete catalogue within. The text was immaculately typewritten, in the unappealing mauve ink of the time, but with – could it be an illusion? – something not quite right about the upstrokes of the capital letters. I pushed my nose even closer to the case, and, no, it was no illusion, the capital letters in the text were indeed virtually as thick as the small-case ones. I stepped back and smiled slightly. The field was narrowing. Just then a gust of businesslike voices came to me from one of the ends of the corridor, and I whipped my magnifying glass back into the inside pocket of my greatcoat, and, adopting a more relaxed posture, I applied myself to an engrossed study of the display-case until the pair swept past behind me and the distant slamming of a door confirmed that I was alone again in the corridor. I took a last look at the nameplate: 'A. Miller, Timber Importer', then made my way to the stairs.

I knew that Violet would have been making her own enquiries that afternoon, and we had arranged to meet for tea at home at four, so, with an hour in hand, I took a cab and returned to Henrietta Street, where I found my wife all a-bustle.

'A lead, James, a definite lead!' she muttered, a lethal-looking pin clamped between her teeth as she put up her tow-coloured hair.

'Oh?' I exclaimed. 'In connection with what?'

'The young girl whose existence we were speculating about

the other day – a possible offering to Ostyankin in Poland Street on the night of the murder.'

'What! You have found her?'

'As to that, we shall see,' Violet said briskly, as, her hair up, she thrust the pin decisively through her little tarred sailor's hat, and I fought down my recently married man's impulse to go round and gather her in my arms like a good harvest.

'I have been going the rounds of the orphanages and foundlings' refuges since one o'clock,' she went on as I helped her put on her caped coat, 'and I think I may at last have found something definite.'

'Where?'

'St Crispin's Mission in Bevis Marks.'

'Ah, yes, Miss Carlin,' I said. 'You were colleagues at the New Women's Hospital, weren't you?'

Violet nodded, then, locking my arm in hers, led me downstairs to the front door, and out into the street, where she stepped out on to the road and waved her umbrella in the path of a disengaged cab. As we got into the cab she bade the driver take us to Pembridge Square, Bayswater, and, after we were comfortably seated, continued her narrative.

'Sophie consulted her books for the end of last November, but could find no record of any actual admissions around that time, and I was about to carry on my search elsewhere, when, on an afterthought, she remembered that a gentleman – a Mr Moberley of Bayswater . . .'

'Moberley?' I mused. 'That seems to ring a bell . . .'

'Yes, it is Randall Moberley the eye-surgeon.'

'Of course! He was quite a swell in his day – retired prematurely through illness or something of the kind. Well, well . . .'

'It seems Mr Moberley left a message with her to look out for the people of a girl who had been left – quite literally – on his doorstep. A girl of fifteen, who said she lived in Lamb Street . . .'

'That's just behind Spitalfields Market – not very far from the Whitechapel Dispensary.'

'Yes, anyway Mr Moberley had apparently been round there, but could find no trace of the girl's parents or find anyone who would tell him of their possible whereabouts. He decided to come to Sophie as last court of appeal, so to speak. I thought we might pay him a call before evening surgery.'

I concurred willingly, and spent the last five minutes or so of our journey in recounting my findings of the afternoon.

'You think the thickness of the typewritten letters significant, then?' Violet asked.

'We shall see, Violet, we shall see – we must neglect nothing.'

Mr Moberley lived in a fine house amid surroundings of discreet opulence, and, on our producing our cards to the parlourmaid at the door, we were immediately summoned to the drawing-room, where places were laid for us for tea.

Randall Moberley was a square-shouldered man of no more than fifty-five, with a full head of black hair, grey at the sideburns, and parted in the middle in the fashion of Mr Joseph Chamberlain. His square, aquiline-featured face creased in a smile as he rose to shake our hands. He shook Violet's first, and I was somewhat surprised by the feeble way with which he clawed at my hand, then seemed to throw it from him again, as if he had inadvertently picked up something unpleasant.

'Forgive the masonic grip,' he remarked ruefully, clearly having noticed my slight dismay, 'but grasping at shattered carriage-windows doesn't do the tissues any good . . .'

The ex-surgeon held up his right hand, the last two digits of which were withered and bent over, more like hen's claws than fingers. I then vaguely remembered a newspaper article I had read several years before, about a runaway coach and a crash, which had involved the distinguished surgeon.

'Oh, bad luck, sir!' I said. 'That'll account for your early retirement, I take it?'

'Just so, doctor – or d'you prefer plain mister? Says on your card you're one of us . . .'

'Oh, either will do, sir. I'm not coy about it.'

'Very sensible, too. Well, now, please sit down and tell me how I can help you.'

We sat down at the table, and a maid appeared and plied the tea things, while Violet explained our interest, but without mentioning the Poland Street case specifically.

The square face of our host darkened.

'You too suspect the vice-traffic, hey, ma'am? Then I'm with you heart and soul. Filthy business! My late wife's views on the matter were much the same as yours, especially where under-aged girls are involved. Still, I'm glad to say it doesn't seem to have applied in little Emily's case, at any rate. She had a thorough examination after she turned up here – very thorough.'

'Ah, little Emily,' I said. 'May I ask when she was brought to you, sir?'

'End of last November – 27th, or rather the early hours of the 28th. Just appeared on the doorstep, like the Demon King in a pantomime! Whoever brought her simply rang the front doorbell and kept on ringing till someone was roused – Cook, as it happened. She came banging on my bedroom door, and when I'd got up and opened it, there she stood shivering, her hair in papers, and whispering that there was a girl on the doorstep. I went downstairs immediately and led the waif into the kitchen, where there was still some warmth left in the fire, lit the gas and looked her over. Calm little creature, clean, well-nourished and healthy-looking. Neatly and cleanly dressed, too. I asked her her name, how old she was and where she lived, and she said her name was Emily Chaytor, she thought she was fifteen, and she lived in Spitalfields. When I asked her mother's name, she just said Meg. I asked if this Meg had brought her here, and she shook her head, saying that a nice lady had brought her, but that she didn't know who the lady was. She said she didn't know why she had been brought to my door. I was at a loss what to do, but it occurred to me that the girl's people must be frantic, so I dressed and, slipping a life-preserver in the pocket of my greatcoat – I still have a good left-hand swing! – I took Emily out and collared a cab, and, after asking her what part of Spitalfields she lived in, ordered the cabbie to take us to Lamb Street. It must have been half-past four in the morning by the time we got there, and the place Emily led me to was as vile a hole as might be imagined; in fact, for one sticky moment I thought the child might have lured me there to a sandbagging! Anyway, to cut a long story short, there was no sign of this Meg in the hovel Emily finally brought me to, nor did anyone I could rouse there admit to have even known such a person. I met with a veritable wall of silence, so that I was prompted on more than one occasion to ask Emily if she had really lived there, or whether it had all been a bit of make-believe. Perhaps she had run away from home somewhere else, or from school. But the child's denials seemed sincere, so my next stop was Leman Street police station, where I again drew a blank. They'd heard nothing of a missing girl, and in any case, there must be thousands like her in like plight throughout London. By then day was beginning to dawn, and Emily looked done in, so I just put her back into the cab and drove home, and told Cook to give her a slice of pie and a glass of milk, then put her to bed somewhere till a more civilised hour. Cook was rather taken with her, and in fact made up a bed for her in her own room, but later on, after breakfast, I could still get no more out of Emily besides what she'd told me when first she'd been brought to me, except for an odd, dis-jointed rigmarole about what had brought her here that made no sense to me. It sounded like some sort of game.'

'Ah,' I said, 'what was that, sir?'

'Why not have the story from Emily's own lips, doctor?'

'You mean she is still with you, Mr Moberley?' Violet asked.

'Yes but more of that anon,' our host said, turning to the maid, who was standing behind us against the wall. 'Florence, please go down to Cook and ask her to send Emily here.'

It was a matter of a couple of minutes before the little homely cook, with her hair in a grey bun, gently led her small charge into the room. The cook's rather prominent eyes followed ours uncertainly as she waited for her employer to speak. She was clearly as protective of her charge as an old hen.

'All right, Mrs Read, you can leave her with us for now: this lady and gentleman have some questions they would like to put to Emily.'

The cook nodded and bustled out of the room, evidently relieved that we had not come to take the girl away. Emily went up to our host and stood beside him, her pretty, rather long face wearing a calm and placid expression. She was blonde, and her eyes were still and glass-grey. With her slight build, she might have been younger or older than the fifteen she'd professed to Mr Moberley, who took her by the hand, and nodded at us each in turn.

'This is Dr Mortimer, Emily, and the lady is Dr Branscombe. They'd very much like to know about how you came to live here. Would you like to tell them?'

Emily glanced up at our host's face and nodded solemnly, then turned her unwavering stare on me and started to speak in a quiet, cockney voice, though I could discern evidence of her stay in this professional upper-middle-class household in her voiced aitches and already-passable grammar.

'Meg said I had to have a bath, then a lady was coming to take me somewhere where I had to be very good, and I'd be given a new dress, but the lady was going to play a game with me . . .'

'A game, Emily?' Violet interrupted, husky-voiced.

'Yes, I was to wear a thick cloth over my eyes, and then I'd have to guess where I'd been, and if I could, I'd be given toffee direckly. I had the bath, and the lady, er . . . looked at me . . .'

Moberley gave a sort of growl, and went quite red in the face.

'How, Emily?' Violet asked. 'How did she look at you?'

Emily blushed, and cast her eyes down at her long, folded hands, through which one of her apron-strings emerged. She made no reply.

'I see, my dear,' Violet said gently, 'it's all right – don't think about it any more.'

We adults exchanged glances, then Moberley patted Emily's hand, and asked her to go on with her story, without describing the physical examination the toffee-lady had evidently put her through.

'. . . and Meg dressed me in a nice dress I hadn't ever seen before, and the lady came and . . .'

'What did she look like, Emily?' I asked.

'She had a black dress on, and wore a veil, so I couldn't see her face, and she talked a bit funny.'

'A foreign lady, Emily?' Violet asked, and the girl went on in a continuous monotone.

'I don't know. She talked to Meg for a bit, then she took me into a cab with the windows covered, and the lady in the veil asked if Meg had told me about the game we were going to play, and I said yes, and she laughed and tied a cloth round my eyes till the cab stopped, then the lady lifted me out and led me down some stairs, and I heard a door being knocked, then the lady took me into a room, and she was talking to someone else, who didn't say anything to her, then it was quiet for a bit.'

'You were left alone, Emily?' I asked.

'I don't know. I couldn't see or hear anything. Then the nice lady came back . . .'

91

'The lady with the funny voice?' Violet put in.

'No, another lady – the nice lady . . .'

'Ah,' I said, 'the lady who brought you here to Mr Moberley's house?'

Emily nodded gravely at me, and went on.

'She said we were to go on with our game, but in a different room, then she took my hand and took me into a room upstairs, and sat me on the bed and told me to wait a jiffy, and be a good girl, and I'd get something nice when she came back. I heard the door being locked, and I sat there for a long time, then the door was opened again, and I heard the nice lady talking to someone else . . .'

'A man, or a woman, Emily?' I asked.

'I don't know – they didn't answer her back.'

'Do you remember anything they said?' Violet asked.

Emily shook her head, and I thought of the chloroform mentioned at the trial.

'Do you remember what the nice lady smelt like, Emily?'

'She smelt nice, like the things Cookie puts in my bath.'

'She didn't smell a bit like, well . . . medicine – strong medicine?'

The same solemn shake of the head, then, at my prompting, Emily went on.

'Then we went downstairs again, and the nice lady lifted me up into another cab, and it went along for quite a while, then it stopped, and the lady asked me to promise that if she took the cloth off my eyes I would go with her and be a good girl, and I said yes, and she took the cloth off and we got out of the cab.'

'Did you see her face, Emily?' Violet asked.

'No, she had a veil on, too, but she was quite little, in a black dress. We walked a long way, and it was ever so dark and cold, then we came here, and the lady said the game was nearly finished, and started to ring on the door, and she rang and rang till I heard someone shouting behind the door – it was Cookie – then, as the door was opening, the nice lady made me promise to stay there, and she went away. Cookie came and took me to Mr Moberley.'

'Do you remember anything more, Emily?' I asked. 'About the

lady with the funny voice, the nice lady, the cab-drive, the house
you were first taken to?'

The grave, still eyes regarded me, then came the half-expected
shake of the head. Violet smiled at the young girl, and reached
forward towards her.

'Don't you miss Meg, Emily? Wouldn't you like to find her
again?'

The girl pressed herself against Mr Moberley in a gesture that
spoke a thousand words, and shook her head more violently
than ever. Moberley patted her hand.

'Well, that'll be enough for now, my dear,' he said, 'so if you'd
like to make your goodbyes to our guests, you can run down
and join Cookie again.'

Emily bobbed a solemn little curtsey to each of us in turn, and
left the room.

'An extraordinary tale!' Moberley remarked. 'What d'you
make of it?'

'I don't like the sound of the physical examination or the
blindfold,' I said. 'Something was interrupted there, and it was
no harmless game.'

'I felt that myself at first,' Moberley replied. 'Especially when
Emily told me about the examination, yet what went on at this
mystery house – or madhouse – according to the child's account
seems to have been harmless enough, if bizarre. I can make
neither head nor tail of it, though I don't doubt she's telling the
truth.'

'Yes,' Violet said, 'something in her manner compels belief, but
when all's said and done, it does seem a roundabout way of
abandoning someone . . .'

'You're right there, ma'am,' our host conceded. 'Well, that's
about all I know. As I've told you, I've tried the police and the
rescue missions, and I've even been down to Somerset House to
consult the registers, but they've no record there of any Emily –
or Meg – Chaytors within the last twenty years.'

'Really, Mr Moberley,' Violet said, 'I think you have acted with
admirable charity and public spirit, and that anyone else in your
position would by now have simply handed Emily over to the
parish . . .'

Moberley stiffened in his chair, and fairly spluttered his reply.

'God forbid! The child has been bandied about like a parcel, and, and . . .'

My wife smiled.

'You have become fond of her, have you not, Mr Moberley?'

Our host's attitude relaxed immediately, and he spread his hands over his knees.

'There, you've put your finger on it, ma'am! I've no children of my own, and, well . . . she has fairly wound herself round my heart! And she seems happy here. But there's the trouble – the thing is so irregular. I am powerless to take any official steps towards taking Emily under my guardianship unless I can trace her legal parents. I suppose I can only carry on the search, and in the meantime give the child a decent home and pass on to her some rudiments of education.'

We both rose.

'I hope we have been of assistance to you, doctor, ma'am,' our host said, rising and ringing for the maid.

'It has been most interesting, thank you, Mr Moberley.' Violet spoke for us both.

'You have been most helpful.'

'One final thing, sir,' I said, as the maid came in with our outdoor things.

'Yes, Dr Mortimer?'

'Have you really no idea at all why, of all the doorsteps in London, anyone should leave Emily on yours?'

'None, sir, none at all,' Moberley replied as he walked to the corridor with us, while the maid helped us on with our things. 'I have been pondering the business ever since, and can come up with no answer.'

'You have never been involved in social relief work, sir?' Violet asked. 'Your name is not perhaps on the books of any charitable organisations?'

'Well, I have given my professional services free on occasion, as we all do from time to time in especially deserving cases, but as for my name being on any official roster . . .'

Violet nodded and turned away, and, renewing our thanks, we followed the maid to the street door, and were let out. My wife paused for a moment outside, and I saw that her face was drawn, and her eyes hot with anger.

'What is it, dear?' I said.

There was a tremor in her husky voice as she replied through clenched teeth.

'I'd give them toffee, James!'

11

I must own that it was in no very alert frame of mind that I attended next morning at the Old Bailey, for as soon as Violet and I had finished surgery at the Whitechapel Dispensary on the previous evening, we had both been called out on emergency cases, which had occupied us till the small hours, and, of course, given us little opportunity to discuss the fruits of our visit to Mr Moberley in Bayswater that afternoon.

As for the matter in hand, it was now that the crucial advantage enjoyed by the prosecution counsel – to speak after the defence barrister – came fully into play. As to the contents of his speech, the details are scarcely germane to my account, for, like those of Francis Carmody's address the previous day, they merely consisted of a rhetorical rehash of what had already passed in the trial to date. I thought, however, that, despite its forensic verbosity, his counterblast against Carmody's gibes as to the Crown's reliance on coincidence was neat enough to bear verbatim repetition. It came, then, at the very end of his closing peroration.

'My learned friend,' the Solicitor General concluded, 'made great play yesterday as to the Crown's supposed dependence on mere coincidence in this case. In his closing speech, he even paid me the double-edged compliment that I was making the best of a bad job in trying to make bricks without straw. Let me return him the compliment, gentlemen of the jury: let us test the soundness of *his* bricks in the construction of a house of convincing evidence, a house that will stand against the force of the Crown's argument. To sum up, the defendant, Solomon Solomons – who, by his own admission to the police, had been dogging the victim's steps, and moreover had set himself the task of bringing him to some sort of account – is – again by his own admission – keeping watch on the fatal night at the scene of General Ostyankin's appalling murder. A few hours later – and yet again neither Solomons nor my learned friend seeks to deny the fact – he is found clutching eighteen sovereigns, two of them marked colonial coins, as had been drawn at Coutts Bank that same day by the victim. And again – if we credit my learned friend's opinion – by another remarkable fluke, chance, or what you will, the sum that the unfortunate general drew that morning was twenty pounds, which, after some minor purchases made during the day and after he had paid his reckoning at Kettners, had been depleted to . . .'

Sir Edward paused melodramatically as, walking slowly the length of the jury box, he fixed each juror in turn with his eye, then, suddenly swinging on his toe, flung his hand in the air in the gesture a stage magician might use in drawing a coloured handkerchief from a hat.

'Eighteen pounds!' The Solicitor General spat out the words contemptuously. 'And all of these things pure coincidence. I don't know how many of you are racing men, but I think those of you who are will agree with me that three winners in a row like that would constitute a real yankee! Gentlemen of the jury, all of this is not just stretching the proverbially long arm of coincidence, it is wrenching it clean out of its socket!'

On this scornful note the counsel for the Crown finished his speech, and the judge once again dismissed the court till the next morning. I glanced over at the defendant, who would surely know his fate within forty-eight hours, but no marks of anxiety marked his fine, ascetic features. I rose and cast my eyes round the departing crowd of spectators – no familiar faces – then joined the rush to the exits.

Violet and I held another conference later, and, after I had related what had happened in court that day, the first topic she broached was our visit of the previous afternoon to Mr Moberley's in Bayswater.

'I think the child was telling the truth, James, but we cannot of course be certain that the house where she was first taken to was 11, Poland Street.'

'But on that night, and at that hour . . .'

'Too quiet, though – too sedate – for murder. No screams or thumps or mayhem. Just a lady with a funny voice who takes her in, talks to someone who doesn't answer, puts her in a room on her own for a bit, then a nice lady who collects her and takes her upstairs, where she puts Emily alone in another room for a long time, then finally comes back talking to someone who again doesn't answer and takes her out again, to leave her on Mr Moberley's doorstep.'

'The nice lady is "quite little", is veiled and has on a black dress and smells like bath-salts . . .'

'Instead of chloroform,' Violet commented. 'The murderer – or murderess – must have reeked of the stuff, unless he or she'd had a thorough scrub and complete change of clothing immediately after doing the murder.'

'There'd have been the time,' I suggested. 'Remember, Emily said she was alone in the upstairs room for a long time.'

'But the cold-bloodedness of it, James! And with the child only yards away.'

I mused for a little while before speaking again.

'A picture is emerging, Violet: the Portrait of a Nice Lady, if you like . . .'

'Do depict this charming creature, James!'

'She is small, decisive and neat in her appearance, and when she speaks, her interlocutors – or rather non-interlocutors – do not answer her back.'

'A lady who is used to command?'

'Perhaps. Then again, she has a way with children: they will go with her when she coaxes. Perhaps a teacher or a governess.'

'Or a procuress, more like it, with the bath and the examination!' Violet snapped. 'If she was in league with "the lady with the funny voice" who examined Emily. And again – if it *was* No. 11 – perhaps a devilishly cool murderess . . . Think of little Emily, too, if that was indeed the case, and the horrors she may have passed through unawares. She's a dear, solemn little thing, isn't she, and what a turn-up for her, to be taken up by a retired eye-surgeon and his cook!'

'That is about the only good thing that has come out of this whole affair so far.'

'Does this governessy, nice-but-determined little lady in the black dress remind you of someone, James?' Violet asked pensively.

A diminutive, straight-backed figure came to my mind, one whose thin, set mouth and cold blue eyes suggested someone who was ready for anything.

'Our Pocket Venus,' I said, to Violet's confirmatory nod. 'A woman with a purpose – and a grudge – but evidence, my dear, evidence . . .'

Just then time caught up with our speculations, and we had to set off for evening surgery at the dispensary, at the end of which, after I had put Violet into a cab for home, I decided it really was time that I renewed my acquaintance with the Warsaw Café. I well knew the rule of silence that pertained there in criminal matters, but surely at least some ripple must have reached there by now from the great criminal trial that was unfolding at the Old Bailey and was filling the columns of the press, especially considering the fact that at its centre was a familiar face among the café's *habitués*. I set off on foot for Osborn Street, and had soon entered into that little enclave of Eastern Europe, with its newspapers slung over brass rods, and tables covered with chessboards and tall tea-glasses in metal holders. The air was thick with coarse, strong tobacco, and a polyglot murmur filled the spacious room. I paused inside and looked around me, until I had caught the eye of the proprietor.

'Evening, doctor,' he said, 'you're getting to be quite a stranger: after a game?'

I smiled and nodded, and just then a solitary figure rose from one of the tables near the window, and, sawing his belt with his forearm, gave me an ironical bow.

'Ah, Shaffer!' I laughed across the room, going to join my old chess adversary. 'I'm here to claim my revenge!'

'Come on, then, Dr Mortimer,' he replied, as I ordered two lemon teas from the now-attendant waiter, 'but at your own risk! You know I'm always ready to give the bourgeoisie a hammering!'

I laughed again as my opposite number set up the chessboard and rubbed his hands together, his little bright black eyes twinkling with anticipation. Mannie Shaffer was a skilled cabinet-maker by trade, whose services were so much in demand from reproduction-furniture manufacturers that he was able with impunity to indulge his chosen scheme of life, which was to work flat out for six months or so, then to live on the proceeds as an independent man-of-letters and political theorist for the following six. He was a Social Revolutionary, and the Warsaw was his House of Commons and Hyde Park Corner rolled into one. I took a last look round me before we started our game.

Hardly a full house, but par for the course on a Tuesday evening. Apart from the proprietor and Mannie, there was not anyone there I really knew. We played, amid Mannie's triumphant crowing as I gradually lost ground, for a full hour and a half. It was not far off midnight when I finally plucked up courage to broach the subject I had come to pursue. I felt as if I were treading on eggs, such was my anxiety not to lose, by asking unhealthy questions, the credit I liked to think I had built up among those of the café's regulars who were worth knowing. I chose a quiet moment in the game, and spoke.

'Quite a case they're making over that Russian general's murder,' I said, trying to sound unconcerned.

Mannie grunted without looking up, and gave his opinion of the late General Ostyankin in an unprintable Yiddish imprecation.

'Hard lines on Monia Solomons, too,' I ventured. 'You'd have thought someone would have come forward to speak for him on that night, wouldn't you? I mean, it's not as if he wasn't known around here, or had no friends . . .'

There was a notable drop in conversation at the surrounding tables, and an unmistakable tension began to form in the atmosphere.

'*Freg mir bacheirim*, ask me another,' Mannie muttered, again without looking up from the game, but I sensed I had gone too far, this impression being confirmed by the simultaneous breaking up of companies from more than one table around us.

'Checkmate!' Mannie yelped joyfully, breaking some of the tension, and I duly conceded victory and took my leave with a vigorous handshake. I was making rather sheepishly for the door – I was not sure when next I would be coming here – when a loafer in a crumpled cricket cap rose from a table and momentarily blocked my way. He had a wet, pendulous lower lip, to which was attached a soggy cigarette-end. His bleary brown spaniel's eyes searched mine for a moment, then I was engulfed in the odour of garlic and rough black tobacco as he whispered in my ear as I brushed past him and rammed on my hat.

'Ask the copper – Kennedy,' the man said, as he rolled away from me.

I pushed the door shut behind me with a trembling hand, pulled my muffler round my mouth, and, raising the collar of my greatcoat, set off at a brisker pace than usual for the comparative brilliance of the Whitechapel Road. I pondered what the man with the wet lips had muttered to me. He must have overheard the question I had asked Mannie Shaffer, so perhaps Monia Solomons did have a friend of sorts in Whitechapel after all; or at any rate, the underworld had a spokesman. It suggested only one thing to me: PC Kennedy – whom I knew to be a decent man, and one of the few policemen in the division who cared to patrol in Whitechapel alone – must have looked in at the Warsaw at the time of Ostyankin's murder and scanned Solomons' face among the clientele. It must be known to the whole borough by now. It would be an easy enough matter to seek confirmation or otherwise of this from the constable's own lips, for he must be patrolling one of the surrounding streets at that very moment. I decided to retrace my steps, and comb the streets and alleyways till I found him.

I ran into him in Flower and Dean Street forty minutes later, as he was trying the door of a pawn-shop. The tall form swung round, and PC Kennedy raised his lamp, directing it into my face.

'Why, Dr Mortimer!' he exclaimed with a smile. 'Out on a call, then?'

I smiled and shook my head, having decided on the direct approach.

'I've been attending the trial of Solomon Solomons at the Old Bailey, constable,' I said. 'You must have run into him at the Warsaw?'

Kennedy's back stiffened, and the friendliness went out of his eyes as he replied in a cautious tone.

'I know him by sight, doctor – yes.'

'Yes, quite – by sight. That's what I've been hearing about . . .'

The policeman's eyes narrowed.

'Beg pardon, doctor? I'm not quite following you.'

'They're saying that you looked in at the Warsaw,' I bluffed, 'around the time the Russian was being murdered in Soho, and that you saw Solomons there. They're wondering why you haven't come forward as a witness for him, as it would make all the difference to his defence.'

The constable's jaw dropped perceptibly, and for an instant

uncertainty seemed to cloud his eyes. He straightened up and smiled – a rather fixed smile, I fancied.

'Lord, doctor!' Kennedy exclaimed, with an unconvincing effort at a bluff laugh. 'You don't want to believe what you hear in there: thieves' kitchen. Most of 'em would lie away their own mothers' lives just for the fun of it! Second nature!'

I stepped up and brought my face closer to the constable's.

'For God's sake, man!' I spluttered. 'A man's life is at stake! You don't mean to say you're just going to keep mum and see him hanged!'

My eyes locked with Kennedy's for a full five seconds, then he looked away without saying anything. I hardly needed any further explanation, for there was unmistakable shame in the man's eyes. I turned on my heel and walked away, then Kennedy's voice at my back arrested me for a moment. The voice this time had a chastened quality in it.

'I must have been mistaken, doctor . . .'

I glanced back and nodded curtly, before going my angry way. There was at least a spark of manhood left in the constable, after all. I knew that Kennedy had a wife and four children to support, and I surmised that much official pressure – at a high level – must have been brought to bear on him in order to convince him of his 'mistake' in identifying Solomons in the Warsaw that night. As I sought a cab to drive me home, I felt as if I were walking on quicksand.

12

The next morning, which was Wednesday, the 25th, I decided to forgo my customary attendance at the Old Bailey, since the day would be devoted to Lord Justice Calthrop's summing-up, and the proceedings would consequently throw up no new material in the case. On Thursday, Solomon Solomons' fate would in all likelihood be sealed, and, my recent conversation with PC Kennedy having convinced me beyond doubt that the young revolutionary was innocent of Ostyankin's death, I found myself in the grip of a new urgency. It was then with a solid breakfast inside me that I set out on a search round the typewriting agencies of London. My tramp, trade directory in hand, took me round a full circuit of the City, to lead me back to a set of offices in Portugal Street, behind the Strand, and virtually where I had started from. By the waters of Portugal Street I hung up my harp at last, but not to weep, for there I learned from the lady in charge of the agency that they did have a more-than-competent German linguist on their books, and that, yes, as well as being an accomplished commercial translator, she was also a skilled type-writer. When however I broached the matter of the young lady's name and address, I was checked with a frown and a sniff. All work – and payment – was arranged through the agency, and it was not to be assumed that their young ladies could be dropped in on without an introduction. I immediately disclaimed any such notion, accompanying my disclaimer with an explanation that the work was delicate and specialised, and would require a personal meeting between myself and the young lady. Would she then please pass on my card to her, and tell her that it concerned some legal material to do with Herr Müller, who was by way of being a mutual acquaintance, and that it might involve considerable business for the agency. This seemed to do the trick, and the lady took my card with a final dubious sniff then dismissed me with a nod and a good day.

Congratulating myself on a good morning's work, I hurried over to refresh myself at Driver's oyster bar at the top of

Chancery Lane, after which I made for the Old Bailey, only to find Lord Justice Calthrop still busy with the summing-up. I scanned the ranks of my fellow observers, as I squeezed into a row near the back of the crowded chamber, but my glance lit on no familiar face. Solomon Solomons was surveying the scene from the dock, and on his high-boned, ascetic face there was the same expression of calm indifference. Having experienced at second hand something of the weight of state coercion during my interview with PC Kennedy, I felt a new bond of understanding with the young revolutionary in the dock.

'Now much has been made by the defence,' the judge's dry, incisive voice broke into my musings, 'of the issue of circumstantial evidence, which might roughly be defined as circumstances or conditions surrounding an event, but which would pertain in any case, quite apart from the circumstances and conditions involved in the commission of a specific crime. For instance, I may happen to buy a meat-cleaver at an iron-monger's in Houndsditch, a district quite unknown to me, and where I am unknown, and, in trying its edge, I may cut my finger and stain the edge of the implement with my blood. I may then philosophically suck my finger, wrap the cleaver up again in its paper, then proceed on foot up Bishopsgate, pausing in a lonely alleyway to light my pipe. Now what if, minutes later, a man should be discovered dead – murdered in that same alley-way, his wounds being entirely consistent with blows sustained from a heavy, sharp-edged instrument, such as a cleaver? Had I, then, with my wrapped-up cleaver, been spotted and later apprehended – literally red-handed – and brought to trial for the murder, the evidence against me, as you will have seen, would thus have been entirely circumstantial.'

Lord Justice Calthrop paused and surveyed the faces of the jurymen, now screwed up with perplexity, and the ghost of a wintry smile seemed to illuminate the judge's gaunt features. He spread out his hands on the bench in front of him.

'You see the difficulty, gentlemen of the jury? Of terms and definitions – circumstantial or material – there is no end, but take heart, for you are not concerned here today with such difficulties – the law is mine, but the verdict is yours. No, you are not to worry about whether this or that individual piece of evidence is material to the case or merely circumstantial, but to decide whether, taken as a whole, the body of evidence presented on one side or the other is of sufficient relevancy, admissibility – I remind you again most solemnly to disregard all you may have heard or seen written about this case outside the precincts of this court – and weight to enable you to come down on one side or the other. It is with this advice that I now send you away to reach a verdict.'

So that was it! Solomons' fate was to be known today. The jury was dismissed, and I spanned the intermission by reviewing in my mind the aspects of the case I had unearthed to date. I tried all the likely and possible combinations, but all I had were – so I thought – a 'lady with a funny voice' who traded in under-aged girls from – it might have been – 11, Poland Street, and a nice lady who seemingly rescued same. There was also a Pocket Venus and a matronly lady whose attendance at Solomons' trial was in some way connected with a poor wreck in a nursing home in Hampstead. Was this Venus the lady typewriter who did foreign things with capital letters? And what about 'Warwick'? And the defunct lessee of 11, Poland Street, who burnt his walking-stick and packed an extra heavy overcoat which apparently didn't fit him into a weekend bag before suddenly going off to his death in a Belgian dock?

There was a hush and a rustle, and the jury was back. After only forty minutes! Elation gripped me momentarily – of course they were going to throw the thing out: what else could they do on the sort of non-evidence they had been presented with? Then I recalled the judge's deadly little parting parable of the meat-cleaver – of circumstance and coincidence – and I looked at the face of the foreman of the jury, and my heart sank.

'You have reached a verdict?'

'We have.'

A sort of electricity charged the stale air of the chamber, as dead silence fell. Not a cough, not a rustle, not a murmur arose from the stolid, heavily-dressed throng.

'And do you find the defendant guilty or not guilty?'

'Guilty.'

A sort of soughing 'oh' ran through the chamber, and I put my hands over my face. The newspapers had done their work well.

'And that is the verdict of you all?'

'It is.'

Then the solemn mummery of the black cap, the awful words of the sentence. '. . . and that you there be hanged by the neck until you are dead. . .'

There was a hysterical woman's scream, and a man behind me murmured 'Jesus', but I fear these manifestations were far outweighed by the triumphant growlings and gruntings around me, the hissed expletives directed at the dock, the knowing, self-righteous nods from bowler- and billycock-hatted Pharisees with folded arms. I recall now the remark of a distinguished Spaniard thirty years later, to the effect that there was only one savage beast present in the bullring – the crowd. I could well have applied that sentiment to the bulk of my fellow spectators in the Old Bailey that afternoon. And if a sensitive depiction of the accused's demeanour at that dread moment is now required of me, I fear I must disappoint the reader, for on that as well as on a number of similar occasions at the Old Bailey since then, I have never yet been able to look at the face in the dock.

I got up and left the place as quickly as I could, my head in a whirl of disgust, indignation and contempt. So after only seven days it was over. Some official figure must be smirking somewhere: a nice bit of work. Very satisfactory. Well, we should see about that. I was at length spewed out into the Strand with the rest of the crowd, and, when a newsboy thrust a paper under my nose, such was my anger I was hard put to it not to bring my stick down on his shoulders. I calmed down as, the winter breeze lashing my burning cheeks, I strode along, turning up Wellington Street and entering Henrietta Street at last. Calm – I must keep my head. Indignation was not enough. A popular superstition has arisen that there is some ordinance which requires that 'three clear Sundays' must elapse between the passing of the death-sentence and its execution, but this is and always has been pure myth. The time of execution is purely a matter of administrative convenience, and may be set within a few days after sentence. We must work fast.

I arrived home to find Violet in a rare moment of leisure, putting up, with the help of our maid, some splendid new curtains of a bold, oriental design, plunder no doubt of a post-prandial raid on Liberty's in Regent Street. We exchanged glances, and Violet, seeing the concern in my expression, dismounted the kitchen chair on which she had been standing and came up to me.

'Hang on a second, there, do, Lottie,' she said to the maid, while I blurted out my news in an urgent murmur.

'Already!' my wife hissed. 'But the trial has lasted scarcely seven days! Well, I must go immediately to Hackney to break the news to poor Iris before the infernal newspapers do. This will hit her hard, I fear. I shall take some sedatives with me.'

'Do your best to reassure her, Violet,' I said. 'Tell her our efforts to catch the real murderer are proceeding apace . . .'

'Please, mum,' Lottie wailed from her perch on the other kitchen chair, 'can't 'ang on for much longer . . .'

'Up you go, James,' Violet said, as she hurriedly put on her outdoor clothes. 'Help Lottie finish the curtains, and I shall see you at the dispensary later on.'

'Oh, very well,' I muttered to Violet's departing back, and clambered up beside the maid, who directed my faltering hands in the mysteries of curtain-hanging. Something occurred to me.

'Lottie,' I said, 'do you know anything about whist?'

The little pert face frowned, and surprise lit the dark eyes.

'Whist, sir? Lor', yes – I should say I do. In my last place in Primrose 'ill old Mr Bateson used to have his whist party every Saturday evening, reg'lar as clockwork. 'E'd as soon miss church on Sunday as 'is game o' whist.'

'It's a sort of team game, isn't it?' I asked, for I know about as much about card-games as the average Eskimo. 'Involving pairs of partners, or whatnot?'

''Sright, sir – two against two, no bids, no 'ands showing.'

'I'll, er . . . take your word for it. So you must have four to play?'

The trim little torso swung round again, and Lottie spoke as if she were humouring a child.

'Yes, sir, like I said: two and two. One less and it's no go.'

I sank into a brown study.

'Will that be all, sir?' Lottie was saying, this time from the floor. The curtains by now were well and truly hung.

'Mmm . . . oh, yes – first-rate! That will be all, thank you, Lottie.'

I remained teetering atop the kitchen chair like a bespectacled stork, musing the while. Miller had sat in as fourth man, then, in Dr Fedoroff's whist game in Farm Street on the night of Ostyankin's murder, while the physician had gone out on a call, then, as Tvardoffsky leaves the party at twelve thirty – presumably leaving three men behind him – he remarks ruefully to the servant at the door that he's won enough hearts for one night, meaning he's been worsted in a game of Hearts, not whist. But Hearts needs only three people, and . . .

'Are you finished with the chair, sir?' Lottie's voice jolted me out of my reverie. I was surprised she was still there.

'Chair? Oh, yes – quite finished.'

I jumped down, and the maid hauled away the chair I had been standing on. I went up to the window, and, lightly fingering the edge of the bright new curtain, looked out on to the jangling thoroughfare, but my gaze was still turned inward. The arithmetic of the Farm Street card party, as presented by Miller, Cazes and Fedoroff in the witness box, was wrong. Not four, then three, but four, three, then two. If Tvardoffsky, the departing guest, had just left a three-man game, then there were only two left behind him. Had they perhaps changed from whist to Hearts because they had lost the necessary fourth player when another of the company had left – unknown to the manservant – between around midnight, when their host had been called out to a patient, and when he had returned at half-past two on the Friday morning? Now if Alexander Miller had been that first – unofficial – departing guest – and there was no reason why he should not have done whatever he had gone out to do and come back again before Dr Fedoroff had landed back from his patient-call in the early hours of Friday morning – then the urbane timber importer no longer had an alibi. I felt I must seek the further acquaintance of Mr Miller.

13

During the cab-drive home after evening surgery, Violet told me that Iris Starr had taken her sweetheart's death-sentence very hard indeed, and that she had found it necessary to administer a strong sedative. Hilary Venables, who ran the Hackney women's refuge, had promised to keep an especially watchful eye on her during the coming days. It was clear that we should have to strain every nerve and sinew in order to prove Solomon Solomons' innocence.

'I'm surprised the police and the defence didn't make anything of the, er . . . arithmetical discrepancy in Dr Fedoroff's and Miller's testimony, with regard to the card-game on the night of Ostyankin's death,' I mused aloud. 'Whist to begin with would mean four players, then, minus the departing player, Tvardoffsky, three, which would leave enough for a game of Hearts . . .'

'But if Miller had been the first to leave,' Violet capped me, 'not Tvardoffsky, he would have had two full hours to do what he wanted to do, but of course as far as the legal authorities are concerned, that would be purely academic without corroboratory witnesses. I scarcely think Fedoroff could be persuaded to change his testimony now; even less so that the missing players might be lured back from Russia to stand in the witness box. That would have been the first consideration of the police and the lawyers.'

'Yes, and I wonder just how much David Zeinvel knows? There can hardly be a more hardbitten police-court lawyer than he – starry-eyed partiality would be quite alien to his nature – yet he seems to accept Solomons' innocence as a matter of course.'

'Oh, he's a downy bird all right, and I've no doubt we'll be hearing more from him before very much longer. And while we're on the topic of time, we have so little of it, James! The authorities might hang Solomons tomorrow, if it was convenient to them . . .'

'I know, and I was thinking . . .'

'Yes, James?'

'Our resolution to carry on our investigations under the cloak of secrecy – or as far in secret as possible – has I fancy been overtaken by events. There is simply not enough time. I think we must henceforth fight in the open.'

'You mean, approach involved persons directly?'

'Yes, and I suspect that after our typewriter has surfaced – which should be very soon indeed, if my surmise as to who she may be is correct . . .'

'The Venus of Hampstead?'

'Yes, and if it is she, we may see a whole new aspect to the case unfold.'

Violet turned her face away from mine, and gazed out at the shiny-black, greasy February streets.

'And then there is Mr Alexander Miller,' I went on. 'Such a smooth, discreet gentleman, and so vague as to what company he plays cards with . . .'

'Yes, it is essential that we know just what the situation in Farm Street is. It is politics, of course, James . . .'

'Yes, and we must tread very, very carefully. Secrecy as to identity will still be very much in order there . . . My approach will be all-important: I think I shall go as a philanthropist with no particular axe to grind. I have it! – I shall be a campaigner for the abolition of capital punishment!'

God knew I had no enthusiasm for the institution, necessary as it might be.

'Excellent!' Violet said. 'Be sure, though, to betray no interest in Solomons as an individual. You may learn as much from what the Russians don't say as from what they are prepared to tell you!'

Thus armed with some sort of strategy for the following days, we alighted in Henrietta Street for an early supper and a good night's rest, and, as I sat at breakfast the next morning – Violet already having left for the dispensary – Lottie came into the little breakfast parlour and announced a caller.

'A Miss Judith Vulliamy to see yer, sir.'

'You have shown her into the sitting-room?' I asked eagerly, as I sprang up from my chair. My visit to the typewriting agency had evidently borne fruit.

'Yes, sir, she's in there now,' the maid replied, and I dismissed her and stepped out into the corridor and into the sitting-room. My pulses raced as I was confronted by none other than the compact form and bitter little red mouth of the Pocket Venus who had caught my attention among the spectators when Miller had been giving his evidence at the trial, and whom I had spied with her hand on the arm of the unfortunate wretch in the Magnolias that Sunday.

'Dr Mortimer?' she quizzed me in a rather deep, level voice, with a hint of disapproval, and I nodded and motioned her to a chair. She regarded me with slightly raised eyebrows, and I drew up another chair, and, sitting down, confronted my visitor, from whom emanated an indefinable *hauteur*. In her pale blue eyes sat a fixed sadness, and she was dressed all in black.

'I was given your card at the agency when I called in this morning, Dr Mortimer, and I must own that I am at a loss to . . .'

'Pray forgive the eccentricity of my approach, ma'am,' I said, with a self-deprecatory wave of the hand, 'but when you hear of my purpose in attracting your attention, I dare hope that you will help me. Let me explain . . .'

'Please do . . .' the young lady said as she sat ramrod-straight in the high-backed chair.

'I am engaged on behalf of Solomon Solomons, ma'am, whose recent plight can surely not have escaped you.'

'A foreign criminal, I believe, recently condemned for the murder of a Russian general. It is on all the placards. I cannot however share the finer details with you, for I have neither the leisure nor the inclination to read the popular press. Please go on.'

'I hold Solomons to be innocent, ma'am, the pawn of more powerful agencies, and I am engaged in investigations which I hope will succeed in wresting him from the shadow of the gallows.'

'I see, doctor, but what is all this to me? And how do you come to know me?'

'I know nothing of you, Miss Vulliamy, save that you sat in front of me – veiled – in the public gallery at the Old Bailey while Alexander Miller gave his testimony last week, and that you drew up your veil as soon as he had left the court . . .'

'I see. I take it he is the "Herr Müller" the note on your card refers to?'

'The same, ma'am.'

'Very ingenious, but I fail to see what that proves, doctor.'

'Indeed, ma'am, it proves nothing, but it strongly suggests a desire on your part not to be recognised by Miller.'

'Is that all, Dr Mortimer?' the lady said shortly as she rose from her chair. 'If so, I have many calls on my time, and if you will excuse me . . .'

'That is all I know about you, Miss Vulliamy, except that you are on intimate terms with an unfortunate sufferer from a serious nervous ailment, and that, in company with a lady of mature years, you visited him at the Magnolias in Hampstead last Sunday; that you are – forgive me – in straitened financial circumstances; that you are proficient in the German language, and that you undertake typewriting work for Alexander Miller's timber business.'

Miss Vulliamy stood stock still, then sat down again. Uncertainty had crept into the hard, china-blue eyes.

'As to the Magnolias, you could have found out about my visits there by common spying, but straitened financial circumstances, proficient in German . . .'

'It is inconceivable to me that a young lady so scrupulously turned out as yourself should start the day with any but a fresh handkerchief, yet the one you showed at the Magnolias on Sunday was stained with the characteristic purple of typewriting ink. One who must toil at her typewriting machine on a Sunday morning can scarcely be wallowing in affluence . . .'

'And German?'

'I scanned the typewritten list in the case outside Miller's office with a powerful magnifying glass, and the upright strokes of the typewritten capital letters were virtually as thick as those of the small letters, which is not the case with the average English typewritten text – except in a brand new or little-used typewriter, which can scarcely apply to yours. In an English text, the strokes of the small letters tend to be just noticeably thicker than those of the capitals, because used so much more often. Now I know of only one language where capital letters – being used to start *all* nouns – are used frequently enough to cancel out this effect – German. There are many young lady typewriters whose names appear on the books of London agencies, but few who offer technical German, and so my search was considerably narrowed. Come, now, Miss Vulliamy, it is a true bill!'

She sat and studied me for quite half a minute, and I pressed home my advantage.

'I fear in the circumstances that you and Miller are inextricably conjoined in my mind, and I am resolved to know as much as I can about him, with – as I most earnestly wish – your co-operation, or, if not – without it. I must proceed in this matter without regard to the consequences, either to you or to anyone else.'

'This is uncommonly like blackmail, doctor.'

I made no reply.

'Very well, then,' she said at last. 'You force my hand. I shall tell you my story, with one strict proviso: that you will give me an absolute undertaking that anything I may tell you will not be passed on to Miller.'

'I give it without condition, Miss Vulliamy, as God is my witness.'

'I am interested in Miller because he has destroyed the life of my fiancé, Hector Jephson.'

'The young man in the Magnolias?'

Miss Vulliamy nodded.

'And the lady I saw you with there is his mother?'

'Yes: Mrs Lettice Jephson.'

'Of the Soho Working Girls' Club?'

Surprise stole into the blue eyes.

'You are thorough, Dr Mortimer – I will give you that. Mrs Jephson, with her husband, the Reverend Cormell Jephson, manages that establishment on behalf of its trustees. They are people of the most impeccable antecedents and the highest principles. Now, thanks to Miller, Mrs Jephson's heart is broken – a clock without a spring – and Cor – Mr Jephson – is beside himself with grief. Only by working all the hours God sends does he save himself from the abyss. Miller . . .'

For a second the small gloved hands clenched convulsively, and the blue eyes seemed to swim, but Miss Vulliamy quickly regained her composure as she abruptly changed the subject

'My late father was Pastor of the British Seamen's Mission in Hamburg, a post at variance with his background as the son of

113

a field marshal and a lady of title, though irreconcilable differences as to religion led to a clean break between him and his parents just before he went down from the University. There has been no contact with his kin since, and I am not inclined to try to renew it. My mother was German, of a family of minor gentry in East Prussia. She died when I was twelve, and owing to our straitened means, I received my education in Germany, so that, as I heard nothing but English at home, and German at school and among my playfellows, I have grown up to be perfectly at home in both languages. As you have correctly observed, Dr Mortimer, this gift has enabled me to earn a living of sorts since my father's death threw me alone upon the world.'

'And, er . . . Hector Jephson, Miss Vulliamy?'

'I met Hector in the July of '86, while spending the summer on my grandfather's small estate outside Prussian Eylau, now, alas, in the hands of my grandfather's creditors. My grandfather was a much-travelled man, having served in the Schwedt Dragoons, and also knocked about South America in his youth, and his acquaintances were many and varied. He had got to know Hector, who was then part of a British diplomatic mission in Berlin, as a consequence of an argument they had had about politics in a train they had shared. Hector told me later that, on reaching Berlin, Grandfather had turned to him on the platform, thrust his card in Hector's hand and said: "Now, young man, you shall not get off the hook so easily: we shall continue this discussion at my country place next weekend until I've driven some sense into that obstinate skull of yours." That was Grandfather all over: one glance, and he knew his man. Ah, those bright, endless summers – it seems a thousand years ago . . .'

Miss Vulliamy was actually smiling in her narrative, in the way solitary people tend to blossom when once they have the opportunity to talk about themselves, but her brow soon clouded over again, and the lips tightened, as she returned to the topic of her *bête noire*.

'Miller was of the party,' she snapped. 'With a couple of his countrymen. Grandfather had been in Danzig selling yet more of his timber, and he had got in with Miller in the course of his business. They shared a passion for cards and gaming – poor Grandfather – and the Russian also fed his appetite for travellers' tales. That weekend stretched into Hector's annual leave, and soon we were spending virtually all the daylight hours together, chaperoned only by Grandfather's sleepy old coachman. We drove out to the Masurian Lakes, the coast – everywhere – and we resolved to announce our engagement as soon as Hector had finished his mission in Germany, and I was to accompany him – chaperoned by an aunt – to England to meet his people, who then had a house in Ebury Street, as well as their perch in the Soho Working Girls' Club . . .'

'And, er . . . the evenings at Eylau, Miss Vulliamy?'

Her face seemed to snap shut again, like the mouth of a closed purse.

'Cards, and Miller . . . As soon as he learnt that Hector was with the British Foreign Office, Miller drew a bead on him, sounding him out on his politics, his postings and so forth. All very transparent, of course – the man is a spy – but he has a way with him, as if . . . as if he held the key to a whole new way of seeing and enjoying the world, if only one would be guided by him . . .'

'All this will I give unto thee . . .'

'Yes! Like Satan in the Bible – that is what Miller is, doctor, a tempter!'

'And did Hector Jephson succumb at last?'

'At first he regarded Miller as a sort of entertaining joke – "amusing little beggar", as he put it – and persuaded himself that he had the man's measure, while later trotting after him in Berlin, where they frequented the most decadent officers' clubs and nightspots, then, after our engagement, in London, where Hector was attached to the Foreign Office again, and I was staying at the Jephsons' place in Ebury Street in anticipation of our wedding. Our wedding . . .'

Miss Vulliamy paused, biting her lower lip, for a little while, then went on.

'I began to see less and less of Hector as time went on. He would plead pressure of work – the international situation – but then he would talk of Miller, Miller, Miller . . . The Russian would occasionally come to pick him up of an evening in Ebury Street, and I grew to loathe the sickly smile, the wheedling, insinuating manner, the carefully cultivated Slavonic charm. Mrs Jephson detested him at sight, but Cor – Mr Jephson – kept his own counsel, and was quite prepared to put up with him as

Hector's friend. I hope you will forgive me, Dr Mortimer, but I cannot help observing what fools men are!'

'I can only put down your fiancé's gullibility to vanity, Miss Vulliamy: no man cares to think that he has been worsted by someone he deems a figure of fun. I take it a crisis came in your unfortunate fiancé's relations with Miller?'

'Just over two years ago. I confronted Hector about our growing estrangement, the fast life he had been leading, I begged him to draw in the reins, if not for my sake, then for the sake of his career, and it was then that he dropped the bombshell: he suddenly broke down completely and announced that he no longer had a career, that in consequence of a serious indiscretion, he had been obliged to resign from the Foreign Office . . .'

'Miller . . .' I murmured under my breath.

'Yes, doctor – Miller. It was the first thought that came to my mind, but when I taxed Hector with it, he said that the affair was closed, and has never broached the matter since. Since that moment Miller has not communicated with Hector by either word or gesture.'

'I daresay he'd got whatever information he'd wanted out of young Jephson, then had no further use for him. And now, Miss Vulliamy, as to the matter of your unfortunate fiancé's illness . . .'

My visitor's straight back stiffened even more.

'It is a painful matter, Dr Mortimer, and I should rather not . . .'

'Please do not distress yourself, Miss Vulliamy – a nod will be enough.'

'Very well, then, if you think it necessary.'

'I recognised the symptoms as *tabes dorsalis* as soon as I laid eyes on him at the Magnolias,' I went on. 'Am I to assume that it is a consequence of these excursions of Mr Jephson's with Miller into the Berlin demi-monde five years ago that you have just been describing to me?'

Miss Vulliamy nodded, and I reflected that this was one of those cases of the disease which develop very rapidly. I did not press the matter further.

'And how pray did you secure the typewriting and translation work from Miller, Miss Vulliamy? How did you know he gave his typewriting work to Mrs Bennett's establishment in the first place? There are after all a number of such agencies in London.'

'Hers is the first in town for technical translation, and as soon as she heard that I offered German, I was put on the books immediately. Apart from the fact that I needed the income, I knew that much of Miller's timber business was with Germany. It was a while before I was actually given work to do for Miller, but it seems he had found fault with most of the other translators – he is very exacting – so I was eventually tried out, and I have been handling his material for over a year now. He does not know of my identity, of course, since all my work goes out in the name of the agency.'

'Forgive my plain speaking, but why are you dogging Miller? To what end do you seek to learn of his affairs?'

Miss Vulliamy leant forward in her chair, and she spoke with new animation.

'I believe that Miller will eventually make a slip, doctor, and I have made it my mission to find out everything I possibly can about his business and other activities. He is a villain and a spy, and quite apart from what he has done to me and those I hold dear, I cannot doubt that he has been working tirelessly to harm this country and its interests. There is only one way to deal with a rat in a granary . . .'

'Quite, but I recommend that you leave the actual, er . . . control of the pest to the official ratcatchers. And the business in Poland Street, Miss Vulliamy? It is that which I am principally interested in at the moment.'

'As to this Russian general and his fate, I cannot help you, Dr Mortimer. From the little I know of him from the placards, he seems to have been a thoroughgoing brute and bully. To that extent, I am fully on the side of your protégé, innocent or guilty, and will do all I can to help you get him off.'

'I am grateful for that, Miss Vulliamy, but can you then add nothing to my knowledge of the house in Poland Street?'

'Nothing, doctor,' the little Meissen figure of a woman said, then, with the shadow of a smile: 'And I was at home and asleep on the night when your general met his fate.'

I did not doubt it, but why had she found it necessary, unasked, to mention it? And how, if, as she claimed, she had been dealing with Miller's business correspondence, did she

117

know nothing of Ostyankin, who, with his extensive timber interests, must loom fairly large in that department? I should have to bear in mind in any future dealings with her that I had forced Miss Vulliamy's confidences, and see her at best as a very grudging helper, at worst as a potential adversary.

'I really think you should consult the Jephsons on these matters, doctor.' Miss Vulliamy's voice broke in on my thoughts.

'I am much of your opinion, Miss Vulliamy,' I replied. 'Perhaps we may all meet together, and I might introduce you to my wife?'

In rising, Miss Vulliamy gave me a little bow.

'And now,' she said, 'if you will excuse me, I have pressing work.'

'Of course,' I said, hastening to show her out. 'I am most grateful for what you have told me today, though I must tell you fairly and squarely that if we are to work together I cannot do so in the cause of vengeance, but of cold justice.'

A wintry little smile played about the small red mouth, as she paused on the front doorstep.

'Oh, I do not think the two necessarily exclude one another, Dr Mortimer, and in any case, is not revenge a dish which is best eaten cold?'

14

Amid a whirl of considerations as to what I had to do on that busy morning of Thursday the 26th – I found myself counting the days as if condemned myself – in the cause of saving Solomon Solomons, I spent a minute or so weighing up my impressions of Miss Vulliamy. In spite of her obviously deep feeling and concern for her doomed fiancé, which, I felt sure, could scarcely have been feigned, my first impression was one of a certain hardness, the main token of which had been her cut-and-dried judgments of the persons we had discussed: Ostyankin a brute, Miller a spy and villain, men on the whole fools. I did not care to wonder whether she might include me in that category. Clearly a proud, efficient young woman, one who scorned the help of obviously affluent prospective parents-in-law in favour of earning her own living. And in spite of her English father, so German in her thoroughness and Prussian frontierswoman's fear and disdain for the Slavs! Did I consider her capable of calculated, bloody murder? I thought of her parting remark, about revenge being a dish that was eaten cold . . . Whatever her true nature, I fancied Judith Vulliamy would have made a most efficient job of disposing of any 'brute' she thought inimical to the interests of anyone she loved. At all events, a formidable woman to have dealings with, and one who needed watching. We should see about Miss Vulliamy. Time, however, was pressing, and, seizing a carpet bag, which I had carefully packed on the previous evening, and abandoning my trusty stick for an unadventurous umbrella, I set off for Crutched Friars and David Zeinvel.

'There has been a development, doctor,' he said, as, half an hour later, I faced the familiar keen, bird-like features across the desk in his dusty eyrie of an office.

'Ah, thank God for that, Zeinvel!' I exclaimed, leaning back in my chair. 'New evidence? A fresh witness?'

'The latter, doctor; or at least a potential new witness, in this particular instance providing a lead on Klaff, my client's companion on the night of the murder . . .'

'You don't mean you've found him?'

'Unfortunately not, but someone in the Warsaw Café crowd has at last come forward – feeling is now running very strongly in Whitechapel about the affair – with information that Klaff had mentioned to him on more than one occasion that he had been offered a good job in a clothing business by *landsleit* in Arizona, and we have wired the Pinkerton Bureau to look this up.'

'Might you not lodge an appeal on the strength of this, then, Zeinvel? It might gain time if nothing else.'

'I'm afraid not. Although our informant also insists that he saw Klaff and Solomons in the Warsaw together on the night of the murder long after Ostyankin was supposed to have died, we should need Klaff for corroboration.'

I remembered what I had learned on my visit there, and PC Kennedy's subsequent shamefaced denial.

'Has your new informant agreed to testify?'

'Yes, and that would be the basis of our appeal: his and Klaff's corroborative testimony, along with outrageous press prejudice.'

'And if you cannot trace Klaff in America?'

Zeinvel grinned his cockney grin and wagged an admonitory forefinger at me.

'Now what have I said to you before, Dr Mortimer: *nil desperandum!*'

'So we must sweat it out, with the noose ready to be slipped round Solomons' neck at any minute!'

Zeinvel spread out his hands and shrugged his shoulders.

'I am still pursuing other lines of enquiry, doctor, as I'm sure you are.'

There was a clear hint here, and, Violet having given her agreement over supper the previous evening, I revealed to Zeinvel all we had learned to date.

'I've also quizzed PC Kennedy, doctor,' Zeinvel said with a shrug, 'but it's the old story – more than his job's worth to testify on Solomons' behalf.'

'But surely *someone* at the Warsaw besides this new potential witness you've just mentioned should be willing to come forward . . .'

The dapper little man spread out his hands again.

'Depends on what the police have got on them. For a lot of them, it's a case of testify and be deported back to Russia, and then there are others who are acting as police informers already, with money as the carrot and deportation as the stick. And everyone there – whatever his relations with the police – tends to steer clear of the politicals. However, as I've said, feeling's building up, and who knows but that there might not be a break in the logjam soon.'

'Very well, then, Zeinvel, I shall pile on all steam to turn up some new evidence, but this suspense is the very devil!'

'Never say die, Dr Mortimer!' the solicitor said cheerfully, rising to see me to the door, upon which I bade him with a gesture to remain seated. 'And thank you for sharing your findings with me: I shall think them over very carefully.'

I hesitated in the doorway for a moment, until I was quite clear in my mind as to the sequence of tasks I had in front of me. My first stop was the public convenience adjoining Mark Lane station. I emerged arrayed in a soft black hat and clerical collar, and wearing a pair of rather unflattering thick-lensed spectacles, these articles by way of being the first rabbits drawn from the carpet bag which I clutched as I plunged into the forecourt of the station, en route for Brown's Hotel, a hostelry much frequented by men of the cloth. Here I was able to strengthen my new identity at the rather stiff rate of eight shillings a day, by taking a quiet back room and furnishing the wardrobe, albeit sparsely, with such apparel as a clergyman of modest means, up from the country, might be expected to carry. Alongside the Bible which I found in the little bookstand on top of the bedside table, I placed a copy of the capital-punishment abolitionist's *vade mecum*, Christopherson's monumental *In the Shadow of the Rope*, along with the Hon. Frideswide Sykes-Talbot's *Vengeance is Mine* for good measure. Having thus ranged my little mountebank's stock, I surveyed myself with as much accuracy as the ill-suited spectacles would allow in the dressing-table looking-glass, then, clutching the brolly, made my way demurely into the lobby, handed the key to the desk clerk with a benevolent smile, and made for Mayfair.

No. 8, Farm Street was a fine house, with a high-stepped door and a deep area. A mousy-looking little woman with dull, sherry-coloured eyes and brownish hair scraped back into a bun answered my ring. She might have been any age between thirty and fifty. The keys at the belt of her grey dress, along with a certain self-assurance of mien, betokened the housekeeper rather than the run-of-the-mill servant.

'Yes, sir?'

'My name is Flockhart,' I said, 'and I wish to speak to your employer on a matter of the gravest urgency . . .'

'I'm afraid Mr Miller isn't . . .'

'Perhaps I should add that it is to do with the unfortunate affair of the late General Ostyankin . . .'

The woman did not finish her sentence, and I fancied that a spark of animation came into the dull brown eyes.

'If you'd care to step this way, sir.'

The woman in the grey dress took my ulster, along with my hat, gloves and umbrella, and led me past a loudly ticking long-case clock down a long, thick-carpeted corridor. There was a smell of wax-polish and cigar-smoke. After I had covered what seemed like many yards, I was ushered into what was evidently a library, judging by the densely packed shelves on all four walls and the fragrant leather chairs. Chaste winter sunshine streamed through the two high, elegant Georgian window-frames. The woman stood for a moment in a relaxed manner, and eyed me with perhaps a little more nonchalance than I would have preferred from a perfect stranger: evidently no ordinary servant.

'If you care to sit down, sir, I shall go and see if Mr Miller is at home.'

Left alone, I began to inspect the bookshelves, for one may know a man by the books he reads. A couple of walls devoted to Russian texts, which signified nothing to me, then a wall of French, mostly diplomatic history, including Talleyrand's memoirs, Tocqueville and the usual standard works, a block of German classics, and, filling the last wall, a veritable miniature reference library of Shakespeare, with all the Bard's works in several different editions, along with books of criticism in English and German. I compared this European erudition with my typical Englishman's schoolboy French and smattering of German, and smiled wryly to myself.

'Ah!' A familiar high-pitched voice rang out behind me. 'Mr Flockhart, is it not? I trust Mrs Custance has made you comfortable.'

I swung round to confront the blunt, doughy features and scrubby little ginger beard of the man I had last seen in the witness box of the Old Bailey. Alexander Miller was grinning an obsequious grin, but the little dark eyes were fairly boring into me. I felt his pudgy, moist fist close round mine momentarily.

'I, er, thank you – yes, sir, she has. I see from your books that you are a scholar as well as a businessman, and you clearly share our admiration for our national bard.'

'Ah, but I go further, Mr Flockhart,' the squeaky, lightly accented voice went on. 'I actually read him! But please sit down, sir. You will take some refreshment? I shall ring for . . .'

'No, I thank you, sir. I am glad I have arrived at a time when you are not at your office.'

'Not today, Mr Flockhart,' Miller said, consulting a watch, which he had drawn from his waistcoat, 'but I have a series of engagements here, commencing, I fear, in ten minutes' time. Now if I can help you? Mrs Custance tells me you mentioned my unfortunate acquaintance, the late General Ostyankin?'

'Ah, forgive me, sir, I shall be brief. I am an unattached clergyman, resident at Winchcombe in Gloucestershire . . .'

'Ah! Then you will know Sudeley? Such a charming place, and such fine work Lady Hanbury has done in restoring it.'

The little eyes glinted, but I was not to be caught so easily.

'Surely you mean Mrs Dent, Mr Miller – she is chatelaine there now.'

'Yes, yes – just so, sir – it is a long time since I was last there. Please to go on.'

'Well, sir, I have long been a campaigner against the barbarous institution of capital punishment – man is made in the image of God, Mr Miller, and it is sacrilege to seek to destroy that image – and this present glaring example of the condemnation of an innocent man . . .'

'To which man do you refer, Mr Flockhart?'

'To the wretched Solomons, sir! Bad enough that anyone should suffer death in England's name, but a clearly innocent man . . .'

'Yes, yes – I am sure you are not without support, Mr Flockhart – a noble cause but this Solomons is an anarchist, and one who has previously tried to murder the unfortunate general. I must say that the epithet "innocent" sits awkwardly on such shoulders. But that sort of activity seems to be second nature to so many of Solomons' persuasion in my country . . .'

It was on the tip of my tongue to name some of the abominable atrocities committed by wearers of the Tsar's uniform that had caused so many of Monia Solomons' 'persuasion' to embrace the cause of revolution, but I had other fish to fry, so I let the remark pass.

'Do you have a special interest in this man, Mr Flockhart? Perhaps you are appearing on behalf of some principal? His family, perhaps?'

'No, sir, I am pursuing a number of such cases at present – I and my colleagues in the Church – both here and in the provinces. Our numbers grow by the day, Mr Miller, and . . .'

Some of the suspicion seemed to go from Miller's eyes, and, glancing again at his watch, he cut me short.

'What can I do for you, Mr Flockhart?'

'I watched you in the witness box during the trial, Mr Miller, and I wondered if, at this crucial time, when Solomons' life – he is a fellow human being, after all – hangs in the balance, you might even at this eleventh hour recall some fact or detail which may throw fresh light on General Ostyankin's death. It is my hope that somehow, even if conscience cannot stir the hearts of our rulers, enough fresh evidence may yet be uncovered by myself and others like-minded to stay the hand of the hangman.'

'Such as what, Mr Flockhart? I told all I knew of the affair in court – all.'

'Well, sir, for example, anything or anyone you may have noted when you left your game of Hearts in the early hours of the morning after the general's death.'

Miller's jaw fell perceptibly, and his stare became colder.

'Allow me to correct you on that point, Mr Flockhart. It was a game of whist I left that night, not Hearts. I believe I made that clear in court.'

'Ah, I fear you must be right, sir – forgive me.'

The smile returned as Miller gave me a little sideways bow of acknowledgement.

'Mr Miller,' I said, changing tack, 'does the name De Kok mean anything to you?'

My host shook his head, then seemed to ponder a little.

'Ah,' he said brightly, 'was it not mentioned in court? The tenant of the house in Soho, was that not he? They could not find him, as I recall.'

'You did not know this man, or of him?'

'No, sir, I did not.'

I might add that in putting the question to Miller, I had used the correct pronunciation of the name – 'Koe' – which had *not* of course been used in court. A trifle, no doubt, but trifles can sometimes open doors.

'And is the name Desmond Coe familiar to you?'

Again, the little dark eyes betrayed no spark of alertness.

'No, Mr Flockhart: should it be?'

'It is of no consequence, Mr Miller; and now, a final question, if I may . . .'

The little crick-necked bow was again brought into play.

'Please, Mr Flockhart . . .'

'Does the name – or place – "Warwick" – have any special significance for you?'

This time it was a hopeless little shrug, then a wry smile, as Miller rather pointedly consulted his watch again. I took the hint, and rose to my feet.

'I see that you cannot help me further, sir,' I said resignedly, 'but I am nevertheless infinitely grateful for the time and attention you have given me. Should you wish to communicate with me further, Brown's Hotel will find me. In the meantime, may I leave this with you?'

As Miller went over and tugged at the bell-sash, I took out of my pocket a spare copy of *Vengeance is Mine* and laid it on top of the handsome reading table which stood under one of the high Georgian windows. Miller stepped over and looked at the book, then smiled and nodded at me.

'Ah! Such reforming zeal, Mr Flockhart! Perhaps I am too Orthodox to enter into such a moral view of religion. In any case, your Thirty-Nine Articles would always be a stumbling block to my understanding: I would have particular difficulty with Number Twenty-Eight . . .'

The eyes were hard and probing again, and I knew that my chubby inquisitor would require an answer, for what genuine Church of England clergyman would be ignorant of the Thirty-Nine Articles? Beads of sweat pricked from my brow for an

125

instant, then the recollection of an apposite chestnut of my old housemaster's – himself a clergyman – at Clifton came to my rescue.

'Ours is the broadest of churches, Mr Miller, and I think you need have no further difficulties if you stick to Article Six on all occasions: "Holy Scripture containeth all things necessary to salvation."'

'Ha!' Miller laughed, as he took my things from his stolid housekeeper, who had appeared quietly at the library door, and was eyeing me in her disconcerting way. 'Who can resist so wily a theologian! I see I shall be in danger of imminent conversion, the more I see of you!'

My host helped me on with my things in the friendliest possible way, and accompanied me to the front door himself. Something occurred to me.

'You were acquainted with General Ostyankin, Mr Miller,' I said, turning to face him on the threshold. 'What did you make of him?'

Miller shrugged and spread his hands in an eloquent gesture.

'Sometimes a soldier must do hard things, Mr Flockhart. One could almost say that he is in fact seldom responsible for his actions, for he almost always *reacts* to situations. Like an animal – spurred on by fear. But he is always human – he must have his memories – but then there is the bottle . . . How can we judge?'

'How indeed . . . The newspapers have much to answer for. Perhaps after all General Ostyankin's bark was worse than his bite . . .'

Upon my making this seemingly-innocent remark, I was disconcerted to find myself held in the most penetrating stare I had yet received from my host, a stare which changed quickly to confusion, then to dancing merriment. To judge by this response, I had evidently passed some sort of test, a conclusion reinforced when, after he had given me his curious little sideways bow, half-deferential and half-mocking, and closed the door on me, I was even more disconcerted to hear through the immaculately lacquered panels peal after peal of high-pitched laughter.

15

I consulted my watch on Miller's doorstep – twelve thirty already – and redoubled my steps towards the intersection with Davies Street, my thick 'stage' spectacles causing me to misjudge the depth of the kerb there as I started to cross to the other side, with the result that I stumbled and nearly fell over into the path of the traffic. As soon therefore as I was safely on the other side, I reached into the inside pocket of my frock coat for my own pince-nez, so that at least I should not break my neck or be run over before I could keep my luncheon appointment with Violet. To my irritation I could not find the glasses in any of my coat-pockets. I cursed my absent-mindedness, then roundly damned it as, rummaging in the outer pockets of my ulster – which had been in the hands of Miller's beady-eyed housekeeper for more than a quarter of a hour – my gloved hand closed round the pince-nez. I tore off the useless glasses, and, as I clipped my own over my nose, my worst suspicions were confirmed, for a smudge on one of the lenses obscured the clarity of my vision. I paused on the pavement and took off my pince-nez and examined the lens. A small, smudged fingerprint, distinctly narrow at the tip. I had polished the glasses before leaving home that morning, and my fingerprints are rather long and spatulate, besides being about twice the size of the one on the lens.

There could be only one conclusion: Miller's housekeeper had gone through the pockets of my ulster. Would she have noticed the discrepancy between the respective thicknesses of the lenses of the thick glasses I had been wearing in Farm Street and those in the overcoat pocket? There was no help for it now, so, cursing myself anew and thinking on 'the tangled web we weave, when first we practise to deceive', I emerged into the roar of Oxford Street and made quickly for my luncheon-tryst with Violet, where we had arranged – she suitably veiled – to meet in a private room in Mrs Stewart's confectionery shop, where meals could be taken by arrangement.

'I had a visit from Mr Zeinvel just before I left the dispensary,'

Violet announced eagerly as, cosily ensconced in Mrs Stewart's dining-room, we attacked our brown Windsor soup.

'Ah!' I replied, all ears. 'Something has broken on the Solomons front?'

'Yes, Zeinvel has traced Tvardoffsky, the missing card-player who said at the trial that he was first to leave Dr Fedoroff's in Farm Street on the night Ostyankin was murdered.'

'Tvardoffsky is here in London?'

Violet shook her head.

'No, it seems he is now a political exile in Paris, after he got wind in St Petersburg of an imminent move to arrest him as a Turkish agent. It appears that *l'affaire Tvardoffsky* is quite a *cause célèbre* in France at the moment, and Mr Zeinvel's contact in the French capital – a lawyer with extensive British interests who has a reciprocal arrangement with our friend in Crutched Friars – has managed to get Tvardoffsky to sign a legal affidavit to the effect that Miller left the card-game shortly after twelve fifteen on the night of Ostyankin's murder.'

'What!' I exclaimed, letting my spoon drop into my soup. 'But that casts an entirely new light on the case. Surely the authorities here . . .'

We assumed vacant smiles as a maid took away our soup plates, then, once we were alone again, Violet dampened my enthusiasm.

'Corroboration,' she said. 'They still cannot find anyone else who was at the card party to back up Tvardoffsky's allegation, and now that he is under a cloud – under suspicion of spying against his own country – his sole testimony would be scarcely enough to have the verdict against Solomons set aside.'

'Still, this new slant on the case will surely at least give the authorities pause for thought – oh, if only we could find someone else to cast some light on the comings and goings in Farm Street on that night!'

Just then the maid came in again and served our fried plaice.

'Leave that side to Mr Zeinvel,' Violet went on. 'Now what is your news?'

I told her all about my encounter with Miss Vulliamy that morning, then recounted the details of my visit to the unctuous timber-agent in Farm Street.

'Miller knows more than he says,' Violet said. 'Too smug by half. And don't you find it odd that a professed Shakespearean should never have heard of the name Warwick? Warwick the Kingmaker – *Henry VI* and all that? This Vulliamy woman sounds quite formidable, too – quite the Brünnhilde, in fact!'

'No comment, my dear!' I joked, reaching over and squeezing my wife's hand.

'Seriously, James, from the way you have described her, I should say she was capable of anything, and her motive for getting her own back on Miller is of the strongest. So, for that matter, is that of the Jephsons. If someone had led a son of mine to his ruin . . .'

'All the more reason for a, shall we say, guarded alliance with that camp,' I said.

'Yes James, we are in completely uncharted waters. We must arrange a meeting with Miss Vulliamy and the Jephsons before very long. And you clearly caught Miller on the raw when you mentioned the game of Hearts in Dr Fedoroff's house on the night of the murder – it bears out Tvardoffsky's testimony that he left Fedoroff's house in ample time to visit Poland Street around the time of Ostyankin's death. As for the housekeeper's possibly having handled your glasses in your overcoat pocket, in all likelihood she will have taken them for reading-glasses. What do you plan to do next?'

'I propose to set off in search of Sidney Arthur Wellcome.'

Violet paused thoughtfully for a moment, fishknife in hand, then her expression brightened.

'Ah! I remember now. The defence witness at the trial who'd been sleeping on the roof of the baker's outhouse on the night of Ostyankin's death, and who identified Solomons as having arrived in back Poland Street after two in the morning. Do you think he may know more than he said in court?'

'It is just that, with the cut-and-dried attitude the police seem to have taken, he may have volunteered more information when they questioned him than they might have thought suited their purpose – the expeditious conviction of Solomon Solomons.'

The maid came in again and took away our plates, and, as we had arranged beforehand for the sake of speed to forgo the meat course, we were soon tucking into our cabinet pudding.

'And have you any ideas for this afternoon?' I countered.

'I am to accompany Iris from the Hackney women's refuge to Wormwood Scrubs to see Solomons. I must admit, I am absolutely dreading it. Oh, it is so cold-blooded and irrevocable, James! It will be like talking to a dead man. We must – must – get him free! But Iris has worked herself up to the point of hysteria in her insistence on going to see him, and I seriously fear for her sanity if her wish is not granted.'

'Then it is well that you have come veiled. Will Venables be coming with you?'

'Hilary has arranged to follow us close behind in another cab, so that he may see if we are followed and take appropriate action.'

'Mmm, very well. I fear I shall need to keep up my clerical disguise if we are to keep our, er, suspects in separate compartments: let not the left hand know what the right hand is doing, so to speak.'

'Spoken like a curate! And will you be staying in Brown's Hotel for the duration, James?'

'I fear so, my dear, since it would look odd if messages were to come in there for the Reverend Mr Flockhart, and I never to be found. But it should not be for long.'

I paused for an instant, and thought about what I had just said. Then the proud, austere face of the youth in the condemned cell flashed across my inward eye, and I thought of the strain and stress – the unutterable tragedy – of his early life, the hot idealism, however wrongheaded, of his present, warmed by Iris Starr's simple love. I felt my flesh creep as I realised that, perhaps but for me, the light of those dreaming eyes might soon be brutally put out by the hangman's rope, and, to paraphrase Heine's words, that whole passionate world be buried in quicklime.

'By God!' I murmured through clenched teeth, as the horror of it began to sink into me. 'For Solomons' sake, it had better not be long!'

'It is awful, James: the time is so short . . .'

We finished our coffee and parted, but not before we had arranged to meet for a little discreet curaçao that evening in the restaurant of the Charing Cross Hotel. I stayed on for long enough to pay the reckoning, then left Mrs Stewart's and sought the opening to Regent Street, en route for Sackville Street, and the premises of Messrs Gabbitas and Tring, the scholastic agents. I did not suppose the deboshed schoolmaster would still be on their active list, in view of his recent showing in the Old Bailey, but hoped that they might still retain some record of him and his whereabouts.

'Hmph!' the clerk at the filing cabinet sniffed, as, seated in the agents' outer office, my hopes were confirmed. 'Mr Wellcome has recently been taken off our books, sir, and consequently I fear I cannot . . .'

I had come prepared for this, and the urgency and gravity of the cause in which I was engaged drove out all scruple. I started back in my chair, and, letting my jaw fall open, inhaled three rattling breaths.

'Dear me, sir!' the clerk exclaimed, leaving the open filing cabinet as it was and hurrying over to me. 'What can the matter be? May I . . .'

'Water!' I whispered. 'Just a little water, if you please . . .'

'Of course, sir, of course!' the man said. 'It'll only take a jiffy . . .'

The instant he was out of the room, I leapt to my feet and dashed over to the cabinet. The range of cardboard files was open where the clerk had found Wellcome's entry, at the top of which was the name and address of his next-of-kin, a Mrs Louisa Wincott of Boscobel Street, which I knew was somewhere off the Edgware Road, on the way to St John's Wood. Under this entry was a list of schools, with handwritten comments in a broad, lined column on the right of the list, and across the whole, in red rubber stamp, was the word 'deleted'. I just had time to resume my seat, when the clerk bustled in again and began to ply me with a glass of water.

'Thank you, I am much better now,' I said, rising from my chair. 'I am given to these attacks – extrasystole, you know. They cease with as little warning as they come on, and with no ill effects.'

'I see,' the man said uncomprehendingly. 'Well, sir, I'm afraid I cannot help you with the enquiries you are making, since we have a strict policy of not divulging our clients' particulars; and in any case, the person about whom you are asking is in fact no longer on our books, so in any case we could not give you his present address. I'm sorry I've been unable to help you.'

131

'On the contrary,' I said, with my best clerical smile, 'you have been most helpful: I bid you good day.'

Mrs Wincott turned out to be Sidney Wellcome's elder sister, and, no, she had not had contact with her brother since – well, she need not go into that. She had been officially informed, however, that he had come to rest in the infirmary of Lewisham Workhouse, and since it was public knowledge, she felt at liberty to tell me of the fact. That was all.

It was near teatime when, wearily, I arrived at the above-mentioned institution, to find Wellcome propped up, a living skeleton, in a steel-framed bed in a grim ward with limewashed walls. It was clear from the wretch's luminous great eyes, pink, sunken cheeks and sweat-beaded forehead that Lady Life would not have much longer to play her tricks on him. I stood over him quietly for a little while, then the head turned on the pillow and the eyes – painful to look at – turned to mine.

'I thought they at least had the decency to wait until one was dead, padre!'

Wellcome quipped in a sort of rustling whisper, and I admired the man's pluck.

'Please don't worry, Mr Wellcome: I am not here in my official capacity. I am making enquiries on behalf of Solomon Solomons, at whose trial you recently stood witness.'

'Yes, yes, the revolutionary feller – couldn't have done it. Know that, know that . . . Going to get him off, padre?'

'With God's help, Mr Wellcome, and perhaps with yours, too.'

'Yes, anything. Can't hang a chap for nothing: all wrong. What is it you want to know?'

'What you said you saw that night in the witness box: was that everything? You said you saw Solomons arrive in back Poland Street after the church clock had struck two.'

'Yes, St Thomas, St Thomas. Wind was perishing: if it hadn't been for that I'd have got off to sleep straight away, straight away . . .

'How long did you lie awake on the outhouse roof before you saw Solomons at two in the morning? Please try to remember, Mr Wellcome.'

'Hour, two hours, since a quarter-past midnight, I think. Perishing.'

'And did you see anyone else – anyone at all – enter the back lane between that time and the appearance of Solomons?'

The head flopped back on the other side for a while, then turned to face me again.

'Little fat chap – around half-past midnight. Topper and evening togs – little beard, I think. Mincing walk.'

Miller! I stooped low, until poor Wellcome's sickly-sweet, panting breath was in my face.

'Did he go into the building?' I asked eagerly.

'No. Tried the door, then left in the direction of Marlborough Street.'

'Didn't you tell the police about this, Mr Wellcome? It didn't come out in court.'

'Told them at the time, but I couldn't give 'em detailed description of him – face and so on – and when I told 'em he hadn't actually gone into the place, they seemed to lose interest . . .'

They would no doubt have taken him for some upper-class masher or stage-door Johnny, I thought, on the prowl for fun and games, and trying the place on 'spec'. The whole street was notorious in that respect, anyway.

'No,' Wellcome went on in his wheezing whisper, 'after that it was all Solomons, Solomons . . . Feller didn't do it. Put the record straight.'

'Did you attend the rest of the trial, Mr Wellcome?' I pressed. 'Did you see anyone in the court – in the witness box – you thought perhaps you recognised?'

'No, the baker wouldn't let me keep my perch after that – said I'd got him a bad name. I fetched up down here – chap's got to be somewhere, after all. Then the last haemorrhage, and here . . .'

'And you can't remember anything else about that night?'

'No, that's all, padre.'

I grasped the damp, skinny hand for a moment, thanked the poor devil, and, leaving him with my blessing, hurried out of the cheerless place. I was sure that the man in evening clothes must have been Miller, and I felt that it was possible that, on trying the back door of No. 11, Poland Street, he had gone straight round to the front. The question was, had he got in? I should have to give Poland Street my closer attention. But not now, for I still had some unfinished business, my intention that morning having been to kill two birds with one stone in Farm Street, for Miss Vulliamy's visit to our rooms in Henrietta Street earlier on had put out my arrangements somewhat. I had still to call on Dr Fedoroff at No. 19, Farm Street, where my particular interest lay with Cazes, the Russian doctor's French manservant, who had kept the door there on the night of the card-games. The sky was dark and louring, and I could smell snow in the air. I pulled out my watch: five fifteen. Well, no help for it: I pulled up the collar of my ulster and made for the nearest cab-rank.

By the time I had reached the house in Mayfair, an icy sleet was swirling round the already-lit gaslamps, and the pavements were greasy with slush. To my dismay, the house appeared deserted, for none of the front windows, including those down in the area, were lit. I climbed the front steps and knocked firmly, but no answering sound came from within. I waited, my clerical hat soaking in the sleet, for a full minute, then reached up my hand again to the knocker. To my relief the door opened before I could knock again, but my relief turned to consternation when, in the light of the single candle she was carrying, I discerned the impassive features of Mrs Custance, Miller's housekeeper.

'Why, Mr Flockhart!' she said in a fluttering voice. 'Come in – you'll catch your death!'

I thanked her, took off my hat and shook it on the step, then, since Mrs Custance was holding the candleholder with one hand and had a pair of sheets slung over her other arm, I declined her embarrassed offer of help and pulled off my overcoat myself, slinging it over my arm, while I tossed my hat atop a combined coat- and stick-stand which I espied dimly in the hall. The woman grabbed my umbrella deftly in the hand she was using to carry the sheets, then, letting the metal shaft slip through her hand, grasped the head for an instant, as if to steady it, then dropped it into the rack with what in the obscurity looked like at least half a dozen sticks and umbrellas. Mrs Custance led me into a nearby reception-room, where she laid down the candle-holder, then the sheets, on to an occasional table and took my ulster, which she draped carefully over a chair, then indicated another, on which I sat down. The fire was extinct – the grate swept clean – and the room was as cold as a mortuary. I rubbed my gloved hands together.

'I must say I did not expect to find you here, Mrs Custance,' I remarked. 'My business was with Dr Fedoroff's man, Cazes.'

'Oh, then I'm afraid you've come too late, sir. The doctor's gone abroad, and Cazes has gone with him. All the regular staff have left. Mr Miller says I'm to look after the place in the meantime.'

'In pitch darkness?' I said, for the candle only seemed to make the obscurity thicker. 'And in this cold?'

'I've only this minute come in, sir, and you haven't given me time to light the gas, if you don't mind me saying so.'

The voice was discreet, almost apologetic, but there was not a trace of servility or timidity there, and I found the unwavering stare more unsettling than ever. Sitting there in the near-darkness, the old nursery-jingle came involuntarily into my mind: 'Come into my parlour, said the spider to the fly . . .'

'Well I'm sorry I've bothered you, Mrs Custance: I don't suppose your employer could let me know . . .'

'Mr Miller won't be back till very late, sir: he's going straight from business to the Lyceum this evening – Mr Irving's on as Richard the Third.'

'Ah, I remember he said this morning how keen he was on Shakespeare.'

'Especially when Mr Irving's playing, sir – I'm sure I couldn't tell you how many times he's been to see him as Richard the Third! But he's just as keen on Macbeth, Neville the Kingmaker and all that . . .'

I pricked up my ears: this was more like it!

'You must mean Warwick the Kingmaker, Mrs Custance. . .' I remarked in as indifferent a tone as I could dissimulate. I am no playgoer, even less of a bardolator, and I had no definite idea of which play or plays this particular Warwick – there were several in Shakespeare's plays, I seemed to remember from schooldays – figured in. The name which only that morning Miller was pretending had no connotations for him . . .

'Yes, I'm sure you're right, sir,' the woman replied. 'It must be Warwick.'

I got to my feet.

'Well, I shall not keep you from your duties any longer, Mrs Custance. You don't by any chance know when Dr Fedoroff will be back from his travels?'

'I really don't, sir: he left quite suddenly. I can give a message to Mr Miller . . .'

'No matter, but thanks anyway. Now I shall be off – I too have an evening engagement.'

The housekeeper took my ulster off the back of the other chair and gave it a final shake before helping me on with it, then quickly slipped out of the candlelit room into the corridor, and was back with my hat and umbrella in almost the same movement.

'I should light up one of the fires if you're going to be here long, Mrs Custance,' I remarked, as she picked up the candle-holder from the little table and lit me to the street door.

'Oh, it won't take me long, thank you, sir,' she said. 'Just keeping an eye on things, in a manner of speaking.'

There was something dead in the chocolate-brown stare, and I shuddered slightly as the door closed behind me. Something then occurred to me, and, examining my brolly in the light of the nearest gaslamp, I shuddered anew when I realised that in the pitch darkness of the hallway of No. 19, Mrs Custance must have instantly and unerringly picked out the handle of my umbrella from those of at least half a dozen similar sticks and umbrellas in the rack.

16

Brown's Hotel was not far off in Albemarle Street, and I decided to hasten back there on foot rather than hang about in the chilling sleet looking for a cab in that dead part of the evening, too late for tea and too early for dinner. I pulled up the collar of my ulster and strode forth, and within twenty minutes I was in my hotel, lying contemplatively in a steaming bath. I drew on a rather unclerical cigar as I reviewed the case to date. At the top of the list of those with strong motives for killing Ostyankin was, I had to admit, Solomons, though after my brush with PC Kennedy I could no longer entertain the slightest doubt as to his innocence. After all, if a man is not on the scene of a crime he can scarcely have committed it. To counter this was the condemned man's obstinate silence, which in default of further information I chose provisionally to attribute to a desire to protect someone else. But whom? Not surely Iris Starr, who as far as I could see had no other relation to the case than her connection with Solomons. No, politics was still the most likely field of action in which to seek other motives for Ostyankin's murder and Solomons' silence, and I was still far from clear about how wide the ramifications of this might stretch. Let us say, then, a desire to protect revolutionary comrades, but that implied conspiracy, and in the eyes of the law an accessory to murder was as culpable as whoever struck the fatal blow, and bound to suffer the same penalty. I would have to know much more about the politics of the thing.

Then there was Alexander Miller, shrewd man of affairs, and, if the Jephsons and Judith Vulliamy – that hard, passionate young woman – were right, the debaucher and destroyer of poor Hector Jephson. When I compared the golden boy young Jephson must have been on the eve of his Foreign Office career with the emaciated thing I had glimpsed in the sunroom of the Magnolias, I could scarcely repress a shudder . . . If Miller was capable of this in the interests of Tsar and Motherland, he would surely have taken the elimination of Ostyankin as a political obstacle to his country's foreign policy in his stride. But how did one gauge the foreign policy of a closed autocracy? Again it all seemed to boil down to politics: just where did Miller stand in this regard? Perhaps he secretly favoured the Russian war-party, and the blow against Ostyankin might have included him, as far as its perpetrators had been concerned. And the pressure against Solomons' life was being increased like that on a stretched violin-string: perhaps at that very moment Mr Berry the public hangman was sitting quietly in a third-class carriage in some train hurtling towards London, his duty in the provinces fulfilled, his black bag on the luggage-rack above his head. I squashed out the stub of my cigar in the soap-dish, and began to climb out of the bath: whatever else I was going to ferret out, I had better do it quickly.

Seated half an hour later at a discreet corner-table for two at the Charing Cross Restaurant, Violet and I discussed the events of our respective afternoons over curaçaos. Although my wife listened attentively to my account, I could sense from the expectancy of her manner that she had much to tell me.

'I'm sure the stage-door Johnny the wretched Mr Wellcome described to you was Miller,' she agreed. 'If only Wellcome had stayed to see the rest of the trial, he might have been able positively to identify him. I wonder what else he knows.'

'You mean he may know something which he didn't choose to tell me? I must say I didn't think too much about that.'

'Well, what, for instance, if he had found something of value lying in the lane outside the house in Poland Street, after Solomons had gone off with his sovereigns? Do you think a man in such desperate straits as Wellcome would have hesitated before turning whatever it might have been into food, or more likely drink?'

'Dash it all, Violet, the man is clearly a gentleman, in spite of his circumstances, and I hardly think he would have concealed anything of importance on what is clearly his deathbed, especially when he is so transparently eager that Solomons shall have a square deal.'

'Hmph, I hope you are right, James. And that housekeeper of Miller's, Mrs, Mrs. . .'

'Custance,' I prompted.

'Mrs Custance, then. From your description, she seemed, well, too much at home with Miller to be a simple housekeeper. You are aware that that term can cover a multitude of sins, especially in the household of a man who is almost certainly a foreign spy. And does one lend one's housekeeper to a neighbour simply to keep his house aired while he is away? A housemaid would be generous enough, if one could spare her.'

'You mean send someone who can be relied upon to be discreet: keep it in the spying family, so to speak?' I suggested.

'Precisely. And again, his denial of any knowledge of the name Warwick sits ill with his pretensions as a Shakespearean! The way I feel about Miller at the moment, James, is that he is a man one cannot hit because he won't keep still!'

'I think I know what you mean,' I remarked, laughing. 'And now for your news, for I know from your Mona Lisa smirk that you have some!'

The smug smile was in no way diminished as Violet drew from her bodice a folded sheet of paper, which she unfolded into an important-looking foolscap document.

'Wired to Mr Zeinvel this morning,' she said. 'From his French legal associate in Paris . . .'

'Ah, yes!' I exclaimed, galvanised. 'Tvardoffsky the missing card-player's flight from St Petersburg. Do read on.'

'So evidently Mona Lisas have their uses . . . Very well, then, I shall translate as I go along: "I, the undersigned, hereby depone that at approximately 10 p.m. on the evening of Thursday November 27th, 1890, I was admitted to No. 19, Farm Street, London, where I had been invited to join a party of whist, my partner being Lieutenant Alexander Nikolayevich Kostromin, Engineer Officer in the Imperial Russian Army, the other partners in the game being Dr Alexey Nikiforovich Fedoroff, medical practitioner and tenant of the property, and Lieutenant Grigoriy Yefimovich Yevdokimoff, adjutant to the Imperial Russian Military Attaché in London. I further depone that at about eleven fifty-five on the same night, my host Dr Fedoroff was obliged to leave the party, having been called out to a medical emergency some distance from the house, and that he returned only a minute or so after in the company of Alexander Vissarionovich Miller, an export agent, who took Dr Fedoroff's place in the game of whist opposite Lieutenant Yevdokimoff. Dr Fedoroff then went out on his call, and I did not see him thereafter. The said Alexander Miller continued to play whist until approximately ten-past midnight, when Lieutenant Yevdokimoff asked him if he had a cigarette, since he had left his case behind. Miller then produced a cigarette-case of the nugget-type, and, removing the lid and holding it up level with Yevdokimoff's eyes, turned it slowly upside down, and said the one word: 'finished.' Lieutenant Yevdokimoff then nodded, and Miller got up from his chair, announcing that he had remembered an appointment and must leave, whereupon Lieutenant Kostromin engaged in badinage with Miller as to the physical excellences of his so-called appointment. Miller then left us, and, being left three-handed, we continued with a game of Hearts. I lost heavily, and left the game and the house at about half-past midnight. I had no further contact with the participants in the card party, and at about three the same afternoon of Friday the 28th of November, I was summoned from a meeting in the Russian Embassy by the Ambassador, who informed me that a grave development had occurred there in London in the early hours of the morning, and that in consequence I was to leave immediately and incognito for St Petersburg, where I was to hold myself at the disposal of the War Ministry until further notice. I was to ask no questions about the development in London, nor was I to speak to anyone of my tour of duty in Great Britain. I then left England immediately. Signed: Ivan Ivanovich Tvardoffsky, Major. Witnessed: Eustache Fabre-Lebreuil, Public Notary." It is dated yesterday, the 25th, James.'

'Then that settles it: Miller left the party well within the medical time-limits of General Ostyankin's death. And what was the meaning of that rigmarole with the, what was it?'

'"Cigarette-case of the nugget-type", James.'

'And what pray is that when it's at home?'

'A good question, and it's a piece of capital good luck that Sam Marshack lives so near the dispensary . . .'

I pause to explain that Samuel Marshack, originally of Odessa, was by way of being a freelance jeweller of considerable acumen, and, since his means of subsistence were not of the visible variety, and since, moreover, he chose to ply them in Thrawl Street – possibly the most *louche* of all the streets of the East End – he was the regular object of the attentions of the local police. Be that as it might, in view of our credit in the district as

trustworthy persons, Sam had early on retained us as his con-
sultant physicians, though up till then our only fee had been – of
all things – a crate of canned greengage jam, of God knew what
provenance. Violet had promptly distributed the tins among our
needier patients. But one good turn deserved another.

'Ah, the omniscient Mr Marshack!' I exclaimed. 'No doubt he
had it all taped. I trust you made an appropriate barter: a gross
of uncut clothes-pegs, perhaps?'

'You may scoff, James, but Sam was most helpful. According
to him, the object referred to in the deposition is a *samorodok*, or
nugget-shaped cigarette-case – something like a stylised metal
pine-cone with a lid. He says that Russians of standing vie to
have theirs designed and made by Morosoff, one of Fabergé's
rivals.'

'Mmm . . . I'm not surprised that Miller should have such a
fancy whatnot about him – in character with the man – but
I can't at the moment see any significance in it.'

'Ah, but there was something else . . .'

'Yes, what was that, then?'

'Sam told me that *samorodok* – nugget – also means an uncultivated person with natural talent, just as in English we say of an
unprepossessing but fundamentally good person that he's a
rough diamond.'

'That's interesting. It may be that when Miller turned this
cigarette-barrel affair upside down and said "Finished!" to his
whist-partner he wasn't referring to his cigarettes, but to a
person.'

'Ostyankin?'

'Mmm . . . rough enough by all accounts, but uncultivated? An
aristocrat, who'd presumably been through all the academies
and cadet-establishments of the Russian Empire? His natural
talent seemed above all to be one for spreading as much political
turmoil and mayhem as he could. We must file this away in our
memories for future reference – the active file. And your visit to
Wormwood Scrubs?'

Violet sighed, glass in hand, and briefly raised her eyes to
heaven.

'Awful! I had to wait outside in the corridor, but I could hear
it all, even through the heavy door. Iris went quite to pieces, and

finally a female officer had to be called to restrain her: luckily I was able to give her something.'

'You could then learn nothing from her as to Solomons' position?'

'Scarcely – the poor man would hardly want to discuss anything serious with Iris with her in that state. But there was something . . .'

'Yes, go on.'

'I think I may have seen another of Solomons' prison visitors.'

This really made me sit up and take notice.

'Yes, how is that?'

'As a condemned man, Solomons has separate arrangements for visitors. One waits in an ante-room until the officers are ready to take one to see him. Well, as we were being escorted back through the ante-room after our visit today, there was someone waiting; or rather pacing up and down the room as if he were a condemned man himself!'

'Did you get a good look at him?'

'Only a glimpse, since as soon as we came into the room, he turned his back to us. He was a tallish, wiry, red-haired man of about sixty, in a tight-fitting overcoat, and wearing a billycock hat. He had restless, rather bloodshot eyes.'

'Interesting!' I murmured, then: 'But there are no doubt other condemned men in Wormwood Scrubs.'

'No, James. I asked the escorting officer, and he told me that Solomons was the only one there at present due to "swing", as he put it, as soon as the hangman and his assistant have done their work "up north".'

'And Solomons has given neither Iris nor you any inkling as to who this might be?'

'None: he would tell us nothing of his affairs, and he was merely kind and reassuring towards Iris, as one might be towards a child or an animal. I cannot for the life of me see them as equal comrades . . .'

'But he must realise by now that Iris is in safe hands, and effectively out of the reach of reprisals by any revolutionary cronies, if that is what is keeping his mouth shut . . .'

'No, I don't think it is that. I am convinced that for Solomons, one is either of his philosophical and political totem, or one is not, and so beyond the pale. He is a true fanatic.'

142

' "Them and us", hey? Well, I say again: I've never met anyone so determined not to be saved! Confound it, Violet, but we cannot seem to get to grips with this business!'

'Courage, James! We seem to be in the wilderness now, but perhaps there will be water over the lip of the very next sand-dune!'

And so it happened, for, as I rather disconsolately saw my wife into a cab after our tête-à-tête, it dawned on me that I would have to spend the rest of the evening – it was just after nine thirty – within the sedate confines of Brown's Hotel. I decided then to stroll back as slowly as possible, take a night-cap and turn in. I sauntered across the road to the opening of Craven Street, which was almost deserted in the damp chill, and, idly tapping my brolly against each lamp-post as I walked along, stared vacantly at the shopfronts and alleyways. Then I saw a sign I recognised: Nevill's Turkish Baths. I recalled Mrs Custance's little gaffe over the name of Shakespeare's famous Kingmaker, then remembered the message impressed in the blank page of the notepad I had found in the former Pimlico rooms of the late Desmond Coe, alias De Kok, and erstwhile nominal tenant of the murder house in Poland Street: 'Warwick Wednesday seven fresh parcel.' I stood stock still. Of course! Nevill's – Richard Neville, Earl of Warwick: Coe had met his principal amid the naked anonymity of the Turkish bath!

17

Next morning I took an early breakfast amid the sobre representatives of cloth and county, then went back up to my room, to re-emerge bearing a small attaché case, in which reposed the outward accoutrements of my identity as James Mortimer. I had a cab summoned, then repaired in it to the bottom of Regent Circus, whence I walked circumspectly, with several – I hoped – innocent-seeming glances into shop-windows to see in their reflections if I was being followed, to the premises of the Express Messenger Company. I took a final sweeping glance round me, and, reassured, went inside and asked that a message be sent in the name of the Rev. Thomas Riddell of Balaclava Lodge, Barry – but not by the very next boy – to the offices of the *Daily Telegraph*. The clerk then wrote to my dictation a request that the following words be inserted in the agony column of the next day – Saturday's – edition: 'Warwick Monday seven value nugget.' I handed the clerk a half-sovereign, and left the office. That should start a hare or two, provided my guess as to the meaning of 'Warwick' turned out to be accurate.

I then made my way to Charing Cross station, where, in the privacy of the gentlemen's retiring-room, I effected my transformation back to James Mortimer, after which I hailed a hansom to take me to the Whitechapel Dispensary, where I thought I had better put in ten minutes in my occasional capacity of works supervisor at the new institute. When I got there, I found what I had known all along – that the builders were proceeding to time without outside interference. Indeed, if Napoleon's dictum that an army marches on its stomach applies equally to jobbing builders, then Bill Postgate's gang that very morning had found a staunch caterer in Mrs Chinnery, a handsome Boadicea of a woman with an air to her, and, if a written testimonial she had handed to an amused Violet, along with a free, piping-hot sample of her wares, had aught of truth in it, a veritable queen among piewomen. With the inner man thus fortified, how could the builders' men fail to work with a will? But, pies aside, the news Violet had for me made my journey worthwhile.

'We have a call to pay after lunch, James: the Working Girls' Club in Soho.'

'Miss Vulliamy and the Jephsons!' I exclaimed. 'Capital! This is our first real lead in the case – barring those that have led us merely to a corpse or to the cold trails of political fugitives!'

'I got a letter from Miss Vulliamy this morning: we are to call at our very earliest convenience.'

'At last we may be about to enter into the truth of this affair, from people whose paths have actually crossed Miller's.'

'I advise caution, James: remember you took Miss Vulliamy unawares yesterday, but now they have had time to get their heads together.'

I put in my stint in the pharmacy that morning while a growing sense of anticipation surged within me, and begrudged the time spent on the sandwich luncheon which was all we took that day. At last, we were able to lock the doors of the dispensary behind us, and, after Violet had shot a basilisk stare at the workmen on the other side of the court, we made for Aldgate East station.

At two o'clock we were received at the front portal of the Soho Working Girls' Club by a lean, red-haired man of fifty-five or more. His pale-blue eyes were reddened behind the gold-wire rimmed spectacles, and there was a searching sort of restlessness in them. I sensed Violet's arm stiffen in mine as the man said our names, then, with the curtest of nods, and not offering his hand, he ushered us through the offices and workrooms to the small back parlour. There Miss Vulliamy and the middle-aged lady we had seen her with at the Magnolias half-rose from their seats at either side of a plush-clothed table under a window, then sat down again in response to our nods and Jephson's curt words of introduction. Miss Vulliamy eyed us with that coldness I have remarked upon while describing our meeting of the previous day, while the other lady – whose Christian name we now knew was Lettice – seemed to look beyond us through some private fog of grief and distraction. A pair of hard upright chairs were indicated to us, then, after we had sat down, Cormell Jephson strode over to the mantelpiece and seized a framed photograph, which he thrust into my hand, before resuming his restless pacing over the snug-piled carpet of the little room. I shared the photograph with Violet, and in it we saw depicted a handsome, blond athlete of a youth with a confident smile on his lips. He was in rowing kit, sitting under a pair of crossed oars. I could not repress a little groan as I recognised the young man in the emaciated wreck I had studied through the window of the sunroom of the Magnolias nursing home. With a shake of the head, I handed back the photograph to Jephson, who replaced it on the mantelpiece as jerkily as he had taken it down.

'My son, Hector,' he said, with obvious emotion in his voice, then, still pacing up and down, and like a schoolmaster warming up to his lesson: 'Judith has told me of how you forced her hand the other day, Dr Mortimer.'

'I assure you, sir, it was for the very best of reasons . . .'

The wiry man waved away my excuse with a curt gesture, and continued his promenade.

'No doubt, doctor, and no matter now. What you know, you know. Of course I shall help if that poor wretch, what's his name . . .'

'Solomons, sir: he lies in the condemned cell of Wormwood Scrubs at this very moment. You will appreciate that I can afford to indulge no niceties of etiquette or fine feeling if I am to make the best of whatever time still remains to me – or to him – in order to get justice for him.'

'You will allow me to observe, Dr Mortimer, that your zeal in this man's cause seems to go far beyond that of a good citizen towards a possible injustice to one of his fellows.'

'My wife here owes her life to, to . . . one to whom Solomons is dearer than life itself, Mr Jephson, just as my wife is all-in-all to me. For the sake of that person, and for that same cause of justice to which you have alluded, I shall strain every nerve in my body in his behalf.'

'Mph,' the cleric grunted, pausing in mid-pace and studying me for an instant, then glancing at Violet. 'Reason enough, I should think . . .'

Violet blushed and inclined her head, and it seemed that some of Jephson's original guarded hostility had gone out of his manner towards us.

'Very well, then, what can I do for you both?'

'It has occurred to me that the murder of General Ostyankin

146

may have some bearing on the fate of your unfortunate son, in the light of his profession and of what Miss Vulliamy told me about the malign influence Miller had over him in Berlin and here in London. I feel strongly that we are dealing with espionage.'

Jephson came to an abrupt halt, and, stepping over to the window, twitched at the curtains with nervous fingers, before swinging round to face me. His blue eyes seemed on fire, and he was convulsively drawing back his lips round his teeth. I noticed for the first time the characteristic blueing or cyanosis of the lips which betokened some labouring valve or possible calcification of the heart. The owners of such lips do well to take life calmly.

'Miller!' the clergyman hissed. 'If you could know the sorrow that name has brought to this house, the extent to which its owner has challenged my very faith in Christ.'

'Do not take on so Cor!' Mrs Jephson urged plaintively from her corner. 'You know it is bad for you. And remember, a Christian cannot hate.'

Jephson stepped over to the table and flopped into an empty chair.

'Yes, yes, Lettice my dear, you are right: that above all. A Christian must not hate. Tell me what you wish to know from me that Judith has been unable to tell you, doctor,' the clergyman said quietly, the storm having evidently passed.

'Did you ever meet Ostyankin or other Russians in Miller's company, sir?'

'Never, doctor, neither the man nor his compatriots meant anything to me.'

'And Miller never mentioned Ostyankin to you?'

'Neither I nor my wife sought Miller's further acquaintance, after Hector had introduced him to us at the theatre, shortly after my son's return from his posting in Germany, Dr Mortimer. He made a most unfavourable impression on us, and we only tolerated him afterwards because he was our son's friend.'

The theatre again, I thought.

'And Miller never called on you in – was it Ebury Street, Mr Jephson?'

'Mmm . . . once, I remember. It was a purely formal call, and the ice was not broken. We met him only at the theatre – he is an ardent theatregoer – and in other public places of resort after that one and only call.'

'And did your son entertain Miller in your house in Ebury Street?'

'He may well have done in our absence – we are very busy here at the club at all times – but I did not question him on the matter. My son was of age, after all.'

'There was no question of your having forbidden Miller the house?'

'No, no, it is as I have told you: he was Hector's friend, and I respected that.'

'And Miller did not come here to the Working Girls' Club on any occasion?'

'Certainly not! Besides, it was after the truth of poor Hector's illness had come out, and Miller's part in his contracting it, that we shut up our house and came to stay here permanently. The ghosts of happy laughter, Dr Mortimer . . .'

And here I am afraid the poor man quite broke down. At this point, Mrs Jephson bustled over to a side-table, whence she came to her husband and plied him with medicine in a spoon.

'What must you think of me, doctor,' Jephson remarked brusquely as, regaining his composure, he dashed the flat of his hand briefly over his eyes and gave me his attention once again. Mrs Jephson resumed her chair.

'It grieves me to have to pursue what is so evidently a painful subject to you, Mr Jephson,' I went on, 'but did your son correspond with you during his stay in Germany? Send you his *impressions de voyage*, so to speak?'

Jephson heaved a sigh, and turned to his wife.

'Shall we, my dear?' he said.

'I am sure that Dr Mortimer will not mind giving us his solemn word that he will return the letters,' she said, searching my eyes keenly with hers.

'Unconditionally, ma'am!' I exclaimed.

Jephson rose from his chair, went over to a small bureau, rummaged for a while in a little drawer, then selected a bundle of envelopes, which he tossed on to the plush tablecloth in front of me.

'My dear sir,' I murmured, 'I hardly expected . . .'

'It is liberal, indeed, Mr Jephson,' Violet echoed my gratitude.

'No, doctor, please take them. I cannot bear to look at them now.'

'They are all I have of him, now,' Lettice Jephson said, and covered her face with her handkerchief.

'We are greatly obliged to you both,' I replied, 'and I shall return them to you just as soon as we have looked through them.'

'As you please, Dr Mortimer, as you please,' Jephson said with a weary sigh. I picked up our epistolary prize from the plush table-top and slipped it into the inside pocket of my frock coat, and we both rose with Jephson. We said our farewells to the ladies, Lettice Jephson responding with a wan little smile, and Judith Vulliamy, who had said not a word throughout the proceedings, merely gave the ghost of a nod. Jephson then escorted us solemnly to the street door again, this time dismissing us with a slight handshake apiece.

'Pray take care of the letters, Dr Mortimer – for Lettice's sake,' was his parting remark, then: 'And may justice be done for the poor fellow in Wormwood Scrubs. He shall be in our prayers.'

'What a tragedy!' I exclaimed as we found ourselves alone again on the raw, dirty streets of Soho. 'And how they detest Miller! And what a stroke of luck their allowing us to borrow these letters . . .'

But for the moment my wife did not seem to be interested in my remarks, for she responded by grasping my arm so tightly that I could have winced.

'James!' she whispered hoarsely. 'The man I saw in the visitors' waiting-room in Wormwood Scrubs – it was Cormell Jephson!'

149

18

Violet having no afternoon engagements until evening surgery at Whitechapel at five, we returned to Henrietta Street, arriving there at about ten to two, with the intention of studying at leisure the ill-starred Hector Jephson's German letters. We ensconced ourselves in facing easy chairs in the sitting-room, and I sorted out the envelopes according to the order of the dates of the postmarks, then took out the first letter. It was dated the 6th of May, 1886, a couple of months before the young man's first meeting with Judith Vulliamy on her grandfather's estate in East Prussia. The envelope was postmarked Berlin, and the contents, prefaced – as were all of them – with the words 'Dear Old Things,' were taken up with young Jephson's impressions of that capital. It was a lively, colourful account, couched in the succinct prose of the professional report-writer, and its author was clearly possessed of first-rate powers of observation, which were also displayed in the subsequent letters up to that describing his meeting with Miss Vulliamy. He had been clearly bowled over by her, though he expressed his feelings with the breezy inconsequence cultivated by young Foreign Office swells. It soon became apparent that Hector Jephson had possessed tact and professional discretion in equal measure to his gift for observation, for there was not a single mention of politics, and obviously political personalities were mentioned briefly by name, only to be passed over as soon as they had served to place the scenes the writer had been describing in proper context, rather like stage props. The name of a colleague, Ned Coram, cropped up more than once, but there was no mention of Russians at all until the appearance of that 'most amusing little beggar you'd ever clapped eyes on', during the weekend at Eylau. The 'little beggar's' amusing tricks, in which young Jephson became an increasingly frequent participant after his return to Berlin later in July, figured in letters sent twice a week to his parents, until an abrupt break in the correspondence, marked by the omission of one of the serially reported episodes of a Berlin wheeze jointly performed by the writer and the 'amusing little beggar', Miller, occurred near the end of July. My suspicions aroused, I quickly riffled through the letters I had read, then through those I had not yet arrived at, to see if I had got one of them out of sequence, but in vain. Violet shared my speculations as to what might have been the significance of that week or so at the end of July, 1886. It was with a creased brow that I read through the rest, which were similarly unrevealing to our purpose, until the series ended on the eve of Hector Jephson's home posting in October of that year as the result of the successful completion of the barely-referred-to conference behind the scenes of which he had served as a minor adjutant. His last letter described how Miller was to be in London, too, and expressed the hope that his 'dear old things' and the Russian would get on like a house on fire, a wish whose fulfilment was to fall so wide of the mark.

'One can only guess at the nature of the less harmless "wheezes" Miller might have led young Jephson into in Berlin . . .' Violet remarked when I had finished.

'Yes, the gap in the correspondence may well be accounted for by one of them.'

'Or the letter may simply have been lost or mislaid,' Violet countered. 'You will have noticed that Miss Vulliamy volunteered no letters during our interview in the Working Girls' Club in Soho.'

'Nor any word about anything else, for that matter.'

'She will not forgive you for stealing her thunder the other day, James – springing what you'd learned about her on her in such a cavalier fashion!'

'And are you absolutely sure it was Cormell Jephson you saw in the ante-room in Wormwood Scrubs prison?' I asked, returning to an earlier subject.

'Positive: it was he, James, down to the nervous pacing up and down.'

'Then this reverend gentleman is a barefaced liar, asking me to repeat Solomons' name, as if he hardly knew it. But what possible connection or affinity could there be between a clergyman from Ebury Street and a Russian anarchist from Whitechapel?'

'Unless they met over a game of chess at the Warsaw!' Violet chaffed me.

I then told her about my theory, founded on Mrs Custance's

verbal gaffe of the previous afternoon, that 'Warwick' was code for Nevill's Turkish Baths at Charing Cross, and of my insertion of the advertisement in the *Daily Telegraph* inviting whoever might be able to interpret it to a rendezvous.

'A capital idea!' Violet replied. 'Who knows what it may not smoke out! You are not thinking of going alone?'

I knew what was coming.

'It is out of the question that you should be hanging about a Turkish bath after nightfall, Violet,' I protested, 'and what's more, I do not think it will suit our goal of anonymity in the affair if you are to be seen to be too much associated with the Reverend Flockhart. It would turn the business into a carnival.'

'But the danger, James . . .'

'Rest assured I shall be discretion itself, and remember it is only a theory. It is more than possible that the whole thing may be no more than a wild goose chase after all, but we must act on every possibility, the time being so short.'

'If the law takes its course, it will kill poor Iris,' my wife remarked with a shudder. 'I should never forgive myself, after what I owe her. I should feel like a useless fraud, an impostor!'

'Do not even think of it, Violet!' I urged, then she was pensive for a moment before making her next remark.

'Do you think, James, can it be possible . . .'

'Yes?'

'That it was in fact Miller who was the intended victim in Poland Street? It is suspicious that he should leave the card-game in Farm Street, then be seen trying the back door of the house in Poland Street just as Ostyankin was being murdered there. It looks as if Miller might have been lured there.'

'But how? For one thing, Ostyankin bore no resemblance to him at all, and for another, I doubt if some casual hired assassin who didn't know Miller from Adam and had merely been pointed in the direction of the room where his intended victim was would have carried out his task with such horrible vehemence. I've no experience of the breed, but surely a cool head is required in such a calling, as well as a cold heart. This was a crime not just of passion, but of insane fury!'

'Yes, I suppose you're right – it was just a feeling. It is just that Miller seems to be so hated.'

'Yes, I know what you mean, but aren't we – haven't we been

from the start – neglecting the man who should be the leading player in this drama?'

'Ostyankin, you mean?'

'Precisely. Alias Monsieur Lefranc, alias Lord-knows-what in the years he's been intriguing and trouble-making over three continents.'

'But how are we to learn about the recent ways and doings of a man to whom secrecy and dissimulation have been a way of life? You will have noticed how the press have had a field day over the general's reported public misdeeds, but about the man himself – virtually nothing. We have seen how quickly his compatriots and cronies here in London disappeared as soon as the news of his murder broke. Are we then to go to Russia? To Bulgaria? To the steppes of Central Asia? Short of that, there seems nothing but the public record, seen for the most part through the eyes and pens of jingo reporters. We now have Tvardoffsky, of course . . .'

'Yes, we have!' I exclaimed. 'Friend Zeinvel once again proves his worth! But Tvardoffsky is in Paris, and – confound it yet again! – we haven't the time! Still, Crutched Friars shall be one of my ports of call later: after Cook's office . . .'

'Cook's! But did I not just hear you say that we had not time to travel?'

'No, it has nothing to do with travel. It is an idea I've had concerning the apparent gap in Hector Jephson's German letters: where might a young English rowing blue go on a few free summer days in Germany?'

'Ah, I see. That might be worth looking into, James.'

'What are your plans for this afternoon, Violet?'

'I shall be free till evening surgery at five. Why? What have you in mind?'

'That you go straight from here to the British Museum Reading Room, and follow the public life and times of General Ostyankin in the contemporary history shelves.'

'Very well, then. Is there anything in particular I should be looking for?'

I pondered for a moment.

'The facts surrounding the attempt on his life in Odessa in '84, in which Solomons is supposed to have had a hand – everything you can learn about it. I shall come and pick you up after the close of evening surgery, then perhaps a little supper at Gatti's: we can talk things over then.'

And so it was agreed. By now it was after half-past three, so we went on our occasions without more ado. The young man behind the counter at Cook's, my first call, proved a live wire and most helpful.

'Something to do in Germany round the last week in July, sir? What part of the country had you in mind?'

'Oh, north – Berlin, Prussia – the Baltic – way.'

'Thinking of taking the family, sir?'

'Mmm . . . no, actually me and some chaps at the office've got a spot of holiday coming up then, and, well, between you and me, the idea is to get away from the dear ones, don't you know . . .'

The youth grinned conspiratorially, and for a moment I feared he was about to lean over the counter and dig me in the ribs. I quickly sought to correct any possible misconception on his part.

'It was a bit of outdoor sport we had in mind, in fact – rowing, messing about in boats sort of line.'

'Ah, in that case, I think we may have the very thing, sir – if you'll hang on a tick . . .'

The young spark riffled through a batch of brochures, then, pulling one out, opened it and jabbed his forefinger at an entry.

'There you are, sir – week commencing the 23rd – the Kiel Regatta. Ferry from Hull to Hamburg, thence by rail. A sight worth seeing, with all the great racers, fireworks and a ball on the closing evening. Cream of society – everyone's there. Capital fishing to be had around there, too, if you like a quiet life – quaint fishing-villages – hire a boat – Frisian Islands . . .'

'Yes,' I said, interrupting his flow of eloquence, 'it sounds just the ticket. Many thanks to you – I'll talk it over with the chaps.'

I touched the brim of my topper with the tip of my umbrella, and, accepting the brochure, left the bureau. Yes, the date fitted perfectly, and it was just the sort of way a spirited young diplomatist might choose to spend a few free days. And in whose company? That of the 'most amusing little beggar you'd ever clapped eyes on', perhaps? Or some much heavier Slavonic

154

company? This was all very well, but as things stood, it was all merely a shimmering tower of conjecture: I needed verification, facts, evidence. Whom did I know who was knowledgeable about yachting? I knew nobody at present who was given to the hobby, and the only one of my school-companions I had known to be interested in messing about in boats had been Frederick 'Napper' Whale, whose exploits in Brixham harbour in the late seventies had been legendary, but as far as I knew, Napper was at that time running a sheep-range out in Namaqualand. I must go, then, to the fountain-head: the Royal Thames Yacht Club, and there I succeeded beyond my expectations, for their excellent library yielded me a complete programme for the Kiel Regatta for the year in question. The English contingent had evidently been heavy swells indeed, but I found no familiar names among their crew-lists, and the same applied to the Germans, but that of one of the two Russian cutters entered – the *Kronstadt* – gave me what I was looking for. Among the boat's company figured Jephson, H., Lefranc, A. and Miller, A. Lefranc was of course one of the pseudonyms the late General Ostyankin had gone under. I now knew that, whether or not Hector Jephson had been privy to any of Ostyankin's darker activities, he had at least once been a shipmate of his. It was therefore with a new purpose in my step that I re-emerged into Knightsbridge, and, turning sharp left down Sloane Street, made for Sloane Square station and the Metropolitan Line, which would take me to Mark Lane, whence I would walk to Zeinvel's legal eyrie in Crutched Friars. Here I was to be disappointed, however, for it turned out that Zeinvel was out briefing some barrister, but his clerk assured me that he would be back in half an hour or so, and would be at his desk until at least eight that evening.

It was now about twenty past four, and a calm winter dusk was already settling over the City. I decided to fill in the time before Zeinvel arrived back by strolling up into the nearby East End to Dorset Street, the scene of Solomons' arrest the previous November. A sort of mental disengagement, passing into a dreamy reverie, gradually stole over me as lawyers' warrens and Dickensian offices and warehouses started to give way to huddled, mean residential streets as I entered the Minories, on the very marches of the City. Ten minutes' walk due north brought me into Aldgate, whence I continued in a north-easterly direction till I at last found myself in Dorset, or 'Dossen' Street, as most of the inhabitants called it, where, on that fateful late-November afternoon, Solomon Solomons had been 'took', in Iris's words, by the police. In front of the 'Scotch baker's', to be precise, before he had made his fruitless dash through the common passage of No. 44, and had had the darbies clapped on him by the other, alerted, waiting bobby. And what had been the name of the tenant of No. 44, through whose rooms Solomons had dashed? Yes: Flitterman, Isaac Flitterman.

I arrived at the baker's shop – Logan's – and was momentarily surprised by the knot of people bearing pots and bundles outside the shop-door. Surely rather late in the day – dusk, in fact – to buy bread? Then I recalled: dusk on Friday evening, when the light was not enough to allow one to distinguish between a black and a white thread before one's eyes, marked the start of the Jewish Sabbath. It was just before that hour when observant Jews would take their cooking-pots to the nearest Gentile baker – who, of course, would be working through the night – to have their meats and stews cooked in the baker's ovens, ready for collection on Saturday. It was the same everywhere in the East End. It struck me that Solomons had tried to give PC Seddon the slip here on just such a Sabbath eve the previous November, only to fall into the waiting arms of PC Yeatman.

Perhaps there was a clue here – 'he who runs may read' – but just then I could make no connection, nor did the depressing passageway of No. 44, into whose stygian gloom I briefly poked my nose, set off any fruitful train of thought. I gave a last look down the street in the direction of Logan's bakery, where the patient knot of the pious was rapidly shrinking, then, turning on my heel, made for the broader thoroughfares of Aldgate. I strolled aimlessly southward for ten minutes or so, when the cry of some distant cantor brought with it the resonance of the passion and grief of two thousand years of exile. I felt a sort of truce in the air in this hallowed dusk. The strange fancy took me that a faraway voice was calling to me, but I could not make out the words of the message.

A growing awareness that I was attracting the attention of passers-by, some even grunting and spitting as they crossed my path, broke my reverie at last, and it dawned on me how ominous, barely two years after the last 'Jack the Ripper' murder had taken place in this very district, must be the sight of a top-hatted man looking speculatively around him and carrying a little black bag! I tucked the bag awkwardly under my arm, and hurried in the direction of Crutched Friars.

I found no consolation from Zeinvel, though. Major Tvardoff-sky, it seemed, had been served a deportation order by the French authorities, in the wake of pressure brought to bear by the Russian government, and the wayward witness of Farm Street was now at large somewhere in greater Europe. Nor had there been any fresh leads as to the whereabouts of Semyon Klaff, though Pinkerton's were still on his trail. I thanked the lawyer, and left his eyrie to hail a cab, in which I was finally conveyed to the Whitechapel Dispensary, where I helped Violet and our invaluable assistant and colleague, Dr Jane Bonsor, through the rest of evening surgery, until she was picked up by her trusty swain, and we made our way to Aldgate station and a westbound train, discussing our respective findings during the journey towards Gatti's and supper. Violet began with Ostyankin.

'A bloody business, and a bloody man!' my wife announced with characteristic forthrightness. ' "December, 1872",' she read from the foolscap sheet that contained her notes, ' "took part in Vinnitza pogrom, but got shot through the throat for his pains. Recovered – the devil looks after his own. January, 1878, known to have perpetrated appalling atrocities against Bulgarian Moslems during taking of Sofia by the Tsar's forces. June, 1884, hundreds slaughtered – women and children burned alive in their houses – by Cossacks in Kozodieffka pogrom directed by Black Hundreds nationalist secret society, of which Ostyankin is known to be the directing force." And there is more – much more.'

'The late general was evidently not prominent among the forces of enlightenment,' I remarked, 'but it is the last event which is of interest to us: the Kozodieffka pogrom, in which Solomon Solomons' mother and young sister are supposed to have perished; that and the subsequent attempt on Ostyankin's life by revolutionaries, including Solomons. What have you on that?'

' "August the 4th, 1884, Odessa",' Violet read out, after turning over the sheet of foolscap. ' "Carriage carrying State Counsellor

157

Pamphiloff and General Ostyankin to a review of the Black Sea Fleet intercepted at a turning by six revolutionaries armed with revolvers. Pamphiloff shot through the head – dies immediately – Ostyankin through the left lung – lies in hospital in critical condition for three months, but eventually recovers. Four of the assassins captured, two denouncing Solomons – described as a rabbinical student – at trial, but he's already out of the country, along with the last assassin, Mark Diamant, a stonemason."'

'Shot through the throat in '72,' I said, thinking of Ostyankin's earlier wound sustained in the Vinnitza pogrom. 'A wound like that would change a man.'

'How do you mean, James? His personality?'

'No, his voice, depending on the affected parts.'

'Do you see any significance in that?'

'Not at the moment, but I think we might bear it in mind.'

'The more I think about it, James – and especially in the light of what I've just learned in the British Museum – the more I'm convinced it is politics.'

'But when all's said and done, Violet, London is not the Balkans . . .'

'And that gap in poor Hector Jephson's correspondence with his father might well have been an oversight on his part. Still, it is intriguing to know that young Jephson sailed in the Kiel Regatta with Miller and Ostyankin in his "Monsieur Lefranc" persona.'

We had had a tiring day, and our conversation during our bite to eat at Gatti's – we were there for scarcely half an hour – was of the desultory variety, until, at just ten to eight, I put Violet into a cab home, and once again found myself facing another sedate night among the gaitered crowd at Brown's. I looked down at my silly little case, and felt like flinging it down the nearest area, then summoned up my resolve and started to look for a suitable place where I might effect my transformation into the Reverend Flockhart. As I went along I thought ahead to Monday's strategem at Nevill's Turkish Baths. I considered Miller's housekeeper, Mrs Custance's, gaffe in the matter of 'Neville the Kingmaker', then wondered if it had been a gaffe, after all . . . I cudgelled my brain, raking my store of schoolday-memories for the play Shakespeare's Kingmaker had figured in. If only I had been more attentive during Eng. Lit. lessons. Then it came to me: *Henry VI*, but whether it was Part One, Two or Three – for all I could recall, there might have been four or even five parts to the blessed thing – I had no idea. As will often happen when one's mind is disengaged, an idea, once it does come, will usurp everything else, but how could I find out at this hour? Just then some devil seemed to get into me. I tugged out my watch: just coming up to eight o'clock. In for a penny, in for a pound: Henry Irving would know.

19

'Why, sir, you can't be serious!' the gaping man at the stage door of the Lyceum in Wellington Street said to me, as, breathless after my dash up the Strand, I urged my visiting-card on him. 'The guv'nor's on in ten minutes – the Funeral Scene's already started. Really, sir, it's out of the question! Now if you'd just care to write in to Mr Stoker tomorrow . . .'

'It is a most vital matter,' I insisted, 'and I know from his reputation that Mr Irving's heart is as great as his genius. When he sees the note I have written on the back of this card, I'm sure he'll spare me at least a minute, which will be more than enough time for my question to be answered. One minute . . .'

'Very sorry, sir, but I really cannot . . .'

I added half a crown to the card, and, seizing the astonished man's hand in both of mine, pressed the objects into it.

'Then at least give the card to Mr Irving's dresser – anyone near him – and I will not think my efforts in vain.'

The man tossed the coin up and caught it, while he held the card in his free hand, then shook his head and smiled ruefully.

'I warn you, sir, there isn't a hope . . .'

'But you will do it?'

For answer, the man sighed, pocketed the coin, then, reading from the card, muttered my name to himself. He then looked me up and down again.

'You're a surgeon, hey, sir?'

I nodded impatiently.

Another sigh, then: 'Hang on a jiffy, sir,' and the man was gone.

Some philosopher has said that there is magic in boldness, and so it was in this instance, for, hardly two minutes later, the doorkeeper was back again, and gazing at me with evident new respect.

'Guv'nor'll see you, sir, but he can only give you five minutes – if you'll come this way. Oh, and I'll take care of that case and umbrella, if you don't mind . . .'

There followed a minute's upping and downing through narrow, ill-lit corridors, until I was finally ushered, my heart pounding, into the 'Guv'nor's' dressing-room, the great man being seated at a small table against the far wall, where he was applying a colour stick to his long, sad visage while gazing into a looking-glass lit by two powerful gas-jets. There was a thick, pungent smell, rather like that of the linseed oil which we used to rub on our cricket bats at school. I realised that, for the first time, I was in the presence of Glamour. The guv'nor went on applying the greasepaint, unperturbed, until it occurred to me that about two-and-a-half of my five minutes had gone.

'I'm greatly obliged to you, Mr Irving,' I stammered, 'for sparing me some of your precious time, and . . .'

The deep, resonant voice cut me short with a perfectly phrased declaration.

'Which man worthy of the name, Mr, er . . .' – he looked down at my card on the table-top – '. . . Mortimer, would not have a few minutes to spare for the sake of a condemned man? A most affecting note: "heart as big as me genius" – mph . . . I've followed the case – your man's antecedents are dead against him. Give a dog a bad name. What is it you want of me? I fear I have but little time – me public . . .'

'Just this, sir: did you ever play Warwick the Kingmaker here at the Lyceum?'

The actor swung round in his chair and faced me. How much longer and sadder the rather flat face seemed, and what quiet dignity the features held. The great man shook his long locks.

'Henry VI, Part Three, Act Five, Scene Three – never, Mr Mortimer, neither here nor anywhere else, and I don't know that any other production of the play has been put on anywhere since Part Two was staged to mark the Birthday in '64. That was at the Surrey, as I recall. Powerful part, too. Me hump, laddy!'

Mr Irving's last words were roared at the open door, whereupon the 'laddy' in question, a wizened stripling of some sixty winters, bustled in bearing a black velvet doublet with the protuberance mentioned visible on one of its shoulders. He immediately began to help the actor on with the garment, but they had scarcely finished when a voice came urgently in through the open door of the dressing-room.

'Yer on, guv'nor!'

I stepped back hastily to make way for the great thespian, louring-faced and twisted as Richard the Third, as, preceded by the dresser, he got up and made for the door.

'I hope I've been of some assistance, Mr Mortimer – good luck with your man!'

The doorman reappeared and, handing me my case and umbrella, led me back down to the stage-door and into the greasy cold of Wellington Street. Had I really spent five minutes with the greatest actor of the age? I made my way slowly to another sedate evening in Brown's Hotel, with two things clear in my mind. From what Irving had told me, when Mrs Custance mentioned that Miller had seen Irving as Nevill the Kingmaker, she had either made a serious gaffe indeed or she had been lying, for what reason I was unsure. Somehow to serve the ends of her employer? To put me off the scent of something more important? Or had it been off her own bat, so to speak? I had food for thought as, after lingering over a cigar, I finally turned in at a disgustingly healthy hour that night.

The next morning after breakfast, I finally decided that the Reverend Flockhart deserved a weekend in the country, and, having made arrangements accordingly at the hotel desk, I left with my little black case and strolled down to St James's Park station, where in the gentlemen's retiring-room I discreetly effected my metamorphosis back into James Mortimer. I then boarded a train to Charing Cross and thence home, where I changed into the modest country togs and rather battered bowler that formed my Whitechapel *tenue*. I entrained again, and was able to give Jane Bonsor a slightly truncated day's holiday from the dispensary.

Violet and I discussed my findings of the previous evening over luncheon chops in the restaurant of the Great Eastern Hotel near Liverpool Street station. Violet was duly impressed by my relation of my brush with the great actor at the Lyceum, but as irritated as I by the inconclusive nature of my findings.

'We simply do not know enough about Miller and his *ménage* to be able to form any conclusion as to his housekeeper's error,' she remarked, 'if it was an error, but my feeling is that if Miller was behind it, and it is a deliberate attempt to lure you to the Turkish baths, I beg you to reconsider going there alone.'

I recalled Miller's hoots of mocking laughter behind the door of his house in Farm Street as I had left there after my visit on Thursday morning, and smiled.

'Come, my dear, why should they consider a harmless crank of a clergyman worth such pains?'

'Well, I hope you are right, James, and now, what about the witness situation?'

'What indeed?' I answered uneasily, staring down into my plate, for during those tense days it seemed as if the life of the condemned wretch in Wormwood Scrubs was ticking away with each stroke of the clock-hand. 'Zeinvel's quest for Klaff seems to have lost its way on the plains of America, and Tvardoffsky may be in Timbuctoo by now. What are the rumours in the East End? I fear that since I have been ordained into the Church, I'm losing touch with things down there.'

'It is as the man said to you in the Warsaw: the whole district knows that Kennedy saw Solomons and Klaff in the Warsaw around one in the morning of the murder.'

'Mmm . . . no good,' I muttered, remembering in a more judicious light my indignation when Kennedy in my presence denied that he had laid eyes on Solomons that night. 'Ignoring Engineer Gaselee's testimony in court of how he'd spent the time between midnight and 1 a.m. with Solomons and Klaff in the Lord Raglan public house in Limehouse, they – or at least one of them – had just enough time after leaving the Warsaw the first time at eleven thirty-five on Thursday night – remember Iris's and Brummie Ida's joint sighting of them? – to dash up to Soho, do the murder, then be back in the Warsaw again in time for PC Kennedy to look in and spot them around 1 a.m. on Friday.'

'They'd have had to be quicker about it than the quickest of music-hall turns,' Violet replied scornfully. 'And they wouldn't have had a single instant to clean themselves up and get back their nerve and even their breath, let alone pause to pick up a host of golden sovereigns on the way.'

'I know, I know, but that is no doubt the way a panel of judges will see it when considering an appeal.'

'And again,' Violet went on, 'apart from Iris and Brummie Ida right at the beginning, those of our witnesses who are prepared to come forward and speak only come in ones! Single spies! Gaselee the ship's engineer from midnight till one in the morning, Iris – alone – at half-past one on the Friday morning, poor

Wellcome the drunkard at two by the Soho church clock, Shalit the tailor's runner at about the same time. No corroboration.'

And there we had to leave it. Violet had business to attend to at the New Women's Hospital after luncheon, and after we had finished our meal I walked with her to a disengaged cab and saw her off, while I made my way to Crutched Friars and Zeinvel. There I learned that the appeal against Solomons' conviction and sentence was to be heard the following Wednesday, and that there had been no further developments in the hunt for witnesses; furthermore, that PC Kennedy had been given a transfer to parts unspecified, and that he might be ruled out of the equation for the foreseeable future. It seemed that the lips of Whitechapel were firmly sealed. I was on the point of leaving, when I remembered Violet's insistence that she had seen the Reverend Cormell Jephson in the ante-room to the condemned cell in Wormwood Scrubs on Thursday afternoon. I also recalled the anxious cleric's declared unfamiliarity with Solomons' name, and I was prompted to pose Zeinvel a statement and two questions.

'I understand, Zeinvel, that it would be highly improper of me to ask about your financial arrangements with one of your clients . . .'

'Highly,' the wily lawyer said drily, but pleasantly.

'And of course I shouldn't dream of doing so.'

'I'm glad to hear of it, doctor.'

'But your impressions are your own, are they not?'

'They are, Dr Mortimer.'

'I wonder, then, what your impression would be if I suggested that the Reverend Cormell Jephson was paying your fee and expenses for undertaking the defence of Solomon Solomons?'

'My impression would be – if you were to make such a hypothetical suggestion – that you had lost none of your old powers of observation and deduction!'

20

I could now scarcely doubt, after Zeinvel's veiled admission that the clergyman was paying for Solomons' defence, that Jephson was directly involved in the case. I could well understand a well-off clergyman's rendering such a service out of disinterested Christian charity, but then to put on a pretence that one scarcely remembered one's protégé's name! And with what indifference – nay, hostility – Jephson had received my mission of aid for Solomons. I stepped out the short distance to Mark Lane station with renewed vigour: I had some letters to return to Soho.

I was received by the Reverend Cormell Jephson himself at the Working Girls' Club, and it seemed that his manner towards me was a degree or two above the near-freezing point he had shown at our initial encounter on the previous day. He led me into his parlour, where Mrs Jephson was busy with some needlework, and, after I had paid my respects to her, Jephson took back his son's letters without comment, though his lady nodded and smiled sadly at me with evident relief as I thanked them both for their favour. The wiry, red-haired man with the fierce blue eyes behind the gold-rimmed spectacles seemed to study me for a moment, then the ghost of a smile flitted across his care-marked face.

'Dr Mortimer, I confess I was more than a little put out by your rather cavalier intrusion into our most intimate family affairs, but I have had time to consider the matter in the round, and I see now that your motives are of the most praiseworthy. I understand also that, with you and your good wife's mission in Whitechapel, you are a fellow labourer in our vineyard, so to speak. Pax, then?'

'Pax it is, sir, with all my heart!' I exclaimed, taking and wringing the proffered hand, which was hot and dry. The returning grip was of steel.

The cleric tugged his watch from his waistcoat pocket and consulted it.

'Ah! It seems I have an hour in hand: would you care to see some of the workings of the club, doctor?'

I must confess that nothing could have been further from my intentions, but, keen to go along with the reverend gentleman's more cordial attitude, I eagerly assented to the suggestion.

'Capital! Please come along, then.'

I exchanged nods with Mrs Jephson, and was led out briskly by her husband into the public corridors of the building.

'Pray understand that this is a club, Dr Mortimer, not just an institution, a word I have not much time for: so redolent of Calvinism, I always feel, besides that taint of the workhouse – pah! We shall begin with the workrooms, I think – the girls' accommodation is Lettice's province.'

With his characteristic jerky dynamism, Jephson positively whirled me through the excellent establishment, which contained most conceivable facilities for the friendless young girl who might find herself under the necessity of earning her living in the capital. The club was open every evening, and there were classes in a generous array of useful and improving subjects, including needlework, gymnastics and mathematics, added to which were the use of a library, penny savings bank and medical dispensary at costs tailored to the modest means of the club-members. The dispensary of course was of particular interest to me, and Jephson and I spent a good twenty minutes comparing its equipment, stock and *modus operandi* with those of our at present humbler medical outpost in Whitechapel. My host's cares were clearly forgotten – or at least banished from his conscious mind – for the moment as he expatiated enthusiastically on his subject, but disquiet still lurked in his eyes.

'Splendid!' I remarked, as we moved towards what was to prove the sewing-room. 'And you say you also provide accommodation?'

'Yes Dr Mortimer, both in the short- and the long-term. Here, for between three shillings and seven-and-sixpence a week, a girl may enjoy the comforts of a quiet, decent dormitory or a single room, according to means and inclination, clean bedlinen, gas-fires and a cheerful sitting-room.'

I reflected that, in comparison with the five shillings a week a poor artisan in the East End might have to lay out in rent for the vilest room imaginable – strictly no facilities included – in order to house himself, a wife and family, this was munificence indeed.

The sewing-room was deserted at that hour, but it was cosily and cheerfully appointed, with those brave little touches humorous posters on the walls, droll rag dolls and mascots perched in the most incongruous places – inseparable from venturesome youth. I was particularly amused by the improvised needle-cases in the common workbasket which occupied the centre of one of the tables: old pencil cases, lipsalve dispensers, and even a spent cartridge-case or two. A fit training-ground for the future mothers of England.

I could tell the purpose of the last workroom before Jephson had even opened the door, for the characteristic metallic tapping betokened the typewriting machine.

'Those of our girls who enjoy free Saturday afternoons avail themselves with increasing frequency of this class, doctor,' Jephson explained as he rapped on the door and invited me to pop my head inside. 'Typewriting is a very taking profession nowadays – let us not detain them.'

I looked into the room, to behold four misses with aprons over their dresses, sitting straight-backed at tall work-tables, their mutton-chop sleeved arms moving up and down in rhythm over the keys of Remingtons of the latest design, to the stentorian tones of a familiar voice.

'Do not think – strike! Thinking is for those who do not know *how*!'

I glanced in the direction of the voice, to behold Miss Vulliamy, standing with her hands clasped in front of her, surveying her pupils with the air of a drill-sergeant. I smiled in her direction, and she gave me the briefest of nods, then, withdrawing my head, I closed the door and rejoined Jephson in the corridor.

'I see Miss Vulliamy makes her contribution to your excellent work,' I said, as we regained the Jephsons' little private parlour.

'She is invaluable to us, Dr Mortimer, and I see no reason why she should not join us here as a full colleague, but she is such an independent young woman. How many times have we invited her to join us, Lettice?'

'Judith is her own woman in all things, Cor dear: you must have learned that by now. I hope Hector's letters were of some

167

help to you, Dr Mortimer, but as you will have read from them, all very harmless . . .'

'Yes, all . . .' I muttered, half to myself. 'That is what I was wondering . . .'

'Hm, what were you wondering, doctor?' the red-haired man asked in his jerky, awkward way, his eyes averted from mine as he fussed with the cushions of an armchair.

'Whether, perhaps there were more letters . . .'

Mrs Jephson increased the speed of her sewing, and fixed her gaze firmly on her work. One could have cut the atmosphere with a knife.

'More letters, Dr Mortimer?' Cormell Jephson said briskly, as he jerked to his feet again. 'You have seen all the letters in our possession my son wrote to us from Germany. And now, if you will forgive me . . .'

The clergyman pulled out his watch again, and I rose to my feet.

'My thanks again to you both,' I said, dismissing with a smile and a raised hand my host's attempt to accompany me to the door. 'And may I congratulate you on the splendid work you are doing here. You may be sure I shall be carrying home food for discussion concerning our parallel efforts in Whitechapel.'

The latter compliment won me a little bow and another wintry ghost of a smile from Jephson.

'Rest assured, doctor, that as to that, you and your good lady will always find willing advisers here – hey, Lettice, my dear?'

A shy little smile and a nod from the lady, and I took up my hat, cane and gloves, and left, to be assailed by mental self-interrogation as soon as I had closed the parlour door behind me. 'All the letters in their possession' sounded like a Jesuitical cavil to me, worthy even of friend Zeinvel! I felt like the student in Omar Khayyam, who 'evermore came out, by the same door as in I went.'

The time for evening surgery came round quickly enough, and after an unremarkable stint at the dispensary, we slept that Saturday night on no more substantial fare than a vague suspicion over Cormell Jephson's seeming evasiveness about the possible existence of more of his son Hector's German letters. By the following morning, we found ourselves becalmed as far as developments in the Poland Street case went, and we dulled our nagging, ever-present anxiety over the speed with which the sands were running out for Solomon Solomons by throwing ourselves, heart and soul, into our medical duties at the dispensary.

After the last patient had left, and the last bottle had been despatched, we took luncheon at Cohen's, somehow not mentioning the thing that must have been uppermost in my wife's mind as it was in mine. I think we were both ashamed that we had made so little progress in the case over the weekend.

After the meal was over, Violet had to leave for Paddington, where she was engaged to shepherd a pair of elderly West Country aunts from the station to their private hotel in Bayswater, and there spend the rest of the afternoon with them. I decided to spend the time in retracing the steps of Solomons and Klaff, from Wentworth Street to the Lord Raglan public house in Limehouse, and thence back to Dorset Street, where Solomons had been arrested. The bright promise of the morning had given way to scudding clouds and showers of sleet, and the squalid desperation of the scene as, dressed in the shabby country togs I kept in the dispensary for such excursions, I made my way down the Commercial Road, seemed to send my spirits down a degree lower with each step.

How many hopeless eyes had I to evade, as I passed the common passages of slums and sweating-dens, behind which the relentless thump of boot-making machines and the clatter of hammers announced one of the characteristic trades of the district. Well might these denizens snatch a minute or two for themselves out of their twelve-, fourteen- or sixteen-hour working-days in order to seek the comparatively fresh air of the streets, if the effluvia which emerged from the passages were accurate tokens of the sickening miasma within. I began to formulate new Factory and Sanitation Acts in the legislature of my imagination, when my sombre musings were abruptly broken by a rush from the opening of Union Street.

There were at least six of them, clad in fantastic rags, some in pointed caps, others with rats' noses and whiskers, and all with coloured chalk and crayon smeared on their faces in parodies of tribal warpaint. They swarmed round me, gesticulating wildly and jabbering in a gibberish incomprehensible to me. I clutched at my trusty old briar stick, and just then one of the imps thrust his hand under my nose in the age-old gesture.

'Give us a penny, mister!'

And then I remembered that today was the 1st of March: it would be the feast of Purim. At least there was one spark of joy in this waste of woe, and with a lightened heart, I decided that they should have their penny. I reached into my trousers-pocket and pulled out a handful of small change, which I then flung among the Purim guisers. I chuckled as, with their howls of delight dying away behind me, I resumed my walk down the Commercial Road. The incident reminded me of Mrs Snell's account of her lodger, the missing witness Semyon Klaff's being followed in the street by just such a bunch of urchins, though apparently with less good-natured intent. What was that she had told me they had called after him? Yes: 'our better friend.' Again I reflected on what an odd, lame-sounding thing this expression had seemed. 'Our better friend.' Even allowing for that particular bunch of children's possible deficiency in English, surely they could have managed something more scathing than that. And then I stood still in my tracks. If only we would *listen* when people talk to us! 'Our better friend' – no doubt more like 'ahr better friend' to the landlady's cockney ear – was a near-perfect reproduction of the name of the local weekly radical paper *Arbeter Fraint* – the Worker's Friend. Klaff must have been a distributor of the paper, and it would have been the most natural thing in the world for the children to march in step behind this funny little man on his rounds, parroting his cry of '*Arbeter Fraint! Arbeter Fraint!*' I further reflected that the fountainhead of the paper, the International Workers' Educational Club, was in Berner Street, a narrow slum not five minutes' walk from where I was. One could trace the wall fly-sheets advertising the paper there, as in a paper-chase. I shook my stick up half-mast in my hand, and hurried down the road, speculating further as I went.

Would it have been beyond the bounds of possibility that Solomons and Klaff on the fatal night in November had stopped off at the Berner Street Club, that hotbed of immigrant radicalism, in their progress to Limehouse? To see whom?

I ducked into Berner Street, and soon found the entrance to the club, where an event must have been in progress, judging by the other ill-dressed nondescripts who crowded the narrow stairs leading up to the hall. A public event, too, for no-one seemed to be officiating at the foot of the stairs. The hall was packed to capacity, and I took up position quietly at the side of the door, so as not to obscure the view from the crowded narrow wooden benches which occupied the walls as well as the floor of the hall. There must have been a hundred and fifty or more persons crammed into this modest space. I faced a bare deal table before the far wall, above which hung a large framed portrait of Karl Marx. There were also political caricatures of various figures of reaction. Four men sat at the table, one of whom was in the process of rising to introduce a third, and a hushed silence fell on the crowd. I glanced around at the dark, eager faces, among which those of women and girls made a not insignificant number. No one chattered, no one smoked or giggled. The speaker, a squat, bullet-headed man in an ill-fitting tweed suit, launched into an exalted tirade in a German I could not follow, while the audience hung on his words. I found to my dismay that the excitement of the crowd was communicating itself to me. Did these intelligent faces, with their earnest, yearning expressions, really belong to the bloodthirsty red rabble portrayed by the popular press? At length the speech ended, and the audience rose as one and began singing a spirited anthem, to which I could only contribute a sort of hummed gibberish. The crowd dispersed immediately after the anthem, none going up to the table on its raised dais, so I turned and descended the stairs with the first eagerly chattering wave. The affair had been public – no membership-cards demanded – but there was an opportunity to contribute to the cause at the foot of the stairs, where a man in a long-visored cap, its peak pulled conspiratorially over one eye, was selling copies of a paper to the departing comrades. I reached anxiously into my pocket, hoping that I had not given quite all of my loose change to the Purim guisers earlier on, and was relieved to come up with a threepenny piece. Soon I was close enough to the paper-seller to be able to make out the bold Hebrew lettering atop the front page of the paper he was selling: it read the *Arbeter Fraint*. The man in front of me exchanged a few words with the man in the cap, and he glanced up briefly in replying. In that moment I was able to see that the eye that had been largely covered by the peak of his cap was dead – a uniform white – the effect, I mused, that might result from the sort of occupational injury associated with the stonemason's trade.

An instant later, it was my turn to contribute my threepenny piece, and take my copy of the *Worker's Friend*, which I did as quickly and unobtrusively as possible, taking care that my eyes should not meet those of the paper-seller. Having entered the street again, I went straight back the way I had come, without looking back, for, if my surmise as to the identity of the paper-seller was correct, the last thing I wanted to do was to arouse his suspicion. I made for the People's Dispensary, which was now closed, as there was no evening surgery on Sundays, and, letting myself in, I went into the pharmacy and busied myself with a receipt never before prescribed for any patient. The prescription having been made up into several ampoules, I left the pharmacy, locked up the building, then went into the court in search of Charlie Noble, one of the less reputable of our allies among the local street urchins, and who had rendered us sterling service in the Aldgate affair. Charlie's harassed mother informed me that he had 'gone to see the sword-swallower', which entailed a long eastwards tramp to Poplar High Street, but there, right in front of the little crowd I saw round the toothless performer, was Charlie, barefoot and clad in his cricket cap and outsize fisherman's guernsey. He was clearly enraptured by the frankly disgusting nature of the performance, and was revolving ecstatically in his mouth the filthy old pipebowl and inch or so of stem which he habitually carried there.

'You have seen me swallow swords!' barked the toothless showman. 'You have seen me swallow fire! Now you shall see me swallow sawdust!'

I waited till the sorry performance was over, then approached Charlie, who greeted me with his usual impassive indifference, not deigning even to spit out the pipebowl in my honour.

'What's the job, then?' he muttered, his bright little blue eyes shining slyly up at me from the wizened, dirty face.

I explained my requirements, and as I went on Charlie grinned one of his rare satanic grins: this was clearly work to his taste.

'Yer on!' he said, taking out the pipebowl and jabbing the stump of stem in my general direction, whereupon I handed him the ampoules, with an injunction not on any account to drop them, along with an earnest of wages, and he ran off, his little bandy legs flailing. I allowed myself a brief smile of satisfaction, then addressed the weary task of finding a cab in those eastern wastes, to take me back to Henrietta Street and the comfort of a late tea.

I found Violet at home, she having conducted her aunts safely to Bayswater, where she had already had tea. I told her of my revelation in the Berner Street Club, and she was all ears.

'Diamant's profession was indeed given as that of a stone-mason,' she said, 'and a stonemason might well lose an eye in the course of his trade, but it is a long shot.'

'Shortened considerably when one reflects how unlikely it would be for both of the escapees from the Odessa murder trial to live hardly three streets from each other in London and be unaware each of the other's existence there. Where more naturally, too, would Solomons and Klaff have stopped on their way to Limehouse on the night of Ostyankin's murder than at the International Workers' Educational Club, as it would have been directly on their route? It is surely inconceivable that Mark Diamant should have known nothing of the Ostyankin affair at that time.'

'But James, do you not see where this is leading? If it can be demonstrated that the very two men who had previously tried to kill the general in Russia had put their heads together in the East End on the night when he was murdered in Soho, you will only be helping to tighten the noose round Solomons' neck as a potential accomplice and accessory!'

'Yes, I see that, Violet, but we must go where the facts lead us: we can do no other.'

'And how amid the teeming streets of the East End will you find out the lair of this one-eyed, paper-selling revolutionary – how keep a watch on him? – when you have no idea where he lives, except that he occasionally plies his wares in Berner Street?'

I smiled a mysterious smile, and Violet listened aghast as I explained my purpose. 'As a patriotic Englishman, I have decided it is my bounden duty to instigate a bomb-attack on the International Workers' Educational Club!'

173

21

Next morning – the Monday of the advertised evening rendez-vous at Nevill's Turkish Baths – I helped out at the Whitechapel Dispensary until Charlie Noble reported there on the success of the mission with which I had entrusted him on the previous afternoon. It was with some excitement, then, that, shortly after the last patient had left at about ten past twelve, we heard the flip-flop of Charlie's bare feet on the linoleum of the stairs. He rapped on the inner door of the consulting-room, and Violet called him inside.

I dragged a chair up to our ragged young visitor, and, revers-ing and mounting it like a saddle, with the back as an armrest, began my interrogation.

'Well, how did it go, Charlie?'

The urchin pulled the eternal pipebowl from his mouth, and, pocketing it, began a droning monologue.

'We went rahnd ter Berner Street as soon as it was light, then we started up wiv va dustbin lids – good an' lahd! – then after a minute or so this geezer shove 'is 'ead aht of one of va upstairs winders, an' started yellin' at us in foreign, then we started up wiv "Gawd Save Va Queen", an' frew pebbles up at va winders that wasn't open. Another geezer opened va third winder along, then we chuck up va stink-bombs frew both va open winders, then up came va third winder, and another geezer – talk abaht Ally Sloper! – leant aht and emptied a po on us. Phew! I let 'im 'ave it then wiv me last bomb, and just then I 'appen ter see another man peep aht of the first winder. One of 'is eyes was all white, like a putty marble . . .'

'You're sure about the eye, Charlie?' I asked urgently.

''E wasn't there long, but I see the eye all right.'

'What happened next?' I asked.

'Well, by then, they was comin' aht o' va front door – not 'im wiv va eye, though – an' one of 'em caught Seppie Frame wiv a belt buckle, an' I got a lump o'coal on me napper – good job me rap's a thick 'un! – so we 'ad ter 'ook it pretty quick, and that's abaht it.'

I handed Charlie enough sixpences to go round his intrepid band, and, scorning Violet's offer of medical assistance for the wounded, he scampered out of the room and downstairs again.

'Diamant does live above the Berner Street Club!' I said, exulting. 'We have him! And mark what Charlie said about his only taking the merest glimpse out of the window, and not coming out after the boys with the other residents: he clearly doesn't wish to be observed.'

'If it is Diamant,' Violet remarked, 'and as to his lying low, if I were a man with only one working eye, I certainly wouldn't be too keen to rush out into a fracas where stink-bombs, pebbles and lumps of coal were being thrown about.'

'Nevertheless, I feel it in my bones that it is he.'

'Then what do you intend to do about it? Go to the police?'

'No – not in the first instance. Diamant is too valuable a cartridge to discharge without one's first finding a prime target. I shall seek Zeinvel's advice.'

We took a sandwich lunch, and, after we had agreed to meet for tea in Henrietta Street, Violet went to visit a patient and I to Crutched Friars and Zeinvel's chambers, where I brought him up to date as to developments from my side of the case.

'And is what I have been telling you about the establishment in Soho new to you, Mr Zeinvel?' was my concluding remark.

The long, narrow face of the young lawyer lit up in a smile of understanding, and he nodded.

'What you have just told me explains a number of things,' he commented.

So Cormell Jephson, who by Zeinvel's previous tacit admission was paying Solomons' legal fees, had told him nothing; no doubt had merely posed as a philanthropist without any axe to grind, anxious to help a friendless young foreigner caught in the toils of the law. Now Zeinvel knew.

'And Diamant?' I asked.

'Interesting and valuable information, if it is Diamant, but again corroboration shakes its hoary locks at us, doctor: the police would certainly like to lay hands on him, if only to arrange his immediate deportation, but as to the case in hand,

175

they would see any move by us in his direction as a tired attempt to drag up yet another rogue of an alien revolutionary to give a peck of uncorroborated – and therefore worthless – evidence. And even if they didn't deport him on the spot, he'd certainly skedaddle before they could get anything on him. As he also would if they raided the Berner Street Club – police raids are usually nets with very large holes. Then we lose our man. No, Dr Mortimer, I think we should hold Diamant in reserve for the moment: I've means of my own of keeping a fairly comprehensive watch on him, now that you've warned me.'

'But don't you think the police would at least like to know more of the case from him? For their records, if nothing else.'

Zeinvel spread out his hands on the desk in front of him.

'Why should they? As far as they are concerned, they have their man – Solomons – and that is the end of the matter.'

'Which brings us to the appeal on Wednesday . . .'

Zeinvel looked graver than usual, and his eyes seemed to evade mine.

'Yes, doctor, the appeal. You know that what we have been looking for above all has been reliable corroboration from other alibi-witnesses, and with Klaff apparently vanished into thin air . . .'

'And PC Kennedy transferred to the sticks . . .'

'Yes, a most, er . . . unsatisfactory development. Well, I'm now hoping that the cumulative effect of such new evidence as you have brought me today, along with some fresh turn of events, may yet swing things our way. I'm still actively pursuing a number of lines of my own, and I hope you will carry on with the excellent work you are doing. Please don't hesitate to call on me at any hour of the day or night, if you think I may be of any assistance.'

A nervous handshake from Zeinvel's long, wiry hand, and I made my way down the crazy stairs into Crutched Friars again. Never before had I heard such a tone of resignation, nay, defeat, in the voice of my learned friend, whose main characteristic up to then had seemed to be a chirpy, dauntless optimism. It was pretty clear, too, what he had been trying to say to me: without new witnesses or a spectacular last-minute turn of events, the game was up. The ball at any rate was in my court, and I felt a great psychological weight descend upon my shoulders.

My next appointment was the retiring-room of St James's station, from which I emerged – briefly, I hoped – as the Reverend Mr Flockhart, in order that I might announce my presence again at Brown's Hotel, and pick up any messages that may have arrived from Barin Street, or, if my disguise had been penetrated, perhaps from elsewhere. To tell the truth, I was more than half-hoping that it would be penetrated, for the irksome charade had long since palled on me, though I remained as convinced as ever that it was necessary if I was to keep my credit with Alexander Miller as a harmless crank. For one thing, I had not the slightest doubt that, one way or another, he must by now have checked on whether I was registered at the hotel under my clerical pseudonym.

There were no messages waiting for me in Albemarle Street, and so, just for the sake of appearances, I went up to 'my' room, and, flinging myself on top of the unused bed, smoked a couple of cheroots while I read *The Times*. The tension and anxieties of the previous days, with their concomitant of wakeful nights, had evidently taken their toll on me, for to my dismay the next thing I recalled was coming to my waking senses amid semi-darkness. I leapt to my feet, and, fumbling for my vesta-box, struck a match and lit the bedside candle, by the light of which I was able to read the time on my watch. Ten past five! Tea with Violet would be out of the question now, as she would already have begun evening surgery in Whitechapel: would there be time for me to go to Henrietta Street and leave my little bag – the *vade mecum* of my two identities – before attending with reasonable time-in-hand at Nevill's Turkish Baths in Charing Cross for my seven o'clock tryst with the unknown?

I hurried over to the wall and turned up the gaslights, then tidied myself up – my hair was standing up like Struwwelpeter's – before the dressing-table looking-glass. By now it was twenty past five – no, if I was to have time to get the lie of the land, I should have to leave directly for Charing Cross, where I would change in the station, before emerging as James Mortimer, then, by some circuitous route, come round to the Turkish baths.

My haste turned out to be fully justified, for by the time I had carried out my emergency plan, it was already twenty to seven, when, my silly little bag – with my umbrella slung along the top – in hand, I crossed into Craven Street from Adelaide Street to the north. I made my way down to Craven Passage, through which I passed to Northumberland Street and the gentlemen's entrance of Nevill's Turkish Baths. Here I paced up and down like a guard on sentry-go, occasionally looking at my watch, and clucking my tongue impatiently against my palate for the benefit of any curious passer-by, after the fashion of one who impatiently awaits a vis-à-vis.

Seven came and went, during which time I recognised no face or demeanour among those who were trooping in for the evening session. I decided it was time to use my *pièce de résistance*, so, squaring my shoulders, I went into the baths and handed my coat and outside things to an attendant, receiving in return a numbered counter in mock-ivory. A florin then bought me the hire of a set of towels and the run of the place till nine the next morning, should I choose to pass the night amid the steamy luxury.

I was directed to the cubicles, where I undressed, and, girding my loins with a towel, emerged into the steam-bath, where I lounged in a seat, with my arm draped casually over my knee, but within sight of any fellow sybarite. It was important to my plan that this arm should be visible, for I had that morning painted on it a most artistic representation of the Three Legs of Man, in three colours of an indelible ink which Woolf the stationer in New Goulston Street had assured me was renowned for its fast dyeing qualities. If anyone did come in response to my advertisement in search of the late Desmond Coe's main distinguishing mark, they should not lack this means of identifying me. I sat in this fashion for what must have been a full hour, then, hope waning, made my way to the plunge, which to my relief the indelible ink survived, but another half-hour in the tepidarium drew no more attention to my splendid false tattoo than had my hour in the steam-room. At last, I repaired to the drying-room, then, finally, to my cubicle, where I dressed and made for the attendant in the front of the baths. I handed over my numbered disc, and the attendant brought round my ulster and outside things, which he helped me to put on, after which I tipped him and stepped out, shivering, into a chilly, damp Northumberland Street.

I looked rather disconsolately around me, while I considered my next move. The Turkish baths, then, had proved to be a mare's nest, but nothing ventured, nothing gained. I neared the mouth of Craven Passage, and was intrigued to see female figures emerging from a door near the farther end. I stopped, and peered into the near-obscurity of the passage, which was lit by a single exiguous gaslamp affixed to the wall over the door. Respectably dressed females they were, and not dawdling in the mission, whatever it was. There was a window set just above my reach, further up the passage. I paused and waited till the coast seemed clear, then strode up to the foot of the window, and, laying down my case and umbrella on the ground, gave myself a lift up by means of the slightly jutting foundation course, and hauled myself up level with the bottom of the window. A dim light came from within, and I was further intrigued by the sound of female laughter. I stretched myself further upwards and forwards, in order to get a better view, when I felt rough arms entwine my legs, and I was dragged down abruptly to the ground.

22

'Right, my lad,' said the voice behind me, a hand gripping my wrist firmly as I scrambled to my feet. 'You'd better come along with me.'

I found myself staring up into the face of a burly constable.

'I assure you, officer,' I stammered, 'I meant no harm. I was merely . . .'

'Yerss?'

On reflection, it was a sticky situation: how did one put a favourable gloss on one's being caught scrambling up a window-ledge in a dark passage?

'Er, I merely wanted to see which building the window belonged to.'

'As if you didn't know it was the ladies' end of the Turkish baths! There's been too much of this sort of thing going on, lately – the complaints we've had . . .'

'Hullo, what's all this, then?'

The constable had been joined by his colleague on the beat.

'Peeping Tom, George, you'd better have a dekko in his bag.'

The other policeman lifted up my bag from the ground, and, opening it, rummaged among my things. He picked out the clerical collar, and, lifting it level with my eyes, rolled it round his forefinger like a hoop, with a quizzical look on his face.

'I, er . . . I'm not really a clergyman . . .' I stammered.

'Get away! I took you for the Archbishop of Canterbury . . .'

I was led away, feebly protesting, between both of them. My humiliation was complete as they led me into the glaring gaslight of Charing Cross and into the presence of the desk sergeant in the police station.

'I am engaged in investigations of a highly confidential nature, sergeant,' I began to protest.

'Oh, I see – a CID man, hey? What division are you attached to? Colney Hatch? I'll have your name, if it ain't too confidential, that is . . .'

'My name is James Mortimer, and, and . . .'

I had an idea.

'Sergeant, will you allow me to send a note to Leman Street police station by cab? Inspector Moultry or Sergeant Wensley will vouch for me.'

The sergeant put down his pen and looked at me with a new seriousness in his expression, and the two arresting officers exchanged uneasy glances.

'All right,' the sergeant said at length. 'You'll have to pay for the cab, then – both ways.'

'Yes, yes, only please do it.'

I kicked my heels in the ante-room for a good hour and a half, with one of the officers in close attendance, until the sergeant came in, accompanied by my old acquaintance, Detective Sergeant Wensley. The latter glanced at me, then nodded brusquely at the desk officer.

'All right, I'll look after this . . .'

I could not help but be struck by the cocky self-confidence, typical of the man, with which Wensley thus dismissed a colleague equal to him in rank and superior in seniority by at least twenty years. Frederick Wensley was very much a young man in a hurry.

'Well, if it isn't Dr Mortimer!' he said with his usual half-sneer. 'Been up to no good at the ladies' Turkish baths, I hear: you've really landed yourself in queer street this time.'

'Thank God you're here, Wensley – a ridiculous misunderstanding. If you'll just tell them to give me back my things, and . . .'

'Not so fast, doctor. First I'd like to know just what it's all about: little birdie tells me that you've been making yourself busy in certain quarters of the East End recently. I hope you haven't been getting yourself out of your depth. Haven't I warned you before not to believe everything you're told . . .'

I felt sure the 'little birdie' could only be PC Kennedy, now in unknown parts, or perhaps one of Wensley's informers among the clientele of the Warsaw Café. The crucial thing, though, was how much the detective sergeant knew. I must tell him something, in order to regain my liberty, as even a day lost in the quest for the real murderer of General Ostyankin might cost

Solomon Solomons his life. I must get out of this, before farce turned into nightmare.

'I am in search of the real murderer of General Ostyankin, sergeant.'

'Oh, that it, is it? Putting in a spot of sleuthing, are we? No doubt in cahoots with Zeinvel, hey? You're getting into bad company, doctor. Take my tip, Dr Mortimer, the "real" murderer of the Russian general's at present in the condemned cell at Wormwood Scrubs, and no amount of shinning up windows'll change that. Why the Turkish baths, anyway?'

I explained about Desmond Coe, and the impression of the 'Warwick' message on the notepad he'd left in his rooms in Porteous Place.

'So you are in this with Zeinvel: I suppose you'll be the "reliable informant" he told us about when he reported the business about Coe. Well, he's not much use to you now as a witness – he's pushing up daisies in Belgium. Too many disappearing witnesses in this case for my liking. For my money, it's a true bill against Solomons – no doubt about that – but I'd have preferred a bit more in the way of evidence. Still, that's out of our hands now.'

I recalled the rather bizarre circumstances of Coe's sudden departure from his Paddington lodgings later on the day of Ostyankin's murder, and decided to try to mine some of the ore of Sergeant Wensley's near-photographic memory.

'Sergeant, when you received the report from Belgium of the discovery of Coe's body, did they send you an inventory of his possessions?'

'Yes, of course they did – routine procedure. Why?'

'Do you remember offhand how many overcoats he was found with?'

'Only one, I think: that was the one he had on when they fished him out of the dock. Inverness cape, I seem to remember: Belgians described it as a "raglan".'

Neither of those garments, I thought, would have remotely fitted Coe's landlady's description of his spare overcoat as a 'baggy black affair'.

'And did they trace the rest of his possessions?'

'Yes, to a little hotel near the docks: there was only a small Gladstone bag.'

'What about a stick?'

'They didn't mention anything about a stick, unless it's still floating about the dock over there. What's so special about Coe's coat and stick, anyway?'

'Oh, just a thought: a man's possessions can tell a lot about his personality and likely actions, sergeant.'

Wensley let out a snort of laughter.

'Taking a leaf out of Sherlock Holmes' book, are we, doctor? Trying his so-called "method", hey? Take my tip: that hare won't run! Fact is, Solomons was pretty well caught in the act, he's had his trial, and he's for the drop. There's nothing you can do about that, and if you're still het up about it, why not leave it to your learned friend, Zeinvel? For one thing, he's getting paid for it. Now why don't you call it a day, and cut along home to your missus?'

'Of course, sergeant, and thank you.'

'Oh, and I may add that if you make a habit of getting into these scrapes, I mightn't always be able to see my way to getting you out of them: good job I happened to be still in the station when your note came this evening.'

A good job, indeed, I reflected, as, thoroughly chastened, and clutching my reclaimed bag and umbrella, I was escorted out of the building by Wensley. But then, why had Desmond Coe burnt his walking-stick before dashing off on that fatal Friday in November, and why, having left behind half a dozen suits in his diggings, had he chosen to stuff an extra overcoat into a week-end bag? And why had he been found with only one overcoat in Antwerp?

My ponderings faded as the dire necessity of returning to my hotel began to reassert itself, and then respite came when I remembered Hector Jephson's professional colleague, Coram, whose name had cropped up several times in the unfortunate young man's German letters to his parents. I would step out to Pall Mall, then, and the Reform Club, to see what I should see.

Being decently turned out, I experienced no difficulty in getting past the doorman of the Temple of Liberalism, and, on handing my card to a flunkey in the outer lobby, was rewarded a couple of minutes later, when the man returned, and told me that if I cared to follow him to one of the sitting-rooms, Mr Coram would see me.

Edward Coram turned out to be a fresh-faced, black-haired young man just on the sunny side of thirty. Evidently, my visit had coincided with one of his home postings. He rose to greet me, and bade me take a leather-bound easy chair next to his while he ordered the flunkey who had accompanied me to bring us brandies and soda. While I introduced myself as a friend of the Jephsons and told him the history of his unfortunate friend since the German episode, his brow darkened, and he shook his head from time to time.

'I've been meaning to look them all up again,' Ned Coram remarked, 'and I must sincerely thank you for sparing me an even greater shock if I had simply turned up on their doorstep unawares. I had thought Jephson's resignation to have been purely on health grounds, though, and as for the, er . . . other, I should have thought he'd have been the very last one to succumb . . .'

'Oh, why is that, Mr Coram?'

The diplomatist chuckled as we were served our drinks.

'Why, you never saw such a pious, demure fellow! D'you know he used to kneel and say his prayers every night, before turning in, at Brasenose? We used to think it too rich for words! Reflection on us, I suppose, but there you are. And as for dissipation, well . . . Jephson! Absurd! I am truly sorry to hear of all this, Dr Mortimer: if there is anything I can do – the nursing home, perhaps . . .'

'No, no, Mr Coram, that is all in order, I assure you – young Jephson's people have that all in hand.'

Coram's eyes seemed to light up.

'And wasn't there a fiancée in the background?'

'Miss Judith Vulliamy?'

'That's the lady! Very formidable – she should surely have kept him on the straight and narrow.'

'You wouldn't have met her in person, I suppose, she being in Hamburg and you and Jephson in Berlin?'

'On the contrary, doctor, I met them both frequently in Berlin; in fact, how he got away from her long enough to er, go astray is beyond me. A young lady of the most impeccable character and professed principles . . .'

184

She was all of that, I had no doubt, but this was not what she had led me to believe when she had painted a picture to me of her Hector, out of her reach in Berlin, being led to his ruin by Miller and his raffish cosmopolitan friends. Where was I being led in all this?

'Ah,' I said, 'I must be mistaken, then. I believe young Jephson had a wide circle of acquaintance in Berlin . . .'

Coram's eyes narrowed, and I had to remind myself that I was after all dealing with a professional diplomatist . . .

'We all tend to do so in our profession, doctor,' the young man said coolly. 'It's what we're for, don't you know . . .'

I sensed that I would get no further on this tack, so I rose, and, thanking Coram for his hospitality, caught the eye of the flunkey, who led me back through the august portals of the club. He presented me with my outdoor things and case, and I stepped meditatively into Pall Mall again. So Judith Vulliamy's story, it would seem, like that of her putative father-in-law, did not quite hold water. I still had to penetrate the true state of things in Soho Square: were shared misfortune and grief the true bonds that held them all together, or were the wells of sorrow defiled by more tainted undercurrents?

As it happened, I did not have long to wait for news of developments in that quarter, for, after an unproductive night in my room at Brown's Hotel, followed by a tensely humdrum Tuesday morning at the Whitechapel Dispensary *in propria persona*, it became evident that Ned Coram had carried out his vow to pay a call on the Soho Square establishment, for our very last 'patient' was Lettice Jephson.

She was clearly agitated as Violet showed her into the consulting-room and sat her in the patients' chair. I took my place at the window which faced Violet's chair, leaning against the sill.

'It is to you, Dr Mortimer, that I have come to make a most urgent request . . .'

'Yes, ma'am? I am entirely at your service.'

'Then you will henceforth desist from making any more enquiries about my poor son, and confine yourself to those who may be concerned in the dreadful business which you are investigating. You can have no conception of the suffering these probings and questions are causing my husband and myself, and

185

especially my husband. Why, Cor is at the end of his tether, and he is not a well man . . .'

'But you seemed at our last meeting in Soho to favour my enquiries, Mrs Jephson; or at least the end to which they are directed.'

'Yes, doctor, no decent person could deny what aid was in their power to help this wretch you are championing, but Hector cannot be of any conceivable help to you: if you could see him now . . .'

'There can be no question of my wishing to quiz your son personally, Mrs Jephson. I am a medical man, and I have seen him; it is rather certain events in his past which touch on the matter I have in hand . . .'

The little stout face with its rather long nose blenched, and Mrs Jephson's jaw dropped slightly.

'Hector's past, Dr Mortimer? What of his past? He was a young man of the brightest promise, but of little experience, whose life was blighted by the machinations of lewd and wicked men. That is all my son's "past", as you put it.'

'I am not suggesting that Hector Jephson's antecedents conceal anything underhand or criminal, Mrs Jephson, and pray do not think that I am making him the centre of my enquiries – no question of that, I assure you – but his life has touched on those of others who may be directly implicated in the affairs I am looking into. Miss Vulliamy, for instance: I am now given to understand that she did after all see your son while he was *en poste* in Berlin five years ago, and see him there rather frequently . . .'

'As for that,' the little lady in the black bonnet positively snapped, 'you must ask Judith herself: I am sure she will give you your answer!'

'I hope I have sufficiently explained, Mrs Jephson, I am merely . . .'

The little rotund figure in black leapt to her feet, and clasped her bag and umbrella to her bombazine bosom.

'I know, I know, doctor! I know what you *think* you are doing, but I tell you things are not what you think they are, and that if you persist in your present direction you will spark off a tragedy – oh, Lord, how long must I be punished? How long? I can bear no more!'

At this point the little woman swayed and finally fell back against the chair, scattering it across the room. Violet got up from her chair, and, briefly rummaging in the table-drawer, drew out a small bottle and rushed over to Mrs Jephson, whom I was raising to a sitting position on the floor. My wife administered the sal volatile, while I loosened the overwrought lady's stays.

'We must do something to reassure her, James: with her build, this sort of agitation . . .'

'Yes, I see that. Ah! She is coming round . . .'

I set the chair upright again, and we lifted the lady gently and replaced her in its seat.

'There, there, now, Mrs Jephson,' I said, 'this will not do, you know. Now what do you say to my not asking another question of anybody about your son?'

'Oh, do you promise, doctor?'

I exchanged glances with Violet, then promised, whereupon Mrs Jephson suddenly leant forward and grasped my hand in both of hers. She locked glances with me, and it seemed as if her eyes were boring into my soul.

'And I absolutely guarantee, doctor,' she said in a sort of vehement whisper, 'that Hector's plight is totally and completely immaterial to your enquiries, and that, whatever the outcome, you will see that it is so! And now I must go.'

I saw the lady down into her cab, and, returning to the consulting-room, discussed Mrs Jephson's visit with Violet.

'Mrs Jephson certainly gives the appearance of not knowing anything about the murder of Ostyankin,' Violet remarked, 'and as for Miller and he, and what they're supposed to have done to young Jephson, all her desire seems to be for reassurance rather than vengeance. Either she is a rare example of Christian forbearance, or a very odd woman indeed.'

'But why must we ask no more about Hector Jephson's plight or antecedents? And is his father or his fiancée privy to all of this?'

Violet paused, and her expression darkened.

'I think this business is moving towards some sort of crisis, James: I feel it in my bones. It will not be a happy outcome.'

'But we must press on, my dear: Solomons' appeal is to be heard on Wednesday, and God alone knows how much time we shall have after that.'

'Yes, of course, and I was wondering if perhaps news of your debacle at the Turkish baths last night might have reached the Jephsons?'

'Oh, I should hardly think so: how would it have reached them?'

'I don't know, but as for your disguise, I cannot help but recall the old saying that more know Tom Fool than Tom Fool knows . . .'

'Mmm . . . after the show I put on at Nevill's, I certainly won't deny the "fool" bit!'

'I didn't mean that!' Violet remarked, laughing. 'And there's another thing, James . . .'

'Yes?'

'You know how I leave the day-book on the pharmacy bench before we leave every night?'

'Yes, well?'

'This morning it was in its place, closed, but face down. It would not be in my nature to leave it like that. I asked Jane and Freddie the errand-boy if they had looked in it last thing, but both denied having done so.'

'You mean, you think someone's been rummaging about in the pharmacy during the night?'

'It would be quite easy to do so – hanging about the common passage, looking for one's chance – and a reasonably active person could easily edge along to the window along the roof of the outhouse.'

'Have you noticed anything missing? Any damage?'

'No, but I cannot help feeling that with your "Warwick" advertisement, you have nailed our colours to the mast. We must now expect the game to move in our direction.'

'But I have only broached the Warwick matter to Miller, and that in my disguise as the Reverend Flockhart. How could he have traced me here?'

'It is not difficult to follow someone – or to have him followed.'

Something occurred to me.

'It is Lottie's night off tonight, is it not?'

'Yes, but what of it?'

'A diligent, er . . . watcher would have taken note of that fact, would he not?'

'Ah, I think I follow you . . .'

'I think we shall dine out tonight, Violet – or so it will seem – and I suspect our cab will be delayed a little while at the door, before we, er . . . go.'

'A capital idea, James – we shall see what we shall see; and in the meantime, what are your plans for this afternoon?'

'I have been pondering the account of little Emily Chaytor, formerly of Lamb Street, the child left on the doorstep of Randall Moberley the surgeon only hours after the murder of Ostyankin in Poland Street . . .'

'Ah, yes – solemn little thing, with her forensic-seeming bath and blindfolded night-flit across London. The girl who was to be given "toffee directly".'

'Yes, first a foreign-seeming lady, who supervised the bath, took her somewhere, then left her there in the care of someone she didn't see, who the foreign lady talked to outside the room, then, after she'd been taken up to another room in the same building by a "nice" lady . . .'

'Who smelt nice . . .'

'Yes! This fragrant lady locks her in the second room for some time, talks to someone – again whom Emily neither sees nor hears – outside, then, after some time, the nice, sweet-smelling lady comes back, lets Emily out of the room, then ushers her – blindfolded again – out into a cab, and apparently dumps her on Moberley's doorstep in Bayswater.'

'Well, what have you in mind?'

'It seems to me that, barring a pointless charade – a possibility I don't entertain for a moment – there was some sort of changing of the guard in that mysterious house, and, judging by the silence that little Emily encountered throughout her experience, a smooth and efficient one.'

'Go on, James.'

'What if it wasn't a changing of the guard, but a turning of the tables – a palace *coup d'état*?'

'I should say the former, since it was all so quiet and orderly, each apparently playing his or her part without fuss.'

'But the object of the operation?'

'I see – Emily. She was not, er . . . used.'

'Quite: that would be the whole idea if, as I suspect, the house was 11, Poland Street, and Ostyankin lay in lustful anticipation in one of those so-quiet rooms . . .'

'Then,' Violet said thoughtfully, 'what happened to the, er . . . guard that had been forcibly relieved?'

'Quite: unless they were party to the plot, they would have had to be got rid of.'

'Then, James, if the relieving guard at Poland Street did go to such extremes, I suggest we use the rest of the afternoon till evening surgery looking up likely reported deaths around the morning of the 28th of November last.'

'Yes, let us divide the city between us. Our acquaintanceship among the coroner fraternity is already extensive, so let us see where it may lead us.'

So passed the afternoon, but our enquiries in that direction proved fruitless, though I suspected from her rather annoyingly smug expression that Violet had also been following a line of her own. It seemed that a lamentable number of souls had passed over in squalid, mysterious and unexplained circumstances on the 28th of November last, as is always the case in London, but we could find none who might fit our bill concerning the Poland Street affair. Either I had been wrong as to the change of personnel in Emily Chaytor's house of blindfolds and toffee, or there had been some sort of collusion. At any rate, on this occasion we could not find the body, but we were not to be given much leisure to discuss this during our customary chat in the Whitechapel Dispensary after evening surgery, for the footsteps of the last patient had scarcely died on the stairs when, apparently following the lead of his good lady that morning, Cormell Jephson chose the moment to pay us a return visit. There was, however, none of the benign interest of the professional colleague in his reddened eyes, as, spurning our offer of a chair, he confronted us in the consulting-room.

'I had thought you both bigger than this, Doctors Mortimer and Branscombe!'

'Oh,' I said gently, 'we have disappointed you in some way, Mr Jephson?'

'My wife has been here.'

'Yes, and then?'

'Do not think I do not see your game, doctor: you seek to divide my wife from me, you hope by dissimulation to worm

190

your way into my house and seek out our family secrets. And after the confidence I had shown you – letting you read my son's letters . . . I demand to know what she has . . .'

'Mr Jephson,' Violet cut across his bows in a calm, hard tone, 'have you been here last night?'

She was clearly referring to her suspicion of that morning that some intruder had broken into the dispensary and rifled through its contents.

'I?' Jephson exclaimed, with what seemed like unfeigned surprise. 'No, madam, I was not here. This is my first visit to your establishment, which I may say I had hoped one day to visit as a colleague, a friend . . .'

'Mr Jephson,' I said, 'allow me to tell you that your wife came here with the self-same purpose with which you have clearly come: to request us to cease our investigations with regard to her family. Nor did she come by our invitation.'

'I do not speak of invitations, doctor,' our ruddy visitor cried, his tone growing warmer, 'but of your infamous conduct in abusing our confidence. The justice of your cause, however patent, does not excuse abuse of hospitality, deceit . . .'

'Stop here, sir!' I said. 'You speak of dissimulation, though we have sought you out openly from the beginning, and stated our cause to you in the plainest of terms, but let us examine your bona fides . . .'

'My what, doctor . . .' Jephson said, alarm joining anger in his tone.

'You lead us to believe you scarcely know the name of Solomon Solomons, yet my wife has seen you in the same waiting-room she occupied while visiting him in Wormwood Scrubs prison . . .'

Dismay replaced indignation in our visitor's eyes, and his lean jaw fell slightly.

'And if that were not a pretty piece of dissimulation in itself,' I said, following up my advantage, 'you are even paying Solomons' legal expenses . . .'

'By God, doctor!' the rufous cleric burst out in open anger. 'The Law Society shall hear of this! Zeinvel has flagrantly broken his professional trust . . .'

'I am prepared to swear before any tribunal in the land that Mr Zeinvel has made no admission to me not in keeping with his professional principles. And as for the letters which you so handsomely lent me, you left out the very one that would have had any bearing on the cause in which I am engaged, the one which would have established beyond doubt that your unfortunate son knew both Miller and the murdered Russian general in Germany. Dissimulation, Mr Jephson?'

This time our visitor slumped back into the chair which he had first spurned. He laid his hat and stick on Violet's desk and stared at both of us in bemused fashion.

'You have proof of that last point?' he asked quietly.

'It is public knowledge to anyone who cares to consult the library-shelves of the Thames Yacht Club.'

'Dear God!' Jephson said in a sort of shuddering groan, as he cradled his head in his hands, then looked up again, fear in his eyes. 'What will you do now?'

'To you and your family – nothing,' Violet put in with husky urgency.

'We make no conditions, impose no terms on you,' I declared, 'but consider: you must know that Solomons' appeal is to be heard tomorrow, and that without fresh evidence, it must inevitably fail.'

Jephson leapt to his feet again, and began his old habit of pacing up and down. He combed his bristly hair with a gesture of his outstretched fingers as he paced the spartan linoleum.

'Do you imagine that I have thought of anything else since Solomons' arrest?' the clergyman said with a sort of derisive snort. 'You cannot conceive the weight of the burden I bear in this. On the one hand, an innocent man's life; on the other, my family's name, and . . .'

At this point, Jephson hesitated, as if he had been on the point of saying too much.

'And more besides,' he said inconclusively.

'Please understand once and for all, Mr Jephson,' my wife said, 'we seek to pry into no intimate affairs of yours or of your family, but if Solomons is hanged in a few days – as he certainly will be if nothing new is forthcoming in the case – where then is your family's reputation? Of what worth is a reputation founded on the sacrifice – nay, the murder – of an innocent man?'

Our visitor paused, and raising both his hands to his head,

pressed his palms against his ears. If ever I saw a man in torment, it was at that moment.

'Mr Jephson,' Violet said gently, 'we swear by all we hold sacred that whatever you say here will not be repeated by us without your express permission.'

'You also have my solemn word to that,' I added.

Jephson's hands fell to his sides again, and he seemed to stand to attention.

'Very well, then,' he said, resuming his pacing, 'this much I will tell you: Hector had occasion to see the real relation in which Miller stood to Ostyankin on the yacht at Kiel: hunter and prey!'

'Please explain yourself Mr Jephson!' I said, all agog.

'It was on the evening of the second day of the regatta. A slight mist had set in, and since they were in shoal water, Ostyankin took his turn with the plumb-line. Hector chanced to come on deck and distinctly saw Miller, belaying-pin in hand, quietly inching up on Ostyankin from behind. Hector stopped in his tracks, then Miller began to raise the belaying-pin above the other Russian's head, and my son yelled out a warning. Miller then pretended to join in the warning, seizing Ostyankin by the arm and telling him he was leaning too far over the side. So the thing passed off; but from that moment on, Hector knew Miller's game . . .'

'And did your son write this to you in the missing letter?' Violet asked.

'No, he told me of it after he had returned to England, and his relations with Miller thereafter were as much those of an investigator as a fascinated young crony. The incident may of course have been a prank on Miller's part, albeit a rather sinister one, but what if Hector had not appeared on the scene?'

'Controversial Russian military man disappears overboard in yachting accident . . .' Violet mused out loud. 'Concealed sighs of relief in a dozen European chancelleries . . .'

'This places things in a rather different light,' I remarked, then, to our visitor: 'And can you not tell us any more, Mr Jephson?'

The unquiet blue eyes regarded me for a moment.

'You ask for answers, Dr Mortimer, but for me the whole affair hinges on a question, one which, were I to put it, might destroy both me and my family. I fear that at this juncture I really cannot say more, except to apologise for my earlier rush to judgment: any deceit that has occurred between us – as you have rightly pointed out – has been on my part. I still honour and applaud your quest on Solomons' behalf, and in all respects which do not touch directly upon my family, I shall be happy to share with you whatever new light might come my way on the matter. You know where I am to be found: I bid you both good evening.'

'That man is burning himself out,' Violet remarked after our visitor had made his abrupt and jerky exit. 'And I wonder what this question is that he must put, if he is to get to the bottom of the affair, though it destroy him and his family? Can it be that it is so simple we have overlooked it?'

'That is as maybe, Violet, but the main thing is that we now know – if Jephson is to be believed – that Miller has previously made an attempt to put Ostyankin out of the way, so Miller definitely joins our list of suspects. Perhaps young Jephson smoked him out in the end, before his illness clouded his wits.'

'Mmm . . . the course of the illness seems to have been remarkably rapid in his case, but then again there is great variation in the rates with which the different stages develop. The study of it is a life's work in itself.'

I rather regretted in passing that I had let my knowledge of the disease lapse, for a doctor knows best the things he is used to treating on a daily basis. We were to have proceeded home to change, in order that we might leave on our bogus night out, with a view to sneaking back and lying in wait for whoever might wish to examine the contents of our Henrietta Street rooms, but fate would have it otherwise.

'Ah,' Violet said, stooping as she led the way to the door at the head of the stairs which was the general entrance to the dispensary. 'A note, James: someone must have slipped it under the door while we were talking in the consulting-room.'

'They might have knocked,' I remarked. 'What is it, a call?'

'Yes, from Mrs Tighe at 6 Frostic Place.'

My wife handed me the piece of cheap notepaper with a resigned sigh, and I read the scrawled, unformed handwriting: 'Please come and oblidge, as May is particler bad tonit.'

'Mph,' I grunted, none too pleased, for I saw our plans for the evening going for a burton. 'Is it serious?'

'Chest, but little May's real illness is Frostic Place. I shall take some linctus and a chest-rub. You may escort me there, James, then if you'd care to go and find a cab and wait for me outside the passage, we may yet be able to carry on with our plan for the evening.'

Violet returned to the pharmacy and got the medicines, then we left the dispensary, and, locking up behind us, we walked the short distance between the opening into the Whitechapel Road and Osborn Street, then, hurrying up there along cold and greasy pavements, arrived in three or four minutes at the mouth of Frostic Place, a cavernous and dismal backwater joined to Old Montague Street by the narrowest and dingiest of passages. I saw Violet into the passage, which was dimly lit on one side by a guttering greenish-yellow gas-jet in a little wire cover, then retraced my steps to the Whitechapel Road in search of a disengaged cab. It took me a full twenty minutes to find one, but, cheered by the thought that I would not have to wait long before Violet had finished administering a chest-rub and a spoonful of linctus to little May Tighe, I ordered the cabbie to proceed to Frostic Place. There I waited in the cab outside the mouth of the passage for ten, then twenty minutes, and finally for half an hour before impatience got the better of me, and, bidding the cabbie wait, I dismounted and walked down the dimly lit alley and knocked at the door of No. 6. A whiff of sizzling suet and distressed humanity greeted me as the door opened and a little thin woman in a filthy apron and with pale, frightened eyes stood in the opening. No, she hadn't sent for no doctor, and May was as well as she might be under the circumstances, what with the cruel weather and the cost of coals; and, no, that wasn't her writing on the piece of paper, neither.

Alarmed, I turned away from the woman, and the door slammed behind me. I tried four of the other five doors in the passage, only to receive non-committal or hostile grunts, then the very last door, at the end of the passage, gave easily under my hand. I flung myself inside, and, fumbling in the pocket of my ulster, drew out my vesta-case, and, withdrawing a match, struck it and held the flaming chip aloft. I beheld a desolate, dirty room, unfurnished save for a three-legged chair and a wooden crate with two or three empty lemonade bottles in its partitions. All around me was the sickly-sweet smell of chloroform.

23

After the first waves of panic had swept over me – better that a thousand Solomonses, be they innocent as grace, should hang than that Violet should be in danger – I felt a steady anxiety grip me by the throat, and with it a measure of returning calm. I must keep a steady head. The onset of sudden pitch blackness and the pain of singed fingers emphasised this need for rational deliberation, and, after I had flung away the extinct vesta and breathed in and out slowly three times, I got out another match, struck it, and stepped over to the mantelpiece, on which I discerned two or three hardened pools of candlewax, each covered with thick dust.

I carefully blew away the dust from the thickest blob of grease, and saw that it contained the flattened end of the wick, and, taking care not to disturb the dust which covered the rest of the shell, I prised the wick up with my thumbnail and passed on to it the dying flame of my match. In the guttering and uncertain light thus afforded, I took a look round the room.

I examined the dilapidated fittings, which included a nailed-down sash window, whose panes were varnished with a patina of encrusted filth, and upon whose sill a thick layer of dust lay undisturbed. The panes were old and unbroken. I then turned my attention to the ceiling, whose plaster was cracked and yellow, with a thick growth of cobwebs at each corner, with, at the centre, a protruding nine or so inches of piping, which at one time must have held a gas-fitting of some kind. No sign, however, of a trapdoor there, any more than there was in the bare boards of the floor, whose dust, I observed, was marked by the signs of a scuffle. I stepped back up to the mantelpiece, whose top contained nothing but old dust and the blobs of candle-grease. I lit another vesta to intensify the available light, and was able to verify that the dust had not been disturbed. This led me to the conclusion that, if, as I feared, my wife had been chloroformed here, virtually under my nose, two persons at least had been involved in the attempt, for, if a lantern had been used by a lone assailant, the only place upon which it could practically have stood would have been the mantelpiece, whose thick layer of dust lay completely unmarked. The equally thick layer of dust over the cakes of candlegrease also ruled out their use as a source of light during the abduction.

Steeling myself against what I might find, and with my heart in my mouth, I bent over the empty fireplace and thrust my arm as far up the chimney-flue as it would go, gasping with relief as I felt on my open hand the icy, unchecked updraught. I straightened myself up again, and examined the broken chair, but it suggested to me no more than any other broken chair might, whereupon I turned my attention to the lemonade crate. The bottles were not quite so dusty as the rest of the room, suggesting that someone had been using the place till fairly recently as an informal empty-bottle store, and the missing stoppers suggested a raid by urchins in search of the glass marbles incorporated in them by the manufacturers as a sales-wheeze. I carefully passed my fingers round each empty partition of the crate, and, at the last, my heart missed a beat as I touched a fragment of cardboard, which I picked up carefully and held up to the light. It was an imperfectly torn-across half of a District line railway-ticket from Whitechapel: imperfectly for the 'Far' of what must have been 'Farringdon Road' was still visible in one corner. I lit another match and peered down at the bottom of the partition, to find that its dust was quite undisturbed. The ticket was clearly one of recent issue. I took out my pocketbook and carefully placed the ticket in it.

I stood and took a last look round the room, the cloying reek of the chloroform-vapour still hanging in the air making me recall with a shudder that Ostyankin had been chloroformed before they had . . . well, it did not bear thinking about. With a final bluish flare, the candle-end on the mantelpiece guttered out, and I was left in the dark. I groped my way to the door, and, shutting it behind me on its useless lock-case, I stepped back down the passage into Old Montague Street and paid off the waiting cabbie. I then walked to the far opening of the passage – into gaslit Finch Street – and stooped to examine the ground. There were clean stone paving slabs as far as the gutter, but just in from it there was a coal-hole cover, and beside it a smudge of wet coal dust about two feet in diameter. I went over and peered at the cake of dust. There were three cleanly marked tracks in it, with gaps of nine or ten inches between them. But what wheeled street-conveyance went on three wheels? The ambulant saveloy- or hot-potato stands commonly seen on the streets came to mind, but surely there would be more breadth between the wheels? The first alternative that suggested itself – a garden barrow – I dismissed as unlikely to the point of absurdity in that district. There only remained – yes! – an invalid's wheeled chair! Hope mingled with the thrill of the chase stirred within me, momentarily suppressing my anxiety. What better way of conveying a chloroformed woman than in an invalid-chair? But in which direction? South-west down Wentworth Street towards Aldgate and the City, or north-east, rejoining Old Montague Street via Casson Street? Taking my bearings, I realised that, three hundred yards farther up Old Montague Street, on the right, was the turn-off down St Mary Street, which led down to St Mary's station on the Whitechapel Road. North-east, then, briskly! There was a policeman patrolling on the corner of the entrance to Dunk Street, and I asked him if he had seen a party being wheeled in an invalid-chair in the vicinity.

'Why, yes, sir, coming up the road from the west: that'd be when I started my beat, about forty minutes ago.'

'Was the party in the chair a lady, constable?'

'Yes, sir: she was all muffled up in a rug, and she was wearing a hat with a veil. Little tubby chap in a cricket-cap was pushing the thing, with a tall, well set-up woman walking at his side.'

'What did this man look like, constable?'

'Oh, can't rightly say, sir – I wasn't all that close, and the light wasn't much to crack on on that stretch. Any trouble, sir?'

'Er, no, no – I'm the lady's doctor, and I forgot to give her some medicine she needs. Which way were they making for?'

'Direction you're going in now, sir – p'raps they were heading for the station.'

'My very thought, constable – much obliged, and good night to you!'

The policeman touched the rim of his helmet, and I hastened along the street, but not without having memorised his number – 144. I finally reached St Mary Street, and dashed down into the Whitechapel Road, dodging my way through the traffic as I crossed over into the maw of St Mary's station.

'It's in the left-luggage, sir,' the ticket-office man said, referring to the invalid-chair, after he had informed me that the berugged lady had been helped into a train by her strapping, veiled companion, after the latter had bought two tickets to Victoria. 'And the man who pushed the chair for them,' I pressed. 'What did he look like?'

'Little fat feller, sir, round face like a dumpling, with a scrubby bit of a ginger beard – what I call a needn't-have-bothered beard, if you see what I mean. Shabbily dressed, with a cricket cap. He didn't say anything – tall lady just gave him half a crown and he touched his cap and went directly. I particularly remember because things were slack after the rush, and there was all the to-do about the chair.'

'What was that?'

'Could they leave it with us, as it wouldn't fit into the train compartment? They said someone'd be round in a jiffy to take it away. That was three-quarters of an hour ago. I told them, normally it's against regulations to . . .'

'May I see it?'

'If you like, sir – just pop round to the left-luggage and ring the bell.'

I did, and the invalid-chair turned out to be an antiquated contraption, with a yellowing bone label bearing the name of a once well-known Southwark firm of surgical-equipment manufacturers, by then defunct. God knew what junk-shop or workhouse had been its last home. I examined it thoroughly, not neglecting to thrust my fingers into all the seams of the upholstery, and to turn it upside-down, but without reward. I finally took out my notebook and wrote down the serial number on the bone label, just in case, tipped the attendant, then returned to the ticket-office and thanked the clerk, solemnly promising him that he would be the first to know if I managed to unearth the owner of the abandoned contraption. I then bought a ticket to Charing Cross, and, three or four minutes later, was ensconced in the corner of a third-class smoker on my way to Henrietta Street. I attacked my cigarette-case, then, eagerly drawing in a draught of mild Virginia, sought to still my racing mind.

'A little fat feller, with a round face like a dumpling, and an apology of a ginger beard', or words to that effect. What a perfect description of Alexander Miller! By God, if he had had a hand in abducting my wife! But surely he could not be as desperate as that – to come out into the glaring gaslight of a busy railway station! But then again, I had no real idea of how desperate that stage of the game – if game it was – might be at that particular time. Perhaps things were moving to a climax, and I all unawares. Just then a grim thought slipped into my mind: Violet had owed her life to Iris Starr's intervention, and perhaps that debt was now about to be repaid in full . . . I shuddered – no, I must not think such thoughts: in the real world, mystical debts were never repaid, any more than gypsies' curses were fulfilled. There were but two earthly deities for the man of science: cause and effect, and in that sign I must conquer. Isolate cause, then follow down the road of effect, and there at the end would be the truth. But now I must pinpoint the whereabouts of Alexander Miller, so that he might be eliminated from the Frostic Place equation. He would now receive another call from the Reverend Flockhart, that tireless campaigner against man's inhumanity to man. And the occasion of the call? I lit another cigarette, and drew deeply on it: yes, a man named Diamant. That might tantalise the smug timber-dealer a little. I really would like to know more about Mark Diamant.

All was quiet and seemingly in order at home – the burglar Violet and I had been half-anticipating after the incident of the turning-over of the pharmacy day-book had evidently not yet made his appearance, but the night was yet young. Not that young, though, I thought, glancing at the clock on the bedroom mantelpiece as I struggled into my clerical rig, and seeing that it was already ten past nine. The odds were that Miller would be out on the town, but, knowing the late hours he kept, I put my hope in his having dined at home before going on to wherever he might have been going. Or perhaps it was a cards evening. At any rate, I must hurry.

At Farm Street, Mrs Custance of the still gaze informed me that her employer was just finishing dinner, but if I'd care to wait a little while, she was sure he would see me. This time she ushered me into a spacious and well-appointed drawing-room, which, so far as I recalled from my last visit, adjoined Miller's study. I waited for some ten minutes, then heard jovial chatter in the corridor: Miller was evidently seeing out a guest. I got up and approached the slightly-open drawing-room door as circumspectly as I could, to be rewarded with a glimpse, through the door-crack, of a thin, moustachioed man with long, greasy black hair. He was talking in a sort of arrogant drawl, while Miller tittered solicitously at whatever witty sallies his departing guest was making. There was something familiar about the man's features: surely I had seen them portrayed – or caricatured – somewhere.

'Monday, then, at nine,' the drawl concluded, and I heard the front door shut, whereupon I hastened back to my chair. Just at that moment, Miller popped his head in at the door.

'Ah, Mr Flockhart: I was wondering when I would have the pleasure again. I have asked Mrs Custance to serve coffee in here. You will join me, I hope?'

I rose from my sofa, and, with a slight bow, murmured my thanks. Just then the telephone could be heard ringing from the adjoining study, and Miller brought his palm to his brow in a gesture of irritation.

'Pfui! I am to be allowed no rest! You will excuse me for one moment, Mr Flockhart, then we may talk about serious matters.'

I nodded again, and Miller ducked back into the corridor. An instant later I heard the study door shut, and soon after that, the drawing-room door opened noiselessly, and the housekeeper appeared with a tray bearing coffee things. Something occurred to me.

'I hope you don't mind me mentioning it, Mrs Custance, but it strikes me that your being surrounded by so much Russian company all the time must require considerable powers of adaptation on your part. How do you manage with the language when Mr Miller is not here to help out?'

The housekeeper seemed to fumble a little as she was laying out the coffee things on the little oriental table in front of me, and I fancied I read evasion in her quick, sideways glance. She laughed rather awkwardly, and drew the empty tray up to her chest.

'Oh, I manage somehow, sir, and so many of the Russian gentlemen know English: why, some of them speak it better than I do!'

'You are perhaps a widow, Mrs Custance?' I pressed.

'Ah, here's Mr Miller now, sir,' she said brightly, parrying my question. 'I'll leave you now, sir, if that's all.'

'Yes, thank you, Mrs Custance.'

The little Russian bounced into an armchair opposite my sofa, and did the honours with the coffee things.

'And how is the good fight going, Mr Flockhart? Have you found any new clues?'

Miller's little dark eyes were like sparkling raisins in floury dough ready for the oven. The fellow looked as clever as a box of monkeys. Our verbal duel was clearly about to recommence.

'Alas nothing a court of law – or rather, at this stage, a court of appeal – would accept as such, Mr Miller, but certain personalities are beginning to recur in my investigations.'

'Personalities, Mr Flockhart?' he asked, passing me a saucer bearing a little cupful of black coffee. 'What sort of personalities? And how can I help?'

'I refer in this instance to a Russian personality, albeit a pretty notorious one . . .'

The little fellow shrilled his feminine laugh.

'"Notorious", hey, Mr Flockhart? And you come straight to me! How my poor reputation seems to precede me!'

'I do not for a moment suggest that you might be personally acquainted with the man, Mr Miller: I allude rather to your wide experience of Russian state affairs.'

'Yes, yes, Mr Flockhart – forgive me for teasing you. It is just that your, er . . . high moral tone tends to intimidate me, make me nervous, you see . . .'

I was more than a little gratified to see that he still did not take the Reverend Flockhart seriously: or was it that he had dined rather too well?

'Diamant,' I said quietly.

My host's coffee cup was arrested for a moment betwixt watch-chain and collar, and a flinty quality seemed to flash over the sly little eyes. The grin died from his lips, with their silly ginger fringe.

'Diamant,' he parroted rather dreamily. 'That is a bad man, Mr Flockhart – a very bad man. What do you know of Diamant?'

'He was one of the gang who got away after the murder of State Counsellor Pamphiloff in Odessa in '84,' I said, my host nodding slowly in confirmation, 'the gang which gravely wounded General Ostyankin in the course of the same attack.'

'Yes, the scum of the earth, Mr Flockhart, and the other swine to get away was your angel of innocence, Solomons. I am very familiar with the details of the trial: it shook all Russia at the time. And what of Diamant? Do not tell me you have found him? Why, the police of three continents . . .'

I took a sip of the heady black coffee, and waved my hand in deprecation. It would not do – if there was any connection between them – if, on my prompting, Miller was to tip the wink to Diamant, and so put him beyond my reach.

'Not at all, Mr Miller: would that I could lay hands on the man, for I suspect that if anyone knows the truth about how General Ostyankin died, it will be Diamant, wherever he may be at this moment. No, it was on a question of the er, sequence of events of the affair: did Solomons and Diamant get clean away after the murder? Or did one or both of them escape from police custody? I have consulted all the available public records, press accounts and so forth, but have not been able to establish this.'

Miller put his cup and saucer down on the table, and stared at me for fully half a minute before replying.

'It is a matter of public record – least in the Russian press,' he said quietly. 'Solomons got clean away after the attempt – it seems he had relations in Odessa itself – but Diamant was arrested a couple of days later at Krivoy Rog. It seems he later managed to hoodwink his escort and jump from a train in the middle of the night. No one has seen hide or hair of him since.'

'I see: so the police had time to, er . . . talk to him before his, er . . . escape.'

'Ah! I see what you mean, Mr Flockhart. You have no doubt read of our dreaded secret police – the Okhrana – in your penny dreadfuls. They, er . . . get to work on Diamant – perhaps they even hold his loved ones as hostages – then set him on the trail of Solomons . . . Very thrilling, but in reality our secret police are not so very secret, and I doubt if there would be enough of them to detail for a mission as far away as Odessa . . .'

In a gesture that was becoming familiar to me, Miller whipped out his watch and, glancing at it, shrugged his shoulders rather theatrically, and smiled with apologetic helplessness, upon which I put down my cup and saucer and rose to my feet.

'I had thought to call on you around seven,' I said, in as casual a tone as I could muster, 'but I was not sure whether you would be dining early, or . . .'

'But Brown's Hotel have the telephone, do they not, Mr Flockhart?' Miller remarked silkily. 'Such a useful apparatus, don't you think?'

'Ah, I daresay,' I said, reminding myself just in time of my supposed London residence, 'but for the life of me I cannot get the hang of the contraption!'

'Ha!' Miller exclaimed, as I felt his hot little paw on my shoulder, and he started to conduct me to the front door. 'We must keep up with the times, Mr Flockhart, but in any case, you would not have found me at home: I was in conference till after eight in Leadenhall Street – the annual get-together of our Baltic factors, you know . . .'

It was too circumstantial an aside not to be an alibi-statement, I thought, but, if true, what of the little, chubby, ginger-bearded man who, according to the ticket-clerk at St Mary's station, had pushed the invalid-chair containing what I now had no doubt had been a chloroformed Violet to the train at seven forty? Or would these so-called Baltic factors be as reliable witnesses as the defaulting Russians at the famous card-game last November? And where had I seen Miller's flashy dinner-guest before? He of the arrogant drawl and the mustachios?

My musings continued on the cab-journey back to Henrietta Street, as I enumerated the possible strong suspects in Ostyankin's murder: Miller, who according to Cormell Jephson had already made an attempt on the general's life aboard the *Kronstadt* off Kiel; Diamant, who, whatever his relations with the Russian authorities might be, had also previously tried to kill the militarist; then the Soho ménage of Cormell and Lettice Jephson, now that I had torn away their pretence of not knowing that Ostyankin had been part and parcel of their son's Russian imbroglio in Berlin. And Judith Vulliamy, so clearly capable and ruthless enough to have squashed the 'brute' who might have helped destroy her fiancé's life and her happiness. Which of them might have been prompted to move against Violet? And why at this particular juncture?

I decided to fight down my disquiet by giving my mind and energies a definite object. The railway ticket-stub I had found in the lemonade crate in the hovel in Frostic Place. Whitechapel to

Farringdon Road by the District line. The ticket must not have been handed to the collector at Farringdon Road, though it had been torn in half. Or had there been a rush of people leaving the platform, and he perhaps had carelessly let the stub fall from a fistful of others – it may have been into the hem of Violet's skirt or some fold or pleat of her clothing? For I was sure that the ticket had been bought by Violet that day. One would have to change at Tower Hill to a train of the Circle line. I drew a rough mental boundary round Farringdon Road station at a radius approximately halfway from the surrounding stations, the northern limit being the House of Correction in Upper Farringdon Road, beyond which it would have been more logical to approach from King's Cross. Grays Inn Road would form the western limit, taking its normal serving stations as Euston and King's Cross, and Goswell Road and Aldersgate Street the eastern, with Moorgate station forming the centre of counterattraction beyond. I set my southern limits at Holborn Viaduct, since the Strand-cum-Fleet Street area to the south could be approached by anyone coming from the east more conveniently by way of the Temple station.

And what was there to be found of note within the imagined boundaries of my little Republic of Farringdon? Certainly several churches, whose parish registers might conceivably have been consulted by Violet as part of her search for the names of those who had died on November the twenty-eighth in the previous year. As for my suspicion that she had had another purpose in mind this afternoon, the results of which, Violet-like, she had decided to keep to herself in order to surprise me, where then? The Houses of Correction and of Detention? A possibility, but surely she would have to have known – and concealed from me – rather a great deal of new information in the case, to have had such definite destinations in mind? The Charterhouse, up Goswell Road way? And which of the thirty decayed but deserving gentleman residents would she have wished to interview within those venerable walls? The only other notable places in the area I could call to mind were Smithfield Market and the gasworks, Barts and the church of St Bartholomew the Great being so far south as to be better served by the Temple station. I should have to consult my directories at home. Then the germ of hope began to arise in me: perhaps the whole nightmare had all been imagination on my part, and I would find Violet waiting for me at home. After all, the use of chloroform for nefarious purposes was far from unknown in the darker recesses of the East End. I banged the head of my stick on the canopy of the cab and yelled at the driver to go faster.

When I did arrive at our rooms in Henrietta Street, I found yet no signs of the burglary Violet had anticipated, though of course the night was by no means over, but there was a shabby little brown paper packet waiting for me on the doormat. It was simply a scrap of stout brown paper held together by string. I examined it for clues – nothing unusual, no superscription whatever, so obviously delivered by hand – then undid the string and opened the package. All my hopes were dashed when I found a lock of my wife's tow-coloured hair and her pince-nez. My hands began to shake with rage, and I started to make insane vows – calm, calm . . . I placed the objects on a side-table under a dimmed gas-mantle, and, straightening out the paper, I turned up the gas and raised the paper towards the light. There were a couple of irregular lines of crude capital letters, made with some warehouseman's stencil. The letters read: 'Your wife is safe and well. Do not go to the police or it is death for her. Remember the general. You shall hear from us soon.'

I took the objects from the table, and, replacing them gently in the folds of brown paper, walked automaton-like into our little sitting room, poured myself out a liberal glassful of brandy, and flung myself into an armchair. 'Remember the general . . .' I certainly did, along with Sir James Ettrick the great patholo-gist's words at the trial, concerning Ostyankin's wounds: 'the worst injuries I have ever known any human being to inflict on another.' I shuddered: no, I should not be going to the police.

24

There could have been no question of my retiring that wretched night: for one thing, the dread of how I would feel on waking up to find an empty space beside me in the bed would have banished all possibility of any worthwhile sleep.

Instead, I sprang up from the armchair, stirred the fire up, then went over to the bookshelves in search of trades directories, the invaluable Ward's at the top of the list. It was then that I pulled myself up: I was neglecting method, that *sine qua non* of detection. Before consulting any particular volume, I went carefully through all the dozen shelves of the wall-case, noting if markers had been placed in any book that I could not recall placing there myself. Perhaps I should thereby attune myself to Violet's last train of thought. At last I came to the last volume on the lowermost shelf: nothing save markers in a couple of medical textbooks, one beside articles on syphilis, the other in the second book, this time at a place which dealt with affections of the eye. The former could easily be explained by Violet's desire to know more about poor Hector Jephson's predicament, the latter no doubt in connection with one of her own patients.

I passed on to the directories, but of course they were arranged in trades and professional and other specialisations, not by district. I should have to wade blindly through each one, page by page, if I was to find any suggestive reference to the area of research I had outlined for myself around Farringdon Road station, in line with the clue of the ticket-stub. With a sigh, then, I took out Ward's Directory for 1890 – the most up-to-date in the series – and returned to my armchair to begin my labours. At about eleven thirty, I was electrified by the banging of the area door, and I leapt up and ran out into the corridor, my spirits borne aloft by I know not what hopes. These were only to be dashed by my hearing Lottie's cheerful humming as she bolted the area door behind her, presently to pop her head into the sitting-room to ask if there was anything I wanted.

'No, Lottie,' I replied, 'nothing more for tonight: you'd better run along to bed.'

With the maid's unconcerned goodnight echoing in my ears, I slumped back into the armchair and attacked the next page of Ward's Directory. Soon I was nodding over the book, and I reached out for my box of cheroots to see what Lady Nicotine would do for my fading wits. And so I devilled, far into the watches of the night, Ward's eventually giving way to Kelly's and the other standard works of those who would find their way round the trades and avocations of London. All in vain, and at the end I was left with what I had set out with: the half-dozen or so most notable institutions in the district. Putting the book I had been reading down, I lit my umpteenth cheroot and stared into the dying embers of the fire, while the gas-jets popped and spluttered above the mantelpiece. I closed my eyes, the better to concentrate, and began with Farringdon Road station itself. You turned left up the road, and . . .

I woke up with a jerk and a racking cough, amid the devil's own fug, a dirty grey light illuminating the room. Shivering with cold, I glanced at the mantelpiece clock, noting with alarm that it was after eight. My coughing got worse, and I went over to the window and thrust the sash up to its fullest height, a draught of air from behind billowing the bright, new Liberty curtains out into Henrietta Street. I looked behind me, and saw that the door was open, and, with a little curse, went over and shut it, then, having excluded the draught, went over and pulled the curtains back in again. As the cold fresh air filled the room, I felt I could breathe easily again, and pulled the window-sash down to a reasonable gap. Something troubled my mind slightly as I did so: it was as if I were repeating an identical action, performed long before. There was no time for psychological reflections, though, for in spite of my returning sense of nagging anxiety and loss, there was the People's Dispensary to be opened in far-off Whitechapel: the first patients would be arriving in an hour and a half. I dashed into the corridor and called down to Lottie.

'Did you leave the sitting-room door open, Lottie?'

'Yes, sir,' came the reply from the bowels of the building. 'I saw you was asleep and didn't want to wake you up – I've been up and about since 'alf-six. Dr Branscombe out on a night-call, then, sir?'

'Yes, Lottie,' I said, trying to keep the desolation I felt out of my voice, 'she's out on a call. Will you bring up some hot water to the bedroom, please, as soon as you like, and then I'd like a pot of the strongest coffee you've ever made in your life!'

'Right you are, sir,' came the maid's laughing reply. 'I won't spare the grains!'

I dashed off my toilet as soon as the hot water arrived, then went down to the kitchen and more or less finished off the coffee before hurrying out. On my way to the station, I realised that I had quite smoked myself out during my night-vigil, and popped into Oliver's, my usual tobacconist, near Charing Cross station. I laid in a stock of Virginia rolling tobacco and Trichin-opoly cheroots, then, in my haste, dropped my money all over the polished counter. Old Oliver clucked his tongue solemnly against his upper palate, then, producing a shiny metal object like a police whistle from a display-case at the side of the counter, flourished it gently under my nose, as I scrabbled up my loose money.

'Why, sir,' he said with true chapman's unction, 'you really should look after your money better than that! Especially where sovereigns is concerned. This is the very thing you need.'

I took the metal tube from the shopman and examined it. It was sealed at one end, and there was a slot-arrangement at the other. I twisted the slot-end and the cap moved to one side.

'That's the ticket, sir!' Oliver said encouragingly. 'You just feed your coins in from the top-end, close it to, and there's a spring at the bottom that pushes 'em up to the slot when you need 'em. A tanner to you, sir!'

I grunted assent, then paid for and pocketed my purchases, which included the patent coin-case. I then hurried out of the shop and made for the station, and was just in time to catch the 8.32 to Whitechapel. If only we could recognise at the time we encounter them the trifles that are to change our lives.

Going over the events of the previous day during the train-journey to Whitechapel, I remembered with a sinking feeling that I had come directly from Miller's house to Henrietta Street in my clerical garb. Anyone watching would have seen the Reverend Flockhart go into our rooms, and, just now, Dr James

Mortimer leave them. What price now my disguise? A deceit, if it is to succeed, must above all be sustained and consistent. I sat back and groaned inwardly, then the vision came to me of the dinner-guest Miller had seen out shortly after my arrival in his house in Faith Street. Someone famous, I was sure. The lank black hair and moustachios, along with the drawling speech, called the artist Whistler to mind, but there had been something not of the 'greenery-yallery' cut of the contemporary artist about him. Not a businessman, I was sure, but what? I chewed the matter over in my mind, for anything connected with a figure as important as Miller to the drama in which I was involved might be of vital relevance. And what was to happen at their 9 p.m. rendezvous on Monday?

My musings were broken as, dead on time at 8.53, the train screeched into Whitechapel station. I would have just seven minutes to get to the dispensary before Jane Bonsor arrived, but as it happened, she was already in the pharmacy, setting the new lad to work, when I ran up the stairs.

'Ah, Violet is not with you?' the wide-eyed English rose queried in her soft, rapid voice. At twenty-six, she was the baby of the trio of English girls who had shared diggings in Paris while studying for their medical degrees at the Sorbonne, the other two being Violet and Eleanor Ramsbotham, then a leading light at the New Women's Hospital in Seymour Place.

'Jane,' I murmured, gently taking her by the elbow and leading her the two steps that led into the empty consulting-room, whose inner door I closed behind us, 'Violet is missing.'

'Missing, James?' she said, the eyes opening even wider. 'She has not returned from a call, you mean? Why, you know as well as I that that can take . . .'

'No, there has been a note – an anonymous note . . .'

'What can I do, James?'

'Carry on here as usual – as it is you are virtually running the place already – but be extra vigilant. I want you to notice everything out of the ordinary, however insignificant it may seem: any new patients, old patients who seem to be acting strangely, or asking more questions than usual. Any unusual comings and goings down in the court or among the builder's men working on the new dispensary – anything and everything.

And not a word of what I have just told you to anyone. Do you understand?'

'Of course, but you must be on your way – every second counts in your search for Violet . . .'

I needed no further admonition on that score, and, scarcely forty minutes later, I was standing on the platform of Farringdon Road station. Armed with a photograph of Violet, and beginning with the station itself, I sought out and questioned staff who had been on duty the day before as to whether a short, tow-haired lady in pince-nez had been making enquiries of them. Thus I passed the entire morning and early afternoon, and I must have repeated the process in every public building – hospitals, churches, workhouse and infirmary – and major retail business within a one-and-a-half mile radius of the station. It was just before three o'clock when, footsore and depleted from my fitful three or so hours' sleep of the night before, at the north-easternmost boundary of my circumscribed area of operations, my efforts were rewarded by the manager of the Sadler's Wells Theatre.

'That's the lady, sir!' the dapper man with the middle parting exclaimed from behind his desk after I had assured him of my identity and *bona fides* and passed the photograph across to him from the visitor's chair. 'Called in around two. Most specific she was in her enquiries. Missing, you say? I am sincerely sorry to hear it. If there is anything I can do . . .'

'May I ask what these specific enquiries were, Mr Maidment?'

'I don't see why not, sir – wanted to know if I had photographs of all the performers who had appeared here between ten and fifteen years ago. I can't claim to have them all, but I think I can rightly pride myself on having most.'

'And did the lady find what she was looking for?'

'She certainly did, sir: signed portrait of Miss Cora Raines – a "visiting card" as they called such photographs in those days.'

'And have you any idea when this would have been taken, Mr Maidment?'

'I do, sir: '78, it would have been. Saw her myself in *Fair Maid of Seville*. Small part, you understand – Hetty Baskombe had the leading part – but Cora had tons of talent, and such energy. Pity she didn't go on in the profession – marriage, I suppose. The old story: they hit a bad patch somewhere on the shady side of thirty, and decide to settle for comfortable domesticity. She'll be pushing forty now, and as we say in the profession: nobody loves a fairy when she's forty!'

I summoned up a sickly sort of effort at a smile in response to the man's guffaw.

'Would Cora Raines have been a stage-name, d'you think?'

'Oh, yes, I should think so – has the ring to it.'

'Do you think I might see that photograph, Mr Maidment?'

The dapper man chuckled.

'If you can find the lady, sir – I lent it to her yesterday.'

My heart sank: it was fairly certain that whoever had got Violet would also have the photograph now, unless she had left it somewhere in the dispensary before we had left on our wild goose chase on the previous evening after little May Tighe and her supposed bad chest. If only she had discussed it with me, but it was always Violet's way to keep something to herself until she had all the evidence she needed to produce it with as conclusive an effect as possible. But still, I felt I was that much further forward – Miss Cora Raines was evidently the lady in the case.

'Did the lady say when she would return the photograph, Mr Maidment?'

'Just said as soon as possible. I lent it her without question: a real lady, sir. I know the breed. Important, is it?'

'That may well be, Mr Maidment,' I said, beginning to rise from my chair. 'Well, I shall detain you no longer. I'm very much obliged to you, sir.'

The manager leant across his desk and shook my hand.

'Not at all, sir – any time. And when you do see the lady again – as I have no doubt you will – do give her my regards. May I ask you a personal question, sir?'

'By all means.'

'Have you been long married?'

'Er, seven months and a bit.'

'Say no more, sir! I may say, *entre nous*, that my own good lady has on more than one occasion, er . . . disappeared as a result of some trifling little difference between us. It is the ladies' way of paying us out, God bless them! In such cases, sir, always look to the mother-in-law! And, er . . . the matter of the photograph.

Much though I am pleased to let your wife borrow it, such mementoes are impossible to replace . . .'

'Rest assured, sir, it will be the very first thing I shall ask her about! And may I thank you for your most reassuring advice.'

Bathed in the afterglow of Mr Maidment's knowing smirk, I left the theatre and set off for Farringdon Road station as briskly as my swollen feet and aching joints would allow. It was already half-past three, and evening surgery was at five. I must search the dispensary from top to bottom. It was already twenty to five by the time I got there, and I threw myself into my task, the empty rooms resonating with the noise of flung-aside packing-crates, ransacked shelves, and pulled-up linoleum. I searched high and low in pharmacy, consulting-room and waiting-room, not omitting the rough coir doormat at the threshold at the head of the common stairs, but found no photograph. Could it be that our burglar had, instead of turning his attention to Henrietta Street, revisited the dispensary last night? But who could be behind it? Miller? The Berner Street crowd? The Jephsons – all in the name of religion, of course, and for our own good? Or that hard little Meissen figurine Miss Vulliamy? Or had some obscure little understudy in the drama been working quietly behind the wings?

Jane Bonsor arrived just then, and, after I had given her an account of my day's activities, I asked her if anything out of the ordinary had happened at the dispensary that morning.

'Nothing, I'm afraid – just the usual patients, and nothing worthy of note in the court or road. You look absolutely done in – have you eaten?'

'Far from my mind, Jane, but I must confess I could do with one of Mrs Chinnery's meat pies at this moment!'

'Ah, that reminds me – there were rumblings among the builder's men in the new dispensary this morning, since she was nearly an hour late with their dinnertime pies! First time it had happened, it seems.'

'Well, absence makes the heart – and appetite – grow fonder, I suppose. And there was absolutely nothing else?'

'I'm afraid not; or at any rate, I didn't notice anything. If there's anything I can do, James . . .'

'In keeping the dispensary going as you have been doing for

so long, Jane, you are doing quite enough as it is. I am sure that it will be foremost in Violet's mind now, wherever she is.'

Just then we were interrupted by a sharp knocking at the waiting-room door. I stepped through to the waiting-room and opened the main door, to be confronted by Zeinvel's junior clerk. And then I remembered. Good grief! In my anxiety over Violet's disappearance, I had quite forgotten that today was the day when Solomons' appeal was to have been heard!

'Mr Zeinvel's compliments, sir, and would you care to step over to his office immediately – I've a cab waiting. Mr Zeinvel says it's urgent, sir . . .'

I felt tension grip my throat.

'Yes, of course – I'll be down presently.'

The lad scuttled downstairs, and I dashed back in and explained to Jane where I was going, with the promise that I should be back as soon as possible. Perfect silence reigned during the cab-drive, and Zeinvel received me, poker-faced, in his chamber in Crutched Friars. He rose and shook my hand, then indicated the visitor's chair and sat down.

'Solomons' appeal has been turned down, doctor, on grounds of insufficient new evidence. The law is to take its course.'

25

'Is it final, then?'

Zeinvel nodded, and the mean thought flitted across my mind that, with Solomons hanged and out of the way, perhaps Violet would be released.

'My wife has been kidnapped,' I said simply, handing the brown paper package to the lawyer, who carefully opened it, examined the hair and pince-nez, then read the irregularly stencilled message in silence for a moment.

'Have you any strong suspicion as to who might be behind this?' he asked at last.

'Anyone connected with the Poland Street affair,' I said wearily.

'Normally I should advise you to go straight to the police,' came the dry, Cockney voice.

'Why "normally"?'

'I've been making enquiries in Hamburg. I received this cable this afternoon.'

I took the offered flimsy, and read it. First came details of the death certificate, issued by the Hamburg *Standesamt* in the November of 1884, of the Reverend Crispin Vulliamy. No next of kin was signified. Next was a digest of a marriage certificate, issued on the 4th of June, 1884, by the same office, between Judith, only daughter of the Reverend Crispin Vulliamy, and Eugen Balasz-Monteiro, described as a landed proprietor, of Recife, Brazil. The last sentence of the cable was to the effect that to date no record had been established of either a Judith Vulliamy or a Judith Balasz-Monteiro having been in Germany since then.

'This business evidently has far wider ramifications than we had thought,' Zeinvel said, as I handed him back the cable, 'and we shall have to proceed very carefully indeed in the matter of Dr Branscombe's disappearance.'

I let the implications of the cable sink into my mind for a moment. So Judith Vulliamy – whatever her real name was – had simply hooked herself on to Hector Jephson in Germany. Her fine old Junkers of a grandfather must presumably have also been an impostor. I voiced my speculations to Zeinvel.

'They were clearly using him,' he said, then with a shrug: 'As to why, you may take your choice.'

I chose politics: the mystery seemed to deepen as its successive layers were peeled away.

'You are still pursuing your enquiries on behalf of Solomons, then,' I asked, changing the subject, 'in spite of the failure of the appeal?'

'Those are my instructions,' Zeinvel said, not a trace of emotion showing on his thin, mobile features, 'and besides, I was never one for striking my colours while there was still a game to play.'

I nodded, then brought the young solicitor up-to-date with my enquiries.

'I shall try the theatres,' he said. 'In seeking out this Cora Raines, it's possible that your wife has trodden on someone's toes. Meanwhile, Dr Mortimer, I would advise you to look out very carefully in case anyone is watching you or your movements. I'm fairly sure the abduction of Dr Branscombe has been the work of more than one person. In my experience, a watcher always plays a crucial role in such disappearances. Find the watcher, and he may lead us to the kidnapper, and, ultimately, to your wife.'

'You've had no luck in tracing the missing witnesses in Solomons' case?'

Zeinvel shook his narrow, aquiline-featured head.

'My enquiries continue, though, and remember: please keep me informed about anything which may turn up concerning Dr Branscombe. I share your concern about her, and wish you the best of luck.'

We both rose and shook hands, then I was in the cab again, and on my way back to the dispensary. On the way, my thoughts returned to the cruel-mouthed typewriter: what exactly was her game? After evening surgery had finished, and Jane Bonsor had left, I decided to have one last rummage round for anything Violet might have left behind that her kidnappers might have been interested in laying their hands on. This time I reversed the

217

order of my search, since approaching familiar things from an unfamiliar perspective will sometimes yield results.

It was no use, however, and at length I flung myself into Violet's chair behind the consulting-room desk and began to devour the pressed-beef sandwiches and ale Jane had so considerately ordered in for me after I had left with Zeinvel's clerk. I must say that the meal – my first that day – did me good, and I sat back briefly, while I polished off the last of the ale. As I did so, my eye lit on the glass-fronted bookcase against the wall to my left. The volumes therein were all medical tomes, which I had already turned over twice that day. I stretched my arm across and pulled open the glass door, then took out the only book with a marker in it, noticing at the same time that its immediate companion was not one of our little collection, but was stamped with the cartouche of the medical library of the Charing Cross Hospital. This book I also drew out, and laid them both on the desk in front of me.

I opened the first book at the marked page, which was the end of a chapter-section on syphilis, which, I recalled, was the topic marked in one of the reference books I had noticed that morning at home in Henrietta Street. I laid the book aside for a moment, and, remembering the wheeze one used with a book to find out on what page it had last been read, I lightly tossed the other – from the Charing Cross Hospital library – onto the desk, and it fell open at a page which dealt with throat wounds. I read idly on, then my attention was gripped: it seemed that one of the effects that could result from a certain type of wound was a pronounced bark in the sufferer, which would be set off by excitement or strong emotion. Could Ostyankin, after receiving a bullet through his neck during the Vinnitza pogrom in '82, have been such a barking man? At that moment I felt the vague unease we experience when we suspect there is something we *ought* to remember – like a fly buzzing impotently behind the pane of a closed window – but the mental correspondence did not come through, and I pressed on with my researches.

I turned again to the first, marked, book, and read on in the marked section, hoping to catch up with my knowledge – so rusty and deficient since student days, as one seldom encounters the disease in rural Dartmoor practices – of syphilis. I reached the paragraphs distinguishing between the respective bodies of symptoms which marked the two main variants of the scourge: *tabes dorsalis*, or, as it was alternatively known, *locomotor ataxia*, and general paresis or paralysis of the insane. I related what I was reading to what I had seen that Sunday afternoon a fortnight previously through the shrubbery of the Magnolias in Hampstead: poor Hector Jephson, attempting with the jerky, high-stepping gait of a stilt-walker to escape the restraint of his mother and the woman who called herself Judith Vulliamy. But there was something wrong here: the typical, uncontrolled, jerky, movements of *tabes dorsalis* belonged to the congenital form of the disease. It was not to be picked up casually in some *louche* Berlin night-spot. I remembered Cormell Jephson's unexplained remark about the question he had said he dared not put, a question that might shake his world on its foundations, and I wondered whether perhaps I now knew what it was . . .

I cursed myself for falling asleep in the early hours of that morning, and not leaving myself time to read on in the corresponding textbook in Henrietta Street. That morning . . . I recalled in my musing the chill dawn dimity-light, the stale tobacco-fug of the sitting-room, then the billowing curtains as I flung up the sash to let in the fresh air, only to bring it down again after I had closed the door in order to retrieve the sucked-out curtains. Then the hurried toilet, the gulped coffee, the dash to Charing Cross station, and my purchase, en route, under the blandishments of Oliver the tobacconist, of the patent, spring-bottomed coin-case. I reached dreamily into my pocket, and, drawing the case out, laid it on top of the desk with the two medical books. It was not unlike a cartridge-case: where had I seen a cartridge-case recently? I was sure I had seen one, only it had not housed a bullet.

What use was a cartridge without a bullet? I mused on, and what use was the former in any case, without a gun?

I sat bolt upright. Suddenly everything fell into place. A cartridge without a bullet could nevertheless kill, and it did not need a charge or even a gun to propel it towards its target . . . I jumped to my feet, and, barely lingering to turn down the gaslights and lock up the dispensary, I rushed out in search of a cab that would take me to Soho Square and the Working Girls' Club. I found Mrs Jephson at home in the little private parlour at the back of the building.

'I fear my husband is out on rescue-work, Dr Mortimer,' the sad lady explained to me, after she had asked me to sit down. 'We dine early here, and if you had only come half an hour earlier . . .'

'No matter, ma'am, I am hoping you may be able to help me on this particular occasion.'

The lady's eyes took on the hunted expression I was becoming used to seeing in them.

'Oh, have no fear, ma'am,' I hastened to reassure her. 'I recall my promise to you – I am not here to trespass on, er . . . certain topics . . .'

'That is a relief, doctor – now how may I help you?'

I took out the patent coin-case from my pocket, and held it up in front of my hostess. For an instant she showed no recognition, then something dawned in her eyes.

'Ah, you have one, too, doctor: it is not by any chance the one that . . .'

'The one that Miller asked about after his visit to you in Ebury Street?' I put in. 'After his arrival back from Germany '86?'

'It is quite a long time ago, but, let me see . . . yes, but it was not he who called about it, but his housekeeper what was her name?'

'Mrs Custance.'

'Yes, a quiet, self-possessed woman – quite the lady. She brought a note from Miller: had any of us perhaps found it after his visit? I couldn't find the thing – I don't think I did, anyway. That is really all I remember about it. Is it important?'

'That remains to be seen, Mrs Jephson – oh, and I don't think we need trouble Mr Jephson about the matter. Yes, there was another thing . . .'

'What is that, doctor?'

'I should be most grateful if you could see your way to giving me Miss Vulliamy's address – there is a little matter I would like to discuss with her.'

'Ah, Dr Mortimer, there you place me in a rather difficult position. The fact is, Judith is most particular about receiving unexpected callers. Her clients, you see many have the notion she is a professional interpreter to be called upon – or out – at any hour of the day or night. She most strongly prefers callers to inform her in advance, so that she may call on them. I can give her a message, though, if it is so urgent.'

'That will be perfect, thank you. It is just that, the way things stand with me now, I am not sure when I will be available to receive her call. If you would be so good, then, as to ask her if she might call on me tomorrow at, say, ten?'

'And if she should ask the nature of your business, doctor?'

I rose and smiled.

'Just Brazil, Mrs Jephson.'

My hostess's eyebrows rose perceptibly, and she smiled faintly in return.

'Very good, Dr Mortimer: Brazil it shall be.'

I saw myself out, and made my way wearily home, hoping that a walk in the night air would revive my energies, but by the time I got to Henrietta Street, I was dead on my feet, and it was all I could do to play about with the late supper Lottie insisted on preparing for me before I staggered up to bed at the early hour of a quarter to ten. I kicked off my boots somehow, flung off my clothes, and, falling into bed, let sleep take me.

I breakfasted late that Thursday morning, and at ten o'clock – just as I had anticipated – I received no call from Judith Vulliamy. I did not tarry long, but, refreshed by my long sleep, dashed out in the direction of theatreland for memories of Miss Cora Raines. I should have taken comfort from the fact that Zeinvel's agent was at that moment duplicating my effort, but all I was conscious of was the stunning weight of my loss. I was prepared to run myself into the earth in my quest for Violet.

Nearest home, I looked in at Covent Garden, then the Haymarket, before going on to Leicester Square, nearer the heartland of that territory, and braving doorkeepers and angry audition-directors at the Empire, Daly's and the Garrick across the Charing Cross Road. Thence down into the Strand, heartland of the Kingdom of Greasepaint. On the north side, neither the Adelphi, the Gaiety, the Vaudeville nor the Olympic knew Cora, nor, on the south side, did Terry's, the Savoy or the Strand, but at the Tivoli Music Hall my efforts were requited. There, the man inside the little glass booth which stood guard within the portals of the stage door – aided, no doubt, by the small consideration I gave him – asked me to wait till he saw if Stanley was available. The gentleman referred to, a wiry little man with his forelock greased into a calf-lick – I was learning to recognise the dresser-breed – appeared with the booth-dweller five minutes later, bearing an album.

''E's got 'em all in there, 'as Stanley,' the doorkeeper said, as I poked my nose eagerly between their shoulders, and the dresser riffled in a leisurely way through the pages of signed photographs, enumerating in a precious voice the intimacies which the great ones in the photographs had shared with him over the years.

'And there she is, sir!' he lisped at last. 'Cora herself. Lovely she was then – boy's figure, I used to tell her. Unspoilt – that was the word. And so quiet, with it. Not that that sister of hers would have let anyone spoil her, sir, if you get my meaning . . . Real tartar the sister was – you only had to look at her, and she'd look as if she was going to knock you into next week.'

I craned even farther forward. A little fair thing in tights and an elfin sort of confection of a body-tunic, making an arch curtsey with her forefinger to her chin. Lithe like a boy, too, just as the dresser had said. The face appealing enough, but her physical appeal in the round would have been her main attraction. Something sombre in the eyes, I fancied, despite the high candlepower of the professional smile. At the bottom I read, in a round, childish hand: 'Truly yours, Cora Raines.' The handwriting was as unfamiliar to me as the face.

'Could I persuade you to part with this photograph for a little while, Mr, er . . . Stanley?' I said in a tone of controlled urgency. 'I shall leave my card with you, of course.'

The mannikin closed the album with an air of finality.

'Why, sir, I wouldn't part with any of my photographs for a minute, not if you were to offer me a gold sovereign for it.'

I offered him two, and it was mine for the duration. I rushed out, elated, into the Strand, with the photograph in my trembling hand, then disillusion crept in with the common light of day. I had the photograph of someone I didn't know from Adam, signed in a hand that meant nothing to me: what on earth was I going to do with it? Just then, a gnawing at the pit of my stomach reminded me that I was human, and I made my way down to Simpsons for a very late luncheon.

Half an hour later, I sat back, replete, in my pew, and took out the photograph. I laid it on the table beside my tankard, and looked into the dark, troubled eyes of Cora Raines, who had had the body of an Ariel, and who, as far as they knew at Sadler's Wells, had stopped dancing around the age of thirty and sought refuge from the world's uncertainties in marriage. Thus do our dancing days end, I reflected. But had it really been so? I made a sort of invocation: Cora, tell me where you are now.

But this nonsense was bringing me no nearer to finding Violet. Stanley the dresser had said that there had been a formidable sister in the wings – a sort of watchful duenna. It took at least two to chloroform a hefty soldier and dismember him alive, just as it would have taken two to overpower a young woman as physically robust and spirited as my wife. How long might they have been watching us? In Henrietta Street? At the dispensary? At both places? Would they have identified me as the Reverend Flockhart? The watcher was possibly someone perfectly humdrum, someone whom one would not give a second glance among the ranks of the Professional Unnoticed. Catching the waiter's eye, I paid the reckoning, and, leaving the chophouse, made thoughtfully for the Temple station.

26

It was half-past three when I reached the deserted dispensary, where my search lay this time among the invoices and other business papers in Violet's American roll-top desk in the consulting-room. There might be something. I ransacked all the drawers and compartments, until I found, wedged between two penny account-books, a rather creased letter, with a trade-name and address, in green, embossed print, at the head. This was of a Tilbury boatyard, but it was the handwritten testimonial which formed the text that interested me. In brief, 'Albert Cutliff General Foreman,' testified that 'you would have to go a long way to find pies that tasted like the holder's . . .' There was other stuff in this vein. The testimonial of Mrs Chinnery, the pie-woman who catered to the builder's men.

I flung the screed on to the desk-top in disgust, and, dis-heartened, began to swing myself back and forth on the swivel seat. In an idle gesture, I took out the photograph of Cora Raines and ran my gaze over it, as if a mere image could . . . But wait a moment! Surely not! I grabbed up the testimonial again with a trembling hand and compared the two sets of handwriting. I sucked in my breath, for the writing on the testimonial was simply a more mature version of the hand that had written the dedication on the photograph of Cora Raines! If Cora Raines had written the testimonial . . . I dropped everything and dashed down into the court, where I found Charlie Noble, who was rhythmically kicking a rusty can against a miniature chalked-out goal mouth on the wall of the close he lived in.

'Charlie!' I gasped. 'The piewoman who comes here at dinner-time . . .'

'Yus?' the urchin muttered, still absorbed in his one-man foot-ball game.

'Do you know where she lives?'

'No: you 'ungry, then?'

I knew my man.

'I could do with one of those steak pies right now – how about you?'

Kick-clang, clang-kick . . .

'Wouldn't mind . . .'

'Think you could find her?'

Charlie glanced up at me, wrinkling up his blackhead-pimpled snub nose.

'She wuz rahnd 'ere Monday night – I see her, didn't I?'

It was on the Tuesday that Violet had noticed that the dispensary day-book had been tampered with since she had left on the Monday evening.

'Did you follow her, Charlie?'

'Nah, why should I? Anyway, them's Foggie's pies from Brick Lane – know 'em anywhere. She don't make 'em.'

'You're sure of that?'

'Course I am – 'e puts rabbit in 'em – you can taste it. Lahvley . . .'

'Thanks, Charlie, I think I'll be off now. I won't forget your pie!'

I hastened back up into the dispensary, where I changed into my disreputable country togs and a battered tweed cricket cap. I selected my knobbiest loaded stick, then, leaving a note for the pharmacy lad to take to Zeinvel, informing the indefatigable lawyer of my day's luck, I locked up, and, plodding along at an easy slouch, with the stick under my elbow, I set off for Fogg's the butchers in Brick Lane.

The shop was opposite the Police House, at the corner with Fashion Street, and I decided to take up position in Blitz's eating-house, two doors down, where I secured a corner table near the window. I ordered coffee and a cheesecake, and waited for about half an hour, when, at twenty to five, a strapping woman in a tarred sailor's hat and tartan shawl could be seen striding up to the butcher's opposite. It was Mrs Chinnery. She was carrying a flat object under one arm. She went into the shop, to re-emerge five minutes later, the flat object evidently having translated itself into a pieman's tray, which was strapped round the woman's neck.

I got up, and, tossing a shilling on to the counter on my way out, left the eating-house, and began carefully to retrace my steps back to the dispensary, on a parallel course to that of the piewoman, ducking into alleyways or finding things of absorbing interest in shop windows whenever she was stopped by a chance street customer, or, as happened from time to time, she looked round her, no doubt to see if anyone was following her. The woman's route led back to the immediate area of the dispensary, where, as I was able to watch from a vantage point behind the giant wheels of a furniture-dealer's pantechnicon in the White-chapel Road, she cried her wares round the entrance to the court in which the dispensary was situated, then slipped into the court itself. Evidently, I had caught the evening watch . . . I knew I could rely on Charlie – if he was still there – to keep his mouth shut, inveterate foe as he was to the direct question. Ten minutes later, the woman reappeared in the Whitechapel Road, her now empty tray tucked under her elbow again. She made purpose-fully up the Whitechapel Road in the direction of St Mary's station.

I used all my craft, all my guile, to dog her footsteps, helped as I was by the fact that I was already on the station side of the road. Encouraged by this fact, I decided to back my own wager and go on ahead of the woman I knew as Mrs Chinnery to the station, for there can be few who see a pursuer in someone who is ahead of them, and on the other side of the road. I strode along briskly, and soon entered the station portal, and, like the stalwart woman who, accompanied by the little, fat, ginger-bearded man who pushed her companion in the invalid-chair two nights before, bought a ticket to Victoria. I joined the little crowd on the platform.

The seconds ticked away, and, gripped by doubts as to whether my gamble was going to pay off, I was on the point of hurrying out again in order to cut my losses – she could not have got that far up Whitechapel Road – when the piewoman marched on to the platform. She rested her tray, edge-up, on the ground, and waited with the rest of us. I cursed myself as I remembered a vital accessory to the railway-compartment Paul Pry, and hurried over to the station kiosk and bought a paper, returning to the platform just as the train was rumbling into the station. I followed the piewoman into a third-class compartment, and, installing myself in a seat two or three rows behind hers, put up my newspaper barrier, while peeping round its edge from time to time to see which way the land lay.

226

I counted off the intermediate stations: Mark Lane, the Monument, Mansion House, Blackfriars, Temple, Charing Cross, then, Westminster, where, as the train pulled into the station, a clunk of wood against the piewoman's seat put me on the alert. I peeped round the edge of my paper. She was getting off. I followed suit, allowing her to move as far ahead of me as I dared, without losing sight of her. The chase took me past the Houses of Parliament, and up the broad, important expanse of Victoria Street, until my quarry ducked abruptly into the huddle of Strutton Ground. By now it was nearly dark, and I hesitated before following the woman into the side-street. In that narrow thoroughfare, she had only to turn smartly on her heel, and the game would be up. I chose the bolder path, and, pulling the peak of my cap over my eyes, forged ahead and up into the turning into Old Pye Street, quickly crossing to the other side, from the corner of which I might spy back down Strutton Ground. I found myself alone on the corner, and peeped, ever so carefully, round it. My caution turned out to have been justified, for the woman chose just that moment to look round her before entering a passage at the side of the Kilkenny Cat public house.

I leant back against the street-corner, loafer-like, and, taking out my tobacco tin, rolled and lit a cigarette in leisurely fashion, all the while fuming and fretting inwardly, so great were the stakes in the game. What if, emerging into the other end of the passage, she was to give me the slip? But to be spotted by her entering the passage would surely be fatal to my purposes, and, more importantly, perhaps literally fatal to someone else . . .

I dithered mentally in this fashion for quite three or four minutes, until flicking the fag-end of my cigarette into the gutter, I strolled over into Strutton Ground and approached the head of the passage. I glanced cautiously down it, to see the piewoman's back – this time minus her tray – disappearing in the direction of Artillery Row. She must have spent the last few minutes in one of the properties that led off the passage.

My heart beating faster, I slipped into the gloom, and, huddling myself against the wall at the lip of the opposite entrance, saw the woman crossing the expanse of the Artillery Ground site. There I could not follow, for in that broad expanse of open ground, the woman must know – even in this twilight – that

I was dogging her steps. I was dismayed for a moment, then logic came to my aid: if I had kidnapped someone, then observed that the addressee of my ransom note was not in his usual place, what would be my first action? To see that my captive was still securely in place.

I examined the only building whose door was actually in the passage, the other side being occupied by the blank wall of the Kilkenny Cat. The entrance to the building was by an area doorway down a flight of steps, which I descended into the rubbish-strewn area. There was a dingy signboard above the door: 'Jos. Eagles, the London Furrier', and on either side of the door a tall, wide window, its panes dark with grime, and tacked over with a sort of veil made of rusty chicken wire. There was not a soul in sight, nor any sound to be heard. I approached the door, and examined the padlock which secured it. There was neither rust nor dirt on its stout securing-ring.

I looked round me to make sure the coast was clear, then inserted the ferrule of my stick into the half-moon bar of the padlock. I thrust the stick as far down into the half-moon as it would go, then wrenched at it with all my might, splitting and snapping off the ferrule and end of the stick in the process, but also breaking open the padlock, and leaving my way clear into the building.

The door opened easily – evidently not barred from inside – and I slipped into a dingy passageway, the soles of my boots crunching on straw and broken glass. There was a cool draught running from somewhere, and a smell of soot. Lighting my way with vestas, protected from the draught by my cupped hand, I opened each of the doors leading off the passage, quietly calling Violet's name into each before entering, but they were empty, until, at the foot of a flight of stairs, I came upon a locked door.

'Violet!' I barked nervously through the keyhole, and, to my unutterable excitement, heard the squeaking of what sounded like bedsprings, then a dull banging, as if something was being knocked against a wall. I stood back, then kicked with all my might at the door. The lock did not yield, so I turned my efforts to the panel below it, and kicked for dear life till the deal gave way. I lit my umpteenth vesta, and, stooping, peered through the shattered panelling. I could make out a bed against the opposite wall, and on it a wriggling figure. I flung down stick and vesta, and, wriggling like a ferret, got through the gap in the door.

Inside the room, I struck another vesta, and held it over the figure in the bed, to behold my wife's disarrayed tow hair spread over a coverless, rust-stained pillow. There was a gag in her mouth, and her trunk and arms were constrained in a tightly laced lady's corset, her reddened wrists, as well as her still-booted ankles, being secured by cords to the frame and posts of the old iron bedstead. There was a little cane table at one side of the bed, upon which stood a cheap paraffin lamp, alongside a half-full water-carafe. I pulled up the lamp-funnel with one hand and applied the dying flame of the vesta to the wick, then replaced the funnel. By the warm yellow light so produced, I got out my penknife and set to work on Violet's gag and bonds, then helped her gently to her feet. With joyous thanks in my heart, I gathered her in my arms, and quite forgot for the moment that I was a cold, relentless, calculating machine.

27

After I had assured myself that Violet had not come to any serious harm from her imprisonment – apart, as she had said, from acute indigestion caused by an exclusive diet of meat pies – we made our way out into Scrutton Ground, then managed to hail a cab in Victoria Street. We piled in, and I bade the cabbie make haste for Crutched Friars.

'Why Sadler's Wells?' was my first question to Violet after we had settled down on our journey.

'I had been following my own line of enquiries with regard to the apparently random dumping of little Emily Chaytor on the doorstep of Randall Moberley the eye surgeon in Bayswater, on the morning after Ostyankin's murder.'

'How many times, Violet,' I said angrily, 'have I urged – begged – you to share your lines of enquiry with me!'

'That, my dear James,' my wife replied with a little laugh, 'I will willingly do when you show signs of returning the compliment!'

I was too relieved for further recriminations, and urged her to go on with her story.

'I became more and more convinced,' Violet went on, 'that the choice of Moberley's house had been no accident, but the tribute paid by some witness to his former kindness . . .'

'A former patient?'

'Just so, but who? Now Emily's case had all the elements of a rescue, in which case, it seemed to me that an official rescuer would have come out into the open about it – stayed to tie up loose ends, if you like. Which rescuer, then, would have acted so furtively? A rescuer, moreover, with a reason to be grateful to Moberley?'

'One perhaps on the shady side the law – maybe even one who had been involved – willingly or unwillingly – in the vile trade that led Emily to Poland Street.'

Violet nodded.

'Or someone,' she went on, 'who had suffered what Emily had

been about to suffer, and had taken things into her own hands. I went to see Mr Moberley, and he kindly let me look among his papers, where I sought out the records of his cases around 1873, the year of Ostyankin's first publicly acknowledged visit to Britain . . .'

'And the year after the one in which he got his throat-wound, which left him in moments of excitement with a pronounced bark!'

'Yes – I see you have read the book I borrowed from the Charing Cross Hospital library. Well, Ostyankin was here in '73 for one of the many Balkan conferences of that decade. I found records in Moberley's journals of nearly thirty operations during that year, and pursued them all in the various hospitals and clinics indicated. One proved of special interest at Barts: Cora Raines, aged sixteen – just about the age Emily Chaytor will be now – in the care of St Dunstan's Blind Institution in Marylebone. The operation, performed in the October of that year, had been for a simple corneal scrape . . .'

'Mmm . . . cleaning away hardened scar-tissue formed by the healing-over of continual infections.'

'Yes, well, the operation was a complete success, and Cora Raines' sight was restored.'

'She will be thirty-four now,' I mused aloud.

'I next checked at St Dunstan's, and their records revealed that the police in one of their periodic sweeps against beggars had taken two young girls off the streets in the March of '73. The elder – she was seventeen – was called Dinah, and the younger – Cora – fifteen, and Cora was blind. She was accordingly sent to St Dunstan's, and Dinah to the local workhouse. On routinely examining Cora not long after, the medical officer at the Blind Institution recognised the possibilities for a cure, and the wheels were set in motion for Moberley's charitable intervention in October. This happy ending, however, had a sting in its tail, for having regained her sight, Cora no longer qualified for residence in the Blind Institution, and promptly rejoined her sister in the workhouse! The order of release was not far off, however, for a year later both girls were indentured into domestic service by the wife of the manager of Collins' Music Hall, where it soon became obvious that Cora, as well as having developed a most graceful person, had a marked talent for dancing . . .'

231

'And that was what led you to search the theatres, ending up chloroformed in Frostic Place.'

'Yes, and a very neat and well-judged job the doping was: as you'll appreciate, not even all trained physicians can handle chloroform with confidence.'

'I think we know the why – your picking up Cora Raines' trail at Sadler's Wells – but I'm still not sure of the who, especially in respect of the little, fat, Miller-shaped man who seems to have pushed you, unconscious, in the wheeled chair to St Mary's station . . .'

'Perhaps the notion of someone who had no love for Miller . . . I strongly suspect, James, that the hand that wielded the chloroform-pad in Frostic Place belonged to Dinah Raines, Cora's sister-cum-manageress, duenna and general watchdog.'

'But how? How would they have known by Tuesday evening that you'd been at Sadler's Wells at two o'clock? And how when they called you out on the wild goose chase would they have known about May Tighe's bad chest?'

'As to the first part of your question, it remains to be seen, but as to the second: why do you think the dispensary day-book – with all our patients' call-details – was tampered with on Monday evening?'

'Of course! Mrs Chinnery the piewoman alias Dinah Raines! She'll have got the Tighes' address there. So if Cora Raines did suffer as a child at the hands of Ostyankin, we have another strong suspect for his murder.'

'But she would have been blind then, James: how would she have recognised him in later life?'

'By hearing, Violet. What more memorable than a man who barks!'

'But on what possible occasion – how came it that their paths crossed?'

'That too remains to be seen. But did your captors say anything to you?'

'Not a word, and there was only one captor I remember: the big, raw-boned woman who administered the chloroform. She wore a red bandanna wrapped all round the lower part of her face and up over her nose like a highwayman's mask. She growled pretty eloquently, though, whenever I tried to struggle free at feeding times. Those pies . . . Then it was the gauze pad again . . .'

'My poor Violet: it must have been awful for you. It's been hell for me too.'

'Mustn't think about that now, James, my dearest,' Violet said, giving my hand a squeeze. 'We have much to do Now tell me what you have discovered in my absence.'

I took out the tubular tin coin-case Oliver the tobacconist had forced on me, and slipped it into her hand.

'This is the means by which Solomon Solomons came to find Ostyankin's sovereigns in back Poland Street without ever having been inside the murder house . . .'

'But how? Was it thrown down to him from the window, then?'

'No – by the laws of gravity and ballistics, under the strong influence of the north-west wind!'

'I still don't understand, but, wait, are you telling me that this is the very container Solomons found in the street?'

'No, but I've an idea where I might find it, and that'll be our next stop after Crutched Friars – ah, here we are . . .'

Just then the cab had turned into the street in question from Mark Lane, and we were not long after ushered into Zeinvel's chambers. As soon as we came into the room, the lawyer leapt out of his chair and rushed over to shake Violet's hand.

'Dr Branscombe!' he exclaimed, with a gleeful laugh. 'Why, this is a sight for sore eyes! But please sit down, both of you. I got your note about Cora Raines five minutes ago, Dr Mortimer, but first tell me all about Dr Branscombe's deliverance: I can't tell you how relieved I am!'

Zeinvel resumed his seat, and I told him the whole story, showing him the photograph of the younger Cora Raines in the process, but he merely glanced at it.

'I daresay she could be traced,' he said indifferently; 'that is, if she's still alive and in the country, but it would involve the expenditure of much shoe-leather and lots of time, which of course is exactly what we haven't got.'

'You have news of Solomons?' Violet asked eagerly, but Zeinvel merely nodded solemnly and averted his gaze.

'I understand Berry the hangman is at Nottingham at the

233

moment: Critchley the Beeston arsonist is to be executed there, probably tomorrow morning, then . . .'

'How soon?' Violet demanded hoarsely, leaning forward and gripping the edge of the lawyer's desk. 'You don't mean it could be Saturday morning?'

'No, it's customary for the executioner to spend the night before the execution in the actual prison. He needs to test and adjust the, er . . .. apparatus, for one thing, then he'll want to view Solomons thoroughly – through a peep-hole in the cell door – in order to judge his height and weight for the drop . . .'

'God!' Violet exclaimed with a shudder. 'In spite of all our blundering efforts, it has come to this! It could be Monday morning – it will destroy Iris.'

'Chin up, Dr Branscombe!' the dapper young lawyer remarked, with his usual cockney chirpiness. 'You and Dr Mortimer have done wonders in the last few days, and we may yet pull this particular chestnut out of the fire. You say you may be able to lay hands on the coin-case in question, Dr Mortimer? That would be a crucial piece of evidence: I suggest you have the police in attendance at the actual finding; otherwise there'll be no proof as to where you found the object – if you do find it.'

'Sound advice as usual, Zeinvel,' I remarked, though my heart sank at the prospect of trying to convince Sergeant Wensley and his superiors of the validity of what would no doubt seem to them to be my latest mare's nest. I exchanged glances with Violet, and we rose to our feet.

'Leman Street police station, then,' I said as we both took our leave of Zeinvel for the moment, our waiting hansom soon bringing us to that address, and the sceptical presence of Detective Sergeant Wensley.

'And just how did this flying coin-case of yours get out of the window of No. 11, Poland Street?' was his first response to our story, as we sat in one of the bleak, green-and-buff painted interview rooms of the Leman Street station. 'You're suggesting the wind made the curtains sweep it out – how? Was it lying conveniently on the windowsill? And didn't the murderer think it worth his while to go down and get it back, especially if his name was on it?'

'I tell you, sergeant,' I insisted, 'I believe I can lay my hand on it now . . .'

'Oh, yes?' Wensley replied, with maddening indifference. 'Where will that be, then? Not the ladies' Turkish baths, I hope . . .'

'At 144, Dorset Street,' I said, ignoring the sergeant's dig. 'Hardly a stone's throw from here. We've a cab waiting outside. A matter of fifteen minutes, sergeant, and a man's life at stake . . .'

Wensley's sole response was to fling his legs up, and, crossing them, rest his boots on the edge of the table.

'Flitterman's place,' he said wearily. 'I should've known: why, we went through it from top to bottom after Solomons was taken. Back yard, too. With a fine-tooth comb.'

I realised the time had come to stake all.

'But that's the whole point, Sergeant Wensley,' I said vehemently. 'The case wasn't there when you searched the place!'

The detective swept his legs off the table, and turned flinty eyes on us.

'I've warned you two before about concealing evidence . . .' he began grimly.

'But my dear man,' Violet erupted, 'how in God's name can we be concealing evidence when we're sitting here begging you to come and help us collect it!'

Wensley, evidently shaken by the logic behind my wife's remark, got up from the table and took a couple of paces, as if in thought, then stopped and turned to us again.

'Take time to get a warrant made out – Chief Inspector's gone home, and . . .'

'Hopefully we might not need a warrant,' I said. 'Let me make the initial approaches. Just an informal visit . . .'

Wensley finally led us into the corridor.

'Here we go,' I heard him mutter. 'Up the wall . . .'

The Flittermans were domestic outworkers, in the cheap melton overcoat line, and their workshop, which also served as living-room and kitchen, formed the principal of their two rooms on the ground-floor back, which, as I have described before, overlooked the yard over whose wall Solomon Solomons had dropped into the arms of the police on the afternoon of the day of General Ostyankin's murder. Besides Flitterman – a yellow, wasted-looking individual – and his stocky, raven-haired wife, there sat at the long table which occupied the centre of the room a young apprentice-improver – a 'greener', in the vernacular – a young woman coat-machinist and four sallow, dark-eyed children. There were piles of shaped, navy-blue broadcloth everywhere, and everyone around the table had a job to do, including the children, who were now staring solemnly at us like a row of marmosets, after we had knocked briskly on the open door and stepped into the room. No one got up to greet us, and the young woman's machine thumped and stuttered uninterrupted.

I introduced myself to Flitterman, and tried to make myself heard above the racket.

'I believe the police came to see you here last November, Mr Flitterman,' I shouted above the row, only to receive an anxious, uncomprehending stare. I was glad that Wensley had left the questioning to me, for I was sure his more direct methods of intimidation would instantly have sealed the lips of the whole household.

'He don't speak such goot English,' the raven-haired woman said to me. 'What do you want?'

'When your Sabbath stew came back from the baker's on the morning after the police came here last November, Mrs Flitterman, I believe you found something in it which wasn't there when you left it out for the man to collect just before Solomons had been chased down the passage outside. I'm right, aren't I?'

The woman stared at me intently, but said nothing.

'If you can remember, Mrs Flitterman, I believe that thing you found in your stew on the Saturday morning might be able to save an innocent man from being hanged.'

'Oh, please help, Mrs Flitterman!' Violet said beseechingly. 'You don't want to have blood on your hands, do you?'

The black-haired woman fixed her dark eyes on my wife's.

'I know you,' she said. 'You are the lady doctor from the Whitechapel Road. He is your man . . .'

The coat-maker's wife nodded in my direction, then Flitterman muttered something in his wife's ear. She waved him away, and seemed to ponder for a moment.

'There was no money in the thing – on my mother's life . . .'

My heart fairly sang with relief as Violet dug her fingers into my arm.

'Oh, we know that, Mrs Flitterman,' I said as reassuringly as

I could. 'The case was empty when Solomons dropped it in your stew.'

'Come with me,' the lady of the house said, and we trooped into the bedroom with her, where she went over to a dilapidated dressing-table, on which lay a flat wickerwork basket. She opened it, to reveal bobbins of thread and many-coloured wools. Mrs Flitterman rummaged in the little basket for a moment, then, taking out a coin-case identical to the one Oliver the tobacconist had sold me, slipped back the lid and spilt out a selection of sewing-needles and bodkins on to the table-top.

'The lid was loose when I found it,' she said, handing the case to me. 'I just cleaned it up, and used it for what you see.'

'God bless you!' Violet said fervently.

'Don't mention it,' the woman said with a shrug, as I eagerly examined the case. It had had some wear, but the initials stamped on its cap were still clearly outlined.

I gave a low whistle, and handed it to Violet, whose eyes widened as she read the stamped inscription on the tin. Finally Wensley, having finished his notes, and got Mrs Flitterman to sign them, looped the elastic back round his notebook and turned to us. Violet handed him the coin-case without comment.

Wensley rolled the metal tube in his fingers, weighed it in his palm, then slipped back the lid and angled it into the gaslight so that he could examine the inside, before turning his attention to the initials on the lid. He sucked his teeth audibly, and looked at each of us in turn with an intent air of speculation that seemed to have quite replaced his former scepticism.

'We shall have to look into this,' Wensley said quietly.

l

28

There followed a conference at Leman Street, to which Chief Inspector Moultry was summoned from home. He greeted Violet and me in friendly fashion – Moultry had led the official side in the Aldgate affair in which we had been involved the previous year – then, after Wensley had given him the details of the matter in hand, his blunt features knitted in concentration.

'This is going to be a tricky one,' Moultry said glumly. 'I want you to go straight away to the Scrubs, Wensley, and confront Solomons with the article – see if that loosens his tongue a bit. As for the initials . . .'

It occurred to me that Solomons had exercised considerable ingenuity, as well as presence of mind, in concealing the coin-case from his police pursuers; he was unlikely now to acknowledge the thing, and give away the associate whose initials were possibly stamped on it. But this consideration scarcely occupied the forefront of our minds after the revelation of those initials.

' But Chief Inspector,' Violet began to protest, 'surely you have your man now: the initials on the lid are A. M. – Alexander Miller . . .'

'Or Archie McTavish, Dr Branscombe,' Moultry replied with his genial good humour, 'or Ah Ming or whatever you like. Failing circumstantial corroboration from Solomons or someone else involved, that 'un won't run yet.'

'And we don't want to put Miller on his guard,' Wensley growled. 'We don't want him going on his travels like the other Russian witnesses . . .'

'But surely you're not just going to leave it at that,' I protested. 'Solomons won't talk, and . . .'

Moultry's pale, doughy features creased round the little peasant eyes as he positively beamed on us.

'Still hot for justice, hey, doctor? It's quite like old times. Oh, and I'd very much like to hear your explanation of just how the coin-case found its way into the back alley of Poland Street. Something about the curtain being swept out by the wind, and carrying it with it, wasn't it? Well, where was the case in the first place? On the windowsill?'

Just then, Wensley gave a ritualistic tap with his gloved hand against the side-pocket of his ulster, touched the brim of his bowler with his finger for his boss's benefit, and left on his errand. In the slight pause that followed, I mastered the feeling of deflation caused by Moultry's commonsense dismissal of the value of the initials on the coin-case as evidence, and had an idea.

'As to exactly how the coin-case found its way into the alley,' I said, taking up the thread of my conversation with Moultry again, 'I hope to be able to demonstrate to you, Chief Inspector. With your help, that is . . .'

'Well,' Moultry murmured, 'what had you in mind?'

'Is there still a police guard on the house in Poland Street, Chief Inspector?'

'Mmm . . . not since Solomons was sentenced last Wednesday: as far as we were concerned, we had no further official interest in the matter. Why?'

'Because I feel sure that whoever left the case there – whether it was the owner of the initials inscribed on it or someone else – will want very much to find out if it is still there.'

'If he knows it was there in the first place, that is, and another thing: where in the murder room would we plant it to make sure he went straight to it? No good just nabbing somebody for trespassing in the house. We'd need to nab him with the thing on him. Again, if he's been reading his papers, he'll know the place has been sifted from cellar to attic, and he'll have had to hide it pretty cleverly to think it was worth his while to come back and look for it after the official police search.'

I felt very much as Oscar Wilde must have felt when he coined his saying to the effect that using brute reason in argument was tantamount to 'hitting below the intellect'.

'I see the difficulty, Chief Inspector,' I said, my ardour considerably dampened, 'but won't you have the place put under surveillance again? Discreet surveillance?'

Moultry sat back in his chair, and, thrusting out both arms, laid the tips of his fingers on the edge of the table. He seemed to consider for a moment.

'All right, then, but I'll have to persuade the local division to chip in – can't spare men at this end – and this'll have to be after I've made representations higher up . . .'

We were much relieved to have Moultry's co-operation, however grudging, and, thanking him for his promise of help, we rose to go. The Chief Inspector's voice however interrupted our progress into the corridor.

'Now if you do manage to dream up exactly where the coin-case was left in the murder room, let me know straight away, will you?'

We gave our promise, and went out and rejoined our cab. I insisted on taking Violet home to Henrietta Street, and took supper with her there, after which I made her promise to make an early night of it, asking Lottie to bolt the front door after me, and to check that our bedroom door was locked from the inside before she turned in later on. I then set off for Soho Square, in search of Judith Vulliamy, who seemed to have an aversion to the mention of Brazil.

Again it was Lettice Jephson who received me at the Working Girls' Club, where, after I had made my apologies about the lateness of my visit, she told me that her husband had retired soon after they had had supper, on account of the strain the events of the past weeks had been having on his heart. I remembered his unhealthily high colour, and the blue tinge about his lips.

'As a medical man, Mrs Jephson,' I said, 'I should recommend that he take a long sea-voyage, with no duties whatsoever.'

'Not while we are needed here, Dr Mortimer. And have you news of your unfortunate, er . . . protégé?'

'No, ma'am, it is not Solomons' plight that I have come here about tonight, but to tell you that Miss Vulliamy has not kept the appointment you so kindly offered to suggest to her during my last visit here, and to ask if you can further help me in the matter . . .'

'Dear me, it is not at all like her to be unpunctual: I wonder what can be the matter? Well, I suppose I shall have to give you her address. She has a room at No. 22, Maddox Street, near Hanover Square.'

'Tell me, Mrs Jephson, has Miss Vulliamy ever mentioned Brazil to you?'

Real perplexity came into the lady's eyes.

'Why, no, Dr Mortimer, and I am bound to say that when I gave Judith that word as your message the other day, she was plainly as puzzled by it as I.'

'Pray what other response did she make concerning my message?'

'None save to thank me for telling her about it.'

'Did you ever meet her father, the Reverend Crispin Vulliamy, or visit him in his mission in Hamburg?'

'No, never – neither my husband nor myself has ever been to Germany – and Judith's father died before Hector and she became engaged.'

'I see – thank you, Mrs Jephson. I shall not keep you any longer – oh, but before I go . . .'

'Yes, Dr Mortimer?'

'You have not by any chance remembered anything else regarding my query of the other day – about the object Alexander Miller sent to enquire about at your old house in Ebury Street – the thing he claimed to have left behind on his one-and-only visit there?'

'The coin-case, you mean? No, I told you all I could remember about it.'

'I see – well, my thanks for your help at this late hour, and pray give my advice to your husband about the sea-voyage. I can see myself out.'

I got up to leave, and, as I stepped through the parlour door into the ground-floor corridor, I fancied I heard the discreet click of a door being shut stealthily. It occurred to me that Cormell Jephson might well have retired after dinner, but not to bed.

My visit to Judith Vulliamy's lodgings in Maddox Street was greeted by a grudging withdrawal of bolts, and the yawning advice of a general maid that Miss Vulliamy had left word that she would be going away for a few days, and that, no, she had left no forwarding-address. Back on the pavement, I took out my watch, and found it to be twenty past eleven. I felt tired, but all of a sudden felt a sort of premature sunrise in my heart: my wife was safe at home again. I hurried briskly up towards the cab-rank in Hanover Square.

Next morning, Violet insisted on going to the dispensary as usual, protesting that she was absolutely none the worse for her ordeal at the hands of the chloroformers. I saw that my protests were in vain, but nevertheless prevailed on her to take on her journey a packet of pepper and a small life-preserver, which I urged her not to hesitate to use against any stranger who might accost her on the way. I further insisted that she travel from door to door in a hansom which I went out after breakfast to engage at Charing Cross, the cabbie of which was known to me. Having next secured her Bible-oath that she would not stir out from the dispensary until I had arrived there to collect her later, I saw her into the waiting cab, and, sternly enjoining the cabbie to stop for no one on the way, waved my wife off to work.

I set off at once for the house-agents in Berkeley Square who handled 11, Poland Street, and was not at all surprised to learn that the house was still on their hands. Indeed, the clerk was not a little chopfallen to hear that I was not interested in renting it, for I had thought better of his offer of an order to view in consideration of the fact that, hopefully, Chief Inspector Moultry's plain-clothes watch would now be in place there, and I did not wish to compromise their efforts. One thing reassured me above all else: the clerk's confirmation that the house had come fully furnished, and that none of the fittings or furnishings had been changed in any way since General Ostyankin's murder. He further informed me that, since the previous Wednesday, the same cleaner that had found the general's body had been able to resume her duties there. All then, would seem to be back to normal, and it was my fervent hope that this situation would soon be appreciated by someone who would want to search discreetly through the former house of assignation for a lost object.

Moultry confirmed that the watch on No. 11 was already in place when I arrived at his office in Leman Street police station forty minutes later.

'And the cleaner?' I asked. 'You are quite sure about her?'

'Absolutely in the clear, doctor, and has been all along. Cast-iron alibi. She knows nothing of what we're up to at present, either – better that way.'

'And Solomons? Did he tell Sergeant Wensley anything in Wormwood Scrubs?'

'Not a sausage! Seemed to look straight through the coin-case, then told Wensley he didn't talk to capitalist mercenaries! It's as if he wanted to swing . . .'

'And the Home Office won't stay their hand?' I asked, hoping against hope, for I knew that the coin-case alone would not be enough to spring Solomons from jail.

'We're to keep the Permanent Secretary informed from hour to hour, but as things stand, the law will still be taking its course.'

'What do we do, then, Chief Inspector?'

'We wait.'

And that, in a nutshell, is what we did, as the weekend drew in and we went about our everyday business on a sort of nerve-stretching mental tiptoe. I learned from Zeinvel on the Saturday morning that Berry the public executioner had done his awful duty in Nottingham on the previous day, my legal friend leaving it to my imagination what that gentleman's next job of work might be. No message came from Judith Vulliamy, and a final visit on my part to Soho Square drew no more from the now wasted-away Cormell Jephson than the statement – made with averted eyes – that to his inexpressible sorrow, he could offer me no more help in the matter. It really did look as if, barring a miracle, Solomon Solomons would be dead by Monday morning.

29

After morning surgery on Sunday, Violet and I took luncheon at Gatti's, then retired to Henrietta Street and put our heads together over the case to date. We began with the murder of Ostyankin itself.

'The first person to make an appearance on the scene at 11, Poland Street,' Violet began, 'or rather, the first person to come out into the open – the cleaner – is in the clear, with an established alibi.'

'She finds the doors locked,' I went on, 'just as they should be.'

'But the shut windows have their catches off.'

'Which suggests a hurried retreat by whoever opened them: either the murderer, or one of the murderers, or a later arrival.'

'The cleaner finds the body,' Violet said.

'Yes, but what else?'

'Certainly not the coin-case: Solomons picks that up from the street below, and, pursued later by the police, drops it into the Flittermans' waiting Sabbath stewpot. We still don't know exactly how the coin-case got down into the street, except that the opened window, the curtains and the wind must have played parts.'

'Who do we know has been to the house in Poland Street since Ostyankin's arrival there ten minutes or so after eleven thirty on the Thursday night?' I asked.

'Miller could have been there about an hour later, if the poor drunkard Wellcome is to be believed, and at least four others, including little Emily Chaytor, if her story about the foreign lady, the nice-smelling lady and the blindfold-game holds water – and it took place in the house in Poland Street.'

'I no longer seriously doubt that, Violet – the dumping of the child on Randall Moberley's doorstep can scarcely have been a random act, after what you found out about Cora Raines and her background.'

244

'But again,' Violet said, 'if Cora Raines rescued Emily, did she also murder Ostyankin?'

'Well, Ostyankin's murder and your abduction had one thing in common . . .'

'Chloroform.'

'Yes and skilfully administered chloroform at that. Really, we may take our choice as to which of our *dramatis personae* may have been at the scene of the crime within two hours or so of its commission.'

'We can include Cormell Jephson, with his nocturnal rescue-missions.'

'And the elusive Miss Vulliamy, who is so sensitive about revealing her whereabouts and movements, and who would seem to have a *doppelgänger* in Brazil . . .'

'And there is also Lettice Jephson,' Violet added, 'who is also no stranger to Soho at night.'

'Then there are Solomons' movements, both before and after his golden windfall: he is seen by Iris Starr and Brummie Ida coming out of the Warsaw Café in Osborn Street in company with Semyon Klaff at about half-past eleven on the night of the 27th of November. They adjourn for a minute or so to Klaff's lodgings a bit farther down Osborn Street, then they set off in a south-easterly direction, arriving, according to Gaselee the sea-going engineer, at the Lord Raglan public house in Limehouse around midnight.'

'The most logical route would be along Commercial Road,' Violet added, 'and there would have been time for them to look in at the Berner Street Club, and on our one-eyed friend Diamant.'

'Yes, it is scarcely conceivable that he would have played no part in the affair. Perhaps Solomons and Klaff were given orders there . . .'

'Or made arrangements for their departure from England – the dockland setting would seem strongly to suggest this.'

'Yes,' I said, 'and the Lord Raglan in Limehouse would further suggest a meeting with some seafaring man.'

'But not Gaselee!' Violet remarked with her deep chuckle. 'I can well understand the rather chilly reception he said they gave him there if in barging in on them he'd wrecked their agreed rendezvous with someone else!'

'Quite! Let's assume that when they left the public house around one, they somehow made other arrangements. Perhaps there was an alternative rendezvous, in case of just such a setback – the Warsaw, say, where PC Kennedy spotted Solomons around that time. Then Solomons reappears, sighted again by Iris, making his way along Wentworth Street at one thirty, and going in the direction of Liverpool Street station.'

'To be lost to view,' Violet said, 'until Wellcome espies him from his perch on the outhouse roof at around two, at which time Ostyankin is already cold meat.'

'Our protégé, then, is in the clear – at least as far as the actual killing is concerned. We must piece together something plausible out of this jumble.'

'And we must prove it!' Violet said tartly.

'Yes – God! It may only be a matter of hours . . .'

'I know, I know – think, James, think . . .'

Just then Lottie came in with the tea things, and we set to solemnly.

'James,' Violet said in an absent-minded tone, after she had taken her first bite of eccles cake.

'Yes, dear?'

'Did you ever find out why De Kok – or Coe – took an extra overcoat with him when he fled to Belgium with only a Gladstone bag for luggage, and why they never found his stick?'

That was a detail that had been rather pushed aside by other events in my mind, a detail which made me remember my ludicrous visit to the Turkish baths. Turkish baths . . .

'Counters!' I spluttered, putting my cup down with a clatter in its saucer.

'What's that, James?'

'One is given them – numbered ivory counters – at the Turkish baths when one hands one's outside things over to the attendant on entering.'

'Go on . . .'

'Don't you see? Two identical coats – Miller's and Coe's – and sticks ditto. The sticks would have screw-tops and metal tubes inside for holding brandy or whisky . . .'

Violet's eyes widened, and she put down her cup into her saucer.

'I see, James! Instead of brandy – sovereigns. If the, er . . .

wares provided by Coe for one of Miller's lecherous clients – or high-life dupes – prove satisfactory, payment is collected simply by the discreet and silent exchange of ivory cloakroom counters in the anonymity of the Turkish baths . . .'

'Yes! On leaving, Coe hands in Miller's counter, to receive Miller's coat and stick loaded with ill-gotten gains. It would also explain the bagginess of the coat on Coe – both garments must have been made to Miller's measure, to make room for his plumpness.'

'A minor-seeming point, but our theory is further buttressed. Then there's the cleaning woman in Poland Street . . .'

I was still thinking about walking-sticks . . . I recalled, not a walking-stick, exactly, but an umbrella, and the meticulous way someone had handled it . . .

'James!' Violet's voice interrupted my reverie. 'You are not listening!'

'I am, my dear – you were talking about the cleaning woman . . .'

'Yes the cleaning woman in Poland Street: it occurs to me that, if she was not party to the murder of Ostyankin, whoever arranged the murder would have had to take account of her arrival there first thing in the morning.'

'Yes, go on.'

'And barring accidents – such as someone's finding the sovereign-case in the street below after some interloper had opened the windows and the curtains had swept it out – the cleaner would have been the first to find anything that had been left behind after the murder.'

A light dawned on me.

'What if the coin-case was *meant* to be found, but by the police, not the cleaner?'

'To incriminate someone else? Then the windowsill would have been a pretty poor place to hide it, and this in fact was proved when the case was swept out by the billowing curtain when someone opened the window.'

'But what if the case wasn't on the windowsill at all, but was nevertheless blown out by the curtain?'

'But surely that's impossible. Something that isn't there can't be swept out!'

'Not if the coin-case had been slipped into the hem of the

curtain, so that the police would find it when they gave the room the fine-tooth-comb treatment!'

'Ah, yes!' Violet exclaimed huskily. 'I see. When the cleaner came into the room, all unsuspecting, and found a bloodsoaked corpse on the bed, her first thought would hardly have been to go and feel the curtains!'

'Leman Street police station, I think!' I cried, leaping to my feet, and we prepared to set off immediately.

Chief inspectors are not usually to be found on duty on Sundays, and Moultry was no exception, but fortunately Sergeant Wensley was still on the prowl – somewhere in the vicinity of Pennyfields, we were told – and we were invited by the duty sergeant to await his return in an interview room. Wensley did not show up till a full hour later, at twenty to five, but his manner clearly told us that he was ready to give us his full attention. He pushed his bowler back on his head, and, not pausing to take off his ulster, bestrode a seat at the interview table while I told him of my new theory.

'It was when Dr Branscombe here pointed out to me that the murderers would have had to take the arrival of the Poland Street cleaning woman in the morning into account that I hit on the only way I could envisage that incriminating evidence might be left in the murder room – safe from her notice – but in a way that would allow it to land – completely fortuitously – at Solomon Solomons' feet when the plot in fact went wrong.'

'What d'you mean, doctor, "incriminating evidence"? I thought we were dealing with murder here, not conspiracy.'

'In my firm view, sergeant, we are dealing with both: Ostyankin was to have been murdered, and someone else incriminated for the deed.'

'What went wrong, then?' Wensley demanded gruffly. 'Somebody put his oar in, did he?'

'In a nutshell, sergeant. The interloper had his own fish to fry in No. 11 that night, and, realising that things were going wrong, he goes upstairs to investigate. He finds the murder room filled with suffocating smoke, caused by a back-draught blowing down the chimney – you may recall how windy it was that night – and blowing out into the room the smoke caused by smouldering cloth in the grate . . .'

'Bloodstained gear the murderer'd put on the fire before hooking it, you mean?'

'Yes, and after the interloper had flung up the windows – unwittingly sending the coin-case flying when the curtains billowed out – and waited till the smoke had cleared, then seen what was lying on the bed . . .'

'Someone had already done his work for him!' Violet interjected.

'Yes – only too well! Well, when he saw that, he'd have slammed the windows down pretty smartly, and made himself scarce, without staying to secure the catches again.'

'Yes,' Wensley said irritably, 'that's fairly in line with the known evidence, but you still don't say how, if the coin-tube thing was hidden away so cleverly, it got down to Solomons in the street below.'

'If you'll just come over to the window, sergeant, I shall demonstrate with my coin-case.'

Wensley and Violet followed me over to the nearest window, where I lifted the foot of one of the coarse green curtains, and held it up towards the sergeant.

'Curtains come with a lower hem, sergeant, some tightly stitched back, others not. This one – in common, I suspect, with the one in the murder room – is not tightly stitched back.'

I took out my coin-case, which I had previously loaded with shilling-pieces, and slid the smooth, metal tube – for all the world like a rifle-cartridge – easily into the rolled-up hem of the curtain. I then pushed it nine inches or so along the hem for extra security.

'Well, I'll be . . .' Wensley muttered, but then, apparently checking himself: 'Our men would have looked there, of course – matter of routine . . .'

'I don't doubt it, sergeant,' I said, 'and I'm equally sure the conspirator was relying on it, too.'

'With you!' Wensley barked, getting up and perching on the edge of the table. 'He wanted our chaps to find it, but not the charwoman! First thing I'd have thought of on finding it would've been that the char had arrived, seen the body, then, having dashed straight back out and come back with the constable, had spotted the coin-case near the scene of the crime before he had – say just under the bed. She'd have recognised it

249

as a coin-case – maybe her old man has one – and, thinking she might do herself a bit of good, but not wanting to be caught with it on her if they searched her, picked it up nippy-like as soon as the constable's back was turned and shoved it into the curtain-hem, hoping to come back and collect the dibs later. I'd have suspected it had been dropped there accidentally by the killer, then, when I'd looked at the initials stamped on it . . .'

'It is nearly six, sergeant!' Violet snapped. 'You know what is going to happen first thing tomorrow: now will you go along with my husband's plan?'

'Very well, then,' Wensley said, slipping off the edge of the table, and, adopting a more alert posture, addressed me.

'D'you want us to use the original coin-case?'

'Yes, sergeant, I think it would be more, shall we say, authentic. And now, do let us be going . . .'

'"Us", Dr Mortimer?' the sergeant quizzed, with an unpleasant little smile. 'This is a matter for the force now. You may rest assured that if anything can be made out of all this, we are the men to do it.'

'Hmph!' Violet snorted. 'Trust you to sniff promotion, sergeant!'

Wensley chuckled, and pulled the rim of his bowler down over his eyes.

'Well, I'll tell you what I'll do, seeing as you've both put such an effort into this: if we do make a pinch tonight – and there's no particular reason why we should on this night above any other – you'll be the first to know. Well, after Zeinvel, that is – he being Solomons' solicitor, and much though I regret the necessity. As I say, if anything does turn up, I'll send word straight away, and you can come with us to the Scrubs afterwards – if Zeinvel has no objection – after I've made the pinch . . .'

In spite of all our entreaties to be allowed on the scene in Poland Street – unreasonable as they were, as we saw on cold reflection – Wensley proved adamant, and we were left to stew in our own juice for the rest of the evening. We took – or rather, pecked at – dinner in the Charing Cross Hotel, then retired to Henrietta Street, prepared to pass the night in anxious vigil. We did not care to think of the morrow . . .

'Wensley was perfectly right,' I reflected aloud at one point. 'There's no particular reason why the murderer should choose to appear tonight of all nights in Poland Street, just because we wish it so . . .'

But I was wrong, and, as it was soon to turn out, there was to be a very simple reason why the case was to be resolved where it had started – in No. 11, Poland Street that very night. At around four in the morning, we were both nodding in our armchairs in our little smoke-filled sitting-room, when a sharp rapping at the street door was followed in short order by the hurried padding of Lottie's bare feet on the stairs. I heard the bolts being drawn downstairs, then a hard, clear man's voice. The rapid padding on the stairs recommenced, and, seconds later, panting and wide-eyed, her hair in paper twists and her thin hands clutching the waist of her nightrobe, Lottie appeared before us.

'It's the perlice, mum!' she gasped at Violet, who had been the first to bestir herself 'They say you're both to step downstairs and come with them in a Black Maria!'

The journey to Poland Street was swift, and passed inside the police van in tense silence. When we pulled into the actual street we saw that something had indeed turned up. There was a knot of men in plain clothes, with Wensley prominent among them, around a stationary ambulance in the mouth of back Poland Street. The constable who had accompanied us in the van jumped out and helped Violet down, then I jumped down after them, and we hurried over to Wensley. By the light of the nearby lamp-post I could make out Zeinvel among the group. The detective sergeant spotted us, and, with a grim smile, touched the brim of his bowler in recognition.

'You've made an arrest?' I asked excitedly.

'See for yourself,' Wensley replied, with triumph in his voice, nodding behind him into the alley. A stretcher was being borne towards the ambulance by two orderlies in hospital whites.

'You couldn't have come at a better time,' the sergeant remarked, chattering rapidly in his excitement. 'Two doctors on the scene – I didn't think he was going to flake out on us . . . He went straight for the window. Got his signature in my notebook before he keeled over, though. Full confession. Congratulations, Dr Mortimer and Dr Branscombe – I suppose I've got to include you in that, too, Zeinvel – your man Solomons is as good as sprung now . . .'

Just then the strapped-down figure on the stretcher came into full view under the street-lamp. I peered into the ashen face and let out a gasp of dismay and sheer disbelief.

30

Violet and I gave what medical help we could to Cormell
Jephson in the ambulance on the way to Charing Cross Hospital,
while Wensley and Zeinvel rumbled off in the police van to set
the wheels of the law in motion with regard to Solomons. It was
clear, however, as the ambulance sped down Poland Street, that
nothing much could be done for the hapless clergyman on the
stretcher, whose straps we had by then undone. His breathing
was laboured and stertorous, and his skin leaden and beaded
with sweat, as he lay in a sort of half-coma. He had, we learned
later, gone straight for the window after forcing the back door of
the house, and had been taken while fumbling with the curtain.
The syncope which had evidently seized his already strained
heart when Wensley and his colleagues had nabbed him must
have been the signal for the inevitable. But Jephson . . . I exchanged glances with Violet, and read confirmation in her eyes
that she was thinking along the same lines. Suddenly there was
a stirring on the stretcher, and I felt my hand gripped by the
clammy hand of the stricken man.

'Dr Mortimer,' he whispered. 'The pain is in my back . . . my
back. I never thought it would . . .'

'Never mind, Mr Jephson,' I murmured, 'you will soon be in
the most expert hands in the kingdom . . .'

'No, doctor, it is all for the best. Solomons must not die . . .'

The clammy grip grew tighter, and Jephson tried to rise from
the stretcher.

'He will not be hanged, Dr Mortimer? I am not too late – for
Jesus' sake . . .'

'No question of Solomons hanging now,' I murmured, gently
coaxing Jephson back down on to the stretcher. He then seemed
to reach out towards something on his left.

'Open the . . . open the . . .' he gasped, then, twisting himself
up in a sort of hoop, he slumped, face-down on to the stretcher
again. The eye visible on my side was glazed and unblinking.
Violet took Jephson's wrist.

'It is over, James,' she said quietly, as she leant forward to help me rearrange the body more decently.

'Dead is he?' the accompanying plain-clothes man said with professional indifference, then, at our nods, took out his note-book, then consulted his watch.

I made no attempt in the CID man's presence to express my shock and surprise. It was better so, as the situation could not be altered. We arrived presently at the Charing Cross Hospital – my alma mater – and I quickly arranged with the head porter to have Jephson's body placed in the hospital mortuary, then we left the plain-clothes constable to do what was officially necessary.

'If we jump in a cab immediately,' Violet suggested, 'we may be able to get to Wormwood Scrubs ahead of Wensley and his party. Lord knows how long it'll take them to get their official red tape sorted out, and by the time they do, Solomons might already have been hanged!'

I needed no further prompting, and, hardly two minutes later, we succeeded in hailing one of the disengaged hansoms which even at that early hour of the morning were to be found before the portals of the busy hospital. Once on our way – our journey considerably speeded up by the offer of a florin tip to the driver, if he should get us there in half an hour – we gave vent in the privacy of the cab to our up-till-then suppressed reactions to the arrest of poor Cormell Jephson.

'So it had to be tonight – or rather, last night – after all,' I said.

'To save Solomons from the scaffold this morning, you mean?' Violet asked. 'Then whom was he trying to shield? He must have known about the coin-case.'

I remembered my last interview with Lettice Jephson at the Soho Working Girls' Club, and the soft closing of the door in the private passage as I had left. Horror seized me, as the implications of Cormell Jephson's possible eavesdropping of that talk sank into me. On my quizzing Mrs Jephson about the coin-case, might the eavesdropping clergyman have been confirmed in a suspicion that it had been his wife who, during his absence on some night-rescue mission, had avenged herself on Ostyan-kin, one of the architects of the ruin of her only son's career and life? And that it had been she who had planted Miller's coin-case on the scene of the murder? I was aghast. I had prompted the clergyman to sacrifice himself in order to protect his wife . . . But it might be worse yet, for I recalled my identification while browsing in the marked medical books of Hector Jephson's form of syphilis – *tabes dorsalis*, the congenital form of the disease. What if Lettice Jephson herself had passed on this awful inheritance to her son while he was still in the womb? How she had implored me to desist from further enquiry into Hector Jephson's condition on her visit to the dispensary . . .

'But how did Jephson know that the coin-case was in the curtain-hem?' Violet went on. 'Wensley said he went straight to the curtain . . .'

'No, Wensley's actual words were that he went straight for the *window*. He needn't have known the coin-case was there.'

'But why then start at the window? He'd nothing to go on.'

'The window-catches. When the police arrived the windows were shut but the catches were off. That was the only anomalous fact about the room that came out during the trial – it was really *all* Jephson had to go on. That being so, it made sense that he should start his search at the window, and to examine a window you've first to draw aside the curtains. As for the "full" confession – allegedly made by a semi-comatose, dying man – I'm sure Wensley would have worked the fact of the coin-case being in the hem of the curtain into Jephson's statement, ready for his "nabs'" signature. You've some idea of Wensley's methods . . .'

'I see now,' Violet said, then, consulting her watch: 'Lord! Seven already . . .'

I banged on the canopy with my stick, and the flap swung up.

'Make that florin five shillings if you can get us there in ten minutes!' I shouted up to the cabbie, and we were jerked back in our seats as the cab went even faster. Seven minutes brought us to the gate of the prison, and, thrusting a five-shilling piece into the cabbie's hand, along with his fare, I dashed up and began to belabour the wicket-gate with the tip of my stick, thanking God that there was no fresh notice affixed to the massive timbers . . .

''Ere, 'ere, now . . .' came a voice from an opened judas-window.

'I demand to see the governor immediately!' I cried. 'The

police are on their way. They have full authority – the Home Office has been informed.'

''E's got a job to do at the moment,' the man said, clearly humouring me. 'I might try 'im after breakfast for yer, if yer'd . . .'

'That'll be too late!' Violet exclaimed. 'It's Solomons' execution – it's to be stopped. For God's sake let us in!'

I saw the man's eyes widen through the judas-window.

'Got papers, 'ave yer?'

I took a spare visiting-card out of the pocket of my ulster and pushed it through the judas-window. The man grabbed it from inside, but I heard no answering grinding of drawn bolts.

'This is no good,' he mumbled at length. 'Yer'll 'ave ter . . .'

'I warn you,' Violet said coldly, 'if an innocent man dies because of your shilly-shallying, your superiors will be only too glad to let you take the full blame.'

That did it. The door opened grudgingly, and we both barged through.

'Yer'd better come this way, an' I'll talk to the duty warder.'

We followed the man upstairs and through various corridors, then briefly across a sort of safety-netted nave with tiers of cells leading out on to metal walkways, until we came to a small duty-room, into which our guide disappeared for a minute with my visiting-card. I heard the words 'medical man', 'administration block', and 'all set up and ready', then a big, hairy-faced man in uniform emerged from the room with the doorkeeper. He glared at us for a moment, then dismissed the doorkeeper with a nod.

'If you'll both follow me,' the big man said.

We were conducted in silence to a secluded corridor, then asked to wait in a room which led off from it. The moment the warder had left us, I thrust my head through the door, and watched him, slightly bowed down, knocking gently at the door which lay at the end of the corridor.

'It must be the governor's office,' I said. 'We can't afford to take chances . . .'

So saying, I rushed into the corridor, and, before the warder had time to protest, grabbed the handle of the door, which, I noticed at a glimpse, bore a brass plate with the words: 'Captain Sutton Kirkpatrick, Governor', and rushed into the room.

There I fell under the angry stare of a straight-backed gentleman in morning dress, who was standing, top hat in hand, by the side of a desk, as if just about to leave for somewhere else.

'What is the meaning of this?' he demanded sharply.

'He was on me before I could . . .' the hairy-faced man began to excuse himself, as he seized me roughly by the arm.

'A chair for the lady, Rosser!' the man by the side of the desk said as Violet came into the room, and I felt the warder's hand let go of my arm.

'. . . and the police are following behind me in a heavy van . . .' I concluded, after I had blurted out the details of our business at the prison.

'I don't know you from Adam, sir,' the impassive man in the morning coat said, with a glance at my visiting-card, 'and I give you fair warning that if this is a stunt, and you are bent on inflicting further mental torture on a condemned man . . .'

'It is no stunt, Captain,' Violet said with husky earnestness. 'The astonishing turn of events my husband has just described to you is perfectly genuine.'

'I shall give you ten minutes,' the governor said, putting his hat on the desk, then taking out a pencil-case and scribbling a note, which he gave to Warder Rosser, who nodded and hastened out of the room. The governor then paced the room in silence for seven agonising minutes, while Violet tore at her handkerchief, and I tapped my foot like a paralytic. It came like a reprieve, when, preceded by another prison officer, Wensley and his party erupted into the room.

'You've cut it rather fine, Wensley . . .' Captain Kirkpatrick said grimly.

'It's not too late, is it, sir?' Wensley said, handing the governor a folded document, which he took without replying, broke the seal, and read.

'The execution will be stopped,' Kirkpatrick said. 'I shall go now . . .'

Violet's gloved hand shot out immediately and clasped mine, then things started to move quickly. I felt, as they say, dizzy with success, and so did Violet, to judge by her shining, brimming eyes. One scene stands out: our making way for a little party in one of the inner corridors of the prison, a party centred round a haggard, white-faced Solomon Solomons. He paused as he came upon us waiting by the side, and for a moment his eyes met mine. I felt as if I were looking into the Pit.

'Thank you, Dr Mortimer,' he said simply, before his official companions hurried him down the corridor and out of our ken.

'Oh, thank God, James!' Violet exclaimed, dabbing her eyes with her handkerchief. 'As soon as it is made official, we must go to Hackney to tell Iris.'

It was not until after eleven that morning that Solomons was bundled out of Wormwood Scrubs by two men in plain clothes, and into a cab to Victoria station. It was the last we were ever to see of him, and when we did arrive with the news at the Hackney refuge where his sweetheart Iris Starr was being sheltered, the street-girl's joy at her lover's deliverance was about equally countered by her dismay at not being able immediately to join him.

'Be sure he'll write as soon as he arrives at wherever it is they're sending him,' Violet sought to reassure Iris as they shared a sofa in the Reverend Hilary Venables' neat parlour. 'The main thing is, he's alive.'

''S'right, mum!' Iris exclaimed, cheering up. ''E'll be writin', sure as apples!'

On that bright note we left her in Hilary Venables' care till things became clearer. We felt absolutely wrung out after the release of the sustained nervous tension which had had us in its grip for so long, and it was as if in a dream that we made our way home for food and rest that afternoon. We were not to be allowed much rest, though, for at three o'clock we were summoned to Leman Street for further questioning, so that, by the time we were free again, it was time for evening surgery. I bought evening papers, and on all the front pages was the story of Cormell Jephson's sensational capture, confession and death – 'Clergyman the Russian Ripper!' – and of Solomons' release and abrupt departure from England.

That night, in the cab home after evening surgery, I got out my paper and glanced idly through the rest of the day's news. A report of a Parliamentary debate caught my eye; or rather the accompanying sketch of its prime mover. In the languid, dandified features, I recognised the departing visitor who had made

258

the appointment with Miller for nine o'clock this very evening in the passage of his house in Farm Street on my last visit there.

I showed the page to Violet, and tapped the sketch with my finger.

'Do you recognise this man Le . . . Le Tou . . . .whatsisname?' I asked.

'It is Le Thuillier, the Liberal MP,' Violet said with a sniff. 'He fought tooth and nail against the Criminal Law Amendment Bill. A cynic and a libertine . . .'

I then recalled that one of the provisions of that bill – now the law of the land – was the raising of the age of consent from thirteen to sixteen. Now having seen Le Thuillier with Miller, I began to wonder if the former's opposition to the bill might have sprung from a more personal motive than the world had hitherto suspected. A dark suspicion took hold of me, and, on our reaching home, and to her evident surprise, I told Violet that I had one last urgent piece of business to attend to in Farm Street before I could put the day behind me.

'But what, James?' my wife quizzed me on our doorstep, as I returned to the cab.

'To prevent two further murders, my dear . . .'

31

I arrived at Alexander Miller's house in Farm Street just in time
to find the timber-agent with his foot on the step of a cab, a
lightly slung cloak hardly concealing his full evening dress. He
was evidently on his way to some evening engagement, and,
turning on the cab-step, he gave me his little sideways bow and
smug smile.

'So! The Reverend Mr Flockhart has abandoned his clerical
garb for the evening; or perhaps he is in disguise? And what a
relief it must be for him not to have on those so absurd spectacles – to be able to see again! I do not know who you are, sir,
but I must say it has been a most charming masquerade . . .'

The man's complacent mockery goaded me to fury, and I cried
out wildly, shattering the respectable calm of Farm Street.

'By God, you shall know me, Miller! You shall rue the day you
ever set eyes on me!'

The plump little man only laughed, and was about to turn into
the cab, when I reached into my pocket, and, pulling out my tin
coin-case, flung it in his face. Cursing under his breath, he
managed a fumbling catch, then, when he had looked at the
object he had caught, the smirk died from his face and his jaw
fell. It was as if Blind Pew, in *Treasure Island*, had pressed the
Black Spot into his palm.

Seeing the effect my gesture had had on him, I exulted in my
rage.

'Not the one you're looking for, Miller,' I shouted, laughing,
'the one with your initials on it. But never fear, it will soon find
you . . .'

I had reasoned that, with Jephson's confession to Ostyankin's
murder in their pocket, the police would not have hurried over
questioning Miller about how a coin-case with his initials
stamped on it had been found in the murder room in 11, Poland
Street.

The Russian, ashen in the glare of the nearby streetlamp,
grasped the coin-case in his pudgy fist, and, glaring at me, flung

it violently on the pavement, where it rolled, ringing, at my feet.

'You are mad!' he growled through clenched teeth, and, shouting at the cabbie to drive on, he got into the hansom, and it moved away.

I was conscious of being watched, and I glanced up at one of the ground-floor windows of the house, to see, framed in the window, the form of Miller's housekeeper, Mrs Custance. Her eyes met mine, and they seemed to be dancing with excitement. On her lips was a little smile of unmistakable glee. I picked up my coin-case and strode up to the front door and hammered the knocker on its iron base. The door was opened by the housekeeper.

'Why, it's Mr Flockhart,' she began. 'As you can see, sir, Mr Miller's just gone . . .'

'My business is not with Mr Miller,' I said curtly, 'it is with you. Oh, and you can cut out the 'Mr Flockhart', now: you know perfectly well who I am, as you and your sister know who my wife is . . .'

'I'm sure I don't know what you're talking about, sir.'

'Aren't you going to let me in – Miss Raines?'

That seemed to settle it. The woman's eyes became very still as she quietly stepped aside, and, closing the front door behind us as I stepped inside, she led me into the nearest reception room, where we stood and confronted one another on the Turkey carpet. Mrs Custance – or Cora Raines, as I was sure she was or had been – stood straight before me, her hands clasped in front of her, and stared at me impassively.

'I don't know what was the immediate cause of you and your sister being cast out on the streets all those years ago, but I think I can name the prime cause – Miller . . .'

The knuckles of the clasped hands whitened, and Cora Raines' brown eyes seemed to turn a shade darker.

'Miller,' I repeated, 'no doubt in search of a new sensation for one of his most distinguished clients – later to become his prospective victim – General Ostyankin. Here was a pretty young girl, perfectly formed, and blind. A charming novelty for a jaded palate . . . But I will say no more of that. Then, after the agonising nightmare and the eventual rescue, Randall Moberley's charitable knife restored your sight, then you were

261

reunited with your sister. Soon after you are both taken into service by the wife of a music hall manager. Your graceful body and your talent for dancing are noticed, then follows a career on the stage. You are never quite top of the bill, but are still well-remembered by many in the business. One day, though, in the years of your early maturity, a sound causes you momentarily to freeze on the stage, while you acknowledge the applause of the audience. A man barks from one of the boxes. Barks like a dog. It is an unmistakable sound to you, a sound which is burned into your very soul . . .'

I could not but pause in my narrative as I envisaged the ultimate loneliness of the poor blind girl, as she was pushed into the room where she would be introduced in the most brutal fashion to the worst in man.

'Shaken,' I went on, 'but still a trouper, you take a curtain-call, and this time your eyes are carefully scanning the boxes, and when you hear the bark again you are able to link it with a bearded face, one which has a dumpling-featured companion. The faces mean nothing to you, but the bark . . . You make a vow on the spot. Perhaps your stage career is waning anyway, for *gamin* charm can scarcely last much beyond twenty-five. Anyway, Cora Raines disappears from public view, along with her formidable sister. I don't know through which byways your eventual transformation into Mrs Custance, indispensable housekeeper of 8, Farm Street, led you, but I strongly suspect from the way you handle chloroform that nursing was one of them . . .'

'How could you possibly know I'd been blind?' Cora Raines asked coldly.

'From the way you handled my umbrella when I found you in Dr Fedoroff's closed-up house at No. 19,' I said. 'Caressing the head all round in your hand and slipping your hand down the shaft as if measuring it before dropping it in the rack, then, as I was leaving, picking it out instantly from half a dozen other sticks and umbrellas in the rack in a pitch dark hallway. You evidently thought the "Reverend Flockhart" too much of a fool to notice.'

'Well, what if I had been blind? What of it? That doesn't prove anything.'

'There was the matter of "Warwick". As no doubt on many

other occasions, you must have had your ear to the keyhole when I discussed the possible significance of the word with your employer. You then decided that "Mr Flockhart" might have his uses after all. Seeing your opportunity to incriminate your master, you fed me with some stuff about your employer's devotion to Shakespeare performances, including that of so-called "Neville the Kingmaker", knowing full well as a veteran of the boards yourself that no play featuring the character of – more accurately – Warwick the Kingmaker had been staged in decades. Just as again you saw your chance when Miller sent you to Ebury Street to ask Mrs Jephson if she had found his sovereign-case – stamped with his initials – which he thought he had left behind on his one and only visit there. I picture you slipping your hand – very discreetly – down chair- and sofa-upholstery, when Mrs Jephson's back was turned. It would be a handy thing to keep against the day of reckoning with Miller, along, no doubt, with enough supplementary "evidence" to land him in the dock.'

'I didn't mean anything to happen to old Jephson,' the woman in the black dress said sombrely, but without noticeable regret in her voice.

'No,' I said, 'that was a new twist to the plot. But in these things anything can happen – there is no going back. Jephson must have remembered the Ebury Street enquiry,' – I did not choose to tell her *who* had inadvertently reminded him – 'and put two and two together, identifying the coin-case as the projectile which carried the dead general's sovereigns to Solomons' feet. You put Ostyankin's loose sovereigns into Miller's long-lost case, which you then slipped into the curtain-hem of the murder room, so that the cleaner wouldn't spot them and be tempted to filch them when she arrived later on that morning. You wanted above all for the police to find Miller's case – you could have fixed up a bogus rendezvous for him, so that they could have picked him up on the spot. What a glorious revenge! As it happened, your murder plot against Ostyankin had driven a coach-and-horses through someone else's – Miller's, by a wry twist of fate – for there could scarcely have been a time when Ostyankin would be more vulnerable than on that particular night – incognito as he was in the Poland Street house of assignation, and leaving no word with anyone where he would be that night. But it all went wrong.'

'Why did Miller want to do him in, anyway?' Cora Raines asked sullenly. 'They were like Tweedledum and Tweedledee . . .'

'Politics,' I said. 'The Tsar's government had evidently decided that Ostyankin's particular form of war-mongering-by-proxy was no longer in line with their present policy, so who better to deal with him than his old friend and loyal agent of the house of Romanoff, Alexander Miller?'

Just then the thought of Judith Vulliamy's mislaid identity and sudden disappearance made me wonder whether another European Emperor – the Kaiser – might also have been interested in Ostyankin's elimination . . .

'Miller's plot,' I went on, 'also provided a golden opportunity for getting rid of another thorn in the side of the Russian government – Solomon Solomons, code-name "*samorodok*" or "nugget" – "rough diamond", we might say . . .'

'How could you possibly know that?'

'A gesture Miller was reported as having made at the card party at Dr Fedoroff's house, when he turned down his empty *samorodok* cigarette-case and said: "Finished . . ." That suggested a likely reason for Solomons' presence outside No. 11, Poland Street – a willing, but misled – and betrayed – accomplice in Miller's murder plot, who was to be the scapegoat for the crime.'

'How can he have been a "willing" accomplice? He was doing his best to get clear of the Russians and everything to do with them . . .'

'Miller used a revolutionary Judas in London called Mark Diamant to inveigle Solomons into the plot. Diamant had been one of the gang – along with Solomons and others – who had tried to assassinate Ostyankin in Odessa in '84. Solomons had escaped arrest, but the fact that Diamant had allegedly escaped from police custody some time after having been captured suggested to me that the Russian secret police might have got at him – offered him his life and a place on their payroll if he would "escape" and stalk Solomons back to England.

'But as we know, things didn't go according to plan on the night in Poland Street, and first Miller, then another, more expendable conspirator – perhaps Diamant – went to investigate, the latter actually entering the house and flinging up the window-sashes to release the smoke given off by your and your sister's bloodsoaked clothes in the grate . . .'

'My sister had nothing to do with it – you can't prove a thing against her . . .'

'The wind blew out the curtains,' I went on regardless, 'and the coin-case shot out into the night, beginning the process that brought Solomons into the dock at the Old Bailey.'

'Dirty little pimp!' Cora Raines snapped. 'I'd hang the lot! He'd have hung anyway – you've just said yourself he was an accomplice.'

'Solomon Solomons did not kill Ostyankin,' I was content to reply. 'You and your sister did.'

'We wouldn't have hurt your wife, if that's what's behind all this. I, er . . . overheard Miller talking to someone on the telephone about her having been to Sadler's Wells, and I thought she was getting a bit too close for comfort. We'd just have kept her till . . .'

'Till you'd killed Miller and perhaps Le Thuillier, too,' I put in. 'Was the MP to go the way of Ostyankin for opposing the raising of the age of consent? So that helpless children might go on suffering as you did? Were they both to receive the Poland Street treatment tonight? The rendezvous in some shabby, secluded house in one of the more run-down residential districts of central London, then the chloroform-pad, followed by the ghastly, help-less awakening, then – vivisection?'

The sallow woman sniffed and cocked her head up.

'And let me assure you,' I went on, 'if I'd thought for an instant that you *had* meant my wife any serious harm, you would not now be needing the services of the hangman . . .'

'What are you going to do, then?'

'It is not what I am going to do that should concern you, but what I *might* do. Now listen to what I am going to tell you. After the challenge I've flung in his face this evening, along with impending police enquiries – timber-agents do not enjoy diplo-matic immunity – I've little doubt that your employer will be leaving rather abruptly for foreign parts. Among other things, he will probably be missing his little rendezvous with Le Thuillier. Be that as it may, as soon as I have finished talking to you, you will pack your possessions, and I will order a cab, in which you

265

will go and collect your sister: I take it she is within reasonable call?'

The black-dressed Nemesis nodded, and stared unwaveringly at me as I took out my notebook and pencil-case and scribbled a note, which I tore out of the book and gave her. I then pulled out my watch: it was nine o'clock precisely.

'On the note I have just given you is the address of a safe refuge in Hackney for women in trouble. I will give you three hours' law, and if within that time you have not – with your sister – joined me at the address on the note, or have failed to send word to me to explain any delay, I shall go directly to the police and lay before them all the facts which I have outlined to you this evening, along with your true identity, and that of your sister. Do you accept?'

The dark woman smiled.

'Aren't you forgetting something?' she asked quietly. 'Proof. Up to now you haven't offered a shred of evidence to back up this story of yours. Why should I do what you say?'

'Consider the consequences for yourself and your sister if I go to the police. Though, as you say, I cannot actually prove my accusation up to the point of causing them to arrest you, they would be obliged after hearing my story to warn the MP Le Thuillier to be on his guard. Now he is a powerful man – a leading figure in his party and in society – but it is what he represents that counts: a sizeable chunk of the British ruling-class. You will have seen for yourself the calibre of men Miller hobnobs with . . . Make no mistake: they will pull all the strings at their command in order to have you both silenced. At best, you would live henceforth as marked women, on a sort of unofficial ticket-of-leave, hounded from pillar to post, hauled in continually for questioning whenever a society blackmail scandal broke. You would find it near-impossible to obtain decent employment or lodging, and would find yourselves moving on endlessly. At worst – well, remember where Desmond Coe ended up . . .'

Cora Raines eyed me coldly for quite half a minute before she answered.

'All right.'

'Very well,' I said, 'and the same terms will apply should you, your sister or both of you abscond from the address on the note before a decision has been reached about your future. Do you understand?'

'Yes.'

Without giving a thought to the gesture, I attempted to take her gently by the elbow, so that I might lead her into the corridor, but such was her answering shudder of revulsion that I immediately withdrew my hand. Ten thousand words could not better have expressed what a man's touch must have come to mean to her. I waited, saddened and abashed, till, fifteen minutes later, Cora Raines reappeared with a trunk and hatbox. After we had turned down the gas, we locked the house behind us, and I whistled up the next passing cab. The cabbie first hauled up her trunk and hatbox for her, then, stooping, she whispered something in his ear and entered the cab. As it drove away into the night, we exchanged brief glances through the side-window, but her eyes gave nothing away.

The weather had turned mild and balmy, and a touch of spring sadness stole into my heart as I turned homewards. I cheered up somewhat at the thought of my dearest Violet, now so happily restored to me, but then I fell to musing on what I had just done. I was sure that Hilary Venables at the Hackney women's refuge would back my action to the hilt, but I could not conceal from myself that in making my unlawful covenant with Cora Raines alias Mrs Custance, I had committed a grievous wrong; or at best, a deeply uncivic act in allowing such a fell murderess to carry on uncensured amid an unsuspecting public. Two things, however, kept me steady on my – no doubt – reprehensible course; namely, the firm conviction that, deprived of access to the main surviving object of her undying hatred and resentment – Alexander Miller – Cora Raines would never kill again, and a persistent image in my mind, one that would haunt me for many a day to come. It was a picture of a young girl, blind and frightened, and deprived of all means of help, locked in a frowsty room with a coarse, lecherous, sixteen-stone man, a man who barked when excited. No, I knew I would never, as long as I lived, give away Cora Raines' secret. As for her crime, I would heed the injunction of the Ghost in *Hamlet*, and 'leave her to heaven'.

Envoi

With the self-imposed martyrdom of poor Cormell Jephson, and the sudden release and deportation of Solomon Solomons, the Poland Street case passed into history; or rather, until the publication of this account – into myth. The press and its readers soon ran after other scandals, other sensations, and the election of the Liberal government in the following year of 1892, with the unfolding drama of Ireland, drove out all the other issues which had engaged the public attention up till then.

As for the mere groundlings in the Poland Street affair, Iris Starr was overjoyed to receive near the middle of March, 1891, a letter with a United States date-stamp on its envelope, and containing a message of love and hope, along with a money order, from her lover. There was a succession of such letters, and not a few money orders, until the correspondence ceased abruptly in the summer of '93, ominously coincidental with the time of the great Scranton Lockout, in the course of which eighteen Pennsylvanian coal-miners and labour agitators fell victim to the carbine-bullets and pickaxe-handles of professional strike-breakers. I fear Solomon Solomons found a hero's death there, shoulder-to-shoulder with his revolutionary comrades. It was as he would have wished.

Iris took this the only way she knew: by leaving the Hackney refuge and returning to the drunken oblivion of the public houses and mean streets of the East End. There was, however, a possibly happier sequel to this, for one day about five years later, when occasion took me down the Ratcliff Highway, I happened to pass by the open doorway of Sisterson's seamen's lodging house. Judging by the shrill, cockney barracking he was receiving from a familiar female voice within, the giant Swede had evidently taken a new wife . . . I hope things went not-too-badly for Iris and him.

Lettice Jephson had of course to leave her co-wardenship of the Working Girls' Club when the scandal of her husband's arrest and confession broke. After her unfortunate son had paid his debt to nature a year later, she retired to the quiet hills of Radnorshire, to keep house for a widowed brother. Let us hope for both of them that a grief shared was a grief halved.

As for the enigmatic Miss Vulliamy – whatever her real name was – I am sure the Kaiser's secret service found other work for her, and I often wondered later which other impressionable young diplomatist might be in her toils . . .

Cora Raines and her sister Dinah kept to our agreement, and presently no poor woman rescued from the streets of the Cardiff dock-area found a stauncher friend than in the new housekeeper of Canon Nuttall's celebrated mission there, nor any marauding drunkard or hooligan a sterner rebuff than from his stalwart matron.

I hope that Cora Raines' bitter hatred cooled with the demise of its last object, when, in the course of the appalling bomb outrage outside the door of the Uniate Cathedral of Lemberg in '94, what was left of Alexander Miller somehow managed to drag itself into the gutter, where he bled to death before help could reach him.

As for my own feeling of guilt over being the possible indirect cause – when he had overheard me question his wife about the incriminating coin-case – of Cormell Jephson's tragic and misguided sacrifice, I received a degree of consolation from a completely unsuspected source. It seems that word of my part in the solution of the Poland Street affair reached the ear of the Turkish authorities, who had come increasingly under attack from the baying wolves of the Russian war-party, who tried to lay the death of their bloody hero Ostyankin at Turkey's door. The reader will readily imagine my surprise and gratification, when, not long after the events I have been describing, a heavy parcel was handed to me by our maid Lottie over the breakfast table in our rooms in Henrietta Street. Intrigued, I undid the parcel, to reveal a finely chased silver ewer of great age, with a letter from the Turkish Ambassador, Rustem Pacha. After reading – not without blushes – the gracious sentiments expressed in the letter, I examined the ewer more closely, to find the rim covered in writing in the ancient Kufic script. I later sent my transcription of these characters to the British Museum, and the translation I received in due course did much to console me in my misgivings as to the part I had played in the events I have described in this record. The translation read: 'Only Allah is All-Knowing.'